THE FEAR INDEX

Robert Harris

WINDSOR
PARAGON

First published 2011
by Hutchinson
This Large Print edition published 2012
by AudioGO Ltd
by arrangement with
The Random House Group Ltd

Hardcover   ISBN: 978 1 445 88976 4
Softcover   ISBN: 978 1 445 88977 1

British Library Cataloguing in Publication Data available

Printed and bound in Great Britain by
MPG Books Group Limited

THE FEAR INDEX

This book must be returned by the date specified at the time of issue as the DATE DUE FOR RETURN.
The loan may be extended (personally, by post, telephone or online) for a further period if the book is not required by another reader, by quoting the above number / author / title.

Enquiries: 01709 336774

www.rotherham.gov.uk/libraries

To my family
Gill,
Holly, Charlie, Matilda, Sam

ACKNOWLEDGEMENTS

I wish to thank all those whose expertise, generously given, has made this book possible: first and foremost Neville Quie of Citi, who made many helpful suggestions and introductions and who, along with Cameron Small, patiently helped me through the labyrinth of shorts and out-of-the-money puts; Charles Scott, formerly of Morgan Stanley, who discussed the concept, read the manuscript and introduced me to Andre Stern of Oxford Asset Management, Eli Lederman, former CEO of Turquoise, and David Keetly and John Mansell of Polar Capital Alva Fund, all of whom provided useful insights; Leda Braga, Mike Platt, Pawel Lewicki and the algorithmic team at BlueCrest for their hospitality and for letting me spend a day watching them in action; Christian Holzer for his advice on the VIX; Lucie Chaumeton for fact-checking; Philippe Jabre of Jabre Capital Partners SA for sharing his knowledge of the financial markets; Dr Ian Bird, head of the Large Hadron Collider Computing Grid Project, for two conducted tours and insights into CERN in the 1990s; Ariane Koek, James Gillies, Christine Sutton and Barbara Warmbein of the CERN Press Office; Dr Bryan Lynn, an academic physicist who worked at both Merrill Lynch and CERN and who kindly described his experiences of moving between these different worlds; Jean-Philippe Brandt of the Geneva Police Department for giving me a tour of the city and answering my queries about police procedure; Dr Stephen Golding, Consultant Radiologist at the John Radcliffe Hospital in Oxford, for advising me on brain scans and putting me in touch with Professor Christoph Becker and Dr Minerva Becker who in turn helpfully arranged a tour of the Radiological Department of the University Hospital in Geneva. None of these, of course, is responsible for the errors of fact, misguided opinions and Gothic flights of fantasy that follow.

Finally a special word of thanks to Angela Palmer, who selflessly allowed me to borrow the concept of her stunning art works and bestow them on Gabrielle Hoffmann (the originals can be seen at angelaspalmer.com), and also to Paul Greengrass, for wise advice, good friendship and the sharing of numerous Liquidity Replenishment Points along the way.

Robert Harris
11.7.11

1

Learn from me, if not by my precepts, at least by my example, how dangerous is the acquirement of knowledge, and how much happier that man is who believes his native town to be the world, than he who aspires to become greater than his nature will allow.

MARY SHELLEY, *Frankenstein* (1818)

Dr Alexander Hoffmann sat by the fire in his study in Geneva, a half-smoked cigar lying cold in the ashtray beside him, an anglepoise lamp pulled low over his shoulder, turning the pages of a first edition of *The Expression of the Emotions in Man and Animals* by Charles Darwin. The Victorian grandfather clock in the hall was striking midnight but Hoffmann did not hear it. Nor did he notice that the fire was almost out. All his formidable powers of attention were directed on to his book.

He knew it had been published in London in 1872 by John Murray & Co. in an edition of seven thousand copies, printed in two runs. He knew also that the second run had introduced a misprint—'htat'—on page 208. As the volume in his hands contained no such error, he presumed it must have come from the first run, thus greatly increasing its value. He turned it round and inspected the spine. The binding was in the original green cloth with gilt lettering, the spine-ends only slightly frayed. It was what was known in the book trade as 'a fine copy', worth perhaps $15,000. He had found it waiting for

1

him when he returned home from his office that evening, as soon as the New York markets had closed, a little after ten o'clock. Yet the strange thing was, even though he collected scientific first editions and had browsed the book online and had in fact been meaning to buy it, he had not actually ordered it.

His immediate thought had been that it must have come from his wife, but she had denied it. He had refused to believe her at first, following her around the kitchen as she set the table, holding out the book for her inspection.

'You're really telling me you didn't buy it for me?'

'Yes, Alex. Sorry. It wasn't me. What can I say? Perhaps you have a secret admirer.'

'You are totally sure about this? It's not our anniversary or anything? I haven't forgotten to give you something?'

'For God's sake, I didn't buy it, okay?'

It had come with no message apart from a Dutch bookseller's slip: 'Rosengaarden & Nijenhuise, Antiquarian Scientific & Medical Books. Established 1911. Prinsengracht 227, 1016 HN Amsterdam, The Netherlands.' Hoffmann had pressed the pedal on the waste bin and retrieved the bubble wrap and thick brown paper. The parcel was correctly addressed, with a printed label: 'Dr Alexander Hoffmann, Villa Clairmont, 79 Chemin de Ruth, 1223 Cologny, Geneva, Switzerland.' It had been dispatched by courier from Amsterdam the previous day.

After they had eaten their supper—a fish pie and green salad prepared by the housekeeper before she went home—Gabrielle had stayed in the

2

kitchen to make a few anxious last-minute phone calls about her exhibition the next day, while Hoffmann had retreated to his study clutching the mysterious book. An hour later, when she put her head round the door to tell him she was going up to bed, he was still reading.

She said, 'Try not to be too late, darling. I'll wait up for you.'

He did not reply. She paused in the doorway and considered him for a moment. He still looked young for forty-two, and had always been more handsome than he realised—a quality she found attractive in a man as well as rare. It was not that he was modest, she had come to realise. On the contrary: he was supremely indifferent to anything that did not engage him intellectually, a trait that had earned him a reputation among her friends for being downright bloody rude—and she quite liked that as well. His preternaturally boyish American face was bent over the book, his spectacles pushed up and resting on the top of his thick head of light brown hair; catching the firelight, the lenses seemed to flash a warning look back at her. She knew better than to try to interrupt him. She sighed and went upstairs.

Hoffmann had known for years that *The Expression of the Emotions in Man and Animals* was one of the first books to be published with photographs, but he had never actually seen them before. Monochrome plates depicted Victorian artists' models and inmates of the Surrey Lunatic Asylum in various states of emotion—grief, despair, joy, defiance, terror—for this was meant to be a study of *Homo sapiens* as animal, with an animal's instinctive responses, stripped of the mask of social

3

graces. Born far enough into the age of science to be photographed, their misaligned eyes and skewed teeth nonetheless gave them the look of crafty, superstitious peasants from the Middle Ages. They reminded Hoffmann of a childish nightmare—of grown-ups from an old-fashioned book of fairy tales who might come and steal you from your bed in the night and carry you off into the woods.

And there was another thing that unsettled him. The bookseller's slip had been inserted into the pages devoted to the emotion of fear, as if the sender specifically intended to draw them to his attention:

The frightened man at first stands like a statue motionless or breathless, or crouches down as if instinctively to escape observation. The heart beats quickly and violently, so that it palpitates or knocks against the ribs . . .

Hoffmann had a habit when he was thinking of cocking his head to one side and gazing into the middle distance, and he did so now. Was this a coincidence? Yes, he reasoned, it must be. On the other hand, the physiological effects of fear were so directly relevant to VIXAL-4, the project he was presently involved in, that it did strike him as peculiarly pointed. And yet VIXAL-4 was highly secret, known only to his research team, and although he took care to pay them well—$250,000 was the starting salary, with much more on offer in bonuses—it was surely unlikely any of them would have spent $15,000 on an anonymous gift. One person who certainly could afford it, who knew all about the project and who would have seen the

4

joke of it—if that was what this was: an expensive joke—was his business partner, Hugo Quarry, and Hoffmann, without even thinking about the hour, rang him.

'Hello, Alex. How's it going?' If Quarry saw anything strange in being disturbed just after midnight, his perfect manners would never have permitted him to show it. Besides, he was accustomed to the ways of Hoffmann, 'the mad professor', as he called him—and called him it to his face as well as behind his back, it being part of his charm always to speak to everyone in the same way, public or private.

Hoffmann, still reading the description of fear, said distractedly, 'Oh, hi. Did you just buy me a book?'

'I don't think so, old friend. Why? Was I supposed to?'

'Someone's just sent me a Darwin first edition and I don't know who.'

'Sounds pretty valuable.'

'It is. I thought, because you know how important Darwin is to VIXAL, it might be you.'

''Fraid not. Could it be a client? A thank-you gift and they've forgotten to include a card? Lord knows, Alex, we've made them enough money.'

'Yeah, well. Maybe. Okay. Sorry to bother you.'

'Don't worry. See you in the morning. Big day tomorrow. In fact, it's already tomorrow. You ought to be in bed by now.'

'Sure. On my way. Night.'

As fear rises to an extreme pitch, the dreadful scream of terror is heard. Great beads of sweat stand on the skin. All the muscles of the body

5

are relaxed. Utter prostration soon follows, and the mental powers fail. The intestines are affected. The sphincter muscles cease to act, and no longer retain the contents of the body . . .

Hoffmann held the volume to his nose and inhaled. A compound of leather and library dust and cigar smoke, so sharp he could taste it, with a faint hint of something chemical—formaldehyde, perhaps, or coal-gas. It put him in mind of a nineteenth-century laboratory or lecture theatre, and for an instant he saw Bunsen burners on wooden benches, flasks of acid and the skeleton of an ape. He reinserted the bookseller's slip to mark the page and carefully closed the book. Then he carried it over to the shelves and with two fingers gently made room for it between a first edition of *On the Origin of Species*, which he had bought at auction at Sotheby's in New York for $125,000, and a leather-bound copy of *The Descent of Man* that had once belonged to T. H. Huxley.

Later, he would try to remember the exact sequence of what he did next. He consulted the Bloomberg terminal on his desk for the final prices in the USA: the Dow Jones, the S&P 500 and the NASDAQ had all ended down. He had an email exchange with Susumu Takahashi, the duty dealer in charge of execution on VIXAL-4 overnight, who reported that everything was functioning smoothly, and reminded him that the Tokyo Stock Exchange would reopen in less than two hours' time following the annual three-day Golden Week holiday. It would certainly open down, to catch up with what had been a week of falling prices in Europe and the US. And there was one other thing: VIXAL was proposing to short another three million shares in Procter & Gamble at $62 a share, which would bring their overall position up to six million—a big trade: would Hoffmann approve it? Hoffmann emailed 'OK', threw away his unfinished cigar, put a fine-meshed metal guard in front of the fireplace and switched off the study lights. In the hall he checked to see that the front door was locked and then set the burglar alarm with its four-digit code: 1729. (The numerals came from an exchange between the mathematicians G. H. Hardy and S. I. Ramanujan in 1920, when Hardy went in a taxi cab with that number to visit his dying colleague in hospital and complained it was 'a rather dull number', to which Ramanujan responded: 'No, Hardy! No, Hardy! It is a very interesting number. It is the smallest number expressible as the sum of two cubes in two different ways.') He left just one lamp lit downstairs—of that he was sure—then climbed the curved white marble staircase to the bathroom. He took off his spectacles, undressed, washed, brushed his teeth and put on a pair of blue silk pyjamas. He set the alarm on his mobile for six thirty, registering as he did so that the time was then twenty past twelve.

In the bedroom he was surprised to find Gabrielle still awake, lying on her back on the counterpane in a black silk kimono. A scented candle flickered on the dressing table; otherwise the room was in darkness. Her hands were clasped behind her head, her elbows sharply pointed away from her, her legs crossed at the knee. One slim white foot, the toenails painted dark red, was making impatient circles in the fragrant air.

'Oh God,' he said. 'I'd forgotten the date.'

'Don't worry.' She untied her belt and parted the silk, then held out her arms to him. 'I never forget it.'

*   *   *

It must have been about three fifty in the morning that something caused Hoffmann to wake. He struggled up from the depths of sleep and opened his eyes to behold a celestial vision of fiery white light. It was geometrically formed, like a graph, with thinly spaced horizontal lines and wide-apart vertical columns, but with no data plotted—a mathematician's dream, but not in fact a dream, he realised after squinting at it for a few seconds; rather the result of eight five-hundred-watt tungsten-halogen security lights shining brilliantly through the slats of the window blinds—enough wattage to light a small soccer ground; he had been meaning to have them changed.

The lights were on a thirty-second timer. As he waited for them to turn off, he considered what might have interrupted the infrared beams that criss-crossed the garden to trigger them. It would be a cat, he thought, or a fox, or a piece of overgrown foliage waving in the wind. And after a few seconds the lights were indeed doused and the room returned to darkness.

But now Hoffmann was wide awake. He reached for his mobile. It was one of a batch specially produced for the hedge fund that could encrypt certain sensitive phone calls and emails. To avoid disturbing Gabrielle—she detested this habit of his even more than she hated him smoking—he switched it on under the duvet and briefly checked the Profit & Loss screen for Far Eastern trading. In Tokyo, Singapore and Sydney the markets were, as predicted, falling but VIXAL-4 was already up 0.3 per cent, which meant by his calculations that he had made almost $3 million since going to bed. Satisfied, he turned off the device and replaced it on the nightstand, and that was when he heard a noise: soft, unidentifiable, and yet oddly disturbing, as if someone was moving around downstairs.

Staring at the tiny red dot of light of the smoke detector fixed to the ceiling, he extended his hand cautiously beneath the duvet towards Gabrielle. Lately, after they had made love, if she couldn't sleep, she had got into the habit of going down to her studio to work. His palm traversed the warm undulations of the mattress until his fingertips brushed the skin of her hip. Immediately she muttered something unintelligible and rolled her back to him, pulling the duvet tighter around her shoulders.

The noise came again. He raised himself on his elbows and strained his ears. It was nothing specific—an occasional faint thump. It could just be the unfamiliar heating system, or a door caught in a draught. At this stage he felt quite calm. The house had formidable security, which was one of the reasons he had bought it a few weeks earlier: apart from the floodlights, there was a three-metre-high perimeter wall with heavy electronic gates, a steel-reinforced front door with a keypad entry system, bulletproof glass in all the ground-floor windows, and a movement-sensitive burglar alarm, which he was sure he had turned on before he came up to bed. The chances that an intruder had got past all that and penetrated inside were tiny. Besides, he was physically fit: he had long ago established that high levels of endorphins enabled him to think better. He worked out. He jogged. An atavistic instinct to protect his territory stirred within him.

He slid out of bed without waking Gabrielle and put on his glasses, robe and slippers. He hesitated, and peered around in the darkness, but he could not recall anything in the room that might be useful as a weapon. He slipped his mobile into his pocket and opened the bedroom door—a crack at first, and then fully. The light from the lamp downstairs shed a dim glow along the landing. He paused on the threshold, listening. But the sounds—if there had ever been sounds, which he was beginning to doubt—had ceased. After a minute or so he moved towards the staircase and began to descend very slowly.

Perhaps it was the effect of reading Darwin just before he fell asleep, but as he went down the stairs he found himself registering, with scientific detachment, his own physical symptoms. His breath was becoming short, his heartbeat accelerating so rapidly it was uncomfortable. His hair felt as stiff as fur.

He reached the ground floor.

The house was a belle époque mansion, built in 1902 for a French businessman who had made a fortune out of extracting oil from coal waste. The whole place had been excessively interior-designed by the previous owner, left ready to move into, and perhaps for that reason Hoffmann had never felt entirely at home in it. To his left was the front door and immediately ahead of him the door to the drawing room. To his right a passage led towards the house's interior: dining room, kitchen, library and a Victorian conservatory that Gabrielle used as her studio. He stood absolutely still, his hands raised ready to defend himself. He could hear nothing. In the corner of the hall, the tiny red eye of the movement sensor winked at him. If he was not careful, he would trigger the alarm himself. That had already happened twice elsewhere in Cologny since they moved in—big houses wailing nervously for no reason, like hysterical rich old ladies behind their high ivy-covered walls.

He relaxed his hands and crossed the hall to where an antique barometer was mounted on the wall. He pressed a catch and the barometer swung outwards. The alarm control box was hidden in a compartment behind it. He reached out his right forefinger to enter the code to switch the system off, and then checked himself.

The alarm had already been deactivated.

His finger stayed poised in mid-air while the rational part of his mind sought for reassuring explanations. Perhaps Gabrielle had come down after all, had switched the system off and had forgotten to turn it back on again when she returned to bed. Or he had forgotten to set it in the first place. Or it had malfunctioned.

Very slowly he turned to his left to inspect the front door. The gleam of the lamplight reflected in its glossy black paint. It appeared to be firmly closed, with no sign it had been forced. Like the alarm, it was of the latest design and also controlled by the same four-digit code. He glanced back over his shoulder, checking the stairs and the corridor leading to the interior of the house. All was still. He moved towards the door. He tapped in the code. He heard the bolts click back. He grasped the heavy

11

brass handle and turned it, then stepped out on to the darkened porch.

Above the inky expanse of lawn, the moon was a silvery-blue discus that seemed to have been thrown at great speed through scudding masses of black cloud. The shadows of the big fir trees that screened the house from the road swayed and rustled in the wind.

Hoffmann took a few more paces out into the gravel drive—just far enough to interrupt the beam of the infrared sensors and set off the floodlights at the front of the house. The brightness made him jump, pinning him to the spot like an escaping prisoner. He put up his arm to shield his eyes and turned to face the yellow-lit interior of the hall, noticing as he did so that a large pair of black boots had been placed neatly to one side of the front door, as if their owner had not wanted to trail in mud or disturb the occupants. The boots were not Hoffmann's and they were certainly not Gabrielle's. He was also sure they had not been there when he arrived home almost six hours earlier.

His gaze transfixed by the boots, he fumbled for his mobile, almost dropped it, started dialling 911, remembered he was in Switzerland and tried again: 117.

The number rang just once—at 3.59 a.m., according to the Geneva Police Department, which records all emergency calls, and which subsequently issued a transcript. A woman answered sharply: *'Oui, police?'*

Her voice seemed to Hoffmann very loud in the stillness. It made him realise how visible he must be, standing exposed under the floodlights. He stepped quickly to his left, out of the line of sight of

12

anyone watching from the hallway, and at the same time forward, into the lee of the house. He had the phone pressed very close to his mouth. He whispered: *'J'ai un intrus sur ma propriété.'* On the tape his voice sounds calm, thin, almost robotic. It is the voice of a man whose cerebral cortex—without his even being aware of it—is concentrating all its power entirely on survival. It is the voice of pure fear.

'Quelle est votre adresse, monsieur?'

He told her. He was still moving along the facade of the house. He could hear her fingers typing.

'Et votre nom?'

He whispered, 'Alexander Hoffmann.'

The security lights cut out.

'Okay, Monsieur Hoffmann. Restez là. Une voiture est en route.'

She hung up. Alone in the darkness, Hoffmann stood at the corner of the house. It was unseasonably cold for Switzerland in the first week of May. The wind was from the north-east, blowing straight off Lac Léman. He could hear the water lapping rapidly against the nearby jetties, rattling the halliards against the metal masts of the yachts. He pulled his dressing gown tighter around his shoulders. He was shaking violently. He had to clench his teeth to stop them chattering. And yet, oddly, he felt no panic. Panic was quite different to fear, he was discovering. Panic was moral and nervous collapse, a waste of precious energy, whereas fear was all sinew and instinct: an animal that stood up on its hind legs and filled you completely, that took control of your brain and your muscles. He sniffed the air and glanced along the side of the mansion towards the lake.

13

Somewhere near the rear of the house there was a light on downstairs. Its gleam lit the surrounding bushes very prettily, like a fairy grotto.

He waited for half a minute, then began to move towards it stealthily, working his way through the wide herbaceous border that ran along this side of the house. He was not sure at first from which room it was emanating: he had not ventured down here since the estate agent showed them round. But as he drew closer he realised it was the kitchen, and when he came level with it, and edged his head around the window frame, he saw inside the figure of a man. He had his back to the window. He was standing at the granite-topped island in the centre of the room. His movements were unhurried. He was taking knives from their sockets in a butcher's block and sharpening them on an electric grinder.

Hoffmann's heart was pumping so fast he could hear the rush of his own pulse. His immediate thought was Gabrielle: he must get her out of the house while the intruder was preoccupied in the kitchen. Get her out of the house, or at the very least get her to lock herself in the bathroom until the police arrived.

He still had his mobile in his hand. Without taking his eyes from the intruder, he dialled her number. Seconds later he heard her phone start to ring—too loud and too near for it to be with her upstairs. At once the stranger looked up from his sharpening. Gabrielle's phone was lying where she had left it before she went to bed, on the big pine table in the kitchen, its screen glowing, its pink plastic case buzzing along the wood like some tropical beetle turned on its back. The intruder cocked his head and looked at it. For several long

14

seconds he stayed where he was. Then, with the same infuriating calmness, he laid down the knife—Hoffmann's favourite knife, the one with the long thin blade that was particularly useful for boning—and moved around the island towards the table. As he did so, his body half turned towards the window, and Hoffmann got his first proper glimpse of him—a bald pate with long, thin grey hair at the sides pulled back behind the ears into a greasy ponytail, hollow cheeks, unshaven. He was wearing a scuffed brown leather coat. He looked like a traveller, the sort of man who might work in a circus or on a ride in a fair. He stared in puzzlement at the phone as if he had never seen one before, picked it up, hesitated, then pressed answer and held it to his ear.

Hoffmann was convulsed by a wave of murderous anger. It flooded him like a light. He said quietly, 'You cocksucker, get out of my house,' and was gratified to see the intruder jerk in alarm, as if tugged from above by an invisible wire. He rapidly twisted his head—left, right, left, right—and then his gaze settled on the window. For an instant his darting eyes met Hoffmann's, but blindly, for he was staring into dark glass. It would have been hard to say who was the more frightened. Suddenly he threw the phone on to the table and with surprising agility darted for the door.

Hoffmann swore, turned and started back the way he had come, sliding and stumbling through the flower bed, along the side of the big house, towards the front—hard going in his slippers, his ankle was twisted, each breath a sob. He had reached the corner when he heard the front door slam. He assumed the intruder was making a dash

15

for the road. But no: the seconds passed and the man did not appear. He must have shut himself in.

Oh God, Hoffmann whispered. *God, God.*

He flailed on towards the porch. The boots were still there—tongues lolling, old, squat, malevolent. His hands were shaking as he keyed in the security code. By this time he was yelling out Gabrielle's name, even though the master bedroom was on the opposite side of the house and there was little chance she could hear him. The bolts clicked back. He flung open the door on to darkness. The hall lamp had been switched off.

For a moment he stood panting on the step, imagining the distance he had to cross, calculating his chances, then he lunged towards the staircase, screaming, 'Gabrielle! Gabrielle!' and was halfway across the marble floor when the house seemed to explode around him, the stairs tumbling, the floor tiles rising, the walls shooting away from him into the night.

2

*A grain in the balance will determine which individual
shall live and which shall die . . .*

CHARLES DARWIN, *On the Origin of Species* (1859)

Hoffmann had no memory of anything after that—
no thoughts or dreams disturbed his normally
restless mind—until at last, from out of the fog,
like a low spit of land emerging at the end of a long
voyage, he became aware of a gradual reawakening
of sensations—freezing water trickling down the
side of his neck and across his back, a cold pressure
on his scalp, a sharp pain in his head, a mechanical
jabbering in his ears, the familiar sickly-sharp floral
smell of his wife's perfume—and he realised that he
was lying on his side, with something soft against his
cheek. There was a pressure on his hand.

He opened his eyes and saw a white plastic bowl,
inches from his face, into which he immediately
vomited, the taste of last night's fish pie sour in his
mouth. He gagged and spewed again. The bowl was
removed. A bright light was shone into each of his
eyes in turn. His nose and mouth were wiped. A
glass of water was pressed against his lips.
Babyishly, he pushed it away at first, then took it
and gulped it down. When he had finished, he
opened his eyes again and squinted around his new
world.

He was on the floor of the hall, laid out in the
recovery position, his back resting against the wall.
A blue police light flashed at the window like a

17

continuous electrical storm; unintelligible chatter leaked from a radio. Gabrielle was kneeling next to him, holding his hand. She smiled and squeezed his fingers. 'Thank God,' she said. She was dressed in jeans and a jersey. He pushed himself up and looked around, bewildered. Without his spectacles, everything was slightly blurred: two paramedics, bent over a case of gleaming equipment; two uniformed gendarmes, one by the door with the noisy radio on his belt and another just coming down the stairs; and a third man, tired-looking, in his fifties, wearing a dark blue windcheater and a white shirt with a dark tie, who was studying Hoffmann with detached sympathy. Everyone was dressed except Hoffmann, and it suddenly seemed terribly important to him to put on some clothes as well. But when he tried to rise further, he found he had insufficient strength in his arms. A flash of pain arced across his skull.

The man in the dark tie said, 'Here, let me help,' and stepped forward with his hand outstretched. 'Jean-Philippe Leclerc, inspector of the Geneva Police Department.'

One of the paramedics took Hoffmann's other arm and together he and the inspector raised him carefully to his feet. On the creamy paintwork of the wall where his head had rested was a feathery patch of blood. More blood was on the floor— smeared into streaks, as if someone had skidded in it. Hoffmann's knees sagged. 'I have you,' Leclerc reassured him. 'Breathe deeply. Take a moment.'

Gabrielle said anxiously, 'He needs to go to a hospital.'

'The ambulance will be here in ten minutes,' said the paramedic. 'They've been delayed.'

'Why don't we wait in here?' suggested Leclerc. He opened the door on to the chilly drawing room.

Once Hoffmann had been lowered into a sitting position on the sofa—he refused to lie flat—the paramedic squatted in front of him.

'Can you tell me the number of fingers I'm holding up?'

Hoffmann said, 'Can I have my . . .' What was the word? He raised his hand to his eyes.

'He needs his glasses,' said Gabrielle. 'Here you are, darling.' She slipped them over his nose and kissed his forehead. 'Take it easy, all right?'

The medic said, 'Can you see my fingers now?'

Hoffmann counted carefully. He ran his tongue over his lips before replying. 'Three.'

'And now?'

'Four.'

'We need to take your blood pressure, *monsieur.*'

Hoffmann sat placidly as the sleeve of his pyjama jacket was rolled up and the plastic cuff was fastened around his bicep and inflated. The end of the stethoscope was cold on his skin. His mind seemed to be switching itself back on now, section by section. Methodically he noted the contents of the room: the pale yellow walls, the easy chairs and chaise longues covered in white silk, the Bechstein baby grand, the Louis Quinze clock ticking quietly on the mantelpiece, the charcoal tones of the Auerbach landscape above it. On the coffee table in front of him was one of Gabrielle's early self-portraits: a half-metre cube, made up of a hundred sheets of Mirogard glass, on to which she had traced in black ink the sections of an MRI scan of her own body. The effect was of some strange, vulnerable alien creature floating in mid-air.

19

Hoffmann looked at it as if for the first time. There was something here he ought to remember. What was it? This was a new experience for him, not to be able to retrieve a piece of information he wanted immediately. When the paramedic had finished, Hoffmann said to Gabrielle, 'Aren't you doing something special today?' His forehead creased in concentration as he searched through the chaos of his memory. 'I know,' he said at last with relief, 'it's your show.'

'Yes, it is, but we'll cancel it.'

'No, we mustn't do that—not your first show.'

'Good,' said Leclerc, who was watching Hoffmann from his armchair. 'This is very good.'

Hoffmann turned slowly to look at him. The movement shot another spasm of pain through his head. He peered at Leclerc. 'Good?'

'It's good that you can remember things.' The inspector gave him the thumbs-up sign. 'For example, what's the last thing that happened to you tonight that you can remember?'

Gabrielle interrupted. 'I think Alex ought to see a doctor before he answers any questions. He needs to rest.'

'What is the last thing I remember?' Hoffmann considered the question carefully, as if it were a mathematical problem. 'I guess it was coming in through the front door. He must have been behind it waiting for me.'

'He? There was only one man?' Leclerc unzipped his windcheater and with difficulty tugged a notebook from some hidden recess, then shifted in his chair and produced a pen. All the while he looked encouragingly at Hoffmann.

'Yes, as far as I know. Just one.' Hoffmann put

20

his hand to the back of his head. His fingers touched a bandage, tightly wound. 'What did he hit me with?'

'By the looks of it, a fire extinguisher.'

'Jesus. And how long was I unconscious?'

'Twenty-five minutes.'

'Is that all?' Hoffmann felt as if he had been out for hours. But when he looked at the windows he saw it was still dark, and the Louis Quinze clock said it was not yet five o'clock. 'And I was shouting to warn you,' he said to Gabrielle. 'I remember that.'

'That's right, I heard you. Then I came downstairs and found you lying there. The front door was open. The next thing I knew, the police were here.'

Hoffmann looked back at Leclerc. 'Did you catch him?'

'Unfortunately he was gone by the time our patrol arrived.' Leclerc flicked back through his notebook. 'It's strange. He seems simply to have walked in through the gate and walked out again. Yet I gather you need two separate codes to access the gate and the front door. I wonder—was this man known to you in some way, perhaps? I'm assuming you didn't let him in deliberately.'

'I've never seen him before in my life.'

'Ah.' Leclerc made a note. 'So you did get a good look at him?'

'He was in the kitchen. I watched him through the window.'

'I don't understand. You were outside and he was inside?'

'Yes.'

'I'm sorry—how could that be?'

21

Haltingly at first, but with growing fluency as his strength and memory returned, Hoffmann relived it all: how he had heard a noise, had gone downstairs, had discovered the alarm turned off, had opened the door, seen the pair of boots, noticed the light shining from a ground-floor window, worked his way round the side of the house, and watched the intruder through the window.

'Can you describe him?' Leclerc was writing rapidly, barely finishing one page before turning it over and filling another.

Gabrielle said, 'Alex . . .'

'It's all right, Gabby,' said Hoffmann. 'We need to help them catch this bastard.' He closed his eyes. He had a clear mental picture of him—almost too clear, staring out wildly across the brightly lit kitchen. 'He was medium height. Rough-looking. Fifties. Gaunt face. Bald on top. Long, thin grey hair, pulled back in a ponytail. He was wearing a leather coat, or maybe a jacket—I can't remember which.' A doubt swam into Hoffmann's mind. He paused. Leclerc stared at him, waiting for him to continue. 'I say I've never seen him before, but now I come to think of it, I wonder if that's so. Perhaps I have seen him somewhere—a glimpse in the street, maybe. There was something familiar . . .' His voice trailed off.

'Go on,' said Leclerc.

Hoffmann thought for a moment, then fractionally shook his head. 'No. I can't remember. Sorry. But to be honest—you know, I'm not trying to make a big deal of it—I have had an odd feeling of being watched just lately.'

Gabrielle said in surprise, 'You never mentioned anything to me about it.'

'I didn't want to upset you. And besides, it was never anything I could put my finger on, exactly.'

'It could be that he's been watching the house for a while,' said Leclerc, 'or following you. You may have seen him in the street without being aware of him. Don't worry. It'll come back to you. What was he doing in the kitchen?'

Hoffmann glanced at Gabrielle. He hesitated. 'He was—sharpening knives.'

'My God!' Gabrielle put her hand to her mouth.

'Would you be able to identify him if you saw him again?'

'Oh yes,' said Hoffmann grimly. 'You bet.'

Leclerc tapped his pen against his notebook. 'We must issue this description.' He stood. 'Excuse me a moment,' he said. He went out into the hall.

Hoffmann suddenly felt too tired to carry on. He closed his eyes again and leaned his head back against the sofa, then remembered his wound. 'Sorry. I'm ruining your furniture.'

'To hell with the furniture.'

He stared at her. She looked older without her make-up, more fragile and—an expression he had never seen before—scared. It pierced him. He managed to smile at her. At first she shook her head, but then—briefly, reluctantly—she smiled back, and just for a moment he dared to hope the whole thing wasn't that serious: that it would turn out to be some old tramp who had found the entry codes on a scrap of waste paper in the street, and that one day they would laugh about it—his knock on the head (a fire extinguisher!), his mock heroics, her anxiety.

Leclerc came back into the drawing room carrying a couple of clear plastic evidence bags.

23

'We found these in the kitchen,' he said, resuming his seat with a sigh. He held them up. One contained a pair of handcuffs, the other what looked to be a black leather collar with a black golf ball attached to it.

'What's that?' asked Gabrielle.

'A gag,' replied Leclerc. 'It's new. He probably bought it in a sex shop. They're very popular with the S and M crowd. With luck we may be able to trace it.'

'Oh my God!' She looked in horror at Hoffmann. 'What was he going to do to us?'

Hoffmann felt faint again, his mouth dry. 'I don't know. Kidnap us?'

'That's certainly a possibility,' agreed Leclerc, glancing around the room. 'You're a rich man, that's obvious enough. But I must say that kidnapping is unheard of in Geneva. This is a law-abiding city.' He took out his pen again. 'May I ask your occupation?'

'I'm a physicist.'

'A physicist.' Leclerc made a note. He nodded to himself, and raised an eyebrow. 'That I did not expect. English?'

'American.'

'Jewish?'

'What the hell has that got to do with it?'

'Forgive me. Your family name . . . I only ask in case there may be a racist motive.'

'No, not Jewish.'

'And Madame Hoffmann?'

'I'm English.'

'And you've lived in Switzerland for how long, Dr Hoffmann?'

'Fourteen years.' Weariness once again almost

overtook him. 'I came out here in the nineties to work for CERN, on the Large Hadron Collider. I was there for about six years.'

'And now?'

'I run a company.'

'Called?'

'Hoffmann Investment Technologies.'

'And what does it make?'

'What does it make? It makes money. It's a hedge fund.'

'Very good. "It makes money." How long have you been here?'

'Like I said—fourteen years.'

'No, I meant *here*—here, in this house?'

'Oh . . .' He looked at Gabrielle, defeated.

She said, 'Only a month.'

'One month? Did you change the entry codes when you took over?'

'Of course.'

'And who apart from the two of you knows the combination for the burglar alarm and so forth?'

Gabrielle said, 'Our housekeeper. The maid. The gardener.'

'And none of them lives in?'

'No.'

'Does anyone at your office know the codes, Dr Hoffmann?'

'My assistant.' Hoffmann frowned. How sluggishly his brain moved: like a computer with a virus. 'Oh, and our security consultant—he checked everything before we bought the place.'

'Can you remember his name?'

'Genoud.' He pondered for a moment. 'Maurice Genoud.'

Leclerc looked up. 'There was a Maurice

25

Genoud on the Geneva police force. I seem to remember he went into the private security business. Well, well.' A thoughtful expression crossed Leclerc's hangdog face. He resumed his note-taking. 'Obviously all the combinations will need to be changed immediately. I suggest that you don't reveal the new codes to any of your employees until I've had a chance to interview them.'

A buzzer sounded in the hall. It made Hoffmann jump.

'That's probably the ambulance,' said Gabrielle. 'I'll open the gate.'

While she was out of the room, Hoffmann said, 'I suppose this is going to get into the press?'

'Is that a problem?'

'I try to keep my name out of the papers.'

'We'll endeavour to be discreet. Do you have any enemies, Dr Hoffmann?'

'No, not that I know of. Certainly no one who'd do anything like this.'

'Some rich investor—Russian, perhaps—who's lost money?'

'We don't lose money.' Still, Hoffmann tried to think if there was anyone on his client list who might possibly be involved. But no: it was inconceivable. 'Is it safe for us to stay here, do you think, with this maniac on the loose?'

'We'll have our people here most of the day, and tonight we can keep an eye on the place—perhaps put a car in the road. But I have to say that generally we find that men in your position prefer to take precautions of their own.'

'You mean hire bodyguards?' Hoffmann grimaced. 'I don't want to live like that.'

'Unfortunately, a house like this is always going to attract unwanted attention. And bankers are not especially popular these days, even in Switzerland.' Leclerc looked around the room. 'May I ask how much you paid for it?'

Normally Hoffmann would have told him to go to hell, but he didn't have the strength. 'Sixty million dollars.'

'Oh my!' Leclerc pursed his lips in pain. 'You know, I can't afford to live in Geneva any more. My wife and I have moved to a house just over the border in France, where things are cheaper. Of course it means I have to drive in every day, but there it is.'

From outside came the noise of a diesel engine. Gabrielle put her head around the door. 'The ambulance is here. I'll go and find you some clothes we can take with us.'

Hoffmann tried to rise. Leclerc came over to help him, but Hoffmann waved him away. The Swiss, he thought sourly: they pretend to welcome foreigners but really they resent us. Why should I care if he lives in France? He had to rock himself forward a couple of times before he had gained sufficient momentum to escape the sofa, but on his third attempt he managed it and stood swaying on the Aubusson carpet. The clamour in his head was making him feel nauseous again.

Leclerc said, 'I do hope this unpleasant incident hasn't put you off our beautiful country.'

Hoffmann wondered if he was joking, but the inspector's face was perfectly straight.

'Not at all.'

Together they went out into the hall, Hoffmann taking exaggerated care with each step, like a drunk who wishes to be thought sober. The house had become crowded with people from the emergency services. More gendarmes had arrived, along with two ambulance personnel, a man and a woman, wheeling a bed. Confronted by their heavy government-issue clothing, Hoffmann once again felt naked and vulnerable; an invalid. He was relieved to see Gabrielle coming down the stairs with his raincoat. Leclerc took it from her and draped it around Hoffmann's shoulders.

By the front door, Hoffmann noticed a fire extinguisher, wrapped in a plastic bag. The mere sight of it gave him a twinge of pain. He said, 'Are you going to put out an artist's impression of this man?'

'We might.'

'Then now I think of it, there's something you should see.' It had come to him suddenly, with the force of a revelation. Ignoring the protests of the ambulance people that he should lie down, he turned and walked back along the hall to his study. The Bloomberg terminal on his desk was still switched on. Out of the corner of his eye he registered a red glow. Almost every price was down. The Far Eastern markets must be haemorrhaging. He switched on the light and searched along the shelf until he found *The Expression of the Emotions in Man and Animals*. His hands were trembling with excitement. He flicked through the pages.

'There,' he said, turning to show his discovery to Leclerc and Gabrielle. He tapped his finger on the page. 'That's the man who attacked me.'

It was the illustration for the emotion of terror—an old man, his eyes wide, his toothless mouth agape. Electric calipers were being applied to his facial muscles by the great French doctor Duchenne, an expert in galvanism, in order to stimulate the required expression.

Hoffmann could sense the others' scepticism—no, worse: their dismay.

'I'm sorry,' said Leclerc, puzzled. 'You're telling us that this is the man who was in your house tonight?'

'Oh, Alex,' said Gabrielle.

'Obviously I'm not saying it's *literally* him—he's been dead more than a century—I'm saying it *looks* like him.' They were both staring at him intently. They believe I have gone mad, he thought. He took a breath. 'Okay. Now this book,' he explained carefully to Leclerc, 'arrived yesterday without any explanation. I didn't order it, right? I don't know who sent it. Maybe it's a coincidence. But you've got to agree it's odd that a few hours after this arrives, a man—who actually looks as though he's just stepped out of its pages—turns up to attack us.' They were silent. 'Anyway,' he concluded, 'all I'm saying is, if you want to make an artist's impression of the guy, you should start with this.'

'Thank you,' said Leclerc. 'I'll bear that in mind.'

There was a pause.

'Right,' said Gabrielle brightly. 'Let's get you to the hospital.'

*   *   *

Leclerc saw them off from the front door.

The moon had disappeared behind the clouds. There was barely any light in the sky, even though there was only half an hour until dawn. The American physicist, with his bandaged head and his

29

black raincoat and his thin pink ankles poking out beneath his expensive pyjamas, was helped into the back of the ambulance by one of the attendants. Since his gabbling remarks about the Victorian photograph, he had fallen silent; Leclerc thought he seemed embarrassed. He had taken the book with him. His wife followed, clutching a bag full of his clothes. They looked like a pair of refugees. The doors were banged shut and the ambulance pulled away, a patrol car behind it.

Leclerc watched until the two vehicles reached the curve of the drive leading to the main road. Brake lights briefly gleamed crimson and then they were gone.

He turned back into the house.

'Big place for two people,' muttered one of the gendarmes standing just inside the doorway.

Leclerc grunted. 'Big place for ten people.'

He went on a solitary expedition to try to get a feel of what he was dealing with. Five, six—no, *seven* bedrooms upstairs, each with an en suite bathroom, none apparently ever used; the master bedroom huge, with a big dressing room next to it lined by mirrored doors and drawers; a plasma TV in the bathroom; his-and-hers basins; a space-age shower with a dozen nozzles. Across the landing, a gym, with an exercise bike, a rowing machine, a cross-trainer, weights, another big TV. No toys. No evidence of children anywhere, in fact, not even in the framed photographs scattered around, which were mostly of the Hoffmanns on expensive holidays—skiing, of course, and crewing a yacht, and holding hands on some veranda that seemed to be built on stilts above a coral lagoon of improbable blueness.

Leclerc went downstairs, imagining how it must have felt to be Hoffmann, an hour and a half earlier, descending to face the unknown. He skirted the bloodstains and passed through into the study. An entire wall was given over to books. He took down one at random and looked at the spine: *Die Traumdeutung* by Sigmund Freud. He opened it. Published Leipzig and Vienna, 1900. A first edition. He took down another. *La psychologie des foules* by Gustave le Bon. Paris, 1895. And another: *L'homme machine* by Julien Offray de La Mettrie. Leiden, 1747. Also a first edition. Leclerc knew little about rare books, but sufficient even so to appreciate that this must be a collection worth millions. No wonder there were so many smoke detectors dotted around the house. The subjects covered were mostly scientific: sociology, psychology, biology, anthropology—nothing anywhere about money.

He crossed over to the desk and sat down in Hoffmann's antique captain's chair. Occasionally the large screen in front of him rippled slightly as the shimmering expanse of figures changed: *-1.06, -78, -4.03%, -$0.95*. He could no more decipher it than he could read the Rosetta Stone. If only I could find the key, he thought, maybe I could be as rich as this fellow. His own investments, which he had been persuaded to make a few years back by some pimply 'financial adviser' in order to secure a comfortable old age, were now worth only half what he had paid for them. The way things were going, when he retired he would have to take a part-time job: head of security in a department store, maybe. He would work until he dropped—something not even his father and grandfather had had to do.

31

Thirty years with the police and he couldn't even afford to live in the town where he was born! And who was buying up all the expensive property? Money-launderers, many of them—the wives and daughters of presidents of the so-called 'new democracies', politicians from the central Asian republics, Russian oligarchs, Afghan warlords, arms-dealers—the real criminals of the world, in short, while he spent his time chasing teenage Algerian dope-peddlers hanging round the railway station. He made himself stand up and go into another room in order to take his mind off it.

In the kitchen he leaned against the granite island and studied the knives. On his instructions they had been bagged and sealed in the hope that they might yield fingerprints. This part of Hoffmann's story he did not understand. If the intruder had come prepared to kidnap, surely he would have armed himself properly beforehand? And a kidnapper would have needed at least one accomplice, maybe more: Hoffmann was relatively young and fit—he would have put up a struggle. So was the motive robbery? But a simple burglar would have been in and out as quickly as he could, taking as much as he could carry, and there was plenty portable here to steal. Everything therefore seemed to point to the criminal being mentally disturbed. But how would a violent psychopath have known the entry codes? It was a mystery. Perhaps there was some other way into the house that had been left unlocked.

Leclerc went back out into the corridor and turned left. The rear of the house opened into a large Victorian-style conservatory, which was being used as an artist's studio, although it was not exactly art as the inspector understood that term. It looked more like a radiographic unit, or possibly a glazier's workshop. On the original exterior wall of the house was a vast collage of electronic images of the human body—digital, infrared, X-ray—along with anatomical drawings of various organs, limbs and muscles.

Sheets of non-reflecting glass and Perspex, of various sizes and thicknesses, were stored in wooden racks. In a tin trunk were dozens of files, bulging with computer images, carefully labelled: 'MRI head scans, 1–14 Sagittal, Axial, Coronal'; 'Man, slices, Virtual Hospital, Sagittal & Coronal'. On a bench were a light box, a small vice and a clutter of inkpots, engraving tools and paint brushes. There was a hand drill in a black rubber stand, with a dark blue tin next to it—'Taylor's of Harrogate, Earl Grey Tea'—crammed full of drill heads, and a pile of glossy brochures for an exhibition entitled 'Human Contours' due to begin that very day at a gallery on the Plaine de Plainpalais. There was a biographical note inside: 'Gabrielle Hoffmann was born in Yorkshire, England. She took a joint honours degree in art and French from the University of Salford, and received an MA from the Royal College of Art, London. For several years she worked for the United Nations in Geneva.' He rolled the brochure into a cylinder and stuffed it into his pocket.

Next to the bench, mounted on a pair of trestles, was one of her works: a 3D scanned image of a foetus composed of about twenty sections drawn on sheets of very clear glass. Leclerc bent to examine it. Its head was disproportionately large for its body, its spindly legs drawn up and tucked beneath

33

it. Viewed from the side it had depth, but as one shifted one's perspective to the front it seemed to dwindle, then vanish entirely. He could not make out whether it was finished or not. It had a certain power, he was forced to concede, but he couldn't have lived with it himself. It looked too much like a fossilised reptile suspended in an aquarium. His wife would have thought it disgusting.

A door from the conservatory led out to the garden. It was locked and bolted; no key nearby that he could find. Beyond the thick glass, the lights of Geneva wavered across the lake. A solitary pair of headlights made its way along the Quai du Mont-Blanc.

Leclerc left the conservatory and returned to the passage. Two more doors led off it. One turned out to be a lavatory containing a big old-fashioned water closet, into which Leclerc took the opportunity to relieve himself, and the other a storage room filled with what appeared to be detritus from the Hoffmanns' last house: rolls of carpet tied with twine, a bread-making machine, deckchairs, a croquet set, and, at the far end, in pristine condition, a baby's cot, a changing table, and a clockwork mobile of stars and moons.

3

Suspicion, the offspring of fear, is eminently characteristic of most wild animals.

CHARLES DARWIN, *The Descent of Man* (1871)

According to the records subsequently released by the Geneva medical service, the ambulance radioed to report that it was leaving the Hoffmanns' residence at 5.22. At that hour it was only a five-minute drive through the empty streets of central Geneva to the hospital.

In the back of the ambulance Hoffmann maintained his refusal to obey regulations and lie down on the bed, but instead sat upright with his legs over the side, brooding and defiant. He was a brilliant man, a rich man, accustomed to being listened to with respect. But now suddenly he found he had been deported to some poorer and less-favoured land: the kingdom of the sick, where every citizen was second class. It irritated him to recall how Gabrielle and Leclerc had looked at him when he had showed them *The Expression of the Emotions in Man and Animals*—as if the obvious connection between the book and the attack was merely the fevered product of an injured brain. He had brought the volume with him; it was resting in his lap; he tapped his finger against it restlessly.

The ambulance swerved around the corner and the female attendant put out her hand to steady him. Hoffmann scowled at her. He had no confidence in the Geneva police or in government

35

departments generally. He had no confidence in anyone much, except himself. He searched his dressing gown pockets for his mobile.

Gabrielle, watching him from the opposite seat, next to the ambulance woman, said, 'What are you doing?'

'I'm calling Hugo.'

She rolled her eyes. 'For God's sake, Alex . . .'

'What? He needs to know what's happened.' As Hoffmann listened to the number ringing, he reached over and took her hand to mollify her. 'I'm feeling much better, really.'

Eventually Quarry came on the line. 'Alex?' For once his normally languid voice was strained with anxiety: when is a phone call before dawn ever good news? 'What the hell is it?'

'Sorry to call this early, Hugo. We've had an intruder.'

'Oh, God, I'm so sorry. Are you all right?'

'Gabrielle's okay. I got a whack on the head. We're in an ambulance going to the hospital.'

'Which hospital?'

'The university, I think.' Hoffmann looked at Gabrielle for confirmation. She nodded. 'Yeah, the university.'

'I'm on my way.'

A couple of minutes later the ambulance swept up the approach road to the big teaching hospital. Through the smoked-glass window Hoffmann briefly glimpsed its scale—a huge place: ten floors, lit up like some great foreign airport terminal in the darkness—then the lights vanished as if a curtain had been pulled across them. The ambulance descended along a gently circling subterranean passage and pulled to a halt. The engine was cut. In

36

the silence, Gabrielle gave him a reassuring smile and Hoffmann thought: *Abandon hope all ye who enter here.* The rear doors swung open on to what looked like a spotlessly clean underground car park. A man shouted in the distance, his voice echoing off the concrete walls.

Hoffmann was instructed to lie down, and this time he decided not to argue: he had entered into the system; he must submit to its processes. He stretched out, the bed was lowered, and with a horrible feeling of helplessness he allowed himself to be wheeled along mysterious factory-like corridors, staring up at the strip lighting until, at a reception desk, he was briefly parked. An accompanying gendarme handed over his paperwork. Hoffmann watched as his details were registered, then turned his head on the pillow and glanced across the crowded room to where a television news channel played to a heedless audience of drunks and addicts. On the screen, Japanese traders with cell phones clamped to their ears were shown in various attitudes of horror and despair. But before he could find out any more, he was on the move again, down a short corridor and into an empty cubicle.

Gabrielle sat on a moulded plastic chair, took out a powder compact and started applying lipstick in quick, nervous strokes. Hoffmann watched her as if she were a stranger: so dark and neat and self-contained, like a cat washing her face. She had been doing exactly this when he first saw her, at a party in Saint-Genis-Pouilly. A harassed young Turkish doctor came in with a clipboard; a plastic name tag attached to his white coat announced him as Dr Muhammet Celik. He consulted Hoffmann's notes.

37

He shone a light into his eyes, struck his knee with a small hammer and asked him to name the president of the United States and then to count backwards from one hundred to eighty.

Hoffmann answered without difficulty. Satisfied, the doctor put on a pair of surgical gloves. He took off Hoffmann's temporary dressing, parted his hair and examined the wound, gently prodding it with his fingers: Hoffmann felt as if he were being inspected for lice. The accompanying conversation was conducted entirely above his head.

'He lost a lot of blood,' said Gabrielle.

'Wounds to the head always bleed heavily. He will need a few stitches, I think.'

'Is it a deep wound?'

'Oh, not so deep, but there is quite a wide area of swelling. You see? It was something blunt that hit him?'

'A fire extinguisher.'

'Okay. Let me make a note of that. We need to get a head scan.'

Celik bent down so that his face was level with Hoffmann's. He smiled. He opened his eyes very wide and spoke extremely slowly. 'Very well then, Monsieur Hoffmann. Later I will stitch the wound. Right now we need to take you downstairs and make some pictures of the inside of your head. This will be done by a machine we call a CAT scanner. Are you familiar with a CAT scanner, Monsieur Hoffmann?'

'Computed Axial Tomography uses a rotating detector and X-ray source to compile cross-sectional radiographic images—it's seventies technology, no big deal. And it's not Monsieur Hoffmann, by the way—it's Dr Hoffmann.'

As he was wheeled into the elevator, Gabrielle said, 'There was no need to be so rude. He was only trying to help you.'

'He spoke to me as if I were a child.'

'Then stop behaving like one. Here, you can hold this.' She dropped his bag of clothes on to his lap and walked ahead to summon the elevator.

Gabrielle obviously knew her way to the radiology department, a fact that Hoffmann found obscurely irritating. Over the past couple of years the staff had helped her with her art work, giving her access to the scanners when they were not in use, staying late after their shifts had finished to produce the images she needed. Several had become her friends. He ought to be grateful to them, but he wasn't. The doors opened on to the darkened lower floor. They had a lot of scanners, he remembered. It was the hospital to which they helicoptered the most serious skiing injuries, from Chamonix, Megeve, even Courchevel. Hoffmann had a sense of a huge expanse of offices and equipment extending into the shadows—an entire department stilled and deserted, apart from this one small emergency outpost. A young man with long black curly hair came striding across to them. 'Gabrielle!' he exclaimed. He took her hand and kissed it, then turned to look down at Hoffmann. 'So you have brought me a genuine patient for a change?'

Gabrielle said, 'This is my husband, Alexander Hoffmann. Alex—this is Fabian Tallon, the duty technician. You remember Fabian? I've told you all about him.'

'I don't think so,' said Hoffmann. He looked up at the young man. Tallon had large dark liquid eyes,

39

a wide mouth, very white teeth and a couple of days' growth of dark beard. His shirt was unbuttoned more than it needed to be, drawing attention to his broad chest, his rugby player's chest. Suddenly Hoffmann wondered if Gabrielle might be having an affair with him. He tried to push the idea out of his head, but it refused to go. It was years since he had felt a pang of jealousy; he had forgotten how almost exquisite the sharpness could be. Looking from one to the other he said, 'Thank you for all you've done for Gabrielle.'

'It's been a pleasure, Alex. Now let's see what we can do for you.' He pushed the bed as easily as if it were a supermarket trolley, through the control area and into the room containing the CAT scanner. 'Stand up, please.'

Once again Hoffmann surrendered mechanically to the procedure. His overcoat and spectacles were taken from him. He was told to sit on the edge of the couch that formed part of the machine. The dressing was removed from his head. He was instructed to lie on his back on the couch, his head pointing towards the scanner. Tallon adjusted the neck rest. 'This will take less than a minute,' he said, and disappeared. The door sighed shut behind him. Hoffmann raised his head slightly. He was alone. Beyond his bare feet, through the thick glass window at the far end of the room, he could see Gabrielle watching him. Tallon joined her. They said something to one another that he could not hear. There was a clatter, and then Tallon's voice came loudly over a loudspeaker.

'Lie back, Alex. Try to keep as still as possible.'

Hoffmann did as ordered. There was a hum and the couch began to slide backwards through the wide drum of the scanner. It happened twice: once briefly, to get a fix; the second time more slowly, to collect the images. He stared at the white plastic casing as he passed beneath it. It was like being subjected to some radioactive car wash. The couch stopped and reversed itself and Hoffmann imagined his brain being sprayed by a brilliant, cleansing light, from which nothing could hide—all impurities exposed and obliterated in a hiss of burning matter.

The loudspeaker clicked on and briefly he heard the sound of Gabrielle's voice dying away in the background. It seemed to him—could this be right?—that she had been whispering. Tallon said, 'Thank you, Alex. It's all over. Stay where you are. I'll come and get you.' He resumed his conversation with Gabrielle. 'But you see—' The sound cut out.

Hoffmann lay there for what seemed a long while: plenty of time, at any rate, to consider how easy it would have been for Gabrielle to have had an affair over the past few months. There were the long hours she had spent at the hospital collecting the images she needed for her work; and then there were the even longer days and nights he had been away at his office, developing VIXAL. What was there to anchor a couple in a marriage after more than seven years if there were no children to exert some gravitational pull? Suddenly he experienced yet another long-forgotten sensation: the delicious, childish pain of self-pity. To his horror, he realised he was starting to cry.

'Are you okay, Alex?' Tallon's face loomed above the couch, handsome, concerned, insufferable.

'No problem.'

'Are you sure you're okay?'

'I'm fine.' Hoffmann wiped his eyes quickly on the sleeve of his dressing gown and put his spectacles back on. The rational part of his mind recognised that these sudden lurches in mood were likely to be symptoms of head trauma, but that did not make them any less real. He refused to get back on to the wheeled bed. He swung his legs off the couch, took a few deep breaths, and by the time he walked into the other room had regained control of himself.

'Alex,' said Gabrielle, 'this is the radiologist, Dr Dufort.'

She indicated a tiny woman with close-cropped grey hair who was seated at a computer screen. Dufort turned and gave him a perfunctory nod over her narrow shoulder, then resumed her examination of the scan results.

'Is that me?' asked Hoffmann, staring at the screen.

'It is, *monsieur*.' She did not turn round.

Hoffmann contemplated his brain with detachment, indeed disappointment. The black-and-white image on the screen could have been anything—a section of coral reef being filmed by a remote underwater camera, a view of the lunar surface, the face of a monkey. Its messiness, its lack of form or beauty, depressed him. Surely we can do better than this, he thought. This cannot be the end product. This must be merely a stage in evolution, and our human task is to prepare the way for whatever comes next, just as gas created organic matter. Artificial intelligence, or autonomous machine reasoning as he preferred to call it—AMR—had been a preoccupation of his for more than fifteen years. Silly people, encouraged by journalists, thought the aim was to replicate the human mind, and to produce a digitalised version of ourselves. But really, why would one bother to imitate anything so vulnerable and unreliable, or with such built-in obsolescence: a central processing unit that could be utterly destroyed because some ancillary mechanical part—the heart, say, or the liver—suffered a temporary interruption? It was like losing a Cray supercomputer and all of its memory files because a plug needed changing.

The radiologist tilted the brain on its axis from top to bottom and it seemed to nod at him, a greeting from outer space. She rotated it. She twisted it from side to side.

'No evidence of fracture,' she said, 'and no swelling, which is the most important thing. But what is this, I wonder?'

The skull bone showed up like a reverse image of a walnut shell. A white line of variable thickness encased the spongy grey matter of the brain. She zoomed in. The image widened, blurred and finally dissolved into a pale grey supernova. Hoffmann leaned forward for a closer look.

'There,' said Dufort, touching the screen with a bitten-down, ringless finger. 'You see these pinpoints of whiteness? These bright stars? These are tiny haemorrhages in the brain tissue.'

Gabrielle said, 'Is that serious?'

'No, not necessarily. It's probably what one would expect to see from an injury of this type. You know, the brain ricochets when the head is struck with sufficient force. There is bound to be a little bleeding. It seems to have stopped.' She raised her spectacles and leaned in very close to the screen,

43

like a jeweller inspecting a precious stone. 'All the same,' she said, 'I would like to do another test.'

Hoffmann had so often imagined this moment—the vast and impersonal hospital, the abnormal test result, the coolly delivered medical verdict, the first step on the irreversible descent to helplessness and death—that it took him a moment to realise this was not another of his hypochondriac fantasies.

'What sort of test?' he asked.

'I would like to use MRI for a second look. It gives a much clearer image of soft tissue. It should tell us whether this is a pre-existing condition or not.'

A pre-existing condition . . .

'How long will that take?'

'The test itself does not take long. It's a question of when a scanner is free.' She called up a new file and clicked through it. 'We should be able to get on to a machine at noon, provided there isn't an emergency.'

Gabrielle said, 'Isn't *this* an emergency?'

'No, no, there isn't any immediate danger.'

'In that case, I'd rather leave it,' said Hoffmann.

'Don't be silly,' said Gabrielle. 'Have the test. You might as well.'

'I don't want the test.'

'You're being ridiculous—'

'I said I don't want the goddamned test!'

There was a moment of shocked silence.

'We know you're upset, Alex,' said Tallon quietly, 'but there's no need to talk to Gabrielle like that.'

'Don't you tell me how to talk to my wife!' He put his hand to his brow. His fingers were very cold. His throat was dry. He had to get out of the hospital

44

as quickly as possible. He swallowed before he spoke again. 'I'm sorry, but I don't want it. There are important things I need to do today.'

'*Monsieur*,' said Dufort firmly, 'all patients who have been knocked unconscious for as long as you were are kept here in the hospital for at least twenty-four hours, for observation.'

'That's impossible, I'm afraid.'

'What important things?' Gabrielle stared at him in disbelief. 'You're not going into the office?'

'Yes, I am going into the office. And you're going to the gallery for the start of your exhibition.'

'Alex . . .'

'Yes, you are. You've been working on it for months—think of all the time you've spent here, for a start. And tonight we're going to have dinner to celebrate your success.' He was aware that he was starting to raise his voice again. He forced himself to speak more calmly. 'Just because this guy got into our house, it doesn't mean he has to get into our lives. Not unless we let him. Look at me.' He gestured to himself. 'I'm fine. You just saw the scan—no fracture and no swelling.'

'And no bloody common sense,' said an English voice behind them.

'Hugo,' said Gabrielle, without turning to look at him, 'will you please tell your business partner that he's made of flesh and blood, just like the rest of us?'

'Ah, but is he?' Quarry was standing by the door with his overcoat unfastened, a cherry-red woollen scarf around his neck, his hands in his pockets.

'Business partner?' repeated Dr Celik, who had been persuaded to bring Quarry down from A&E, and was now looking at him suspiciously. 'I thought

45

you said you were his brother?'

'Just have the damned test, Al,' said Quarry. 'The presentation can be postponed.'

'Exactly,' said Gabrielle.

'I promise you I'll have the test,' said Hoffmann evenly. 'Just not today. Is that all right with you, Doctor? I'm not going to collapse or anything?'

'*Monsieur*,' said the grey-haired radiologist, who had been on duty since the previous afternoon and was losing patience, 'what you do, and do not do, is entirely your decision. The wound should definitely be stitched, in my opinion, and if you leave you will be required to sign a form releasing the hospital from all responsibility. The rest is up to you.'

'Fine. I'll have it stitched, and I'll sign the form. And then I'll come back and have the MRI another time, when it's more convenient. Happy?' he said to Gabrielle.

Before she could reply, a familiar electronic reveille sounded. It took him a moment to realise it was the alarm on his mobile, which he had set for six thirty in what felt to him already like another life.

*   *   *

Hoffmann left his wife sitting with Quarry in the reception area of the accident and emergency department while he went back into the cubicle to have his wound stitched up. He was given a local anaesthetic, administered by syringe—a moment of sharp pain that made him gasp—and then a thin strip of hair was shaved from around the wound with a disposable plastic razor. The process of stitching felt strange rather than uncomfortable, as

46

if his scalp was being tightened. Afterwards, Dr Celik produced a small mirror and showed Hoffmann his handiwork, like a hairdresser seeking approval from a customer. The cut was only about five centimetres long. Stitched together it resembled a twisted mouth with thick white lips where the hair had been removed. It seemed to leer at Hoffmann in the glass.

'It will hurt,' said Celik cheerfully, 'when the anaesthetic wears off. You will need to take painkillers.' He took away the mirror and the smile vanished.

'You're not going to bandage it up?'

'No, it will heal quicker if it's exposed.'

'Good. In that case, I'll leave now.'

Celik shrugged. 'That is your right. But first you must sign a form.'

After he had signed the little chit—'I declare that I am leaving the University Hospital contrary to medical advice, despite being informed of the risks, and that I assume full responsibility'—Hoffmann picked up his bag of clothes and followed Celik to a small shower cubicle. Celik switched on the light. As he turned away the Turk muttered, barely audibly, 'Asshole'—or at any rate that was what Hoffmann thought he said, but the door closed before he could respond.

It was the first time he had been alone since he recovered consciousness, and for a moment he revelled in his solitude. He took off his dressing gown and pyjamas. There was a mirror on the opposite wall and he paused to examine his naked reflection under the merciless neon strip: his skin sallow, his stomach slack, his breasts slightly more visible than they used to be, like a pubescent girl's.

47

Some of his chest hair was grey. A long black bruise extended across his left hip. He twisted sideways to examine himself, ran his fingers along the grazed and darkened skin, then briefly cupped his penis. There was no reaction, and he wondered: could a blow on the head render one impotent? Glancing down, his feet seemed to him unnaturally splayed and veined on the cold tile floor. This is old age, he thought with a shock, this is the future: I look like that portrait by Lucian Freud Gabrielle wanted me to buy. He bent to pick up the bag and for a moment the room went fuzzy and he swayed slightly. He sat down on the white plastic chair with his head between his knees.

After he had recovered, he dressed slowly and deliberately—boxer shorts, T-shirt, socks, jeans, a plain white long-sleeved shirt, a sports jacket—and with each item he felt a little stronger, a degree less vulnerable. Gabrielle had put his wallet inside his jacket pocket. He checked the contents. He had three thousand Swiss francs in new notes. He sat down and pulled on a pair of desert boots, and when he stood and looked at himself in the mirror again, he felt satisfactorily camouflaged. His clothes said nothing at all about him, which was the way he liked it. A hedge fund manager with ten billion dollars in assets under management could these days pass for the guy who delivered his parcels. In this respect if no other, money—big money, confident money, money that had no need to show off—had become democratic.

There was a knock on the door, and he heard the radiologist, Dr Dufort, calling his name. 'Monsieur Hoffmann? Monsieur Hoffmann, are you all right?'

'Yes, thank you,' he called back, 'much better.'

'I am going off duty now. I have something for you.' He opened the door. She had put on a raincoat and rubber boots and was carrying an umbrella. 'Here. These are your CAT scan results.' She thrust a CD in a clear plastic case into his hands. 'If you want my advice, you should take them to your own doctor as soon as possible.'

'I will, of course, thank you.'

'Will you?' She gave him a sceptical look. 'You know, you should. If there is something wrong, it won't go away. Better to face one's fears at once rather than let them fester.'

'So you think there *is* something wrong?' He detested the sound of his own voice—tremulous, pathetic.

'I don't know, *monsieur*. You need an MRI scan to determine that.'

'What might it be, do you think?' Hoffmann hesitated. 'A tumour?'

'No, I don't think that.'

'What, then?'

He searched her eyes for a clue but saw there only boredom; she must have to deliver bad news a lot, he realised.

She said, 'It probably isn't anything at all. But I suppose other explanations might include—I am only speculating, you understand?—MS perhaps, or possibly dementia. Best to be prepared.' She patted his hand. 'See your doctor, *monsieur*. Really, take it from me: it is always the unknown that is most frightening.'

4

The slightest advantage in one being, at any age or during any season, over those with which it comes into competition, or better adaptation in however slight a degree to the surrounding physical conditions, will turn the balance.

CHARLES DARWIN, *On the Origin of Species* (1859)

Some in the secretive inner counsels of the super-rich occasionally wondered aloud why Hoffmann had made Quarry an equal shareholder in Hoffmann Investment Technologies: it was, after all, the physicist's algorithms that generated the profits; it was his name above the shop. But it suited Hoffmann's temperament to have someone else, more outgoing, to hide behind. Besides, he knew there would have been no company without his partner. It was not just that Quarry had the experience and interest in banking that he lacked; he also had something else that Hoffmann could never possess no matter how hard he tried: a talent for dealing with people.

This was partly charm, of course. But it was more than that. It was a capacity for bending human beings to a larger purpose. If there had been another war, Quarry would have made a perfect ADC to a field marshal—a position that had, in fact, been held in the British Army by both his great- and great-great-grandfathers—ensuring that orders were carried out, soothing hurt feelings, firing subordinates with such tact they came away believing it was their idea to leave, requisitioning the best local chateaux for temporary staff headquarters and, at the end of a sixteen-hour day, bringing together jealous rivals over a dinner for which he himself would have selected the most appropriate wines. He had a first in politics, philosophy and economics from Oxford, an ex-wife and three children safely stowed in a gloomy Lutyens mansion in a drizzled fold of Surrey, and a ski chalet in Chamonix where he went in winter with whoever happened to be his girlfriend that weekend: an interchangeable sequence of clever, beautiful, undernourished females who were always discarded before there was any sign of gynaecologists or lawyers. Gabrielle couldn't stand him.

Nevertheless, the crisis made them temporary allies. While Hoffmann was having his wound stitched up, Quarry fetched a cup of sweet milky coffee for her from the machine along the corridor. He sat with her in the tiny waiting room, with its hard wooden chairs and its galaxy of plastic stars gleaming from the ceiling. He held her hand and squeezed it at appropriate moments. He listened to her account of what had happened. When she recited Hoffmann's subsequent oddities of behaviour, he reassured her that all would be well: 'Let's face it, Gabs, he's never been exactly *normal*, has he, even at the best of times? We'll get this sorted out, don't worry. Just give me ten minutes.'

He called his assistant and told her he would need a chauffeured car at the hospital immediately. He woke the company's security consultant, Maurice Genoud, and brusquely ordered him to attend an emergency meeting at the office within

51

the hour, and to send someone over to the Hoffmanns' house. Finally he managed to get himself put through to Inspector Leclerc and persuaded him to agree that Dr Hoffmann would not be required to attend police headquarters to make a statement immediately he left hospital: Leclerc accepted that he had already taken sufficiently detailed notes to form a continuous narrative, which Hoffmann could amend where necessary and sign later in the day.

Throughout all this, Gabrielle watched Quarry with reluctant admiration. He was so much the opposite of Alex—good-looking *and* he knew it. His affected southern English manners also got on her Presbyterian northern nerves. Sometimes she wondered if he might be gay, and all his thoroughbred girls more for show than action.

'Hugo,' she said very seriously, when he finally got off the phone, 'I want you to do me a favour. I want you to order him not to go into the office today.'

Quarry took her hand again. 'Darling, if I thought my telling him would do any good, I would. But as you know, at least as well as I, once he gets set on doing a thing, he invariably does it.'

'And is it really so important, what he has to do today?'

'It is, quite.' Quarry twisted his wrist very slightly, so that he could read the time on his watch without letting go of her hand. 'I mean, nothing that can't be put off if his health really is at stake, obviously. But if I'm honest with you, it would definitely be better to go ahead than not. People have come a long way to see him.'

She pulled her hand away. 'You want to be

careful you don't kill your golden goose,' she said bitterly. 'That definitely would be bad for business.'

'Don't think I don't know it,' said Quarry pleasantly. His smile crinkled the skin around his deep blue eyes; his lashes, like his hair, were sandy. 'Listen, if I start to think for *one moment* that he's seriously endangering himself, I'll have him back home and tucked up in bed with Mummy within fifteen minutes. And that's a promise. And now,' he said, looking over her shoulder, 'if I'm not mistaken, here comes our dear old goose, with his feathers half plucked and ruffled.'

He was on his feet in an instant. 'My dear Al,' he said, meeting him halfway across the corridor, 'how are you feeling? You look very pale.'

'I'll be a whole lot better once I'm out of this place.' Hoffmann slipped the CD into his overcoat pocket so that Gabrielle could not see it. He kissed her on the cheek. 'Everything's going to be fine now.'

*   *   *

They made their way through the main reception. It was nearly half past seven. Outside, the day had turned up at last: overcast and cold and reluctant. The thick rolls of cloud hanging over the hospital were the same shade of grey as brain tissue, or so it appeared to Hoffmann, who was now seeing the CAT scan wherever he looked. A gust of wind swirled across the circular concourse and wrapped his raincoat around his legs. A small but egalitarian group of smokers, white-coated doctors and patients in their dressing gowns, stood outside the main door, huddled against the unseasonable May

53

weather. In the sodium lighting their cigarette smoke whirled and disappeared amid flecks of raindrops.

Quarry found their car, a big Mercedes owned by a discreet and reliable Geneva limousine service under contract to the hedge fund. It was parked in a bay reserved for the disabled. The driver—a heavyset and mustachioed figure—levered himself out of the front seat as they approached and held a rear door open for them: he has driven me before, thought Hoffmann, and he struggled to remember his name as the distance between them closed.

'Georges!' He greeted him with relief. 'Good morning to you, Georges!'

'Good morning, *monsieur*.' The chauffeur smiled and touched his hand to his cap in salute as Gabrielle climbed into the back seat, followed by Quarry. '*Monsieur*,' he whispered in a quiet aside to Hoffmann, 'forgive me, but just so you know, my name is Claude.'

'Right then, boys and girls,' said Quarry, seated between the Hoffmanns and squeezing the nearest knee of each simultaneously, 'where is it to be?'

Hoffmann said, 'Office,' just as Gabrielle said, 'Home.'

'Office,' repeated Hoffmann, 'and then home for my wife.'

The traffic was already building up on the approaches to the city centre, and as the Mercedes turned into the Boulevard de la Cluse, Hoffmann fell into his habitual silence. He wondered if the others had overheard his mistake. What on earth had made him do that? It was not as if he usually noticed who his driver was, let alone spoke to him: car journeys were passed in the company of his

54

iPad, surfing the web for technical research or, for lighter reading, the digital edition of the *Financial Times* or the *Wall Street Journal*. It was rare for him even to look out of the window. How odd it felt to do so now, when there was nothing else to occupy him—to notice, for example, for the first time in years, people queuing at a bus stop, seemingly exhausted before the day had properly begun; or the number of young Moroccans and Algerians hanging around on the street corners—a sight that had not existed when he first came to Switzerland. But then, he thought, why shouldn't they be there? Their presence in Geneva was as much a product of globalisation as his was, or Quarry's.

The limousine slowed to make a left. A bell clanged. A tram drew alongside. Hoffmann glanced up absently at the faces framed in the lighted windows. For a moment they seemed to hang motionless in the morning gloom then silently began to drift past him: some gazing blankly ahead, others dozing, one reading the *Tribune de Genève*, and finally, in the last window, the bony profile of a man in his fifties with a high-domed head and unkempt grey hair pulled into a ponytail. He stayed level with Hoffmann for an instant, then the tram accelerated and in a stink of electricity and a cascade of pale blue sparks the apparition was gone.

It was all so quick and dreamlike, Hoffmann was not certain what he had seen. Quarry must have felt him jump, or heard him draw in his breath. He turned and said, 'Are you all right, old friend?' But Hoffmann was too startled to speak.

'What's happening?' Gabrielle stretched back and peered around Quarry's head at her husband.

55

'Nothing.' Hoffmann managed to recover his voice. 'Anaesthetic must be wearing off.' He shielded his eyes with his hand and looked out of the window. 'Turn on the radio, could you?'

The voice of a female newsreader filled the car, disconcertingly bright, as if her script were unfamiliar to her; she would have announced Armageddon through a smile.

'The Greek government vowed last night to continue with its austerity measures, despite the deaths of three bank workers in Athens. The three were killed when demonstrators protesting against spending cuts attacked the bank with petrol bombs . . .'

Hoffmann was trying to decide whether he was hallucinating or not. If he wasn't, he ought to call Leclerc at once, and then tell the driver to keep the tram in view until the police arrived. But what if he was imagining things? His mind recoiled from the humiliations that would follow. Worse, it would mean he could no longer trust the signals from his own brain. He could endure anything except madness. He would sooner die than go down that path again. And so he said nothing and kept his face turned from the others, so that they could not see the panic in his eyes, as the radio jabbered on.

'Financial markets are expected to open down this morning after big falls all week in Europe and America. The crisis has been caused by fears that one or more countries in the eurozone may default on its debts. There have been further steep losses overnight in the Far East . . .'

If my mind were an algorithm, thought Hoffmann, I would quarantine it; I would shut it down.

56

'In Great Britain, voters are going to the polls today to elect a new government. The centre-left Labour Party is widely expected to lose office after thirteen years in power . . .'

'Did you use your postal vote, Gabs?' asked Quarry casually.

'Yes. Didn't you?'

'Christ, no. Why should I bother with that? Who'd you vote for? Wait—no—let me guess. The Greens.'

'It's a secret ballot,' she said primly, and glanced away, irritated that he had got it right.

Hoffmann's hedge fund was based in Les Eaux-Vives, a district just south of the lake, as solid and confident as the nineteenth-century Swiss businessmen who had built it: heavy masonry, wide faux-Parisian boulevards webbed with tram cables, cherry trees erupting from the kerbsides to shower dusty white and pink blossom over the grey pavements, shops and restaurants on the ground floors, seven storeys of offices and apartments stacked imperturbably above. Amid this bourgeois respectability Hoffmann Investment Technologies presented a narrow Victorian facade to the world, easy to miss unless you were looking for it, with only a small name tag on an entryphone to betray its existence. A steel-shuttered ramp, watched by a security camera, led down to an underground car park. On one side was a *salon de thé*, on the other a late-night supermarket. In the far distance the mountains of the Jura still bore a faint rim of snow.

'You promise me you'll be careful?' said Gabrielle, as the Mercedes pulled up.

Hoffmann reached behind Quarry and squeezed her shoulder. 'I'm getting stronger by the minute.

57

What about you, though? You feel okay, going back to the house?'

'Genoud is sending someone round,' said Quarry.

Gabrielle made a quick face at Hoffmann—her Hugo face, which involved turning down the corners of her mouth, sticking out her tongue and rolling up her eyes. Despite everything, he almost burst out laughing. '*Hugo* has it all under control,' she said, 'don't you, Hugo? *As usual.*' She kissed her husband's hand where it lay on her shoulder. 'I won't be stopping anyway. I'll just grab my things and get over to the gallery.'

The chauffeur opened the door.

'Hey, listen,' said Hoffmann. He was reluctant to let go of her. 'Good luck this morning. I'll come over and see how things are going as soon as I can get away.'

'I'd like that.'

He climbed out on to the pavement. She had a sudden premonition that she would never see him again, so vivid she was nearly sick. 'You're sure we shouldn't both cancel everything and take the day off?'

'No way. It's going to be great.'

Quarry said, 'Cheerio then, sweetheart,' and slid his neat bottom over the leather upholstery towards the open door. 'D'you know,' he said, as he clambered out, 'I think I might actually come and buy one of your thingamabobs. Go very well in our reception, I reckon.'

As the car pulled away, Gabrielle looked back at them through the rear window. Quarry had his left arm round Alex's shoulders and was steering him across the pavement; with his right he was gesturing. She could not tell what the gesture meant, but she knew he was making a joke. A moment later they disappeared.

*   *   *

The offices of Hoffmann Investment Technologies revealed themselves to a visitor like the carefully rehearsed stages of a conjuring trick. First, heavy doors of smoked glass opened automatically on to a narrow reception barely wider than a corridor, low-ceilinged, walled by dimly lit brown granite. Next you presented your face to a camera for 3D recognition scanning: it took less than one second for the metric geometry algorithm to match your features to its database (during this process it was important to maintain a neutral expression); if you were a visitor, you gave your name to the unsmiling security guard. Once cleared, you were clicked through a tubular steel turnstile, walked down another short corridor and turned left—and suddenly you were confronted by a huge open space flooded with daylight: that was when it hit you that this was actually three buildings knocked into one. The masonry at the back had been demolished and replaced by a sheer Alpine ice-fall of frameless glass, eight storeys high, overlooking a courtyard centred round a jetting fountain and elaborate giant ferns. Twin elevators rose and fell noiselessly in their soundproofed glass silos.

Quarry, the showman and salesman, had been stunned by the concept the moment he had first been shown round the place nine months earlier. For his part, Hoffmann had loved the computer-controlled systems—the lighting that adjusted in harmony with the daylight outside, the windows that opened automatically to regulate the temperature, the funnels on the roof that drew in fresh air to remove the need for air-conditioning in all open spaces, the ground-source heat-pump system, the rainwater recycling unit with its hundred-thousand-litre holding tank used for flushing the lavatories. The building was advertised as 'a holistic, digitally aware entity with minimal carbon emissions'. In the event of fire, the dampers would be shut off in the ventilation system to prevent the spread of smoke and the elevators sent to the ground floor to stop people boarding them. It was also, most important of all, connected to the GV1 fibre-optic pipe, the fastest in Europe. That clinched it: they took out a lease on the whole of the fifth floor. The corporate tenants above and below—DigiSyst, EcoTec, EuroTel—were as mysterious as their names. Nobody from one firm ever seemed to acknowledge the existence of anyone from another. Elevator rides passed in awkward silence, apart from when passengers stepped in and announced which floor they required (the voice-recognition system could differentiate between regional accents in twenty-four languages): Hoffmann, who made a fetish of privacy and loathed small talk, rather liked that.

The fifth floor was a kingdom within a kingdom. A wall of opaque and bubbled turquoise glass blocked off access from the elevators. To gain entry, as downstairs, it was necessary to present one's relaxed countenance to a scanner. Facial recognition activated a sliding panel, the glass vibrating slightly as it rolled back to reveal Hoffmann's own reception area: low cubes of black and grey upholstery stacked and arranged like child's bricks to form chairs and sofas, a coffee table of chrome and glass, and adjustable consoles containing touch-screen computers on which visitors could browse the web while waiting for their appointments. Each had a screensaver stating the company's rubric in red letters on a white background:

THE COMPANY OF THE FUTURE WILL HAVE
NO PAPER
THE COMPANY OF THE FUTURE WILL CARRY
NO INVENTORY
THE COMPANY OF THE FUTURE WILL BE
ENTIRELY DIGITAL
THE COMPANY OF THE FUTURE HAS ARRIVED

There were no magazines or newspapers in the reception area: it was company policy that, as far as possible, no printed material or writing paper of any sort should pass the threshold. Of course, the rule could not be imposed on guests, but employees, including the senior partners, were required to pay a fine of ten Swiss francs, and have their names posted on the company's intranet, each time they were caught in possession of ink and wood pulp rather than silicon and plastic. It was astonishing how quickly people's habits, even Quarry's, were changed by this simple rule. Ten years after Bill Gates had first preached the gospel of the paperless office in *Business at the Speed of Light*, Hoffmann had more or less brought it about. In a strange way he was almost as proud of this achievement as he was of any of his others.

It was embarrassing, therefore, for him to have

to pass through reception with his first edition of *The Expression of the Emotions in Man and Animals*. If he had caught anyone else with a copy he would have pointed out that the text was readily available online via Project Gutenberg or Darwin.online.org, and asked sarcastically whether they considered themselves to be a quicker reader than the VIXAL-4 algorithm, or had trained their brains to do word search. He saw no paradox in his zeal to ban the book at work and to display it in rare first editions at home. Books were antiques, just like any other artefacts from the past. One might just as well reprimand a collector of Venetian candelabra or Regency commodes for using an electric light or a flush lavatory. Nevertheless he slipped the volume under his coat and glanced up guiltily at one of the tiny security cameras that monitored the floor.

'Breaking your own rules, Professor?' said Quarry, loosening his scarf. 'Bit bloody rich.'

'Forgot I had it with me.'

'Like hell. Your place or mine?'

'I don't know. Does it matter? Okay—yours.'

To reach Quarry's office it was necessary to cross the trading floor. The Japanese stock market would close in fifteen minutes, the European exchanges would open at nine, and already four dozen quantitative analysts—quants, in the dismissive jargon of the trade—were hard at work. None talked above a whisper. Most stared silently at their six-screen arrays. Giant plasma televisions with muted sound carried CNBC and Bloomberg, while beneath the TVs a glowing red line of digital clocks noiselessly recorded time's relentless passage in Tokyo, Beijing, Moscow, Geneva, London and New York. This was the sound that money made in the second decade of the twenty-first century. The occasional soft clatter of strokes on a keyboard was the only indication that humans were present at all.

Hoffmann raised his hand to the back of his head and touched the hard puckered smile of his wound. He wondered how visible it was. Perhaps he should wear a baseball cap? He was conscious of being pale and unshaven and he tried to avoid meeting anyone's gaze, which was easy enough as few bothered to look up as he passed. Hoffmann's force of quants was nine-tenths male, for reasons he did not entirely understand. It was not deliberate policy; it simply seemed to be only men who applied, usually refugees from the twin miseries of academia: low salaries and high tables. Half a dozen had come from the Large Hadron Collider. Hoffmann would not even consider hiring anyone without a PhD in maths or the physical sciences; all doctoral theses were expected to have been peer-reviewed in the top fifteen per cent. Nationality did not matter and nor did social skills, with the result that Hoffmann's payroll occasionally resembled a United Nations conference on Asperger's syndrome. Quarry called it 'The Nerd World'. Last year's bonus brought the average remuneration up to almost half a million dollars.

Only five senior managers got offices of their own—the heads of Finance, Risk and Operations, along with Hoffmann, whose title was company president, and Quarry, who was the CEO. The offices were standard soundproofed glass cubicles with white venetian blinds, beige carpeting and Scandinavian furniture of pale wood and chrome. Quarry's windows looked down on to the street and across to a private German bank, hidden from view behind thick net curtains. He was in the process of having a sixty-five-metre super-yacht built by Benetti of Viareggio. Framed blueprints and artist's sketches lined his walls; there was a scale model on his desk. The hull would be lined all the way round, just below the deck, with a strip of lights he could turn on and off and change colour with his key fob while having dinner in port. He was planning to call her *Trade Alpha*. Hoffmann, who was happy enough in a Hobie Cat, worried at first that their clients might take this ostentation as evidence that they were making too much money. But as usual Quarry knew their psychology better than he did: 'No, no, they'll love it. They'll tell everybody: "D'you have any idea how much those guys are making . . .?" And they'll want to be a part of it even more, believe me. They're boys. They're a herd.'

Now he sat behind his model boat and peered over one of its three model swimming pools and said, 'Coffee? Breakfast?'

'Just coffee.' Hoffmann went straight across to the window.

Quarry buzzed his assistant. 'Two black coffees right away. And you should drink some water,' he suggested to Hoffmann's back. 'You don't want to get dehydrated.' But Hoffmann was not listening. 'And some still water, darling, and I'll have a banana and some yoghurt. Is Genoud in yet?'

'Not yet, Hugo.'

'Send him straight in when he gets here.' He released the switch. 'Anything happening out there?'

Hoffmann had his hands on the windowsill. He was staring down into the street. A group of pedestrians waited on the corner opposite for the lights to change even though there was no traffic coming in either direction. After watching them for a while Hoffmann muttered savagely, 'The goddam tight-assed Swiss . . .'

'Yeah, well just remember the goddam tight-assed eight-point-eight per cent tax rate they let us get away with, and you'll feel better.'

A well-toned freckled woman with a low-cut sweater and a cascade of dark red hair came in without knocking: Hugo's assistant, an Australian— Hoffmann couldn't remember her name. He suspected she was an ex-girlfriend of Hugo's who had passed the statutory retirement age for that position, thirty-one, and been found lighter duties elsewhere. She was carrying a tray. Behind her lurked a man in a dark suit and black tie with a fawn raincoat over his arm.

'Mr Genoud is here,' she said, then added solicitously, 'How are you feeling, Alex?'

Hoffmann turned on Quarry. 'You *told* her?'

'Yes, I called her from the hospital. She fixed us a car. What's it matter? It's not a secret, is it?'

'I'd prefer it if everyone in the office didn't know, if you don't mind.'

'Sure, if that's what you want. You'll keep it to yourself, Amber, right?'

'Of course, Hugo.' She looked at Hoffmann in puzzlement. 'Sorry, Alex.'

Hoffmann raised his hand in benediction. He took his coffee from the tray and returned to the window. The pedestrians had moved on. A tram rattled to a halt and opened its doors, spilling out passengers along its entire length, as if a knife had been passed from end to end, gutting it. Hoffmann tried to pick out faces, but there were too many and they were dispersing too quickly. He drank his coffee. When he turned round, Genoud was in the office and the door was closed. They had been talking to him and he had not realised. He was aware of a silence.

'Sorry?'

Genoud said patiently, 'I was just telling Mr Quarry, Dr Hoffmann: I have spoken to several of my old colleagues in the Geneva police. They have issued a description of the man. Forensics are at your house now.'

Hoffmann said, 'The inspector in charge of the case is called Leclerc.'

'Yes, I know him. He's ready to be put out to grass, unfortunately. This case seems to have him beaten already.' Genoud hesitated. 'May I ask you, Dr Hoffmann—are you sure you have told him everything? It would be wise to be frank with him.'

'Of course I have. Why the hell wouldn't I?' Hoffmann didn't care for his tone.

Quarry cut in: 'I don't give a shit what Inspector Clouseau thinks. The point is, how did this lunatic get past Alex's security? And if he got past it once, can he do it again? And if he got past it at his house, can he get past it here at the office? That's what we pay you for, isn't it, Maurice? Security?'

Genoud's sallow cheeks flushed. 'This building is as well protected as any in Geneva. As for Dr Hoffmann's house, the police say that the codes for the gate, the main door and possibly the alarm itself seem to have been known to the intruder. No security system in the world can protect against that.'

Hoffmann said, 'I'll change the codes tonight. And in future *I'll* decide who knows them.'

'I can assure you, Dr Hoffmann,' said Genoud, 'only two persons in our company knew those combinations—myself and one of my technicians. There was no leak from our side.'

'So you say. But he must have got hold of them from somewhere.'

'Okay, let's leave the codes for now,' said Quarry. 'The main thing is, until this guy is caught, I want Alex to have some proper protection. What will that entail?'

'A permanent guard on the house, certainly— one of my men is there already. At least two other men on duty tonight—one to patrol the grounds, the other to remain indoors downstairs. As for when Dr Hoffmann moves around the city, I would suggest a driver with counterterrorism training and one security officer.'

'Armed?'

'That's up to you.'

'And what say you, Professor?'

An hour ago, Hoffmann would have dismissed each of these precautions as absurd. But the spectre on the tram had jolted him. Little flashes of panic, like brushfires, kept breaking out in his mind. 'I want Gabrielle looked after as well. We keep assuming this maniac was after me, but what if it was her he wanted?'

Genoud was making entries on a personal organiser. 'Yes, we can manage that.'

'Just until he's arrested, okay? Then we can all go back to normal.'

'And what about you, Mr Quarry?' asked Genoud. 'Should we take precautions on your behalf as well?'

Quarry laughed. 'The only thing that keeps me

67

awake at night is the thought of a paternity suit.'

*   *   *

'Right,' said Quarry, when Genoud had gone, 'let's talk about this presentation—if you're still sure you're up for it?'

'I'm up for it.'

'Okay, thank God for that. Nine investors—all existing clients as agreed. Four institutions, three ultra-high net worths, two family offices, and a partridge in a pear tree.'

'A partridge?'

'Okay, not a partridge. There is no partridge, I concede that.' Quarry was in great high spirits. If he was three parts gambler he was also one part salesman, and it was a while since that crucial part of him had been allowed its head. 'Ground rules are: first, they have to sign a non-disclosure agreement regarding our proprietary software, and second, they're each permitted to bring in one designated professional adviser. They're due to arrive in about an hour and a half—I suggest you have a shower and a shave before they get here: the look we require from you is brilliant but eccentric, if you don't mind me saying so, rather than sheer bloody crazy. You walk them through the principles. We'll show them the hardware. I'll make the pitch. Then we'll both take them out to lunch at the Beau-Rivage.'

'How much are we looking to raise?'

'I'd like a billion. Settle for seven-fifty.'

'And commission? What did we decide? Are we sticking with two and twenty?'

'Don't you think?'

'I don't know. That's your call.'

'More than the going rate looks greedy, less and they won't respect us in the morning. With our track record it's a seller's market, but even so I say let's stick with two and twenty.' Quarry pushed back his chair and swung his feet up on to the desk in a single, easy fluid motion. 'It's going to be a big day for us, Alexi. We've waited a whole year to show them this. And they're gagging for it.'

A two per cent annual management fee on a billion dollars was twenty million dollars, just for showing up to work in the mornings. A twenty per cent performance fee on a billion-dollar investment, assuming a twenty per cent return— modest by Hoffmann's current standards—was an additional forty million a year. In other words, an annual income of sixty million dollars in return for half a morning's work and two hours of excruciating small talk in a smart restaurant. Even Hoffmann was willing to suffer fools for that.

He asked, 'Who exactly have we got coming?'

'Oh, you know—the usual suspects.' For the next ten minutes Quarry described each in turn. 'But you don't have to worry about them. I'll handle that side. You just talk about your precious algorithms. Now go and get some rest.'

Hardly any faculty is more important for the intellectual progress of man than ATTENTION. Animals clearly manifest this power, as when a cat watches by a hole and prepares to spring on its prey.

CHARLES DARWIN, *The Descent of Man* (1871)

Hoffmann's office was identical to Quarry's except he had no pictures of a boat, indeed no decoration of any sort apart from three framed photographs. One was of Gabrielle, taken over lunch on the Pampelonne Beach at St-Tropez two years earlier: she was laughing, looking directly into the camera, the sun on her face, a white filigree of dried salt on her cheek from a long sea swim that morning—he had never seen anyone look so vitally alive; it raised his spirits every time he saw it. Another was of Hoffmann himself, taken in 2001, wearing a yellow hard hat and standing 175 metres below ground in the tunnel that would eventually house the synchrotron of the Large Hadron Collider. The third was of Quarry in evening dress in London receiving the award for Algorithmic Hedge Fund Manager of the Year from a minister in the Labour government: Hoffmann, needless to say, had refused even to attend the ceremony, a decision Quarry had approved of, as he said it added to the company's mystique.

Hoffmann closed the door and went around the double-glazed walls of his office lowering all the venetian blinds and closing them. He hung up his raincoat, took the CD of his CAT scan from the pocket and tapped the case against his teeth while he considered what to do with it. His desk was bare except for the inevitable six-screen Bloomberg array, a keyboard and mouse and a telephone. He sat in his two-thousand-dollar high-backed orthopaedic swivel chair with pneumatic tilt mechanism and oatmeal upholstery, opened a bottom drawer and thrust the CD inside out of sight, as far as it would go. Then he closed the drawer and switched on his computer. In Tokyo the Nikkei Stock Average of 225 companies had closed down 3.3 per cent. Mitsubishi Corporation was off by 5.4 per cent, Japan Petroleum Exploration Company 4 per cent, Mazda Motors 5 per cent and Nikon 3.5 per cent. The Shanghai Composite was down 4.1 to an eight-month low. This is turning into a rout, thought Hoffmann.

Suddenly, before he realised what was happening, the screens in front of him blurred and he started to cry. His hands shook. A strange keening note emerged from his throat. His whole upper body shook convulsively. I am coming to pieces, he thought, as he laid his forehead on the desk in misery. And yet at the same time he remained oddly detached from his breakdown, as if he were observing himself from high up in the corner of the room. He was conscious of panting rapidly, like an exhausted animal. After a couple of minutes, when the spasm of shaking had subsided and he was able to catch his breath again, he realised that he felt much better, even mildly euphoric—the cheap catharsis of weeping: he could see how it might become addictive. He sat up, took off his spectacles and wiped his eyes with his trembling fingertips and then his nose with the back of his hand. He blew out his cheeks. 'God,' he whispered to himself, 'God, God.'

He stayed motionless for a couple of minutes until he was sure he had recovered, then he rose and went back over to his raincoat and retrieved the Darwin. He laid it on his desk and sat down before it. The 138-year-old green cloth binding and slightly frayed spine seemed utterly incongruous in the surroundings of his office, where nothing was older than six months. Hesitantly, he opened it at the place where he had stopped reading shortly after midnight (Chapter XII: 'Surprise—Astonishment—Fear—Horror'). He removed the Dutch bookseller's slip, unfolded it and smoothed it out. *Rosengaarden & Nijenhuise, Antiquarian Scientific & Medical Books. Established 1911.* He reached for the telephone. After briefly debating in his mind whether this was the best course, he dialled the bookshop's number in Amsterdam.

The phone rang for a long while without being answered: hardly surprising as it was barely eight thirty. But Hoffmann was insensitive to the nuances of time: if he was at his desk, he assumed everyone else should be at theirs. He let it ring and ring, and thought about Amsterdam. He had visited it twice. He liked its elegance, its sense of history; it had intelligence: he must take Gabrielle there when all this was sorted out. They could smoke dope in a café—wasn't that what people did in Amsterdam?—and then make love all afternoon in an attic bedroom in a boutique hotel. He listened to the long purr of the ring tone. He imagined its bell trilling in some dusty bookshop that peered out through small whorled panes of thick Victorian glass, across a cobbled street, through trees to a canal; high shelves accessed by rickety stepladders; elaborate scientific instruments made of highly polished brass—a sextant, perhaps, and a microscope; an elderly bibliophile, stooped and bald, turning his key in the door and hurrying to his desk, just in time to answer the phone—

'*Goedemorgen. Rosengaarden en Nijenhuise.*'

The voice was neither elderly nor male but young and female; lilting, sing-song.

He said, 'Do you speak English?'

'Yes I do. How can I help you?'

He cleared his throat and sat forward in his seat. 'I believe you sent me a book the day before yesterday. My name is Alexander Hoffmann. I live in Geneva.'

'Hoffmann? Yes, Dr Hoffmann! Naturally I remember. The Darwin first edition. A beautiful book. You have it already? There was no problem with the delivery, I hope.'

'Yeah, I got it. But there was no note with it, so I can't thank whoever it was who bought it for me. Could you give me that information?'

There was a pause. 'Did you say your name was Alexander Hoffmann?'

'Yeah, that's right.'

This time the pause was longer, and when the girl spoke again she sounded confused. 'You bought it yourself, Dr Hoffmann.'

Hoffmann closed his eyes. When he opened them again it seemed to him that his office had shifted slightly on its axis. 'That is not possible,' he said. 'I didn't buy it. It must have been someone pretending to be me.'

'But you paid for it yourself. Are you sure you

73

have not forgotten?'

'Paid for it how?'

'By bank transfer.'

'And how much did I pay?'

'Ten thousand euros.'

With his free hand Hoffmann grasped the edge of his desk. 'Wait a second. How could this happen? Did someone come into your shop and say they were me?'

'There is no shop any more. Not for five years. Only a poste restante. These days we are in a warehouse outside Rotterdam.'

'Well, surely someone must have spoken to me on the phone at least?'

'No, to speak to a customer is very unusual these days. Orders all come from email.'

Hoffmann wedged the phone between his chin and shoulder. He clicked on his computer and went to his email screen. He scrolled through his outbox. 'When am I supposed to have sent you this email?'

'May third.'

'Well, I'm looking here now at my emails for that day and I can assure you I sent no message to you on May third. What's the email address on the order?'

'A-dot-Hoffmann at Hoffmann Investment Technologies dot com.'

'Yeah, that's my address. But I don't see any message to a bookseller here.'

'You sent it from a different computer perhaps?'

'No, I'm sure I didn't.' But even as he uttered the words the confidence leaked from his voice and he felt almost physically sick with panic, as if an abyss was opening at his feet. The radiologist had mentioned dementia as a possible explanation for

74

the white pinpricks on his CAT scan. Perhaps he had used his mobile, or his laptop, or his computer at home, and forgotten all about it—although even if he had, surely some record of it would be here? He said, 'What exactly was in the message I sent you? Can you read it back to me?'

'There was no message. The process is automatic. The customer clicks on the title on our online catalogue and fills in the electronic order form—name, address, method of payment.' She must have heard the uncertainty in his voice; now caution entered hers. 'I hope you are not wanting to cancel the order.'

'No, I just need to sort this out. You say the money was paid by bank transfer. What's the account number the money came from?'

'I cannot disclose that information.'

Hoffmann summoned all the force he could muster. 'Now listen to me. I've clearly been the victim of a serious fraud here. This is identity theft. And I most certainly will cancel the order, and I'll put the whole goddamned thing in the hands of the police, and my lawyers, if you don't give me that account number right now so I can find out just what the hell is going on.'

There was a silence at the other end of the line. Eventually the woman said coldly, 'I cannot give this information over the telephone, but I can send it to the email address given on the order. I can do it immediately. Will this be okay for you?'

'This will be okay for me. Thank you.'

Hoffmann hung up and exhaled. He put his elbows on his desk and rested his head between his fingertips and stared hard at his computer screen. Time seemed to pass very slowly, but in fact it was only twenty seconds later that his email inbox announced the arrival of a new message. He opened it. It was from the bookshop. There was no greeting, just a single line of twenty digits and letters, and the name of the account holder: A. J. Hoffmann. He gawped at it then buzzed his assistant. 'Marie-Claude, could you mail me a list of all my personal bank account numbers? Right away, please.'

'Of course.'

'And you keep a record of the security codes at my house, I believe?'

'Yes, I do, Dr Hoffmann.' Marie-Claude Durade was a brisk Swiss woman in her middle fifties who had been with Hoffmann for five years. She was the only person in the building who did not address him by his Christian name. It was inconceivable to him that she could be mixed up in any kind of illegal activity.

'Where do you keep them?'

'In your personal file on my computer.'

'Has anyone asked for them?'

'No.'

'You haven't discussed them with anyone?'

'Certainly not.'

'Not even your husband?'

'My husband died last year.'

'Did he? Oh. Okay. Sorry. Anyway, there was a break-in at my house last night. The police may want to ask you some questions. Just to let you know.'

'Yes, Dr Hoffmann.'

As he waited for her to send him the details of his accounts, he leafed through the Darwin. He looked up 'suspicion' in the index:

A man may have his heart filled with the blackest hatred or suspicion, or be corroded with envy and jealousy; but as these feelings do not at once lead to action, and as they commonly last for some time, they are not shown by any outward sign . . .

With all due respect to Darwin, Hoffmann felt this was empirically untrue. His own heart was filled with the blackest suspicion and he had no doubt it was evident in his face—in his downturned mouth and sullen, narrowed, shifting gaze. Whoever heard of a case of identity theft in which the thief bought a present for the victim? Someone was trying to screw with his mind: that was what was going on here. They were trying to make him doubt his own sanity, maybe even murder him. Either that or he really was going mad.

He pushed himself on to his feet and prowled round his office. He parted the slats of his blinds and gazed out across the trading floor. Did he have an enemy out there? His sixty quants were split into three teams: Incubation, who composed and tested the algorithms; Technology, who turned the prototypes into operational tools; and Execution, who oversaw the actual trades. Some of them were a little weird, there was no doubt about that. The Hungarian, Imre Szabo, for example—he couldn't walk down a corridor without touching every door handle. And there was another guy who had to eat everything with a knife and fork, even a biscuit or a packet of crisps. Hoffmann had hired them all personally, regardless of their oddities, but he did not know them well. They were colleagues rather than friends. He rather regretted that now. He dropped the slat and returned to his terminal.

The list of his bank accounts was waiting in his inbox. He had eight—Swiss franc, dollar, sterling, euro, current, deposit, offshore and joint. He checked their numbers against the one that had been used to buy the book. None matched. He tapped his finger against his desk for a few seconds, then picked up his phone and called the firm's chief financial officer, Lin Ju-Long.

'LJ? It's Alex. Do me a favour. Check out an account number for me, would you? It's in my name but I don't recognise it. I want to know if it's on our system anywhere.' He forwarded the email from the bookshop. 'I'm sending it across now. Have you got it?'

There was a pause.

'Yes, Alex, I got it. Okay, well, first thing I can tell you right away: it starts "KYD"—that's the Cayman Islands IBAN prefix for a US dollar account.'

'Could it be some kind of company account?'

'I'll run it through the system. You got a problem?'

'No. Just want to check it out, that's all. I'd be grateful if you could keep this just between the two of us.'

'Okay, Alex. Sorry to hear about your—'

'I'm fine,' cut in Hoffmann quickly. 'No harm done.'

'Okay, that's good. Has Gana spoken to you, by the way?'

Gana was Ganapathi Rajamani, the company's chief risk officer.

Hoffmann said, 'No. Why?'

'You authorised a big short on Procter and

78

Gamble last night? Two million at sixty-two per share?'

'So what?'

'Gana is worried. He says our risk limit has been breached. He wants a meeting of the Risk Committee.'

'Well, tell him to go talk to Hugo about it. And let me know about that account, will you?'

Hoffmann felt too tired to do any more. He buzzed Marie-Claude again and told her to make sure he was not disturbed for an hour. He turned off his mobile. Afterwards he lay on his sofa and tried to imagine who on earth would have gone to the trouble of stealing his name in order to buy him a rare volume of Victorian natural history using a Cayman Islands dollar account that he seemed to own. But the bizarreness of the conundrum defeated even him, and very soon he sank into sleep.

*   *   *

Inspector Leclerc knew that the chief of Geneva's Police department, a stickler for punctuality, invariably arrived at police headquarters on the Boulevard Carl-Vogt at 9.00 sharp and that his first act of the day was always to read the summary of what had occurred in the canton overnight. Therefore when the telephone rang in his office at 9.08, he had a fair idea of who might be on the other end of the line.

A brisk voice said, 'Jean-Philippe?'

'Morning, Chief.'

'This assault on the American banker, Hoffmann.'

79

'Yes, Chief?'

'Where are we on this?'

'He's discharged himself from the University Hospital. Forensics are at the house now. We've put out a detailed description. One of our men is watching the property. That's about it.'

'So he's not seriously hurt?'

'Apparently not.'

'That's something. What do you make of it?'

'Bizarre. The house is a fortress but the intruder somehow just wandered in. He came prepared to restrain his victim, or victims, and it looks as though he handled knives while he was on the premises. But then he ended up just hitting Hoffmann on the head and running away. Nothing stolen. To be honest, I have a feeling Hoffmann isn't telling us the full story, but I'm not sure whether that's deliberate or he's just confused.'

There was a short silence at the other end. Leclerc could hear someone moving around in the background.

'Are you going off shift?'

'Just about to leave, Chief.'

'Do me a favour and pull a double, will you? I've already had the Minister of Finance's office on the phone, wanting to know what's happening. It would be good if you could see this one through.'

'The Minister of Finance?' repeated Leclerc in amazement. 'Why's he so interested?'

'Oh, you know, the usual story, I expect. One law for the rich, another for the poor. Keep me up to speed on it, will you?'

After he had hung up, Leclerc let out a string of expletives under his breath. He plodded along the corridor to the coffee machine and got himself a cup of very black and unusually filthy espresso. His eyes felt gritty, his sinuses ached. I'm too old for this, he thought. It was not even as if there was anything much he could do: he had sent one of his juniors to interview the domestic staff. He went back to his office and called his wife and told her he wouldn't be home until after lunch, then logged on to the internet to see if he could find out anything about Dr Alexander Hoffmann, physicist and hedge-fund manager. But to his surprise there was almost nothing—no entry in Wikipedia, no newspaper article and not one image available online. Yet the Minister of Finance himself was taking a personal interest in the matter.

What the hell was a hedge fund in any case? he wondered. He looked it up: 'A private investment fund that may invest in a diverse range of assets and may employ a variety of investment strategies to maintain a hedged portfolio intended to protect the fund's investors from downturns in the market while maximising returns on market upswings.'

None the wiser, he flicked back through his notes. Hoffmann had said in his interview that he had worked in the financial sector for the past eight years; for six years before that he had been employed on developing the Large Hadron Collider. As it happened, Leclerc knew a man, a former inspector in the police, who now worked in security at CERN. He gave him a call and fifteen minutes later he was at the wheel of his little Renault, driving slowly in the morning traffic, north-west past the airport, along the Route de Meyrin, through the drab industrial zone of Zimeysa.

Up ahead, framed by the distant mountains,

CERN's huge rust-coloured wooden globe seemed to rise out of the arable fields like a gigantic anachronism: a 1960s vision of what the future was supposed to look like. Leclerc parked opposite it and went into the main building. He gave his name and clipped his visitor's badge to his windcheater. While he waited for his contact to collect him he studied the little exhibition in the reception area. Apparently sixteen hundred super-conducting magnets, each weighing nearly thirty tonnes, were housed in a twenty-seven-kilometre circular tunnel beneath his feet, shooting beams of particles around it so quickly that they completed the circuit eleven thousand times per second. The collisions of the beams at an energy of seven trillion electronvolts per proton were supposed to reveal the origins of the universe, discover extra dimensions and explain the nature of dark matter. None of it that Leclerc could discern seemed to have anything whatever to do with the financial markets.

*   *   *

Quarry's invitees began to arrive just after ten, the first pair—a fifty-six-year-old Genevese, Etienne Mussard, and his younger sister Clarisse—turning up on a bus. 'They'll be early,' Quarry had warned Hoffmann. 'They're always early for everything.' Dowdily dressed, they were both unmarried and lived together in a small three-bedroomed apartment in the suburb of Lancy that they had inherited from their parents. They did not drive. They took no holidays. They rarely dined in restaurants. Quarry estimated M. Mussard's personal

82

wealth at approximately seven hundred million euros, and Mme Mussard's at five hundred and fifty million. Their mother's grandfather, Robert Fazy, had owned a private bank, which had been sold in the 1980s following a scandal involving Jewish assets seized by the Nazis and deposited with Fazy et Cie during the Second World War. They brought with them their family attorney, Dr Max-Albert Gallant, whose firm conveniently also handled the legal affairs of Hoffmann Investment Technologies. It was through Gallant that Quarry had managed to obtain an introduction to the Mussards. 'They treat me like a son,' said Quarry. 'They're unbelievably rude and do nothing but complain.'

This drab couple was followed closely by perhaps the most exotic of Hoffmann's clients, Elmira Gulzhan, the thirty-eight-year-old daughter of the President of Azakhstan. Resident in Paris and a graduate of INSEAD in Fontainebleau, Elmira was responsible for administering the Gulzhan family holdings overseas, estimated by the CIA in 2009 to be worth approximately $19 billion. Quarry had contrived to meet her on a skiing party in Val d'Isere. The Gulzhans presently had $120 million invested in the hedge fund—a stake Quarry hoped to persuade her at least to double. He had also made friends on the slopes with her long-term lover, François de Gombart-Tonnelle, a Parisian lawyer, who was at her side today. She emerged from her bulletproof Mercedes wearing an emerald silk frock coat with matching head scarf draped lightly over her helmet of glossy black hair. Quarry was waiting in the lobby to greet her. 'Be not fooled,' he had warned Hoffmann. 'She may look like she's off to the races but she could hold down a job at Goldman any day of the week. *And* she can arrange for her daddy to have your fingernails torn out.'

Next to roll up, sharing a limousine from the Hotel Président Wilson on the other side of the lake, were a couple of Americans who had flown over from New York especially for the presentation. Ezra Klein was chief analyst for the Winter Bay Trust, a $14 billion fund-of-funds which, in the words of its prospectus, 'aims to flatten out risk while achieving high returns by investing in a diverse array of managed portfolios rather than individual bonds or equities'. Klein had a reputation for being super-bright, enhanced by his habit of talking at a rate of six words per second (he had once been timed surreptitiously by his bewildered subordinates), roughly twice as fast as normal human speech, and by the fact that every third word seemed to be an acronym or piece of financial jargon. 'Ezra's on the spectrum,' said Quarry. 'No wife, no kids, no sexual organs of any kind, as far as I can tell. Winter Bay could be good for another hundred million. We'll have to see.'

Beside him, not even pretending to listen to Klein's unintelligible jabber, was a bulky figure in his fifties in full Wall Street dress uniform of black three-piece suit and red-and-white striped tie. This was Bill Easterbrook of the US banking conglomerate AmCor. 'You've met Bill before,' Quarry had warned Hoffmann. 'Remember him? He's the dinosaur who looks as if he's just stepped out of an Oliver Stone movie. Since you last saw him, he's been spun off into a separate entity called AmCor Alternative Investments, which is basically just an accounting trick to keep the regulators

84

happy.' Quarry had himself worked for AmCor in London for a decade, and he and Easterbrook went way back—'way, way back', as he dreamily put it: too far to recall, he implied, through the haze of the years—all the way back to the coke-and-call-girl glory days of the 1990s. When Quarry had left AmCor to set up with Hoffmann, Easterbrook had passed them their first clients in return for commission. Now AmCor Alternative was Hoffmann's biggest investor, with close to $1 billion under management. He was another attendee whom Quarry took the trouble to meet personally in the lobby.

And so they all came: twenty-seven-year-old Amschel Herxheimer of the Herxheimer banking and trading dynasty, whose sister had been at Oxford with Quarry, and who was being groomed to take over the family's two-hundred-year-old private bank; dull Iain Mould of what had once been an even duller Fife building society, until it had taken itself public at the beginning of the century and, in the space of three years, run up debts equivalent to half the gross domestic product of Scotland, necessitating a takeover by the British government; the billionaire Mieczyslaw Łukasiński, a former mathematics professor and leader of the Polish Communist Youth Union, who now owned eastern Europe's third-largest insurance company; and finally two Chinese entrepreneurs, Liwei Xu and Qi Zhang, representing a Shanghai-based investment bank, who arrived with no fewer than six dark-suited associates, whom they insisted were lawyers but who Quarry was fairly sure were computer experts, come to inspect Hoffmann's cyber-security—after a furiously polite stand-off the 'lawyers' reluctantly agreed to leave.

Not one existing investor whom Quarry had invited declined the invitation. 'They're coming for two reasons,' he had explained to Hoffmann. 'First, because over three years, even as the financial markets have tanked, we've returned them a profit of eighty-three per cent and I defy anyone to find any hedge fund anywhere that has produced such consistent alpha—I mean, they must be wondering just what the hell it is we've got going on here, yet we've refused to take a single extra cent in investment.'

'And what's the second reason they're coming?'

'Oh, don't be so modest.'

'I don't follow.'

'It's *you*, you daft bugger. They want to take a look at *you*. They want to discover what you've been up to. You're becoming a legend and they want to touch the hem of your garment, just to see if their fingers turn to gold.'

*   *   *

Hoffmann was woken by Marie-Claude.

'Dr Hoffmann?' She shook his shoulder gently. 'Dr Hoffmann? Mr Quarry says to tell you they are waiting for you in the boardroom.'

He had been dreaming vividly, but when he opened his eyes the images vanished like bursting bubbles. For a moment his assistant's face bending over him reminded him of his mother's. She had the same grey-green eyes, the same prominent nose, the same anxious and intelligent expression. 'Thanks,' he said, sitting up. 'Tell him I'll be there in a minute,' and then he added impulsively, 'I'm sorry about your husband. I get'—he twirled his hand helplessly—'distracted.'

'That's quite all right. Thank you.'

There was a washroom across the passage from his office. He ran the cold tap and cupped his hands beneath it. He splashed his face again and again, flailing his flesh with the icy water. He had no time to shave. The skin on his chin and around his mouth, normally bland and smooth, felt as bristly and textured as an animal's. It was a curious fact— no doubt an irrational swing of mood brought on by his injury—but he was beginning to feel exuberant. He had survived an encounter with death— exhilarating in itself—and now he had a boardroom full of supplicants waiting, in Hugo's words, to touch his hem, in the hope that his genius for making money would rub off on them. The rich of the earth had bestirred themselves from their yachts and pools and racetracks, from the dealing rooms of Manhattan and the counting houses of Shanghai, and had gathered together in Switzerland to listen to Dr Alexander Hoffmann, the legendary—Hugo's word again—creator of Hoffmann Investment Technologies, preach his vision of the future. And what a story he had to tell! What a gospel he had to preach!

With such thoughts surging through his damaged head, Hoffmann dried his face, pulled back his shoulders and headed off to the boardroom. As he passed across the trading floor, the lithe figure of Ganapathi Rajamani, the company's chief risk officer, moved smoothly to intercept him, but Hoffmann waved him out of the way: whatever his problem was, it would have to wait.

6

No doubt wealth when very great tends to convert men into useless drones, but their number is never large; and some degree of elimination here occurs, for we daily see rich men, who happen to be fools or profligate, squandering away their wealth.

CHARLES DARWIN, *The Descent of Man* (1871)

The boardroom had the same corporate impersonality—the same soundproofed glass walls and floor-to-ceiling venetian blinds—as the managers' offices. A giant blank screen for teleconferencing took up most of the end wall, looking down on to a big oval table of pale Scandinavian wood. As Hoffmann entered the room, all but one of the table's eighteen chairs was occupied either by the principals or their advisers; the only spare place was next to Quarry at its head. Quarry's gaze followed his progress round the edge of the room with evident relief. 'Here he is at last,' he said, 'Dr Alexander Hoffmann, ladies and gentlemen, the president of Hoffmann Investment Technologies. As you can see, his brain's so big we've had to let out his head to give it some breathing space. Sorry, Alex, only joking. I'm afraid he took a bit of a knock, hence the stitches, but he's fine now, aren't you?'

They all stared. Those nearest to Hoffmann twisted in their seats to look up at him. But Hoffmann, hot with embarrassment, avoided eye contact. He took his position next to Quarry, folded his hands on the table in front of him, and stared fixedly at his interlaced fingers. He felt Quarry's hand grasp his shoulder, the weight increasing as the Englishman rose to his feet.

'Right then, we can at last get started. So— welcome, friends, to Geneva. It's almost eight years since Alex and I set up shop together, using his intelligence and my looks, to create a very special kind of investment fund, based exclusively on algorithmic trading. We started with just over a hundred million dollars in assets under management, a big chunk of it courtesy of my old friend over there, Bill Easterbrook, of AmCor— welcome, Bill. We made a profit that first year, and we've gone on making a profit every year, which is why we are now one hundred times larger than when we started, with AUM of ten billion dollars.

'I'm not going to boast about our track record. I hope I don't need to. You all get the quarterly statements and you know what we've achieved together. I'll just give you one statistic. On the ninth of October 2007, the Dow Jones Industrial Average closed at 14,164. Last night—I checked it before I left my office—the Dow closed at 10,866. That represents a loss over more than two and a half years of almost one quarter. Imagine that! All those poor saps with their retirement plans and their tracker bonds have lost about twenty-five per cent of their investment. But *you*, by placing your trust in *us* over the same period, have seen your net asset value increase by eighty-three per cent. Ladies and gentlemen, I think you'll agree that bringing your money to us was a pretty smart thing to have done.'

For the first time Hoffmann risked a brief glance around the table. Quarry's audience was listening intently. ('The two most interesting things in the world,' Quarry once remarked: 'other people's sex lives and your own money.') Even Ezra Klein, rocking back and forth like a student in a madrasa, was temporarily still, while Mieczyslaw Łukasiński simply could not keep the grin off his plump peasant face.

Quarry's right hand continued to rest on Hoffmann's shoulder; his left was thrust casually in his pocket. 'In our business we call the gap between market performance and fund performance "alpha". Over the past three years, Hoffmann has generated alpha of one hundred and twelve per cent. That's why we've twice been voted Algorithmic Hedge Fund of the Year by the financial trade press.

'Now,' he went on, 'this consistency of performance is not, I can assure you, a matter of luck. Hoffmann spends thirty-two million dollars a year on research. We employ sixty of the most brilliant scientific minds in the world—at least I'm told they're brilliant: I can't understand a word they're on about.'

He acknowledged the rueful laughter. Hoffmann saw that the British banker, Iain Mould, was chuckling particularly hard, and he knew at once that he was a fool. Quarry withdrew his hands from Hoffmann's shoulder and from his own pocket and placed them on the table. He leaned forward, suddenly serious and urgent.

'About eighteen months ago, Alex and his team achieved a significant technological breakthrough. As a result we had to take the very difficult decision to hard-close the fund.' Hard-close meant turning away additional investment even from existing

90

clients. 'And I know that every single one of you in this room—because that is why we've invited you here—was disappointed by that decision, and also bewildered, and that some of you were actually pretty angry about it.'

He glanced at Elmira Gulzhan listening at the opposite end of the table. She had screamed at Quarry down the phone, Hoffmann knew, and had even threatened to withdraw the family's money from the fund or worse ('You hard-close the Gulzhans—the Gulzhans hard-close you . . .').

'Well,' continued Quarry, with the merest hint of a kiss blown in Elmira's direction, 'we apologise for that. But we took the view that we had to concentrate on implementing this new investment strategy based on our existing asset size. There's always a risk with any kind of fund, as I'm sure you're aware, that increasing size translates into decreasing performance. We wanted to be as confident as we could be that that wouldn't happen.

'It is now our opinion that this new system, which we call VIXAL-4, is robust enough to cope with portfolio expansion. Indeed, the alpha generated over the last six months has been significantly greater than it was when we were relying on our original algorithms. Therefore, as of today, I can announce that Hoffmann is moving from a hard-closed to a soft-closed position, and is willing to accept additional investment from existing clients only.'

He stopped and took a sip of water to allow the impact of his words to sink in. There was complete silence in the room.

'Cheer up, everyone,' he said brightly, 'this is supposed to be good news.'

The tension was released by laughter and for the first time since Hoffmann entered the room the clients looked openly at one another. They had become a private club, he realised: a freemasonry bound together by a shared secret knowledge. Complicit smiles spread around the table. They were on the inside track.

'At which point,' said Quarry, looking on contentedly, 'I think the best thing I can do is hand you over to Alex here, who can fill you in a bit more on the technical side.' He half-sat down then stood again. 'With a bit of luck I may even be able to understand it myself.'

More laughter, and then the floor was Hoffmann's.

He was not a man to whom speaking in public came naturally. The few classes he had taught at Princeton before leaving the United States had been torture for lecturer and students alike. But now he felt himself filled with a strange energy and clarity. He touched his fingers lightly to his sewn-up wound, took a couple of deep breaths, then rose to his feet.

'Ladies and gentlemen, we have to be secretive about the detail of what we do in this company, to avoid having our ideas stolen by our competitors, but the general principle is no great mystery, as you well know. We take a couple of hundred different securities and we trade them over a twenty-four-hour cycle. The algorithms we have programmed into our computers pick the positions we hold based on a detailed analysis of previous trends, mostly liquid futures—the Dow, say, or the S and P 500—and the familiar commodities: Brent crude, natural gas, gold, silver, copper, wheat, whatever.

We also do some high-frequency trading, where we may hold positions for only a few milliseconds. It's really not that complicated. Even the S and P two-hundred-day moving average can be a pretty reliable predictor of the market: if the current index is higher than the preceding average, the market is likely to be bullish; if lower, bearish. Or we can make a prediction, based on twenty years of data, that if tin is at this price and the yen at that, then it is more likely than not that the DAX will be here. Obviously we have vastly more pairs of averages than that to work with—several millions of them—but the principle can be simply stated: the most reliable guide to the future is the past. And we only have to be right about the markets fifty-five per cent of the time to make a profit.

'When we started out, not many people could have guessed how important algorithmic trading would turn out to be. The pioneers in this business were frequently dismissed as quants, or geeks, or nerds—we were the guys who none of the girls would dance with at parties—'

'That's still true,' interjected Quarry.

Hoffmann waved aside the interruption. 'Maybe it is, but the successes we have achieved at this firm speak for themselves. Hugo pointed out that in a period when the Dow has declined by nearly twenty-five per cent, we've grown in value by eighty-three per cent. How has this happened? It's very simple. There have been two years of panic in the markets, and our algorithms thrive on panic, because human beings always behave in such predictable ways when they're frightened.'

He raised his hands. '"The space of heaven is filled with naked beings rushing through the air.

Men, naked men, naked women who rush through the air and rouse gale and snowstorm. Do you hear it roaring? Roaring like the wing-beat of great birds high in the air? That is the fear of naked men. That is the flight of naked men."'

He stopped. He looked around at the upturned faces of his clients. Several had their mouths open, like baby birds hoping for food. His own mouth felt dry. 'Those are not my words. They're the words of an Inuit holy man, quoted by Elias Canetti in *Crowds and Power*: when I was designing VIXAL-4 I used them as a screensaver. Can I have some water, Hugo?' Quarry leaned over and passed him a bottle of Evian and a glass. Hoffmann ignored the glass, unscrewed the plastic cap and drank straight from the bottle. He didn't know what effect he was having on his audience. He didn't much care. He wiped his mouth on the back of his hand.

'Around 350 BC, Aristotle defined human beings as *"zoon logon echon"*—"the rational animal" or, more accurately, "the animal that has language". Language, above all, is what distinguishes us from the other creatures on the planet. The development of language freed us from a world of physical objects and substituted a universe of symbols. The lower animals may also communicate with one another in a primitive way, and may even be taught the meaning of a few of our human symbols—a dog can learn to understand "sit" or "come", for example. But for perhaps forty thousand years only humans were *zoon logon echon*: the animal with language. Now, for the first time, that is no longer true. We share our world with computers.

'Computers . . .' Hoffmann gestured towards the trading floor with his bottle, slopping water across

94

the table. 'It used to be the case that we imagined that computers—robots—would take over the menial work in our lives, that they would put on aprons and run around and be our robot maids, doing the housework or whatever, leaving us free to enjoy our leisure. In fact, the reverse is happening. We have plenty of spare, unintelligent human capacity to do those simple, menial jobs, often for very long hours and poor pay. Instead, the humans that computers are replacing are members of the educated classes: translators, medical technicians, legal clerks, accountants, financial traders.

'Computers are increasingly reliable translators in the sectors of commerce and technology. In medicine they can listen to a patient's symptoms and are diagnosing illnesses and even prescribing treatment. In the law they search and evaluate vast amounts of complex documents at a fraction of the cost of legal analysts. Speech recognition enables algorithms to extract the meaning from the spoken as well as the written word. News bulletins can be analysed in real time.

'When Hugo and I started this fund, the data we used was entirely digitalised financial statistics: there was almost nothing else. But over the past couple of years a whole new galaxy of information has come within our reach. Pretty soon all the information in the world—every tiny scrap of knowledge that humans possess, every little thought we've ever had that's been considered worth preserving over thousands of years—all of it will be available digitally. Every road on earth has been mapped. Every building photographed. Everywhere we humans go, whatever we buy, whatever websites we look at, we leave a digital trail as clear as slug-slime. And this data can be read, searched and analysed by computers and value extracted from it in ways we cannot even begin to conceive.

'Most people are barely aware of what has happened. Why would they be? If you leave this building and go along the street, everything looks pretty much as it's always looked. A guy from a hundred years ago could walk around this part of Geneva and still feel at home. But behind the physical facade—behind the stone and the brick and the glass—the world has distorted, buckled, shrunk, as if the planet has passed into another dimension. I'll give you a tiny example. In 2007, the British government lost the records of twenty-five million people—their tax codes, their bank account details, their addresses, their dates of birth. But it wasn't a couple of trucks they lost: it was just two CDs. And that's nothing. Google will one day digitalise every book ever published. No need for a library any more. All you'll need is a screen you can hold in your hand.

'But here's the thing. Human beings still read at the same speed as Aristotle did. The average American college student reads four hundred and fifty words per minute. The really clever ones can manage eight hundred. That's about two pages a minute. But IBM just announced last year they're building a new computer for the US government that can perform twenty thousand trillion calculations a second. There's a physical limit to how much information we, as a species, can absorb. We've hit the buffers. But there's no limit to how much a computer can absorb.

'And language—the replacement of objects with symbols—has another big down side for us humans.

The Greek philosopher Epictetus recognised this two thousand years ago when he wrote: "What disturbs and alarms man are not the things but his opinions and fancies about the things." Language unleashed the power of the imagination, and with it came rumour, panic, fear. But algorithms don't have an imagination. They don't panic. And that's why they're so perfectly suited to trade on the financial markets.

'What we have tried to do with our new generation of VIXAL algorithms is to isolate, measure, and factor into our market calculations the element of price that derives entirely from predictable patterns of human behaviour. Why, for example, does a stock price that rises on anticipation of positive results almost invariably fall below its previous price if those results turn out to be poorer than expected? Why do traders on some occasions stubbornly hold on to a particular stock even as it loses value and their losses mount, while on other occasions they sell a perfectly good stock they ought to keep, simply because the market in general is declining? The algorithm that can adjust its strategy in answer to these mysteries will have a huge competitive edge. We believe there is now sufficient data available for us to be able to begin anticipating these anomalies and profiting from them.'

Ezra Klein, who had been rocking back and forth with increasing frequency, could no longer contain himself. 'But this is just *behavioural finance*!' he blurted out. He made it sound like a heresy. 'Okay, I agree, the EMH is bust, but how do you filter out the noise to make a tool from BF?'

'When one subtracts out the valuation of a stock

as it varies over time, what one is left with is the behavioural effect, if any.'

'Yeah, but how do you figure out what caused the behavioural effect? That's the history of the entire goddam universe, right there!'

'Ezra, I agree with you,' said Hoffmann calmly. 'We can't analyse every aspect of human behaviour in the markets and its likely trigger over the past twenty years, however much data is now digitally available, and however fast our hardware scans it. We realised from the start we would have to narrow the focus right down. The solution we came up with was to pick on one particular emotion for which we know we have substantive data.'

'So which one have you picked?'

'Fear.'

There was a stirring in the room. Although Hoffmann had tried to avoid jargon—how typical of Klein, he thought, to bring up EMH, the efficient market hypothesis—he had nevertheless sensed a growing bafflement among his audience. But now he had their attention, no question. He continued: 'Fear is historically the strongest emotion in economics. Remember FDR in the Great Depression? It's the most famous quote in financial history: "The only thing we have to fear is fear itself." In fact fear is probably the strongest human emotion, period. Whoever woke at four in the morning because they were feeling happy? It's so strong we've actually found it relatively easy to filter out the noise made by other emotional inputs and focus on this one signal. One thing we've been able to do, for instance, is correlate recent market fluctuations with the frequency rate of fear-related words in the media—terror, alarm, panic, horror, dismay, dread, scare, anthrax, nuclear. Our conclusion is that fear is driving the world as never before.'

Elmira Gulzhan said, 'That is al-Qaeda.'

'Partly. But why should al-Qaeda arouse more fear than the threat of mutually assured destruction did during the Cold War in the fifties and sixties— which, incidentally, were times of great market growth and stability? Our conclusion is that digitalisation itself is creating an epidemic of fear, and that Epictetus had it right: we live in a world not of real things but of opinion and fantasy. The rise in market volatility, in our opinion, is a function of digitalisation, which is exaggerating human mood swings by the unprecedented dissemination of information via the internet.'

'And we've found a way to make money out of it,' said Quarry happily. He nodded at Hoffmann to continue.

'As most of you will be aware, the Chicago Board of Exchange operates what is known as the S and P 500 Volatility Index, or VIX. This has been running, in one form or another, for seventeen years. It's a ticker, for want of a better word, tracking the price of options—calls and puts—on stocks traded in the S and P 500. If you want the math, it's calculated as the square root of the par variance swap rate for a thirty-day term, quoted as an annualised variance. If you don't want the math, let's just say that what it does is show the implied volatility of the market for the coming month. It goes up and down minute by minute. The higher the index, the greater the uncertainty in the market, so traders call it "the fear index". And it's liquid itself, of course—there are VIX options and futures available to trade, and we trade them.

'So the VIX was our starting point. It's given us a whole bunch of useful data going back to 1993, which we can pair with the new behavioural indices we've compiled, as well as bringing in our existing methodology. In the early days it also gave us the name for our prototype algorithm, VIXAL-1, which has stuck all the way through, even though we've moved way beyond the VIX itself. We're now on to the fourth iteration, which with notable lack of imagination we call VIXAL-4.'

Klein jumped in again. 'The volatility implied by the VIX can be to the up side as well as the down side.'

'We take account of that,' said Hoffmann. 'In our metrics, optimism can be measured as anything from an absence of fear to a reaction against fear. Bear in mind that fear doesn't just mean a broad market panic and a flight to safety. There is also what we call a "clinging" effect, when a stock is held in defiance of reason, and an "adrenalin" effect, when a stock rises strongly in value. We're still researching all these various categories to determine market impact and refine our model.' Easterbrook raised his hand. 'Yes, Bill?'

'Is this algorithm already operational?'

'Why don't I let Hugo answer that, as it's practical rather than theoretical?'

Quarry said, 'Incubation started back-testing VIXAL-1 almost two years ago, although naturally that was just a simulation, without any actual exposure to the market. We went live with VIXAL-2 in May 2009, with play money of one hundred million dollars. When we overcame the early teething problems we moved on to VIXAL-3 in November and gave it access to one billion. That was so successful we decided to allow VIXAL-4 to take control of the entire fund one week ago.'

'With what results?'

'We'll show you all the detailed figures at the end. Off the top of my head, VIXAL-2 made twelve million dollars in its six-month trading period. VIXAL-3 made one hundred and eighteen million. As of last night, VIXAL-4 was up about seventy-nine-point-seven million.'

Easterbrook frowned. 'I thought you said it had only been running a week?'

'I did.'

'But that means . . .'

'That means,' said Ezra Klein, doing the calculation in his head and almost jumping out of his chair, 'that on a ten-billion-dollar fund, you're looking at making a profit of four-point-one-four billion a year.'

'And VIXAL-4 is an autonomous machine-learning algorithm,' said Hoffmann. 'As it collects and analyses more data, it's only likely to become more effective.'

Whistles and murmurs ran around the table. The two Chinese started whispering to one another.

'You can see why we've decided we want to bring in more investment,' said Quarry with a smirk. 'We need to exploit the hell out of this thing before anyone develops a clone strategy. And now, ladies and gentlemen, it seems to me that this might be a suitable moment to offer you a glimpse of VIXAL in operation.'

*   *   *

Three kilometres away, in Cologny, forensics had completed their examination of the Hoffmanns' house. The scene-of-crimes officers—a young man and woman, who might have been students or lovers—had packed up their equipment and left. A bored gendarme sat in his car on the drive.

Gabrielle was in her studio, dismantling the portrait of the foetus, lifting each sheet of glass out of its slot on the wooden base, wrapping it in tissue paper and then in bubble wrap, and laying it in a cardboard box. She found herself thinking how strange it was that so much creative energy should have flowed from the black hole of this tragedy. She had lost the baby two years ago, at five and a half months: not the first of her pregnancies that had ended in a miscarriage, but easily the longest and by far the most shattering. The hospital had given her an MRI scan when they began to get concerned, which was unusual. Afterwards, rather than stay on her own in Switzerland, she had gone with Alex on a business trip to Oxford. Wandering round a museum while he was interviewing PhDs in the Randolph Hotel, she had come across a 3D model of the structure of penicillin built up on sheets of Perspex in 1944 by Dorothy Hodgkin, the Nobel laureate for chemistry. An idea had stirred in her mind, and when she got home to Geneva, she had tried the same technique on the MRI scan of her womb, which was all she had left of the baby.

It had taken a week of trial and error to work out which of the two hundred cross-sectional images to print off, and how to trace them on to glass, what ink to use and how to stop it smearing. She had sliced her hands repeatedly on the sharp edges of the glass sheets. But the afternoon when she first lined them up and the outline had emerged—the clenched fingers, the curled toes—was a miracle she would never forget. Beyond the window of the apartment where they had lived in those days, the sky had turned black as she worked; brilliant yellow flashes of forked lightning had stabbed down over the mountains. She knew nobody would believe it if she told them. It was too theatrical. It had made her feel as if she were tapping into some elemental force: tampering with the dead. When Alex came home from work and saw the portrait, he had sat stunned for ten minutes.

After that she had become utterly absorbed by the possibilities of marrying science and art to produce images of living forms. Mostly she had acted as her own model, talking the radiographers at the hospital into scanning her from head to toe. The brain was the hardest part of the anatomy to get right. She had to learn which were the best lines to trace—the aqueduct of Sylvius, the cistern of the great cerebral vein, the tentorium cerebellum and the medulla. The simplicity of the form was what appealed to her most, and the paradoxes it carried—clarity and mystery, the impersonal and the intimate, the generic and yet the absolutely unique. Watching Alex going through the CAT scanner that morning had made her want to produce a portrait of him. She wondered if the doctors would let her have his results, or if he would allow her to do it.

She wrapped up the last of the glass sheets tenderly, and then the base, and sealed the cardboard box with thick brown sticky tape. It had been a painful decision to offer this, of all her works, to the exhibition: if someone bought it, she

103

knew she would probably never see it again. And yet it seemed to her an important thing to do: that this was the whole point of creating it in the first place—to give it a separate existence, to let it go out into the world.

She picked up the box and carried it out into the passageway as if it were an offering. On the handles of the doors leading off the corridor, and on the wooden panels, were traces of bluish-white powder where the surfaces had been dusted for fingerprints. In the hall, the blood had been cleaned off the floor. The surface was still damp, showing where Alex had been lying when she discovered him. She carefully skirted the spot. A noise came from inside the study and she felt her skin rise into gooseflesh just as a man's heavy shape loomed in the doorway. She gave a cry of alarm and almost dropped the box.

She recognised him. It was the security expert, Genoud. He had shown her how to use the alarm system when they first moved in. Another man was with him—heavyset, like a wrestler.

'Madame Hoffmann, forgive us if we startled you.' Genoud had a grave professional manner. He introduced the other man. 'Camille has been sent by your husband to look after you for the rest of the day.'

'I don't need looking after . . .' began Gabrielle. But she was too shaken to put up much resistance, and found herself allowing the bodyguard to take the box from her hands and carry it out to the waiting Mercedes. She protested that at least she wanted to drive herself to the gallery in her own car. But Genoud was insistent that it was not safe—not until the man who had attacked her husband had been caught—and such was his blunt professional inflexibility that eventually she surrendered again and did as she was told.

* * *

'Bloody brilliant,' whispered Quarry, catching Hoffmann by the elbow as they left the boardroom.

'You think? I got the feeling I'd lost them at one point.'

'They don't mind being lost, as long as you bring them back eventually to what they really want to see, which is the bottom line. And everyone loves a bit of Greek philosophy.' He steered Hoffmann ahead of him. 'My God, old Ezra's an ugly bugger, but I could give him a kiss for that bit of mental arithmetic at the end.'

The clients were waiting patiently on the edge of the trading floor, all except for young Herxheimer and the Pole, Łukasiński, who had their backs to the others and were talking with quiet animation into their cell phones. Quarry exchanged a look with Hoffmann. Hoffmann shrugged. Even if they were breaking the terms of the non-disclosure agreement, there was not much that could be done. NDAs were bitches to enforce without evidence of breach, by which point it was too late in any case.

'This way, if you please,' called Quarry, and with his finger held aloft, tour-guide-style, he led them in a crocodile across the big room. Herxheimer and Łukasiński quickly ended their calls and rejoined the group. Elmira Gulzhan, wearing a large pair of sunglasses, automatically assumed the head of the queue. Clarisse Mussard, in her cardigan and baggy pants, shuffled along in her wake, looking like her maid. Instinctively Hoffmann glanced up at the CNBC ticker to see what was happening on the European markets. The week-long slide seemed to have stopped at last; the FTSE 100 was up by nearly half of one per cent.

They gathered round a trading screen in Execution. One of the quants vacated his desk to give them a better view.

'So, this is VIXAL-4 in operation,' said Hoffmann. He stood back to let the investors get closer to the terminal. He decided not to sit: that would have allowed them to see the wound on his scalp. 'The algorithm selects the trades. They're on the left of the screen in the pending orders file. On the right are the executed orders.' He moved a little nearer so that he could read the figures. 'Here, for instance,' he began, 'we have . . .' He paused, surprised by the size of the trade; for a moment he thought the decimal point was in the wrong place. 'Here you see we have one and a half million options to sell Accenture at fifty-two dollars a share.'

'Whoa,' said Easterbrook. 'That's a heck of a bet on the short side. Do you guys know something about Accenture we don't?'

'Fiscal Q2 profits down three per cent,' rattled off Klein from memory, 'earnings sixty cents a share: not great, but I don't get the logic of that position.'

Quarry said, 'Well, there must be some logic to it, otherwise VIXAL wouldn't have taken the options. Why don't you show them another trade, Alex?'

Hoffmann changed the screen. 'Okay. Here— you see?—here's another short we've just put on

106

this morning: twelve and a half million options to sell Vista Airways at seven euros twenty-eight a share.'

Vista Airways was a low-cost, high-volume European airline, which none of those present would have dreamed of being seen dead on.

'*Twelve and a half million?*' repeated Easterbrook. 'That must be a heck of a chunk of the market. Your machine has got some balls, I'll give it that.'

'Really, Bill,' said Quarry, 'is it that risky? All airline stocks are fragile these days. I'm perfectly easy with that position.' But he sounded defensive, and Hoffmann guessed he must have noticed that the European markets were up: if a technical recovery spread across the Atlantic, they might be caught by a rising tide and end up having to sell the options at a loss.

Klein said, 'Vista Airways had twelve per cent passenger growth in the final quarter and a revised profits forecast up nine per cent. They've just taken delivery of a new fleet of aircraft. I don't get the sense of that position, either.'

'Wynn Resorts,' said Hoffmann, reading off the next screen. 'A million-two short at one hundred and twenty-four.' He frowned, puzzled. These enormous bets on the down side were unlike VIXAL's normal complex pattern of hedged trades.

'Well that one truly *is* amazing to me,' said Klein, 'because they had Q1 growth up from seven-forty million to nine-oh-nine, with a cash dividend of twenty-five cents a share, *and* they've got this great new resort in Macau that's literally a licence to print money—it turned over twenty billion in table games in Q1 alone. May I?' Without waiting for

107

permission, he leaned past Hoffmann, seized the mouse and started clicking through the recent trades. His suit smelled like a dry-cleaning store; Hoffmann had to turn away. 'Procter and Gamble, six million short at sixty-two . . . Exelon, *three million* short at forty-one-fifty . . . plus all the options . . . Jesus, Hoffmann—is an asteroid about to hit the earth, or what?'

His face was practically pressed against the screen. He produced a notebook from his inside pocket and began scribbling down the figures, but Quarry reached over and deftly plucked it from his hand. 'Naughty, Ezra,' he said. 'You know this is a paperless office.' He tore out the page, screwed it into a ball and put it in his pocket.

François de Gombart-Tonnelle, Elmira's lover, said, 'Tell me, Alex, a big short such as any one of these—does the algorithm put it on entirely independently, or does it require human intervention to execute?'

'Independently,' replied Hoffmann. He wiped the details of the trades from the screen. 'First the algorithm determines the stock it wishes to trade. Then it examines the trading pattern of that stock over the past twenty days. Then it executes the order itself in such a way as to avoid alerting the market and affecting the price.'

'So the whole process is really just fly-by-wire? Your traders are like pilots in a jumbo jet?'

'That's it exactly. Our system speaks directly to the executing broker's system, and then we use their infrastructure to hit the exchange. Nobody telephones a broker any more. Not from this shop.'

Iain Mould said, 'There must be human supervision at some point, I hope?'

'Yes, just like there is in the cockpit of a jumbo—there's constant supervision, but not usually intervention, not unless something starts going wrong. If one of the guys in Execution sees an order going through that worries him, naturally he can put a stop on it until it's cleared by me or Hugo, or one of our managers.'

'Has that ever happened?'

'No. Not with VIXAL-4. Not so far.'

'How many orders does the system handle a day?'

Quarry took over: 'About eight hundred.'

'And they're all decided algorithmically?'

'Yes. I can't remember the last time I did a trade myself.'

'Your prime broker is AmCor, I assume, given your long relationship?'

'We have various prime brokers these days, not just AmCor.'

'More's the pity,' said Easterbrook, laughing.

Quarry said, 'With the greatest respect to Bill, we don't want one single brokerage firm knowing all our strategies. At the moment we use a mix of big banks and specialist houses: three for equities, three for commodities and five for fixed income. Let's take a look at the hardware, shall we?'

As the group moved off, Quarry pulled Hoffmann aside. 'Am I missing something here,' he said quietly, 'or are those positions way out of line?'

'They do look a little more exposed than normal,' agreed Hoffmann, 'but nothing to worry about. Now I think of it, LJ mentioned that Gana wanted a meeting of the Risk Committee. I told him to talk to you about it.'

'Christ, is *that* what he wanted? I didn't have

109

time to take his call. Damn it.' Quarry glanced at his watch, then up at the tickers. The European markets were holding on to their early gains. 'Okay, let's grab five minutes while they're all having coffee. I'll tell Gana to meet us in my office. You go on ahead and keep them happy.'

The computers were housed in a big windowless room on the opposite side of the trading floor, and this time Hoffmann led the way. He stood in front of the face-recognition camera—only a few were cleared for access to this inner sanctum—and waited for the bolts to click back, then pushed at the door. It was solid, fireproof, with a pane of reinforced glass in the centre and rubber vacuum seals on the sides, so that it made a slight whoosh as it opened, the bottom of the seal skimming the white-tiled floor.

Hoffmann went in first; the others followed. Compared to the relative silence of the trading floor, the busy racket of the computers sounded almost industrial. The arrays were stacked on warehouse shelving, their rows of red and green indicator lights flickering rapidly as they processed data. At the end of the room, in a pair of long Plexiglas cabinets, two IBM TS3500 tape robots patrolled up and down on monorails, shooting with the speed of striking snakes from one end to the other as VIXAL-4 instructed them to store or retrieve data. It was several degrees colder than the rest of the building. The noise of the powerful air-conditioning needed to keep down the temperature of the central processing units, combined with the whir of the fans on the motherboards themselves, made it surprisingly difficult to hear. When everyone was inside,

Hoffmann had to raise his voice for the people at the back.

'In case you think this is impressive, I should point out that it is only four per cent of the capacity of the CPU farm at CERN, where I used to work. But the principle is the same. We have nearly a thousand standard CPUs,' he said, resting his hand proudly on the shelves, 'each with two to four cores, exactly the same as those you have at home, except without the casing and repackaged for us by a white box company. We've found this to be much more reliable and cost-effective than investing in supercomputers, and easier to upgrade, which we're doing all the time. I guess you're familiar with Moore's Law? This states that the number of transistors that can be placed on an integrated circuit—which basically means memory size and processing speed—will double every eighteen months, and costs will halve. Moore's Law has held with amazing consistency since 1965, and it still holds. In CERN in the nineties we had a Cray X-MP/48 supercomputer which cost fifteen million dollars and delivered half the power a Microsoft Xbox now gives you for two hundred bucks. You can imagine what that trend means for the future.'

Elmira Gulzhan was clasping her arms and shivering exaggeratedly. 'Why does it have to be so damn cold in here?'

'The processors generate a lot of heat. We have to try to keep them cool to stop them breaking down. If we were to shut off the air-conditioning in here, the temperature would rise at a rate of one degree Celsius a minute. Within twenty minutes it would be very uncomfortable. In half an hour we'd have a total shutdown.'

111

Etienne Mussard said, 'So what happens if there is a power cut?'

'For short-term interruptions, we switch to car batteries. After ten minutes of no mains power, diesel generators in the basement would cut in.'

'What would happen if there was a fire,' asked Łukasiński, 'or this place was attacked by terrorists?'

'We have full system back-up, naturally. We'd trade straight through. But it isn't going to happen, don't worry. We've invested a lot in security—sprinkler systems, smoke detectors, firewalls, video surveillance, guards, cyber-protection. And remember, this *is* Switzerland.'

Most people smiled. Łukasiński did not. 'Is your security in-house, or outsourced?'

'Outsourced.' Hoffmann wondered why the Pole was so obsessed with security. The paranoia of the rich, he guessed. 'Everything is outsourced—security, legal affairs, accountancy, transport, catering, technical support, cleaning. These offices are rented. Even the furniture is rented. We aim to be a company that not only makes money out of the digital age; we want to *be* digital. That means we try to be as frictionless as possible, with zero inventory.'

'What about your own personal security?' persisted Łukasiński. 'Those stitches—I understand you were attacked in your home last night.'

Hoffmann felt an odd stab of guilt and embarrassment. 'How do you know about that?'

Łukasiński said, offhand, 'Someone told me.'

Elmira rested her hand on Hoffmann's arm; her long brown-red nails were like talons. 'Oh Alex,' she said softly, 'how awful for you.'

'Who?' demanded Hoffmann.

'If I could just say,' interjected Quarry, who had slipped in unnoticed at the back, 'what happened to Alex was nothing whatever to do with company business—just some lunatic who I'm sure will be picked up by the police. And to answer your question directly, Mieczyslaw, we have now taken steps to give Alex additional protection until the issue is resolved. Now does anyone have any more questions directly relating to the hardware?' There was silence. 'No? Then I suggest we get out of here before we all freeze to death. There's coffee in the boardroom to warm us up. If you all go ahead, we'll join you in a couple of minutes. I just need to have a quick word with Alex.'

*   *   *

They were midway across the trading floor and their backs were to the big TV screens when one of the quants gave a loud gasp. In a room where nobody spoke in much above a whisper, the exclamation rang out like a gunshot in a library. Hoffmann halted in his tracks and turned to see half his workforce rising to their feet, drawn out of their seats by the images on Bloomberg and CNBC. The physicist nearest to him put his hand to his mouth.

Both the satellite channels were showing the same footage, obviously filmed on a mobile phone, of a passenger airliner coming in to land at an airport. It was clearly in trouble, descending far too quickly, and at an odd angle, with one wing much higher than the other, smoke streaming out of its side.

113

Someone grabbed a remote and pumped up the sound.

The jet passed out of sight behind a control tower and then reappeared, skimming the tops of some low sandy-coloured buildings—hangars, perhaps; there were fir trees in the background. It seemed to graze one of the buildings with its underbelly, a caressing gesture almost, and then abruptly it exploded in a vast expanding ball of yellow fire that carried on rolling and rolling. One of the wings with an engine still attached rose out of the spreading inferno and performed graceful cartwheels up into the sky. The lens followed it shakily until it dropped out of shot, and then the sound of the explosion and the shockwave reached the camera. There were tinny screams and frantic shouts in a language Hoffmann could not quite make out—Russian maybe—the picture shook, and then cut to a later, more stable shot of thick black oily smoke, roiled with orange and yellow flames, unfurling itself above the airport.

Over the images the presenter's voice—American, female—said breathlessly: 'Okay, so those were the scenes just a few minutes ago when a Vista Airways passenger jet with ninety-eight people on board crashed on its approach to Moscow's Domodedovo Airport . . .'

'Vista Airways?' said Quarry, wheeling round to confront Hoffmann. 'Did she just say Vista Airways?'

A dozen muttered conversations broke out simultaneously across the trading floor: 'My God, we've been shorting that stock all morning.' 'How weird is that?' 'Someone just walked over my grave.'

114

'Will you turn that damn thing off?' called Hoffmann. When nothing happened, he strode between the desks and snatched the remote from the hands of the hapless quant. Already the footage was starting to repeat, as it doubtless would throughout the day until familiarity at last eroded its power to titillate. Finally he found the mute button and the room was quiet again. 'All right,' he said. 'That's enough. Let's get on with our work.'

He threw the remote on to the desk and made his way back to the clients. Easterbrook and Klein, hardened veterans of the dealing room, had already lunged for the nearest terminal and were checking the prices. The others were motionless, stunned, like credulous peasants who had just witnessed a supernatural event. Hoffmann could feel their eyes upon him. Clarisse Mussard even made the sign of the cross.

'My God,' said Easterbrook, looking round from the trading screen, 'it only happened five minutes ago and Vista's stock is down fifteen per cent already. It's crashing.'

'Nose-diving,' added Klein, with a nervous giggle.

'Save it, guys,' said Quarry, 'there are civilians present.' He addressed the clients: 'I remember a couple of traders at Goldman who happened to be shorting airline insurance on the morning of 9/11. They did a high-five in the middle of the office when the first plane hit. They weren't to know. None of us knows. Shit happens.'

Klein's eyes were still riveted to the market data. 'Whoa,' he murmured appreciatively, 'your little black box is really cleaning up, Alex.'

Hoffmann stared over Klein's shoulder. The figures in the Execution column were changing rapidly as VIXAL took profits on its options to sell Vista Airways' stock at the pre-crash price. The P&L meter, converted into dollars, was a blur of pure profit.

Easterbrook said, 'I wonder how much you guys are going to make from this one trade—twenty million, thirty million? Jesus, Hugo, the regulators are going to be swarming over this like ants at a picnic.'

Quarry said, 'Alex? We should go and take that meeting.'

But Hoffmann, unable to take his eyes from the figures on the trading screen, was not listening. The pressure in his skull was intense. He put his fingers to his wound and traced his stitches. It felt to him as if they were stretched so tight they might split apart.

7

It can't continue forever. The nature of exponentials is that you push them out and eventually disaster happens.

GORDON MOORE, inventor of Moore's Law (2005)

The Risk Committee of Hoffmann Investment Technologies met briefly at 11.57 a.m., according to a note drawn up subsequently by Ganapathi Rajamani, the company's chief risk officer. All five members of the senior management team were listed as present: Dr Alexander Hoffmann, president of the company; the Hon. Hugo Quarry, chief executive officer; Lin Ju-Long, chief financial officer; Pieter van der Zyl, chief operating officer; and Rajamani himself.

It was not quite as formal as the minutes made it sound. Indeed, afterwards, when memories were compared, it was agreed that nobody had even sat down. They all stood around in Quarry's office, apart from Quarry himself, who perched on the edge of his desk so that he could keep an eye on his computer terminal. Hoffmann took up his former position at the window and occasionally parted the slats of the blinds to check on the street below. That was the other thing everyone remembered: how distracted he seemed.

'Okay,' said Quarry, 'let's keep this quick. I've got a hundred billion dollars on the hoof unattended in the boardroom and I need to get back in there. Close the door, will you, LJ?' He waited until there was no chance of their being overheard. 'I take it we all saw what just happened. The first question is whether by making such a large bet to the down side on Vista Airways shortly before its share price collapsed we're going to trigger an official investigation. Gana?'

'The short answer is yes, almost certainly.' Rajamani was a neat, precise young man, with a strong sense of his own importance. His job was to keep an eye on the fund's risk levels and ensure they complied with the law. Quarry had poached him from the Financial Services Authority in London six months earlier to serve as a bit of window-dressing.

'Yes?' repeated Quarry. 'Even though we couldn't possibly have known what was going to happen?'

'The whole process is automatic. The regulators' algorithms will have detected any unusual activity surrounding the airline's stock immediately prior to the price collapse. That will already be leading them straight to us.'

'But we haven't done anything illegal.'

'No. Not unless we sabotaged the plane.'

'We didn't, did we?' Quarry glanced around. 'I mean, I'm all in favour of people using their initiative . . .'

'What they *will* want to know, however,' continued Rajamani, 'is why we shorted twelve and a half million shares at that precise moment. I know this sounds an absurd question, Alex, but is there any way VIXAL could have acquired news of the crash before the rest of the market?'

Reluctantly Hoffmann let the slats of the blind click shut and turned to face his colleagues.

'VIXAL takes a direct digital news feed from Reuters—that might give it an advantage of a second or two over a human trader—but so do plenty of other algorithmic systems.'

Van der Zyl said, 'Besides, you couldn't do much in that time. A position the size of ours would have taken some hours to put together.'

'When did we start acquiring the options?' asked Quarry.

Ju-Long said, 'As soon as the European markets opened. Nine o'clock.'

'Can we just stop this right now?' said Hoffmann irritably. 'It will take us less than five minutes to show even the most dumb-assed regulator that we shorted that stock as part of a pattern of bets to the down side. It was nothing special. It was a coincidence. Get over it.'

'Well, speaking as a former dumb-ass regulator,' said Rajamani, 'I have to say I agree with you, Alex. It's the pattern that matters, which is why actually I tried to talk to you about it earlier this morning, if you remember.'

'Yeah, well, I'm sorry, but I was late for the presentation.' Quarry should never have hired this guy, Hoffmann thought. Once a regulator, always a regulator: it was like a foreign accent—you could never quite hide where you came from.

Rajamani said, 'What we really need to focus on is the level of our risk if the markets rally—Procter and Gamble, Accenture, Exelon, dozens of them: tens of millions in options since Tuesday night. These are all huge one-way bets we have taken.'

'And then there is our exposure to the VIX,' added van der Zyl. 'That's been ringing alarm bells with me for some days now. I did mention this to you, Hugo, last week, if you remember?' He had once taught engineering at the University of Technology in Delft and retained a pedagogic manner.

Quarry said, 'So where are we on the VIX? I've been so busy preparing for the presentation, I haven't actually checked our positions lately.'

'The last time I looked, we were up to twenty thousand contracts.'

'Twenty *thousand*?' Quarry shot a look at Hoffmann.

Ju-Long said, 'We started accumulating VIX futures back in April, when the index stood at eighteen. If we had sold earlier in the week we would have done very well, and I assumed that's what would happen. But rather than following the logical course and selling, we are still buying. Another four thousand contracts last night at twenty-five. That is one hell of a level of implied volatility.'

Rajamani said, 'I'm seriously worried, frankly. Our book has gone all out of shape. We're long gold. We're long the dollar. We're short every equity futures index.'

Hoffmann looked from one to another—from Rajamani to Ju-Long to van der Zyl—and suddenly it was clear to him that they had caucused beforehand. It was an ambush—an ambush by financial bureaucrats. Not one of them was qualified to be a quant. He felt his temper beginning to rise. He said, 'So what are you suggesting we do, Gana?'

'I think we have to start liquidating some of these positions.'

'That's just about the stupidest goddam thing

120

I've ever *heard*,' said Hoffmann. In his frustration he slapped the back of his hand hard on the blinds, rattling them against the windows. 'Jesus, Gana, we made close to eighty million dollars last week. We just made another forty million this morning. And you want us to ignore VIXAL's analysis and go back to discretionary trading?'

'Not ignore it, Alex. I never said that.'

Quarry said quietly, 'Give him a break, Alex. It was only a suggestion. It's his job to worry about risk.'

'No, actually, I won't give him a break. He wants us to abandon a strategy that's showing massive alpha, which is exactly the kind of illogical, insane reaction to success, based on fear, that VIXAL is designed to exploit! And if Gana doesn't believe that algorithms are inherently superior to human beings when it comes to playing the market, then he's working in the wrong shop.'

Rajamani, however, was unfazed by his company president's tirade. He had a reputation as a terrier: at the FSA he had gone after Goldman. He said, 'I have to remind you, Alex, that the prospectus of this company promises clients exposure to a yearly volatility of no more than twenty per cent. If I see that those statutory risk limits are in danger of being breached, I am obliged to step in.'

'Meaning what?'

'Meaning, if the level of our exposure isn't dialled back, I will have to notify the investors. Meaning I really must talk to their board.'

'But this is *my* company.'

'And the investors' money, or most of it.'

In the silence that followed, Hoffmann started massaging his temples vigorously with his knuckles.

His head was aching badly again: he needed a painkiller. 'Their board?' he muttered. 'I'm not even sure who's on their frigging board.' As far as he was concerned, it was a purely technical legal entity, registered in the Cayman Islands for tax purposes, that controlled the clients' money and paid the hedge fund its management and incentive fees.

'Okay,' said Quarry, 'I don't think we're anywhere near that point yet. As they used to say in the war, let's keep calm and carry on.' He bestowed one of his most winning smiles upon the room.

Rajamani said, 'For legal reasons I must ask that my concerns be minuted.'

'Fine. Write up a note of the meeting and I'll sign it. But don't forget you're a new boy and this is Alex's company—Alex's and mine, though we're both only here because of him. And if he trusts VIXAL then we all should trust it—Christ knows, we can hardly fault its performance. However, I agree, we also have to keep an eye on the risk level—we don't want to be so obsessed watching the instrument panel we fly into the side of a mountain. Alex, you'd accept that? So, given that most of these equities are US-traded, what I suggest is we reconvene in this office at three thirty when the American markets open, and review the situation then.'

Rajamani said ominously, 'In that case, I think it would be prudent to have a lawyer present.'

'Fine. I'll ask Max Gallant to stay behind after lunch. You okay with that, Alex?'

Hoffmann made a weary gesture of agreement.

At 12.08, according to the minutes, the meeting broke up.

'Oh, Alex, by the way,' said Ju-Long, turning in the doorway as they were filing out, 'I almost forgot— that account number of yours you asked about? It turns out it is on our system.'

'What account is this?' asked Quarry.

Hoffmann said, 'Oh, nothing. Just a query I had. I'll catch up with you in a second, LJ.'

The trio walked back to their offices, Rajamani leading the way. As Quarry watched them go, the expression of suave conciliation with which he had ushered them out changed to a sneer of contempt. 'What a pompous little shit that fellow is,' he said. He imitated Rajamani's flawless, clipped English: '"I really must talk to their board." "It would be prudent to have a lawyer present."' He mimed taking aim at him along the barrel of a rifle.

Hoffmann said, 'It was you who hired him.'

'Yes, all right, point taken, and it'll be me who fires him, don't you worry.' He pulled an imaginary trigger a second before the trio rounded a corner and moved out of sight. 'And if he thinks I'm paying Max Gallant two thousand francs an hour to come and cover his ass he's in for a shock.' Suddenly Quarry dropped his voice. 'We are okay here, aren't we, Alexi? I don't have to be worried? It's just that for a second in there I had the same feeling I used to get when I was at AmCor, selling collateralised debt.'

'What feeling was that?'

'That every day I'm getting richer but I'm not sure how.'

Hoffmann regarded him with surprise. In eight

years he had never heard Quarry express anxiety. It was almost as unsettling as some of the other things that had happened that morning. 'Listen, Hugo,' he said, 'we can put an override on VIXAL this afternoon if that's what you want. We can let the positions wind down and return the money to the investors. I'm actually only in this game in the first place because of you, remember?'

'But what about *you*, Alexi?' asked Quarry urgently. 'Do *you* want to stop? I mean we could, you know—we've made more than enough to live out the rest of our days in luxury. We don't have to carry on pitching to clients.'

'No, I don't want to stop. We have the resources to do things here on the technical side that no one else is even attempting. But if you want to call it quits, I'll buy you out.'

Now it was Quarry who looked taken aback, but then he suddenly grinned. 'Like hell you will! You don't get rid of me that easily.' His nerve seemed to revive as quickly as it had wilted. 'No, no, I'm in this for the duration. I suppose it was just seeing that plane—it spooked me a bit. But if you're fine, I'm fine. Well then?' He gestured for Hoffmann to step ahead of him. 'Shall we return to that esteemed bunch of psychopaths and criminals we are proud to call our clients?'

'You do it. I've nothing left to say to them. If they want to put more money in—fine. If not— screw 'em.'

'But it's you they've come to see . . .'

'Yeah, well now they've seen me.'

Quarry's mouth turned down. 'You'll come to the lunch at least?'

'Hugo, I really cannot stand these people . . .'

But Quarry's expression was so forlorn that Hoffmann capitulated at once. 'Oh Christ, if it's really that important, I'll come to the goddam lunch.'

'Beau-Rivage. One o'clock.' Quarry seemed on the point of saying something else, but then looked at his watch and swore. 'Shit, they've been on their own for a quarter of an hour.' He set off towards the boardroom. 'One o'clock,' he called, turning round and walking backwards. He cocked his finger. 'Good man.' He already had his cell phone in his other hand and was entering a number.

Hoffmann pivoted on his heel and headed in the opposite direction. There was no one in the corridor. He quickly put his head round the corner of the alcove and checked the communal kitchen with its coffee machine, microwave and giant refrigerator: also empty. A few paces further on, Ju-Long's office door was shut, his assistant away from her desk. Without waiting for a reply, Hoffmann knocked and went in.

It was as if he had disturbed a group of teenage boys examining pornography on the family computer. Ju-Long, van der Zyl and Rajamani drew back quickly from the terminal and Ju-Long clicked the mouse to change the screen.

Van der Zyl said, 'We were just checking the currency markets, Alex.' The Dutchman's features were slightly too large for his face, giving him the look of an intelligent, lugubrious gargoyle.

'And?'

'The euro is weakening against the dollar.'

'Which is what we anticipated, I believe.' Hoffmann pushed the door open wider. 'Don't let me keep you.'

'Alex—' Rajamani began.

Hoffmann interrupted: 'It was LJ I wanted to speak with—in private.' He stared straight ahead as they filed out. When they had gone, he said, 'So you say that account is on our system?'

'It comes up twice.'

'You mean it's one of ours—we use it for business?'

'No.' Ju-Long's smooth forehead creased into an unexpectedly deep frown. 'Actually, I assumed it was for your own personal use.'

'Why?'

'Because you asked the back office to transfer forty-two million dollars into it.'

Hoffmann studied the other man's face carefully for evidence that he was joking. But Ju-Long, as Quarry always said, though possessed of many admirable qualities, was entirely devoid of a sense of humour.

'When did I request this transfer?'

'Eleven months ago. I just sent you the original email to remind you.'

'Okay, thanks. I'll check it out. You said there were two transactions?'

'Indeed. The money was entirely repaid last month, with interest.'

'And you never queried this with me?'

'No, Alex,' said the Chinese quietly. 'Why would I do that? Like you say, it is your company.'

'Yeah, sure. That's right. Thanks, LJ.'

'No problem.'

Hoffmann turned at the door. 'And you didn't just mention this to Gana and Pieter?'

'No.' Ju-Long's eyes were wide with innocence.

Hoffmann hurried back towards his own office.

126

Forty-two million dollars? He was sure he had never demanded the transfer of such a sum. He would hardly have forgotten. It had to be fraud. He strode past Marie-Claude, sitting typing at her workstation just outside his door, and went straight to his desk. He logged on to his computer and opened his inbox. And there indeed was his instruction to transfer $42,032,127.88 to the Royal Grand Cayman Bank Limited on 17 June last year. Immediately beneath it was a notification from the hedge fund's own bank of a repayment from the same account of $43,188,037.09, dated 3 April.

He performed the calculation in his head. What kind of fraudster repaid the capital sum he had stolen from his victim, plus exactly 2.75 per cent interest?

He went back and studied what purported to be his original email. There was no greeting or signature, merely the usual standard instruction to transfer the amount X to the account Y. LJ would have put it through the system without a second's hesitation, confident that their intranet was secure behind the best firewall that money could buy and that the accounts would in any case be reconciled electronically in due course. If the money had been in the form of bars of gold or suitcases of cash, they might perhaps have been more careful. But this was not really money in the physical sense at all, merely strings and sequences of glowing green symbols, no more substantial than protoplasm. That was why they had the nerve to do with it what they did.

He checked what time he was supposed to have sent his email ordering the transfer: midnight exactly.

He tilted back in his chair and contemplated the

smoke detector in the ceiling above his desk. He often worked late in the office, but never as late as midnight. This message, if genuine, would therefore have had to have come from his terminal at home. Was it possible that if he checked the computer in his study he would find a record of this email, along with the order to the Dutch bookseller? Could he be suffering from some kind of Jekyll-and-Hyde syndrome that meant one half of his mind was doing things the other half knew nothing about?

On impulse he opened his desk drawer, took out the CD and inserted it into the optical drive of his computer. The program took a moment to run, and then the screen was filled with an index of two hundred monochrome images of the inside of his head. He clicked through them rapidly, trying to find the one that had caught the attention of the radiologist, but it was hopeless. Viewed at speed, his brain seemed to emerge from emptiness, swell into a cloudburst of grey matter, and then contract again to nothing.

He buzzed his assistant. 'Marie-Claude, if you look in my personal directory you'll see an entry for a Dr Jeanne Polidori. Will you make me an appointment to see her tomorrow? Tell her it's urgent.'

'Yes, Dr Hoffmann. What time?'

'Any time. Also, I want to go to the gallery where my wife's having her exhibition. Do you know the address?'

'Yes, Dr Hoffmann. When do you want to go?'

'Right away. Can you fix me a car?'

'You have a driver at your disposal at all times now, arranged by Monsieur Genoud.'

'Oh yeah, that's right, I forgot. Okay, tell him I'm

coming down.'

He ejected the CD and put it back in the drawer along with the Darwin volume, then grabbed his raincoat. Passing through the trading floor, he glanced across at the boardroom. Where a section of the blinds was not properly closed he could see Elmira Gulzhan and her lawyer boyfriend through the slats, bent over an iPad, watched by Quarry, who had his arms folded: he looked smug. Etienne Mussard, the curved turtle shell of his back turned towards the others, was entering figures with elderly slowness on to a large pocket calculator.

On the opposite wall Bloomberg and CNBC were showing lines of red arrows, all in the descendent. The European markets had shed their earlier gains and had started falling fast. That would almost certainly depress the opening in the US, which would in turn make the hedge fund much less exposed to loss by mid-afternoon. Hoffmann felt his spirits lighten with relief. Indeed, he experienced a definite thrill of pride. Once again VIXAL was proving smarter than the humans around it, smarter even than its creator.

His good humour persisted as he rode the elevator down to the ground floor and turned the corner into the lobby, where a bulky figure in a cheap dark suit rose to greet him. Of all the affectations of the wealthy, none had ever struck Hoffmann as quite as absurd as the sight of a bodyguard sitting outside a meeting or restaurant; he had often wondered who exactly the rich were expecting to attack them, except possibly their own shareholders or members of their families. But on this particular day he was glad to find himself approached by the polite, thuggish-looking man who flashed his ID and introduced himself as Olivier Paccard, *l'homme de la sécurité*.

'If you would wait just a moment, please, Dr Hoffmann,' said Paccard. He held up his hand in a polite plea for silence and stared into the middle distance. He had a wire trailing from his ear. 'Fine,' he said. 'We can go.'

He moved swiftly to the entrance, hitting the exit button with the heel of his hand precisely as a long dark Mercedes drew up at the kerb, with the same driver who had picked Hoffmann up from the hospital. Paccard strode out first, opened the rear passenger door and ushered Hoffmann inside. His palm briefly brushed the back of the physicist's neck. Before Hoffmann even had the chance to settle himself into his seat, Paccard was sliding into the front, the car doors were all closed and locked, and they were pulling out into the noonday traffic. The whole procedure must have taken less than ten seconds.

They made a sharp left, tyres squealing, and shot down a gloomy side street, which opened at the end on to the lake and the distant view of the mountains. The sun had still not broken through the cloud. The high white column of the Jet d'Eau rose 140 metres against the grey sky, dissolving at its top into a chilly rain that plunged to detonate against the dull black surface of the lake. The flashes from the cameras of the tourists photographing one another at its base winked bright in the gloom.

The Mercedes accelerated to beat a red light and made another sharp left into the dual carriageway, only to come to a halt alongside the Jardin Anglais, held up by some unseen obstruction ahead. Paccard craned his neck to see what was happening.

This was where Hoffmann sometimes went for a jog if he had a problem to solve—from here across to the Parc des Eaux-Vives and back again, two or three times if necessary, until he had found an answer, talking to no one, looking at nothing. He had never really examined the area properly before, so that now he gazed out at the unseen familiarity with a kind of wonder: the kids' play area with the blue plastic slides, the outdoor crêperie under the trees, the pedestrian crossing where he might have to jog on the spot for a minute waiting for the lights to change. For the second time that day he felt as if he were a visitor to his own life, and he had a sudden desire to order the driver to stop the car and let him out. But no sooner had the thought arisen than the Mercedes moved forward again. They entered the busy traffic system at the end of the Pont du Mont-Blanc and emerged from it at speed a few seconds later, weaving westwards through the slower trucks and buses towards the galleries and antique shops of the Plaine de Plainpalais.

8

There is no exception to the rule that every organic being naturally increases at so high a rate, that if not destroyed, the earth would soon be covered by the progeny of a single pair.

CHARLES DARWIN, *On the Origin of Species* (1859)

Contours de l'homme: Une exposition de l'oeuvre de Gabrielle Hoffmann—how much more impressive it sounded in French than English, she thought—was scheduled to run for one week only at the Galerie d'Art Contemporain Guy Bertrand, a small whitewashed space, previously a Citroën auto-repair shop, in a back street around the corner from MAMCO, the city's main contemporary art gallery.

Gabrielle had found herself sitting next to the owner, M. Bertrand, five months earlier at a Christmas charity auction at the Mandarin Oriental Hotel—an event Alex had flatly refused to attend—and the next day he had wheedled his way into her studio to see what she was working on. After ten minutes of outrageous flattery, he had offered to give her an exhibition in return for half of any proceeds, as long as she paid the expenses. Of course she had realised at once that it was Alex's money rather than her talent that was the main attraction. She had observed over the last couple of years how great wealth acted like an invisible magnetic force field, pushing and pulling people out of their normal pattern of behaviour. But she had also learned to live with it. You could go mad trying to guess whose actions were genuine, whose false. Besides, she wanted to have a show—wanted it, she realised, more keenly than she had ever wanted anything in her life, except to have a child.

Bertrand had urged her to throw an opening-night party: it would build interest, he said, and drum up some publicity. Gabrielle had demurred. She knew that her husband would sink into misery for days beforehand at the prospect of such an occasion. In the end, they had compromised. When the doors opened quietly at eleven that morning, two young waitresses in white blouses and black miniskirts stood offering flutes of Pol Roger and plates of canapés to everyone who crossed the threshold. Gabrielle had worried that no one would show up, but they did: the gallery's regulars, who had received an emailed flyer advertising the exhibition; passers-by attracted by the sight of a free drink; and her own friends and acquaintances who she had been calling and emailing for weeks beforehand—names from old address books, people she hadn't seen for years. All had turned up. The result was that by noon, a sizeable party of more than a hundred was in progress, spilling out through the doors and on to the pavement where the smokers gathered.

Halfway through her second glass of champagne, Gabrielle realised she was actually enjoying herself. Her *oeuvre* consisted of twenty-seven pieces— everything she had finished over the past three years, apart from her very first self-portrait, which Alex had asked if they could keep and which remained on the coffee table in the drawing room. And the truth was, once it all was gathered together and properly lit—the engravings on glass especially—it did look like a solid, professional body of work: at least as impressive as most openings she had attended in her time. No one had laughed. People had looked carefully and made thoughtful comments, mostly complimentary. The earnest young reporter from the Geneva *Tribune* had even compared her emphasis on the simplicity of the line with Giacometti's topography of the head. Her only remaining anxiety was that nothing had yet sold, which she blamed on the high prices Bertrand had insisted on charging, from 4,500 Swiss francs—about $5,000—for the CAT scans of the smallest animal heads up to 18,000 for the big MRI portrait, *The Invisible Man*. If nothing had gone by the end of the day, it would be a humiliation.

She tried to forget about it and pay attention to what the man opposite her was saying. It was difficult to hear over the noise. She had to interrupt him. She put her hand on his arm. 'I'm sorry, what did you say your name was again?'

'Bob Walton. I used to work with Alex at CERN. I was just saying that I think you two first met at a party in my house.'

'Oh my God,' she said, 'that's quite right. How *are* you?' She shook his hand and looked at him properly for the first time: thin, tall, neat, grey—ascetic, she decided; either that or just plain severe. He could have been a monk—no, more senior than that, he had authority: an abbot. She said, 'It's funny—I just tagged along to that party with friends. I'm not sure we've ever been formally introduced, have we?'

'I believe not.'

'Well—thank you, belatedly. You changed my life.'

He didn't smile. 'I haven't seen Alex for years. He *is* coming, I assume?'

'I certainly hope so.' Once again her eyes flickered to the door in the hope that Alex would walk through it. So far all her husband had done was to send her the taciturn bodyguard, who had now stationed himself at the entrance like a nightclub bouncer and occasionally seemed to speak into his sleeve. 'So what brings you here? Are you a gallery regular or just a passer-by?'

'Neither. Alex invited me.'

'*Alex?*' She did a double-take. 'I'm sorry. I didn't know Alex sent out any invitations. It's not the kind of thing he does.'

'I was a little surprised myself. Especially as the last time we met we had something of a disagreement. And now I have come to make amends and he isn't here. Never mind. I like your work.'

'Thank you.' She was still trying to assimilate the idea that Alex might have invited a guest of his own, and without telling her. 'Perhaps you'll buy something.'

'I fear the prices are somewhat beyond the means of a CERN salary.' And for the first time he gave her a smile—all the warmer for being so rare, like a flash of sun on a grey landscape. He put his hand into his breast pocket. 'If you ever feel like making art out of particle physics, give me a call.' He gave her his card. She read:

Professor Robert WALTON
Computing Centre Department Head
CERN—European Organisation for Nuclear
Research

'That sounds very grand.' She slipped the card into her pocket. 'Thank you. I might well do that. So tell me about you and Alex—'

'Darling, you *are* clever,' said a woman's voice behind her. She felt someone squeeze her elbow and turned to find herself confronted by the wide pale face and large grey eyes of Jenny Brinkerhof, another Englishwoman in her mid-thirties married to a hedge-fund manager. (Geneva had started to teem with them, Gabrielle had noticed: economic migrants from London, fleeing the UK's new fifty per cent tax rate. All they seemed to talk about was how hard it was to find decent schools.)

She said, 'Jen, how lovely of you to come.'

'How lovely of you to *invite* me.'

They kissed and Gabrielle swung round to introduce her to Walton, but he had moved on and was talking to the man from the *Tribune*. This was the trouble with drinks parties: getting stuck with a person you didn't want to talk to while someone you did was tantalisingly in view. She wondered how long it would be before Jen mentioned her children.

'I do so *envy* you just having the sheer *space* in your life to do something like this. I mean, if there's one thing that having three kids just absolutely *kills*, it's the creative spark . . .'

Over her shoulder Gabrielle saw an incongruous figure, strange yet familiar, enter the gallery. 'Excuse me a minute, Jen, would you?' She slipped away and went over to the door. 'Inspector Leclerc?'

'Madame Hoffmann.' Leclerc shook her hand

politely.

She noticed he had on the same clothes he had been wearing at four in the morning: dark windcheater, a white shirt now distinctly grey around the collar, and a black tie that he had knotted unfashionably close to the thick end, just as her father always did. The stubble of his unshaved cheeks reached up like a silvery fungus towards the black pouches beneath his eyes. He looked utterly out of place. One of the waitresses approached with a tray of champagne, which Gabrielle assumed he would refuse—wasn't that what policemen did when they were on duty: refuse alcohol?—but Leclerc, brightening, said, 'Excellent, thank you,' and took the glass cautiously by the stem, as if he feared he might break it. 'That's very good,' he said, taking a sip and smacking his lips. 'What is it? Eighty francs a bottle?'

'I couldn't tell you. My husband's office arranged it.'

The photographer from the *Tribune* came over and took their picture standing side by side. Leclerc's windcheater gave off the musty smell of ancient damp. He waited until the photographer had moved away and then said, 'Well, I can tell you forensics obtained an excellent set of fingerprints from your mobile telephone and from the knives in the kitchen. Unfortunately we can find no matches in our records. Your intruder does not have a criminal record, in Switzerland at least. Quite the phantom! Now we are checking with Interpol.' He seized a canapé from a passing tray and swallowed it whole. 'And your husband? Is he here? I can't see him anywhere.'

'Not yet. Why? Do you want him?'

'No, I came to see your work.'

Guy Bertrand sidled over, plainly curious. She had told him about the break-in. 'Is everything okay?' he asked, and Gabrielle found herself introducing the policeman to the owner of the gallery. Bertrand was a plump young man dressed from head to toe in black silk—Armani T-shirt, jacket, trousers, holistic Zen slippers. He and Leclerc regarded one another with mutual incomprehension; they might have been different species.

'A police inspector,' repeated Bertrand, in a tone of wonder. 'You would be interested in *The Invisible Man*, I think.'

'*The Invisible Man*?'

'Let me show you,' said Gabrielle, grateful of an opportunity to separate them. She led Leclerc over to the largest exhibit, a glass case lit from beneath in which a full-size nude man, apparently composed of pale blue gossamer, seemed to hover just above the ground. The effect was ghostly, disturbing. 'This is Jim, the invisible man.'

'And who is Jim?'

'He was a murderer.' Leclerc turned sharply to look at her. 'James Duke Johnson,' she continued, rather pleased to have elicited this reaction, 'executed in Florida in 1994. Before he died, the prison chaplain persuaded him to donate his body for scientific research.'

'And also for public exhibition?'

'That I doubt. You're shocked?'

'I am, I confess.'

'Good. That's the effect I wanted.'

Leclerc grunted and set down his champagne. He moved closer to the glass case and put his hands on his hips, staring at it intently. His stomach flopping over his trouser belt reminded her of one of Dalí's melting watches. He said, 'And how do you achieve this impression of floating?'

'Trade secret.' Gabrielle laughed. 'No, I'll tell you. It's quite simple. I take sections from an MRI scan and trace them through very clear glass—two-millimetre Mirogard, the clearest you can get. Only sometimes instead of using pen and ink I use a dentist's drill to engrave the line. In daylight you can hardly see a mark. But if you shine artificial light on to it from the right angle—well, that's the effect you get.'

'Remarkable. And what does your husband think of it?'

'He thinks I've become unhealthily obsessed. But then he has obsessions of his own.' She finished her glass of champagne. Everything seemed pleasantly heightened—colours, noises, sensations. 'You must think we're a pretty strange couple.'

'Believe me, *madame*, my work brings me into contact with people far stranger than you can even begin to imagine.' Suddenly he turned his bloodshot eyes upon her. 'Would you mind if I asked you a couple of questions?'

'Go ahead.'

'When did you first meet Dr Hoffmann?'

'I was just remembering that.' She could see Alex in her mind with perfect clarity. He had been talking to Hugo Quarry—always bloody Quarry in the picture, even right at the start—and she had had to make the first move, but she had drunk enough not to care. 'That would have been at a party in Saint-Genis-Pouilly, about eight years ago.'

'Saint-Genis-Pouilly,' repeated Leclerc. 'A great

139

many CERN scientists live round there, I believe.'

'They certainly did then. You see that tall, grey-headed guy over there—Walton, his name is. It was at his house. I went back to Alex's apartment afterwards and I remember there was nothing in it except computers. It got so hot that one day it showed up on an infrared monitor in a police helicopter and he was raided by the drug squad. They thought he was growing cannabis.'

She smiled at the memory, and so did Leclerc—but for form's sake, she suspected, to encourage her to keep talking. She wondered what he wanted.

'Were you at CERN yourself?'

'God, no, I was working as a secretary at the UN—your typical ex-art student with bad prospects and good French: that was me.' She was talking too fast and grinning too much, she realised. He would think she was tipsy.

'But Dr Hoffmann was still at CERN when you got to know him?'

'He was in the process of leaving to set up his own company with his partner, a man called Hugo Quarry. We all met for the first time on the same night, oddly enough. Is this important?'

'And why exactly did he do that, do you know—leave CERN?'

'You'd have to ask him. Or Hugo.'

'I will. He is American, this Mr Quarry?'

She laughed. 'No, English. Very much so.'

'I assume one reason Dr Hoffmann left CERN was because he wanted to make more money?'

'No, not really. Money never bothered him. Not then, anyway. He told me he could pursue his line of research more easily if he had his own company.'

'And what line was that?'

'Artificial intelligence. But again, you'd have to ask him about the details. I'm afraid it's always been way over my head.'

Leclerc paused.

'Has he sought psychiatric help, do you know?'

The question startled her. 'Not that I'm aware. Why do you ask?'

'It's just that I gather he suffered a nervous breakdown when he was at CERN, which someone there told me is the reason why he left. I wondered if there'd been any recurrence.'

She realised she was staring at him with her mouth open. She clamped her jaw shut.

He was studying her closely. He said, 'I'm sorry. Have I spoken out of turn? You didn't know that?'

She recovered her composure just enough to lie. 'Well, of course I *knew* about it—I knew *something* about it.' She was aware of how unconvincing she sounded. But what was the alternative? To admit that her husband was mostly a mystery to her—that an immense amount of what occupied his mind every day had always been impenetrable territory for her, and that this unknowable quality was both what had attracted her to him in the first place and what had frightened her ever since? 'So you've been checking up on Alex?' she said in a brittle voice. 'Shouldn't you be trying to find the man who attacked him?'

'I have to investigate all the facts, *madame*,' said Leclerc primly. 'It may be that the assailant knew your husband in the past or had a grudge against him. I merely asked an acquaintance at CERN—off the record and in the strictest confidence, I do assure you—why he had left.'

'And this person said he had had a breakdown,

141

and now you think Alex may be making up this whole story about a mysterious attacker?'

'No, I'm simply trying to understand all the circumstances.' He emptied his glass in one swig. 'I'm sorry—I should let you get back to your party.'

'Would you like another drink?'

'No.' He pressed his fingers to his mouth and suppressed a burp. 'I must get on. Thank you.' He bowed slightly, in an old-fashioned way. 'It really has been most interesting to see your work.' He stopped and stared again at the executed murderer in his glass box. 'What exactly did he do, this poor fellow?'

'He killed an old man who caught him stealing his electric blanket. Shot him and stabbed him. He was on death row for twelve years. When his last appeal for clemency was turned down, he was executed by lethal injection.'

'Barbaric,' muttered Leclerc, although whether he meant the crime, the punishment, or what she had made out of it, she was not entirely sure.

*　　　*　　　*

Afterwards Leclerc sat in his car on the opposite side of the street, his notebook on his knee, writing down as much of what he had just been told as he could remember. Through the window of the gallery he could see people milling around Gabrielle, her small dark figure lent an occasional touch of glamour by a camera flash. He decided he rather liked her, which was more than he could say for her exhibition. Three thousand francs for a few bits of glass with a horse's skull scribbled on them? He blew out his cheeks. Dear God, one could buy a decent working animal—the whole thing, mark you, not just the head—for half that amount.

He finished writing and flicked back and forth through his notes, as if by a process of random association he might find some clue that had so far eluded him. His friend at CERN had taken a quick look at Hoffmann's personnel file and Leclerc had jotted down the highlights: that Hoffmann had joined the team operating the Large Electron–Positron Collider at the age of twenty-seven, one of the few Americans seconded to the project at that time; that his head of section had considered him one of the most brilliant mathematicians on site; that he had switched from the construction of the new particle accelerator, the Large Hadron Collider, to the design of the software and computer systems needed to analyse the billions of pieces of data generated by the experiments; that after a prolonged period of overwork his behaviour had become sufficiently erratic for his fellow workers to complain, and he had been asked to leave the facility by the security department; and that finally after extensive sick leave his contract had been terminated.

Leclerc was fairly sure that her husband's mental breakdown had come as news to Gabrielle Hoffmann: another of her endearing qualities was an obvious inability to lie. So it seemed Hoffmann was a mystery to everyone—his fellow scientists, the financial world, even his wife. He circled the name of Hugo Quarry.

His thoughts were interrupted by the noise of a powerful engine, and he glanced across the road to see a big charcoal-coloured Mercedes with its headlights on pulling up outside the gallery. Even

143

before it had come to a stop, a bull-like figure in a dark suit jumped out of the front passenger seat, quickly checked the road ahead and behind and then opened the rear door. The people on the pavement, with their drinks and cigarettes, turned round lazily to see who was emerging, then looked away without interest as the unknown newcomer was escorted swiftly through the doors.

9

Even when we are quite alone, how often do we think with pleasure or pain of what others think of us—of their imagined approbation or disapprobation; and this all follows from sympathy, a fundamental element of the social instincts. A man who possessed no trace of such instincts would be an unnatural monster.

CHARLES DARWIN, *The Descent of Man* (1871)

Hoffmann's non-existent public profile had not been achieved without effort. One day, quite early in the history of Hoffmann Investment Technologies, when the company still only had about two billion dollars in assets under management, he had invited the partners of Switzerland's oldest public-relations firm to breakfast at the Hotel Président Wilson and offered them a deal: an annual retainer of 200,000 Swiss francs in return for keeping his name out of the papers. He set only one condition: if by any chance he *was* mentioned, he would deduct 10,000 francs from their fee; if he was mentioned more than twenty times in a year, they would have to start paying him. After a lengthy discussion, the partners accepted his terms and reversed all the advice they normally gave their clients. Hoffmann made no public charitable donations, attended no gala dinners or industry awards ceremonies, cultivated no journalists, appeared on no newspaper's rich list, endorsed no political party, endowed no educational institution and gave no lectures or speeches. The occasional curious journalist was steered for background to the hedge fund's prime brokers, who were always happy to take the credit for its success, or—in cases of extreme persistence—to Quarry. The partners had always kept their full fee and Hoffmann his anonymity.

It was, therefore, an unusual experience, and frankly an ordeal for him to attend his wife's first exhibition. From the moment he stepped out of the car and crossed the crowded pavement and entered the noisy gallery, he wished he could turn around and leave. People he suspected he had met before, friends of Gabrielle's, loomed up and spoke to him, but although he had a mind that could perform mental arithmetic to five decimal places, he had no memory for faces. It was as if his personality had grown lopsided to compensate for his gifts. He heard what others were saying, the usual trite and pointless remarks, but somehow he didn't take them in. He was conscious of mumbling things in reply that were inappropriate or even downright odd. Offered a glass of champagne, he took water instead, and that was when he noticed Bob Walton staring at him from the other side of the room.

Walton, of all people!

Before he could take evasive action, his former colleague was making his way through the crowd towards him, determined to have a word, his hand extended. 'Alex,' he said, 'it's been a while.'

'Bob.' He shook his hand coldly. 'I don't believe I've seen you since I offered you a job and you told me I was the devil come to steal your soul.'

'I don't think I put it *quite* like that.'

'No? I seem to recall you made it pretty damn clear what you thought of scientists going to the

146

dark side and becoming quants.'

'Did I really? I'm sorry about that.' Walton gestured round the room with his drink. 'Anyway, I'm glad it all turned out so happily for you. And that's sincerely meant, Alex.'

He said it with such warmth that Hoffmann regretted his hostility. When he had first come to Geneva from Princeton, knowing no one and with nothing except two suitcases and an Anglo-French dictionary, Walton had been his section head at CERN. He and his wife had taken him under their wing—Sunday lunches, apartment-hunting, lifts to work, even attempts to fix him up with a girlfriend.

Hoffmann said, with an effort at friendliness, 'So how goes the search for the God particle?'

'Oh, we're getting there. And you? How's the elusive holy grail of autonomous machine reasoning?'

'The same. Getting there.'

'Really?' Walton raised his eyebrows in surprise. 'So you're still going on with it?'

'Of course.'

'Gosh. That's brave. What happened to your head?'

'Nothing. A silly accident.' He glanced over towards Gabrielle. 'I think maybe I ought to go and say hello to my wife . . .'

'Of course. Forgive me.' Walton offered his hand again. 'Well, it's been good talking to you, Alex. We should hook up properly some time. You've got my email address.'

Hoffmann called after him, 'Actually, I haven't.'

Walton turned. 'Yes you have. You sent me an invitation.'

'An invitation to what?'

147

'To this.'

'I haven't sent any invitations.'

'I think you'll find you have. Just a second . . .'

It was typical of Walton's academic pedantry, thought Hoffmann, to insist on such a minor point, even when he was wrong. But then to his surprise, Walton handed him his BlackBerry, showing the invitation plainly sent from Hoffmann's email address.

Hoffmann said reluctantly, for he too hated to admit an error, 'Oh, okay. Sorry. I must have forgotten. I'll see you around.'

He quickly turned his back on Walton to hide his dismay and went in search of Gabrielle. When he finally managed to get across to her, she said—rather sulkily, he thought—'I was starting to think you weren't coming.'

'I got away as soon as I could.' He kissed her on the mouth and tasted the sourness of the champagne on her breath.

A man called out, 'Over here, Dr Hoffmann,' and a photographer's flash went off less than a metre away.

Hoffmann jerked his head back instinctively, as if someone had flung a cup of acid in his face. Through his false smile he said, 'What the hell is Bob Walton doing here?'

'How should I know? You're the one who invited him.'

'Yeah, he just showed me. But you know something? I'm sure I never did that. Why would I? He's the guy who closed down my research at CERN. I haven't seen him for years . . .'

Suddenly the owner of the gallery was beside him. 'You must be very proud of her, Dr

Hoffmann,' said Bertrand.

'What?' Hoffmann was still looking across the party at his former colleague. 'Oh yes. Yes, I am—very proud.' He made a concentrated effort to put Walton out of his mind and to think of something appropriate to say to Gabrielle. 'Have you sold anything yet?'

Gabrielle said, 'Thanks, Alex—it isn't all about money, you know.'

'Yes, okay, I know it isn't. I was just asking.'

'We have plenty of time yet,' said Bertrand. His mobile emitted an alert, playing two bars of Mozart. He blinked at the message in surprise, muttered, 'Excuse me,' and hurried away.

Hoffmann was still half-blinded by the camera flash. When he tried to look at the portraits, the centres were voids. Nevertheless, he struggled to make appreciative comments. 'It's fantastic to see them all together, isn't it? You really get a sense of another way of looking at the world. What's hidden beneath the surface.'

Gabrielle said, 'How's your head?'

'Good. I hadn't even thought about it till you just mentioned it. I like that one very much.' He pointed to a nearby cube. 'That's of you, isn't it?'

It had taken her a day simply to sit for it, he remembered, squatting in the scanner like a victim of Pompeii with her knees drawn up to her chest, her head clasped in her hands, her mouth opened wide as if frozen in mid-scream. When she had first shown it to him at home, he had been almost as shocked by it as he had been by the foetus, of which it was a conscious echo.

She said, 'Leclerc was here earlier. You just missed him.'

'Don't tell me they've found the guy?'

'Oh no, that wasn't it.'

Her tone put Hoffmann on his guard. 'So what did he want?'

'He wanted to ask me about the nervous breakdown you apparently had when you worked at CERN.'

Hoffmann wasn't sure he had heard properly. The noise of all the people talking, bouncing off the whitewashed walls, reminded him of the racket in the computer room. 'He's talked to CERN?'

'About the nervous breakdown,' she repeated more loudly. 'The one you've never mentioned before.'

He felt winded, as if someone had punched him. 'I wouldn't exactly call it a nervous breakdown. I don't know why he has to drag CERN into this.'

'What would you call it, then?'

'Do we really have to do this now?' Her expression told him they did. He wondered how many glasses of champagne she had drunk. 'Okay, I guess we do. I got depressed. I took time off. I saw a shrink. I got better.'

'You saw a psychiatrist? You were treated for depression? And you've never mentioned it in *eight years*?'

A couple standing nearby turned to stare.

'You're making something out of nothing,' he said irritably. 'You're being ridiculous. It was before I even met you, for God's sake.' And then, more softly: 'Come on, Gabby, we shouldn't spoil this.'

For a moment he thought she was going to argue. Her chin was raised and pointing at him, always a storm signal. Her eyes were glassy,

150

bloodshot—she had not got much sleep either, he realised. But then came a sound of metal rapping on glass.

'Ladies and gentlemen,' called Bertrand. He was holding up a champagne flute and hitting it with a fork. 'Ladies and gentlemen!' It was surprisingly effective. A silence quickly fell on the crowded room. He put down the glass. 'Don't be alarmed, friends. I'm not going to make a speech. Besides, for artists, symbols are more eloquent than words.'

He had something in his hand. Hoffmann could not quite see what it was. He walked over to the self-portrait—the one in which Gabrielle was silently screaming—peeled a red spot from the roll of tape concealed in his palm and stuck it firmly against the label. A delighted, knowing murmur spread around the gallery.

'Gabrielle,' he said, turning to her with a smile, 'allow me to congratulate you. You are now, officially, a professional artist.'

There was a round of applause and a general hoisting of champagne glasses in salute. All the tension left Gabrielle's face. She looked transfigured, and Hoffmann seized the moment to take her wrist and raise her hand above her head, as if she were a boxing champion. There were renewed cheers. The camera flashed again, but this time he managed to make sure his own smile stayed fixed. 'Well done, Gabby,' he whispered out of the side of his mouth. 'You so deserve this.'

She smiled at him happily. 'Thank you.' She toasted the room. 'Thank you all. And thank you especially whoever bought it.'

Bertrand said, 'Wait. I haven't finished.'

Next to the self-portrait was the head of a

151

Siberian tiger that had died at the Servion Zoo the previous year. Gabrielle had had its corpse refrigerated until she could get its decapitated skull into an MRI scanner. The etching on glass was lit from below by a blood-red light. Bertrand placed a spot next to that one as well. It had sold for 4,500 francs.

Hoffmann whispered, 'Any more of this, and you'll be making more money than I am.'

'Oh, Alex, shut up about money.' But he could see she was pleased, and when Bertrand moved on and attached another red spot, this time to *The Invisible Man*, the 18,000-franc centrepiece of the exhibition, she clapped her hands in delight.

And if only, Hoffmann thought bitterly afterwards, it had stopped there, the whole occasion would have been a triumph. Why couldn't Bertrand have seen it? Why couldn't he have looked beyond his short-term greed and left it at that? Instead he worked his way methodically around the entire gallery, leaving a rash of red spots in his wake—a pox, a plague, an *epidemic* of pustules erupting across the whitewashed walls— against the horses' heads, the mummified child from the Berlin Museum für Völkerkunde, the bison's skull, the baby antelope, the half-dozen other self-portraits, and finally even the foetus: he did not stop until all were marked as sold.

The effect on the spectators was odd. At first they cheered whenever a red spot was applied. But after a while their volubility began to diminish, and gradually a palpable air of awkwardness settled over the gallery so that in the end Bertrand finished his marking in almost complete silence. It was as if they were witnessing a practical joke that had started out as funny but had gone on too long and become cruel. There was something crushing about such excessive largesse. Hoffmann could hardly bear to watch Gabrielle's expression as it declined from happiness to puzzlement, to incomprehension, and finally to suspicion.

He said desperately, 'It certainly looks as though you have an admirer.'

She didn't seem to hear him. 'Is this *all* one buyer?'

'It is indeed,' said Bertrand. He was beaming and rubbing his hands.

A muted whisper of conversation started up again. People were talking in low voices, apart from an American who said loudly, 'Well, Jesus, that's just completely ridiculous.'

Gabrielle said in disbelief, 'Who on earth is it?'

'I cannot tell you that, unfortunately.' Bertrand glanced at Hoffmann. 'All I can say is "an anonymous collector".'

Gabrielle followed his gaze to Hoffmann. She swallowed before she spoke. Her voice was very quiet. 'Is this you?'

'Of course not.'

'Because if it is—'

'It isn't!'

The door emitted a chime as it was opened. Hoffmann looked over his shoulder. People were starting to leave; Walton was in the first wave, buttoning his jacket against the chilly wind. Bertrand saw what was happening and gestured discreetly to the waitresses to stop serving drinks. The party had lost its point and nobody seemed to want to be the last to leave. A couple of women came over to Gabrielle and thanked her, and she had to pretend that their congratulations were sincere. 'I would have bought something myself,' said one, 'but I never had the chance.'

'It's quite extraordinary.'

'I've never seen anything like it.'

'You will do this again soon, won't you, darling?'

'I promise.'

After they had moved off, Hoffmann said to Bertrand, 'For God's sake, at least tell her it isn't me.'

'I can't say who it is, because to be honest I don't know. It's as simple as that.' Bertrand spread his hands. He was plainly enjoying the situation: the mystery, the money, the need for professional discretion; his body was swelling within its expensive black silk skin. 'My bank just sent me an email to say they'd received an electronic transfer with reference to this exhibition. I confess I was surprised by the amount. But when I got my calculator and added up the cost of all the items on display, I found it came to one hundred and ninety-two thousand francs. Which is precisely the sum transferred.'

'An electronic transfer?' repeated Hoffmann.

'That is right.'

'I want you to pay it back,' said Gabrielle. 'I don't want my work to be treated like this.'

A big Nigerian man in national dress—a kind of heavily woven black and fawn toga with a matching hat—waved an immense pink palm in her direction. He was another of Bertrand's protégés, Nneka Osoba, who specialised in fashioning tribal masks out of Western industrial detritus as a protest against imperialism. 'Goodbye, Gabrielle!' he shouted. 'Well done!'

154

'Goodbye,' she called back, forcing a smile. 'Thank you for coming.' The door chimed again.

Bertrand smiled. 'My dear Gabrielle, you seem not to understand. We are in a legal situation. In an auction, when the hammer comes down, the lot is sold. It's the same for us in a gallery. When a piece of art is purchased, it's gone. If you wish not to sell, don't exhibit.'

'I'll pay you double,' said Hoffmann desperately. 'You're on fifty per cent commission, so you just made nearly a hundred thousand francs, right? I'll pay you two hundred thousand if you'll give Gabrielle her work back.'

Gabrielle said, 'Don't, Alex.'

'That is impossible, Dr Hoffmann.'

'All right, I'll double it again. Four hundred thousand.'

Bertrand swayed in his Zen silk slippers, ethics and avarice visibly slugging it out on the smooth contours of his face. 'Well, I simply don't know what to say—'

'Stop it!' shouted Gabrielle. 'Stop it now, Alex! Both of you! I can't bear to listen to this.'

'Gabby . . .'

But she eluded Hoffmann's outstretched hands and darted towards the door, pushing between the backs of the departing guests. Hoffmann went after her, shouldering his way through the small crowd. He felt as if it were a nightmare, the way she constantly eluded his grasp. At one point his fingertips brushed her back. He emerged on to the street just behind her, and after a dozen or so paces he finally managed to grab her elbow. He pulled her to him, into a doorway.

'Listen, Gabby . . .'

155

'No.' She flapped at him with her free hand.

'Listen!' He shook her until she stopped trying to twist away; he was a strong man—it was no effort to him. 'Calm down. Thank you. Now just hear me out, please. Something very weird is going on. Whoever just bought your exhibition I'm sure is the same person who sent me that Darwin book. Someone is trying to mess with my mind.'

'Oh, come off it, Alex! Don't start on this again. It's you who bought everything—I know it is.' She tried to wriggle free.

'No, listen.' He shook her again. Dimly he recognised that his fear was making him aggressive, and he tried to calm down. 'I promise you. It's not me. The Darwin was bought in exactly the same way—a cash transfer over the internet. I bet you that if we go back in there right now and get Monsieur Bertrand to give us the purchaser's account number, they'll match. Now you've got to understand that although the account may be in my name, it's not mine. I know nothing about it. But I'm going to get to the bottom of it, I promise you. Okay. That's it.' He released her. 'That's what I wanted to say.'

She stared at him and began slowly massaging her elbow. She was crying silently. He realised he must have hurt her. 'I'm sorry.'

She looked up at the sky, gulping. Eventually she got her emotions back under control. She said, 'You really have no idea, do you, how important that exhibition was to me?'

'Of course I do . . .'

'And now it's ruined. And it's your fault.'

'Come on, Gabrielle, how can you say that?'

'Well it is, Alex, you see, because either you

156

bought everything, out of some kind of mad alpha-male belief that you'd be doing me a favour. Or it was bought by this other person who you say is trying to mess with your mind. Either way, it's you—again.'

'That's not true.'

'Okay, so who is this mystery man? Obviously he's nothing to do with me. You must have some idea. A competitor of yours, is he? Or a client? Or the CIA?'

'Don't be silly.'

'Or is it Hugo? Is this one of Hugo's funny public-schoolboy japes?'

'It isn't Hugo. That's one thing I am sure of.'

'Oh no, of course not—it couldn't possibly be your precious bloody Hugo, could it?' She wasn't crying any more. 'What exactly have you turned into, Alex? I mean, Leclerc wanted to know if money was the reason why you left CERN, and I said no. But do you ever stop to listen to yourself these days? Two hundred thousand francs . . . Four hundred thousand francs . . . Sixty million dollars for a house we don't need . . .'

'You didn't complain when we bought it, as I recall. You said you liked the studio.'

'Yes, but only to keep you happy! You don't think I like the rest of it, do you? It's like living in a bloody embassy.' A thought seemed to occur to her. 'How much money have you got now, as a matter of interest?'

'Drop it, Gabrielle.'

'No. Tell me. I want to know. How much?'

'I don't know. It depends how you calculate things.'

'Well try. Give me a figure.'

157

'In dollars? Ballpark? I really don't know. A billion. A billion-two.'

'A billion dollars? *Ballpark*?' For a moment she was too incredulous to speak. 'You know what? Forget it. It's over. As far as I'm concerned, all that matters now is getting out of this bloody awful town, where the only thing anyone cares about is *money*.'

She turned away.

'What's over?' Again he grabbed her arm, but feebly, without conviction, and this time she wheeled on him and slapped him on the face. It was only light—a warning flick, a token—but he let her go at once. Such a thing had never happened between them before.

'Don't you ever,' she spat, jabbing her finger at him, '*ever* grab hold of me like that again.'

And that was it. She was gone. She strode to the end of the street and rounded the corner, leaving Hoffmann with his hand pressed to his cheek, unable to comprehend the catastrophe that had so swiftly overtaken him.

*   *   *

Leclerc had witnessed it all from the comfort of his car. It had unfolded in front of him like a drive-in movie. Now, as he continued to watch, Hoffmann slowly turned around and made his way back towards the gallery. One of the two bodyguards standing with their arms folded outside had a word with him, and Hoffmann made a weary gesture, apparently a signal that he should go after his wife. The man set off. Then Hoffmann went inside, followed by his own minder. It was perfectly easy to

158

see what was happening: the window was large and the gallery was now almost empty. Hoffmann went over to where the proprietor, M. Bertrand, was standing, and clearly began to berate him. He pulled out his mobile phone and waved it in the other man's face. Bertrand threw up his hands, shooing him away, whereupon Hoffmann seized him by the lapels of his jacket and pushed him back against the wall.

'Dear God in heaven, now what?' muttered Leclerc. He could see Bertrand struggling to free himself as Hoffmann held him at arm's length, before once again shoving him backwards, harder this time. Leclerc swore under his breath, threw open his car door and hauled himself stiffly out into the street. His knees had locked, and as he winced his way across the road to the gallery, he pondered yet again the harshness of his fate: that he should still have to do this sort of thing when he was closer to sixty than fifty.

By the time he got inside, Hoffmann's bodyguard had planted himself very solidly between his client and the gallery's owner. Bertrand was smoothing down his jacket and shouting insults at Hoffmann, who was responding in kind. Behind them the executed murderer stared ahead impassively from his glass cell.

'Gentlemen, gentlemen,' said Leclerc, 'we shall have no more of this, thank you.' He flashed his ID at the bodyguard, who looked at it and then at him and very slightly rolled his eyes. 'Quite. Dr Hoffmann, this is no way to behave. It would pain me to arrest you, after all you have been through today, but I shall if necessary. What is going on here?'

Hoffmann said, 'My wife is very upset, and all because this man has acted in the most incredibly stupid way—'

'Yes, yes,' cut in Bertrand, 'incredibly stupid! I sold all her work for her, on the first day of her first exhibition, and now her husband attacks me for it!'

'All I want,' responded Hoffmann, in a voice that struck Leclerc as quite close to hysteria, 'is the number of the buyer's bank account.'

'And I have told him it is quite out of the question! This is confidential information.'

Leclerc turned back to Hoffmann. 'Why is it so important?'

'Someone,' said Hoffmann, struggling to keep his voice calm, 'is quite clearly attempting to destroy me. I have obtained the number of the account that was used to send me a book last night, presumably in order to frighten me in some way—I've got it here on my mobile. And now I believe the same bank account, which is supposedly in my name, has been used to sabotage my wife's exhibition.'

'Sabotage!' scoffed Bertrand. 'We call it a sale!'

'It wasn't one sale, though, was it? Everything was sold, at once. Has that ever happened before?'

'Ach!' Bertrand made a sweeping gesture.

Leclerc looked at them. He sighed. 'Show me the account number, Monsieur Bertrand, if you please.'

'I can't do that. Why should I?'

'Because if you don't, I shall arrest you for impeding a criminal investigation.'

'You wouldn't dare!'

Leclerc stared him out. Old as he was, he could deal with the Guy Bertrands of this world in his sleep.

Eventually Bertrand muttered, 'All right, it's in

my office.'

'Dr Hoffmann—your mobile, if I may?'

Hoffmann showed him the email screen. 'This is the message I got from the bookseller, with the account number.'

Leclerc took the telephone. 'Stay here, please.' He followed Bertrand into the small back office. The place was a clutter of old catalogues, stacked frames, workman's tools; it smelled of a pungent combination of coffee and glue. A computer sat on a scratched and rickety roll-top desk. Next to it was a pile of letters and receipts, skewered on a spike. Bertrand moved the mouse across his computer screen and clicked. 'Here is the email from my bank.' He vacated the seat with a pout. 'I may say, incidentally, I don't take seriously your threats to arrest me. I co-operate merely as a good Swiss citizen should.'

'Your co-operation is noted, *monsieur*,' said Leclerc. 'Thank you.' He sat at the terminal and peered close to the screen. He held Hoffmann's mobile next to it and compared the two account numbers laboriously. They were an identical mixture of letters and digits. The name of the account holder was given as A. J. Hoffmann. He took out his notebook and copied down the sequence. 'And you received no message other than this?'

'No.'

Back in the gallery, he returned the mobile to Hoffmann. 'You were right. The numbers match. Although what this has to do with the attack on you, I confess I do not understand.'

'Oh, they're connected,' said Hoffmann. 'I tried to tell you that this morning. Jesus, you guys

161

wouldn't last five minutes in my business. You wouldn't even get through the frigging door. And why the hell are you going round asking questions about me at CERN? You should be finding this guy, not investigating me.'

His face was haggard, his eyes red and sore, as if he had been rubbing them. With his day's growth of beard he looked like a fugitive.

'I'll pass the account number to our financial department and ask them to look into it,' said Leclerc gently. 'Bank accounts, at least, are something we Swiss do rather well, and impersonation is a crime. I'll let you know if there are any developments. In the meantime, I strongly urge you to go home and see your doctor and have some sleep.' *And make it up with your wife*, he wanted to add, but he felt it was not his place.

10

. . . the instinct of each species is good for itself, but has never, as far as we can judge, been produced for the exclusive good of others.

CHARLES DARWIN, *On the Origin of Species* (1859)

Hoffmann tried to call her from the back of the Mercedes, but he only got her voicemail. The familiar, jaunty voice caught him by the throat: 'Hi, this is Gabby, don't you dare hang up without leaving me a message.'

He had a terrible premonition she was irretrievably gone. Even if they could patch things up, the person she had been before this day began would no longer exist. It was like listening to a recording of someone who had just died.

There was a beep. After a long pause, which he knew would sound weird when she played it back but which he struggled to end, he said finally, 'Call me, will you? We've got to talk.' He couldn't think of anything else to say. 'Well, okay. That's it. Bye.'

He hung up and stared at the mobile for a while, weighing it in his palm, willing it to ring, wondering if he should have said something else or if there was some other way of reaching her. He leaned forward to the bodyguard. 'Is your colleague with my wife, do you know?'

Paccard, keeping his eyes fixed on the road ahead, spoke over his shoulder. 'No, *monsieur*. By the time he got to the end of the road, she was already out of sight.'

Hoffmann let out a groan. 'Is there no one in this goddam town who can do a simple job without screwing up?' He threw himself back in his seat, folded his arms and stared out of the window. Of one thing at least he was certain: he had not bought up Gabrielle's exhibition. He had not had the opportunity. Convincing her, however, would not be easy. In his mind he heard her voice again. *A billion dollars? Ballpark? You know what? Forget it. It's over.*

Across the gunmetal waters of the Rhône he could see the financial district—BNP Paribas, Goldman Sachs, Barclays Private Wealth . . . It occupied the northern bank of the wide river and part of the island in the middle. A trillion dollars of assets was controlled from Geneva, of which Hoffmann Investment Technologies handled a mere one per cent; of that one per cent his personal stake was less than one tenth. Viewed in proportion, why should she be so outraged by a billion? Dollars, euros, francs—these were the units in which he measured the success or failure of his experiment, just as at CERN he had used teraelectronvolts, nanoseconds and microjoules. However, there was one great difference between the two, he was obliged to concede; a problem he had never fully confronted or solved. You couldn't buy anything with a nanosecond or a microjoule, whereas money was a sort of toxic by-product of his research. Sometimes he felt it was poisoning him inch by inch, just like Marie Curie had been killed by radiation.

At first he had ignored his wealth, either rolling it over into the company or parking it on deposit. But he hated the thought of becoming an eccentric

164

like Etienne Mussard, twisted into misanthropy by the pressure of his own good fortune. So recently he had copied Quarry and tried spending it. But that had led directly to the overdecorated mansion in Cologny, stuffed with expensive collections of books and antiques he did not need but which required layers of security to protect: a sort of pharaoh's burial chamber for the living. The final option he supposed would be to give it away—Gabrielle would approve of that, at least—but even philanthropy could corrupt: to distribute hundreds of millions of dollars responsibly would be a full-time job. Occasionally he had a fantasy that his surplus profits might be converted into paper money and incinerated round-the-clock, just as an oil refinery burned off excess gas—blue and yellow flames lighting up the Geneva night sky.

The Mercedes began to cross the river.

He did not like to think of Gabrielle wandering the streets alone. It was her impulsiveness that worried him. Once angered, she was capable of anything. She might disappear for a few days, fly back to her mother in England, have her head filled with nonsense. *You know what? Forget it. It's over.* What did she mean by that? What was over? The exhibition? Her career as an artist? Their conversation? Their marriage? Panic welled inside him again. Life without her would be a vacuum: unsurvivable. He rested the edge of his forehead on the cold glass, and for a vertiginous moment, looking down into the lightless, turbid water, imagined himself sucked into nothingness, like a passenger whipped out through the fuselage of a ruptured aircraft miles above the earth.

They turned on to the Quai du Mont-Blanc. The

165

city, crouched around the dark pool of its lake, looked low and sombre, hewn from the same grey rock as the distant Jura. There was none of the vulgar glass-and-steel animal exuberance of Manhattan or the City of London: their skyscrapers would rise and they would crash, booms and busts would come and go, but crafty Geneva, with its head down, would endure for ever. The Hotel Beau-Rivage, nicely positioned near the mid-point of the wide tree-lined boulevard, embodied these values in bricks and stone. Nothing exciting had happened here since 1898, when the Empress of Austria, leaving the hotel after lunch, had been stabbed to death by an Italian anarchist. One fact about her murder had always stuck in Hoffmann's mind: she had been unaware of her injury until her corset was removed, by which time she had almost bled to death internally. In Geneva, even the assassinations were discreet.

The Mercedes pulled up on the opposite side of the road, and Paccard, his hand raised imperiously to stop the traffic, escorted Hoffmann across the pedestrian crossing, up the steps and into the faux-Habsburg grandeur of the interior. If the concierge felt any private alarm at Hoffmann's appearance, he allowed no flicker of it to show on his smiling face as he took over from Paccard and led *le cher docteur* up the stairs to the dining room.

The atmosphere beyond the tall doors was that of a nineteenth-century salon: paintings, antiques, gilt chairs, gold swag curtains; the Empress herself would have felt at home. Quarry had reserved a long table by the French windows and was sitting with his back to the lake view, keeping an eye on the entrance. He had a napkin tucked into his collar, gentleman's-club style, but when Hoffmann appeared, he quickly pulled it out and dropped it on his chair. He moved to intercept his partner in the middle of the room.

'Professor,' he said cheerfully for the others to hear, and then, more quietly, drawing him slightly apart, 'where the bloody hell have you been?'

Hoffmann started to answer but Quarry interrupted him without listening. He was fired up, eyes gleaming, closing the deal.

'Okay, never mind. It doesn't matter. The main thing is it looks as though they're in—most of them, anyway—and my hunch is for closer to a billion than seven-fifty. So all I need from you now, please, maestro, is sixty minutes of technical reassurance. Preferably with minimal aggression, if you think you can manage that.' He gestured towards the table. 'Come and join us. You've missed the *grenouille de Vallorbe*, but the *filet mignon de veau* should be divine.'

Hoffmann didn't move. He said suspiciously, 'Did you just buy up all Gabrielle's artwork?'

'What?' Quarry halted, turned, squinted at him, perplexed.

'Someone just bought up her entire collection using an account set up in my name. She thought it might be you.'

'I haven't even seen it! And why would I have an account in your name? That's bloody illegal, for a start.' He glanced over his shoulder at the clients, then back at Hoffmann. He looked utterly mystified. 'You know what? Could we talk about this later?'

'So you're absolutely sure you didn't buy it? Not even as a joke? Just tell me if you did.'

167

'It's not my kind of humour, old man. Sorry.'

'Yeah, that's what I thought.' Hoffmann's gaze swept jaggedly around the room: the clients, the waiters, the two exits, the high windows and the balcony beyond. 'Someone's really after me, Hugo. Out to destroy me bit by bit. It's actually starting to bug me.'

'Well yes, I can see that, Alexi. How's your head?'

Hoffmann put his hand to his scalp and ran his fingers over the hard, alien lumps of the stitches. He had a throbbing headache, he realised. 'It's started hurting again.'

'Okay,' said Quarry slowly. In other circumstances, Hoffmann would have found his English stiff upper lip in the face of potential disaster amusing. 'So what are you saying here? Are you saying perhaps you ought to go back to the hospital?'

'No. I'll just sit down.'

'And eat something, maybe?' said Quarry hopefully. 'You haven't eaten all day, have you? No wonder you're feeling peculiar.' He took Hoffmann by the arm and led him towards the table. 'Now you sit here opposite me, where I can keep an eye on you, and perhaps we can all change places later on. Good news out of Wall Street, incidentally,' he added, sotto voce. 'Looks like the Dow's going to open well down.'

Hoffmann found himself being helped by a waiter into a seat between the Parisian lawyer François de Gombart-Tonnelle, and Etienne Mussard. Quarry was flanked by their respective partners, Elmira Gulzhan and Clarisse Mussard. The Chinese had been left to fend for themselves at

168

one end of the table; the American bankers, Klein and Easterbrook, were at the other. In between were Herxheimer, Mould, Łukasiński and various lawyers and advisers exuding the natural bonhomie of men charging hourly fees while simultaneously enjoying a free meal. A heavy linen napkin was shaken out and spread over Hoffmann's lap. He was offered a choice of white or red wine by the sommelier—a 2006 Louis Jadot Montrachet Grand Cru or a 1995 Latour—but refused both. He asked for still water.

De Gombart-Tonnelle said, 'We were just discussing tax rates, Alex.' He broke off a tiny piece of bread roll with his long fingers, and slipped it into his mouth. 'We were saying that Europe seems to be going the way of the old Soviet Union. France forty per cent, Germany forty-five per cent, Spain forty-seven per cent, the UK fifty per cent—'

'Fifty per cent!' cut in Quarry. 'I mean, don't get me wrong, I'm as patriotic as the next chap, but do I really want to go into a fifty–fifty partnership with Her Majesty's Government? I think not.'

'There is no democracy any more,' said Elmira Gulzhan. 'The state is in control as never before. All our freedoms are disappearing and no one seems to care. That's what I find so depressing about this century.'

De Gombart-Tonnelle was still going on: '. . . even Geneva is forty-four per cent.'

'Don't tell me you guys pay forty-four per cent,' said Iain Mould.

Quarry smiled, as if he had been asked a question by a child. 'Theoretically you have to pay forty-four on salary. But if you take your income as dividend and your business is overseas-registered,

169

then four fifths of your dividends are legally tax-free. So you only pay the forty-four on the one fifth. Hence a marginal top rate of eight-point-eight per cent. Isn't that right, Amschel?'

Herxheimer, who lived in Zermatt but by some feat of teleportation was actually based in Guernsey, agreed that it was indeed so.

'Eight-point-eight,' repeated Mould. He looked sick. 'Good for you.'

Easterbrook called down the table, 'I'm coming to live in Geneva!'

'Yeah, but try telling that to Uncle Sam,' said Klein gloomily. 'The IRS will hunt you down to the ends of the earth as long as you have a US passport. And have you ever tried getting rid of American citizenship? You can't do it. It's like being a Soviet Jew trying to emigrate to Israel in the seventies.'

'No freedom,' repeated Elmira Gulzhan, 'as I say. The state will take everything from us, and if we dare to protest, we will be arrested for not being politically correct.'

Hoffmann stared at the tablecloth and let the discussion flow around him. He was remembering now why he didn't like the rich: their self-pity. Persecution was the common ground of their conversation, like sport or the weather was for everyone else. He despised them.

'I despise you,' he said, but nobody paid him any attention, so engrossed were they in the inequities of higher-rate taxation and the inherent criminality of all employees. And then he thought: perhaps I have become one of them; is that why I am so paranoid? He examined his palms under the table, and then the backs of his hands, as if he half-expected to find himself sprouting fur.

170

At that moment the doors swung open to admit a file of eight tail-coated waiters, each carrying two plates capped with domed silver covers. They stationed themselves between their allotted pair of diners, set the plates down before them, grasped the twin covers with their white-gloved hands, and at a signal from the maître d' lifted them away. The main course was veal with morels and asparagus, served to everyone apart from Elmira Gulzhan, who had a piece of grilled fish, and Etienne Mussard, who had a hamburger and chips.

'I cannot eat veal,' said Elmira, leaning confidingly across the table to Hoffmann, offering him a brief glimpse of her pale brown breasts. 'The poor calf suffers so.'

'Oh, I always prefer food that's suffered,' said Quarry cheerfully, wielding his knife and fork, his napkin back in his collar. 'I think fear releases some especially piquant chemical from the nervous system into the flesh. Veal cutlets, lobster thermidor, pâté de foie gras—the nastier the demise the better, that's my philosophy: no pain, no gain.'

Elmira flicked him with the end of her napkin. 'Hugo, you are *wicked*. Isn't he wicked, Alex?'

'He is wicked,' agreed Hoffmann. He pushed his food around his plate with his fork. He had no appetite. Over Quarry's shoulder he could see the Jet d'Eau probing the dull sky on the opposite side of the lake like a watery searchlight.

Łukasiński began calling across the table some technical questions about the new fund, which Quarry laid down his cutlery to answer. All money invested would be subjected to a one-year lock-up, with a redemption day thereafter four times per annum: 31 May, 31 August, 30 November and 28 February; all redemptions would require a notice period of forty-five days. The structure of the fund would be as before: investors would be part of a limited-liability company registered in the Cayman Islands for tax purposes, which would retain Hoffmann Investment Technologies to manage its assets.

Herxheimer said, 'How soon do you require an answer from us?'

Quarry said, 'We're looking to hard-close the fund again at the end of this month.'

'So three weeks?'

'That's right.'

Suddenly the atmosphere around the table was serious. Side conversations ceased. Everyone was listening.

'Well, you can have my answer right now,' said Easterbrook. He waved his fork in Hoffmann's direction. 'You know what I like about you, Hoffmann?'

'No, Bill. What would that be?'

'You don't talk your book. You let your numbers do the speaking. I made up my mind the moment that plane went down. There'll have to be due diligence and all that crap, blah-blah-blah, but I'm going to recommend that AmCor doubles its stake.'

Quarry glanced quickly across the table at Hoffmann. His blue eyes widened. The tip of his tongue moistened his lips. 'That's a billion dollars, Bill,' he said quietly.

'I know it's a billion dollars, Hugo. There was a time when that was a lot of money.'

The listeners laughed. They would remember this moment. It would be an anecdote to savour on the quaysides of Antibes and Palm Beach for years to come: the day old Bill Easterbrook of AmCor put up a billion dollars over lunch and said it used to be a lot of money. The look on Easterbrook's face suggested he knew what they were thinking; it was the reason he had done it.

'Bill, that is so generous of you,' said Quarry hoarsely. 'Alex and I are overwhelmed.' He glanced across the table.

'Overwhelmed,' repeated Hoffmann.

'Winter Bay will be in as well,' said Klein. 'I can't say how much exactly—I'm not cleared to Bill's level—but it will be substantial.'

Łukasiński said, 'That goes for me too.'

'And I shall speak to my father,' said Elmira, 'and he will do as I say.'

'Do I take it that the mood of the meeting is that you're all planning to invest?' asked Quarry. Murmurs of assent ran around the table. 'Well, that sounded promising. Can I ask the question a different way—is anyone here *not* planning to increase their investment?' The diners looked from one to another; several shrugged. 'Even you, Etienne?'

Mussard looked up grumpily from his hamburger. 'Yes, yes, I suppose so, why wouldn't I? But let's not discuss it in public, if you don't mind. I prefer to do things in the traditional Swiss way.'

'You mean fully clothed with the lights off?' Quarry rose to his feet on the tide of laughter. 'My friends, I know we are still eating, but if ever there was a time for a spontaneous toast in the Russian manner—forgive me, Mieczyslaw—then I think this must be it.' He cleared his throat. He seemed on the point of tears. 'Dear guests, we are honoured by

173

your presence, by your friendship, and by your trust. I truly believe we are present at the birth of a whole new force in global asset management, the product of the union of cutting-edge science and aggressive investment—or, if you prefer, of God and Mammon.' More laughter. 'At which happy event, it seems to me only right that we should stand and raise our glasses to the genius who has made it possible—no, no, not to me.' He beamed down at Hoffmann. 'To the father of VIXAL-4—to Alex!'

With a scrape of chair legs, a chorus of 'To Alex!' and a peal of clinking cut glass, the investors stood and toasted Hoffmann. They looked at him fondly—even Mussard managed to curl his lip— and when they had all sat down they carried on nodding and smiling at him until he realised to his dismay that they expected him to respond.

'Oh no,' he said.

Quarry urged him softly: 'Come on, Alexi, just a couple of words, and then it's all over for another eight years.'

'Really I can't.'

But such a good-natured round of 'No!' and 'Shame!' greeted his refusal that Hoffmann actually found himself getting to his feet. His napkin slid off his lap and on to the carpet. He rested one hand on the table to steady himself and tried to think of what he might say. Almost absently he glanced out of the window at the view—which, because he was now elevated, had widened to take in not only the opposite shore, the towering fountain and the inky waters of the lake but also the promenade where the Empress had been stabbed, directly beneath the hotel. The Quai du Mont-Blanc is especially wide at this point. It forms a kind of miniature park with lime trees, benches, small trimmed lawns, elaborate belle époque street lamps and dark green topiary. A semicircular embankment with a stone balustrade radiates out into the water, leading down to a jetty and a ferry station. On this particular afternoon a dozen people were queuing at the white metal kiosk for ferry tickets. A young woman with a red baseball cap skated by on rollerblades. Two men in jeans were walking a large black poodle. Finally Hoffmann's eyes came to rest upon a skeletal apparition draped in a brown leather coat standing under one of the pale green limes. His skull was gaunt and very white, as if he had just vomited or fainted, and his eye sockets were deeply shadowed by his bulging forehead, from which all his hair had been scraped back into a tight grey ponytail. He was gazing directly up at the window from which Hoffmann was looking down.

Hoffmann's limbs locked. For several long seconds he was unable to move. Then he took an involuntary step backwards, knocking over his chair. Quarry, staring at him in alarm, said, 'Oh God, you're going to faint,' and began to rise, but Hoffmann held up his hand to ward him off. He took another step away from the table and his feet became entangled in the legs of the upended chair. He stumbled and almost fell, but that seemed to those watching to break whatever spell he was under, for suddenly he kicked the chair sideways out of his path and turned and ran towards the door.

Hoffmann was barely conscious of the astonished exclamations swelling behind him, or of Quarry calling his name. He ran out into the mirrored corridor and down the sweep of staircase, grabbing the handrail to pivot around the landings. At the bottom he jumped the last few steps, sprinted past his bodyguard—who was talking to the concierge—and out on to the promenade.

11

. . . the struggle [for existence] almost invariably will be most severe between the individuals of the same species, for they frequent the same districts, require the same food, and are exposed to the same dangers.

CHARLES DARWIN, *On the Origin of Species* (1859)

Across the wide highway the pavement beneath the lime was empty. Hoffmann halted amid the rows of guests' luggage, looked left and right, and swore. The doorman asked if he wanted a taxi. Hoffmann ignored him and walked straight past the front of the hotel to the street corner. Ahead was a sign, HSBC Private Bank; to his left, running parallel with the side of the Beau-Rivage, a narrow one-way thoroughfare, the Rue Docteur-Alfred-Vincent. For want of a better idea he set off down it, jogging about fifty metres, past scaffolding, a line of parked motorbikes and a small church. At the end was a crossroads. He stopped again.

A block further along, a figure in a brown coat was crossing the road. The man paused when he got to the other side and glanced back at Hoffmann. It was him, no question of it. A white van passed between them and he was gone, limping off down a side street.

And now Hoffmann ran. A great righteous energy flooded his body, propelling his legs in long, fast strides. He sprinted to the spot where he had last seen the man. It was another one-way street; once again he had vanished. He ran down it to the

177

next junction. The roads were narrow, quiet, not much traffic, a lot of parked cars. Wherever he looked there were small businesses—a hairdresser's, a pharmacy, a bar—people going about their lunchtime shopping. He spun around hopelessly, turned right, ran, turned right again, working his way through the narrow maze of one-way streets, reluctant to give up but increasingly sure that he had lost him. The area around him changed. He registered it only vaguely at first. The buildings turned shabbier; more were derelict, sprayed with graffiti; and then he was in a different city. A teenaged black woman in a tight sweater and white plastic micro-skirt shouted at him from across the road. She was standing outside a shop with a purple neon sign, VIDEO CLUB XXX. Ahead, three more very obvious hookers, all black, patrolled the kerbside while their pimps smoked in doorways or observed the women from the street corner: young, small, thin men with olive skin and cropped black hair—north Africans, maybe, or Albanians.

Hoffmann slowed his pace, trying to get his bearings. He must have run almost to the Cornavin railway station, he realised, and into the red-light district. Finally he stopped outside a boarded-up nightclub covered in a flaking skin of peeling fly-posters: Le Black Kat (XXX, FILMS, GIRLS, SEX). Wincing, his hands on his hips, a sharp pain in his side, he leaned over the gutter trying to recover his breath. An Asian prostitute watched him from a shop parlour window no more than three metres away. She wore a black corset and stockings and sat cross-legged on a red damask chair. She recrossed her legs, smiled and beckoned to him until abruptly some unseen mechanism drew a blind across the scene.

He straightened, conscious of being observed by the girls and their pimps. One rat-faced man, a bit older than the others, with pockmarked skin, was looking at him and talking into a mobile. Hoffmann set off back the way he had come, scanning the alleys and courtyards on either side in case the man had slipped into one of them to hide. He passed a sex shop, Je Vous Aime, and retraced his steps. The window contained a half-hearted display of merchandise: vibrators, wigs, erotic underwear. A pair of crotchless black panties was stretched out and pinned up on a board like a dead bat. The door was open, but the view of the interior was obscured by a curtain of multicoloured plastic strips. He thought of the handcuffs and ball gag the intruder had left behind. Leclerc had said they might have come from such a place.

Suddenly his mobile chimed with an incoming text: 'Rue de berne 91 chambre 68'.

He stared at it for several seconds. He had just passed the Rue de Berne, had he not? He turned around and there it was, right behind him, close enough to read the blue street sign. He checked the message again. The sender was not identified; the originating number was unavailable. He glanced around to see if anyone was watching him. The fronds of plastic fluttered and parted. A fat, bald man wearing braces over a dirty vest emerged.

'Que voulez-vous, monsieur?'

'Rien.'

Hoffmann walked back up the street to the Rue de Berne. It was long and shabby but at least it was busier—two lanes, with tram cables strung

179

above—which made him feel safer. At the junction was a fruit and vegetable shop offering an outdoor display, next to it a forlorn little café with a few empty aluminium chairs and tables set out on the pavement, and a *tabac* advertising *'Cartes telephoniques, Videos X, DVDs X, Revues X USA'*. He checked the street numbers. They ascended to his left. He walked, counting them off, and within thirty seconds had migrated from northern Europe and entered the southern Mediterranean: Lebanese and Moroccan restaurants, swirls of Arabic script on the shop fronts, Arabic music blaring from tinny speakers, a smell of greasy hot kebabs, which turned his stomach; only the freakish absence of litter betrayed that this was Switzerland.

He found number 91 on the northern side of the Rue de Berne, opposite a shop selling African clothes—a dilapidated seven-storey building of peeling yellow stucco, perhaps a hundred years old, with metal-shuttered windows painted green. The building was four windows wide, its name spelt out down the side, almost from top to bottom, by individual letters protruding over the street: HOTEL DIODATI. Most of the shutters were closed, but a few were half-raised, like drooping eyelids, the interiors hidden by a greyish-white cataract of thick net curtains with a floral design. At street level there was an ancient and heavy wooden door that reminded Hoffmann incongruously of Venice; it was certainly older than the building, and elaborately carved with what looked like masonic symbols. As he watched, it swung inwards and from the dim interior a man emerged wearing jeans and trainers, with a hood pulled over his head. It was impossible to see his face. He put his hands in his pockets, hunched his shoulders and set off down the street. A minute or so later the door opened again. This time it was a woman, young and thin, with fluffy dyed orange hair and a short black-and-white-checked skirt. She was carrying a shoulder bag. She paused on the doorstep and opened the bag, searched it, retrieved a pair of sunglasses, put them on and then moved off in the opposite direction to the man.

There was never a moment when Hoffmann made a definite decision to go in. He watched for a while, and then he crossed the road and lingered outside the door. Eventually he pushed it open and peered inside. The place had a stale smell, emphasised rather than disguised by a joss stick burning somewhere. There was a small lobby with a counter, deserted, and a seating area with a black and red sofa with wooden legs and matching armchairs. In the gloom a small aquarium glowed brightly but it seemed devoid of fish.

Hoffmann took a few steps over the threshold. He reasoned that if he was challenged, he could say he was looking for a room: he had money in his pocket, he could pay for it. They probably rented by the hour. The thick door closed behind him, cutting off the sounds of the street. Upstairs someone was moving around, music was playing; the thump of the bass line shook the thin partitions. He moved through the empty reception, across a floor of curling linoleum, and followed a narrow passage to a small elevator. He pressed the call button and the doors opened immediately as though it had been waiting for him.

The elevator was tiny, lined with scratched grey metal like an old filing cabinet, with just about

181

enough room for two people, and when the doors closed Hoffmann was almost overwhelmed by claustrophobia. The buttons offered him a choice of seven floors. He pressed number six. A distant motor whined, the elevator rattled and he began to rise very slowly. It was not so much a sense of danger he felt now as of unreality, as if he were back in a recurrent childhood dream he could not quite remember, from which the only way to wake was to keep on going until he found the exit.

The elevator ride seemed to go on a long time. He wondered what might be waiting at the end of it. When at last it did halt, he put up his hands to protect himself. Jerkily the doors opened on to the sixth floor.

The landing was deserted. He was reluctant to step out on to it at first, but then the doors began to close and he had to thrust his leg out to save himself from being reimprisoned. The doors juddered back and he moved out cautiously on to the landing. It was darker than in the lobby. His eyes had to readjust. The walls were bare. There was the same stale, almost fetid smell of air that had been breathed a thousand times and never refreshed by an open door or window. It was hot. Two doors were opposite him; more led off the passages to either side. An amateurish sign composed of movable coloured plastic letters, of the kind sold in toyshops, indicated that Room 68 was to the right. The clank of the elevator motor restarting behind him made him jump. He listened to the car descend all the way to the bottom. When it shut off, there was silence.

He took a couple of paces to the right and peered slowly around the corner along the passage.

Room 68 was at the far end, its door closed. From somewhere close by came a rhythmic noise of rasping metal, which at first he mistook for sawing but almost immediately realised was bedsprings. There was a thump. A man moaned as if in pain.

Hoffmann pulled out his mobile, intending to call the police. But, curiously for the centre of Geneva, there was no signal. He put it back in his pocket and walked warily to the end of the passage. His eyes were at exactly the same level as the bulging opaque glass of the spyhole. He listened. He couldn't hear anything. He tapped on the door, then put his ear to the wood and listened again. Nothing: even the neighbour's bedsprings had ceased to creak.

He tried the black plastic handle. The door wouldn't open. But it was held by only a single Yale lock and he could see the door jamb was rotted: when he dug his fingernail into the spongy wood, he pulled away a wedge of crumbling orange flakes the size of matchsticks. He stepped back a pace, checked behind him, then barged against the door with his shoulder. It gave slightly. He moved back a couple of feet further and lunged at it again. This time there was a splintering sound and the door opened a couple of centimetres. He worked the fingers of both hands into the gap and pushed. There was a crack and the door opened.

It was dark inside, with just a faint line of grey daylight showing where the bottom of the window shutter had failed to close properly. He edged across the carpet, groped around and through the net curtain for the switch, pressed it, and noisily the shutter began to rise. The window looked out through a fire escape on to the back of a row of buildings about fifty metres away, separated from the hotel by a brick wall and adjacent yards full of waste bins, weeds and rubbish. By the thin light Hoffmann could see the room, such as it was: a single unmade bed on wheels with a greyish sheet hanging down over a red and black carpet, a small chest of drawers with a rucksack resting on top of it, a wooden chair with a scuffed brown leather seat. The radiator under the window was too hot to touch. There was a strong smell of stale cigarette smoke, masculine sweat and cheap soap. The wallpaper around the wall lights had been scorched brown by the bare bulbs. In the tiny bathroom were a small bathtub with a clear plastic shower curtain hung around it, a basin streaked greenish-black where the taps had dripped, and a WC with similar markings; on a wooden shelf was a glass mug with a toothbrush and a blue disposable plastic razor.

Hoffmann moved back into the bedroom. He carried the rucksack to the bed, upended it and emptied out the contents. It was mostly dirty clothes—a plaid shirt, T-shirts, underwear, socks— but buried among them was an old Zeiss camera with a powerful lens, and also a laptop computer which felt warm to the touch. It was in sleep mode.

He put the laptop down and returned to the open door. The frame had splintered outwards around the lock but had not broken, and he found he was able to press the housing of the lock back into place and gently close the door. It would fall open again if pressure was applied from the other side, but from a distance it would look untouched. Behind the door he noticed a pair of boots. He picked them up between thumb and forefinger and examined them. They were identical to the ones he

184

had seen outside his house. He replaced them and went and sat on the edge of the bed and opened the laptop. Then, from the bowels of the building, came a clang. The elevator was moving again.

Hoffmann put aside the computer and listened to the whine of its long ascent. At last it stopped, and then came the rattle of its doors opening close by. He crossed the room quickly and put his eye to the spyhole just as the man came round the corner. He was carrying a white plastic bag in one hand and with the other he was fishing in his pocket. He reached the door and pulled out his key. The distorting lens of the peephole made his looming face seem even more skull-like than before, and Hoffmann felt the hairs rise on his scalp.

He stepped back and looked around quickly, then withdrew into the bathroom. An instant later he heard the key inserted into the keyhole, followed by a grunt of surprise as the door swung open without needing to be unlocked. In the semi-darkness, through the crack between the bathroom door and the door jamb, Hoffmann had a clear view of the centre of the bedroom. He held his breath. For a while nothing happened. He prayed the man might have turned around and gone down to reception to report a break-in. But then his shadow passed briefly across Hoffmann's line of view, heading towards the window. Hoffmann was on the point of trying to make a run for it when, with shocking speed, the man doubled back and abruptly kicked open the bathroom door.

There was something scorpion-like in the way he crouched, legs apart, with a long blade held at head height. He was bigger than Hoffmann remembered, bulked out by his leather coat. There was no way

185

past him. Long seconds elapsed as they stared at one another, and then the man said, in a surprisingly calm and educated voice, '*Zurück. In die Badewanne.*' He gestured with the knife at the bath and Hoffmann shook his head, not understanding. '*In die Badewanne,*' repeated the man encouragingly, pointing the knife first at Hoffmann and then at the tub. After another endless pause, Hoffmann found his limbs doing as they were bidden. His hand pulled back the shower curtain and his legs stepped shakily over the edge into the bath, his desert boots clumping heavily on the cheap plastic. The man came a little further into the tiny room. It was so cramped he took up almost all the floor space. He pulled the light cord. Above the sink a neon strip stuttered into life. He closed the door and said, '*Ausziehen,*' and this time helpfully added a translation: 'Take off your clothes.' In his long leather coat he looked like a butcher.

'*Nein,*' said Hoffmann, shaking his head and holding his palms up in a gesture of reasonableness. 'No. No way.' The man spat out some swear word he didn't understand and slashed at him with the knife, the blade passing so close that even though Hoffmann pressed himself back into the corner under the shower nozzle, the front of his raincoat was slashed and the lower part of it flapped down to his knees. For a ghastly moment he thought it was his flesh and he said quickly, '*Ja, ja,* okay. I'll do it.' The whole situation was so bizarre it seemed to be playing out at one remove from reality, to be happening to someone else. He quickly shrugged the coat off his left shoulder and then his right. There was hardly enough room for him to get his arms out of the sleeves and for a time it was stuck across his back and he had to struggle with it as if escaping from a straitjacket.

He tried to think of something to say, to establish contact with his attacker, to shift this encounter on to a different and less lethal plane. He said, 'You are German?' and when the man didn't respond, he struggled to remember what little of the language he had picked up at CERN: *'Sie sind Deutscher?'* There was no answer.

At last he had the ruined coat off. He let it drop around his feet. He slipped off his jacket and held it out to his captor, who gestured with his knife that he should throw it on to the bathroom floor. He started to unbutton his shirt. He would carry on removing his clothes until he was naked if necessary, but if the man tried to tie him up he resolved that he would fight—yes, then he would put up a struggle. He would rather die than be rendered completely helpless.

'Why are you doing this?' he asked.

The man frowned at him as if he were a slightly baffling child and replied in English: 'Because you invited me.'

Hoffmann stared at him, aghast. 'I didn't *invite* you to do this.'

The knife was flourished again. 'Continue, please.'

'Listen, this is not right . . .'

Hoffmann finished unbuttoning his shirt and let it fall on top of his jacket. He was thinking hard now, evaluating risks and chances. He grasped the bottom of his T-shirt and pulled it up over his head, and when his face emerged and he saw his attacker's hungry eyes he felt his flesh crawl. But

187

here was weakness, he recognised: here was opportunity. Somehow he forced himself to make a ball of the white cotton and to offer it to him. 'Here,' he said, and when the man reached out to take it he slightly adjusted his feet against the back of the bathtub so as to brace himself. He leaned forward encouragingly—'Here you are'—and then launched himself at him.

He landed on his assailant with sufficient force to knock him backwards, the knife went flying, and together they sank down so entwined it was impossible for either man to land a blow. In any case all Hoffmann wanted was to escape the horrible claustrophobia of that squalid bathroom. He tried to haul himself up on to his feet, grabbing at the sink with one hand and the light cord with the other, but both seemed to come away at once. The room went dark and he felt something round his ankle dragging him down again. He hacked at it with his other heel and stamped on it and the man howled with pain. He fumbled in the darkness for the door handle, at the same time lashing out with his feet. He was connecting with bone now—that ponytailed skull, he hoped. Kick a man when he's down, he thought savagely, then kick him and kick him and kick him. His target whimpered and shrank into a foetal ball. When he no longer seemed a threat, Hoffmann pulled open the bathroom door and staggered into the bedroom.

He sat down heavily on the wooden chair. He put his head between his knees and was immediately sick. Despite the heat of the room, he was shivering with cold. He needed to get his clothes. He returned cautiously to the bathroom and pushed at the door. He heard a scuffling noise inside. The man had crawled towards the lavatory bowl. He was blocking the door. Hoffmann gave it a shove and the man groaned and dragged his body out of the way. Hoffmann stepped over him and retrieved his clothes and also the knife. He went back into the bedroom and quickly dressed. *You invited me*, he thought furiously—what did he mean, he had invited him? He checked his mobile phone but there was still no signal.

In the bathroom the man had his head over the lavatory. He looked up as Hoffmann came in. Hoffmann, pointing the knife, gazed down at him without pity.

'What is your name?' he said.

The man turned his face away and spat blood. Hoffmann warily came closer, squatted on his haunches and scrutinised him from a distance of half a metre. He was about sixty, although it was hard to tell with all the blood on his face; he had a cut above his eye. Overcoming his revulsion, Hoffmann transferred the knife into his left hand, leaned forward and opened the man's leather coat. The man lifted his arms and allowed him to search around until he found an inside pocket, from which he withdrew first a wallet and then a dark red European Union passport. It was German. He flicked it open. The photograph was not a good likeness. The text identified him as Johannes Karp, born 14.4.52 in Offenbach am Main.

Hoffmann said, 'And you're seriously telling me you came here from Germany because I invited you?'

'*Ja.*'

Hoffmann recoiled. 'You're crazy.'

'No, fucker, you are crazy,' said the German with

189

a flicker of spirit. 'You gave me your house codes.' Blood bubbled from the corner of his mouth. He spat a tooth into his hand and inspected it. *'Ein verrückter Mann!'*

'Where is this invitation?'

He gestured weakly with his head towards the other room. 'Computer.'

Hoffmann stood. He pointed the knife at Karp. 'Don't move, okay?'

In the other room he sat on the chair and opened the laptop. It came awake immediately and at once the screen was filled with an image of Hoffmann's own face. The quality of the photograph was poor—an enlarged picture-grab from a surveillance tape, by the look of it. He had been captured gazing up into the camera, his expression blank, unguarded. It was so tightly cropped it was impossible to tell where it had been taken.

A couple of keystrokes took him into the hard-drive registry. The program names were all in German. He called up a list of the most recently viewed files. The last folder to be edited, just after six o'clock the previous evening, was entitled *Der Rotenburg Cannibal*. Inside it were scores of Adobe files containing newspaper articles about the case of Armin Meiwes, a computer technician and internet cannibal who had met a willing victim on a website, drugged him and started eating him, and who was currently serving a life sentence in Germany for murder. Another folder seemed to consist of chapters of a novel, *Der Metzgermeister— The Master Butcher*: was that right?—tens of thousands of words of what appeared to be a work of fantasy in an unparagraphed stream of consciousness that Hoffmann could not understand.

And then there was a folder called *Das Opfer*, which Hoffmann knew meant *The Victim*. This was in English and looked like transcripts from an internet chat room—a dialogue, he perceived as he read on, between one participant who fantasised about committing murder and another who dreamed about what it would be like to die. There was something distantly familiar about the second voice, phrases he recognised, sequences of dreams that had once festooned his mind like filthy cobwebs until he had cleaned them out, or thought he had cleaned them out.

Now they seemed to coalesce in front of him into a dark reflection, and he was so absorbed by what was on the screen it was a near-miracle that some slight alteration in the light or air caused him to look up as the knife flashed towards him. He jerked his head back and the point just missed his eye—a six-inch blade, a flick-knife; it must have been hidden in the man's coat pocket. The German lashed out at him with his foot and caught him on the bottom of his ribcage, then lunged forward with the knife and tried to slash at him again. Hoffmann cried out in pain and shock, the chair toppled backwards and suddenly Karp was on top of him. The knife glinted in the pale light. Somehow, by reflex rather than conscious intent, he caught the man's wrist with his left and weaker hand. Briefly the knife trembled close to his face. '*Es ist, was Sie sich wünschen,*' whispered Karp soothingly. *It is what you desire.* The knife-tip actually pricked Hoffmann's skin. He grimaced with the effort, holding the knife off, gaining millimetres, until at last his attacker's arm snapped backwards and with a terrible exultation in his own power Hoffmann flung him back against the metal frame of the bed. It slid briefly on its wheels, banged against the wall and stopped. Hoffmann's left hand still held on to the other man's wrist, his right was clamped to Karp's face, his fingers gouging into the deep sockets of the eyes, the heel of his hand jammed against the throat. Karp roared in pain and tore at Hoffmann's fingers with his free hand. Hoffmann responded by adjusting his grip so that he had his hand entirely around the scrawny windpipe, choking off the sound. He was leaning in to him now; he was able to put the whole weight of his body behind that grip, and his fear and his anger, pinning Karp to the side of the bed. He smelled the animal leather of the German's coat and the cloying rank odour of his sweat; he could feel the unshaved stubble on the neck. All sense of time was gone, swept away in the rush of adrenalin, but it seemed to Hoffmann only a few seconds later that the fingers gradually ceased scrabbling at his hand and the knife clattered to the carpet. The body went slack beneath him, and when he withdrew his hands it toppled sideways.

He became aware of someone pounding on the wall and of a male voice calling out in thickly-accented French, demanding to know what the hell was going on. He heaved himself up and closed the door and as an extra protection dragged the wooden chair over and wedged it at an angle under the handle. The movement set off an immediate clamour of pain in various battered outposts of his body—his head, his knuckles, his fingers, the base of his ribcage especially, even his toes where he had kicked the man's head. He dabbed his fingers to his scalp and they came away sticky with blood. At some point in the struggle his wound must have partially opened up. His hands were a mass of tiny scratches, as though he had fought his way out of an undergrowth of thorns. He sucked his grazed knuckles, registering the salty, metallic taste of blood. The hammering on the wall had stopped.

He was trembling now; he felt sick again. He went into the bathroom and retched into the toilet bowl. The basin was hanging away from the wall but the taps still worked. He splashed his cheeks with cold water and went back into the bedroom.

The German lay on the floor. He had not moved. His open eyes gazed past Hoffmann's shoulder, with an oddly hopeful expression, seemingly searching for a guest at a party who would never arrive. Hoffmann knelt and checked his wrist for a pulse. He slapped his face. He shook him as if that might reanimate him. 'Come on,' he whispered. 'I don't need this.' The head lolled like a bird's on the stem of a broken neck.

There was a brisk knock on the door. A man called out, '*Ça va? Qu'est-ce qui se passe?*' It was the same heavily accented voice that had shouted through the wall from next door. The handle was tried several times and then the knocking resumed. The demand this time was louder and more urgent: '*Allez! Laissez-moi rentrer!*'

Hoffmann levered himself painfully up on to his feet. The handle rattled again and whoever was outside began shoving against the door. The chair moved fractionally but held. The pushing stopped. Hoffmann waited for a renewed assault, but nothing happened. He crept quietly to the spyhole and looked out. The corridor was empty.

And now the animal fear was inside him again,

calm and cunning, controlling his impulses and limbs, making him do things that even an hour later he would look back on in disbelief. He grabbed the dead man's boots and quickly unthreaded the laces, yanking them out and knotting them into a single length a metre long. He seized hold of the wall light but the fixing was too flimsy. The shower curtain rail came away in his hand in a spurt of pink plaster. In the end he settled on the handle of the bathroom door. He dragged the German's body over and propped him up against it. He made a noose out of the end of the laces, slipped the ligature around Karp's neck, looped the line over the handle and yanked. It took some effort, hauling on the cord with one hand and hoisting the corpse under its armpit with the other, but finally he managed to raise it sufficiently to make the scene look at least half-plausible. He looped the line around the handle again and knotted it.

Once he had stuffed the German's possessions back into the rucksack and straightened the bed, the bedroom looked oddly untouched by what had happened. He slipped Karp's mobile into his pocket, closed the laptop and carried it over to the window. He parted the net curtain. The window opened easily, obviously often used. On the fire escape, amid the encrusted swirls of pigeon shit, were a hundred sodden cigarette butts, a score of beer cans. He clambered out on to the ironwork, reached around the window frame and pressed the switch. The shutter descended behind him.

It was a long way down, six floors, and with every clanging step of his descent Hoffmann was acutely aware of how conspicuous he must be—directly visible to anyone looking out from the buildings opposite or who happened to be standing in one of the hotel bedrooms. But to his relief most of the windows he passed were shuttered, and at the others no ghostly faces materialised behind their shrouds of muslin. The Hotel Diodati was at rest for the afternoon. He clattered on down, his only thought to put as much distance between himself and the corpse as possible.

From his high vantage point he could see that the fire escape led to a small concrete patio. A feeble attempt had been made to turn this into an outdoor seating area. There was some wooden garden furniture and a couple of faded green umbrellas advertising lager. He calculated that the best way to get out to the street would be through the hotel, but when he reached the ground and saw the sliding glass door that led to the reception area, the fear-animal decided against it: he couldn't risk running into the man from the next-door room. He dragged one of the wooden garden chairs over to the back wall and climbed up on to it.

He found himself peering at a two-metre drop to the neighbouring yard—a wilderness of sickly urban weeds choking half-hidden pieces of rusting catering equipment and an old bike frame; on the far side were big receptacles for trash. The yard clearly belonged to a restaurant of some kind. He could see the chefs in their white hats moving about in the kitchen, could hear them shouting and the crash of their pans. He balanced the laptop on the wall and hauled himself up to sit astride the brickwork. In the distance a police siren began to wail. He grabbed the computer, swung his leg over and dropped down to the other side, landing heavily in a bed of stinging nettles. He swore. From

195

between the waste bins a youth stepped out to see what was going on. He was carrying an empty slop bucket, smoking a cigarette—Arab-looking, clean-shaven, late teens. He stared at Hoffmann in surprise.

Hoffmann said diffidently, '*Où est la rue?*' He tapped the computer significantly, as if it somehow explained his presence.

The youth looked at him and frowned, then slowly withdrew his cigarette from his mouth and gestured over his shoulder.

'*Merci.*' Hoffmann hurried down the narrow alley, through the wooden gate and out into the street.

*   *   *

Gabrielle Hoffmann had spent more than an hour furiously prowling round the public gardens of the Parc des Bastions declaiming in her head all the things she wished she had said on the pavement to Alex, until she realised, on her third or fourth circuit, that she was muttering to herself like a mad old lady and that passers-by were staring at her; at which point she hailed a taxi and went home. There was a patrol car containing two gendarmes parked in the street outside. Beyond the gate, in front of the mansion, the wretched bodyguard-cum-driver whom Alex had sent to watch over her was talking on his telephone. He hung up and stared at her reproachfully. With his closely shaved domed head and massive squat frame he resembled a malevolent Buddha.

She said to him, 'Do you still have that car, Camille?'

196

'Yes, *madame*.'

'And you're supposed to drive me wherever I want to go?'

'That's right.'

'Bring it round, will you? We're going to the airport.'

In the bedroom she started flinging clothes into a suitcase, her mind obsessively replaying the scene of her humiliation at the gallery. How could he have done such a thing to her? That it was Alex who had sabotaged her exhibition she had no doubt, although she was prepared to concede he would not have meant it maliciously. No, what was absolutely bloody *enraging* was that it would have been his clumsy, hopeless conception of a romantic gesture. Once, a year or two ago, when they were on holiday in the south of France and dining in some ludicrously expensive seafood restaurant in St-Tropez, she had made an idle remark about how cruel it was to keep all those dozens of lobsters in a tank, awaiting their turn to be boiled alive; the next thing she knew he had bought the lot at double the menu price and was having them carried outside to be tipped into the harbour. The uproar that ensued as they hit the water and scuttled away—now that had been quite funny, and needless to say he had been utterly oblivious to it. She opened another suitcase and threw in a pair of shoes. But she couldn't forgive him for today's scene, not yet. It would take at least a few days for her to calm down.

She went into the bathroom and stopped, staring in sudden bafflement at the cosmetics and perfume arrayed on the glass shelves. It was hard to know how much to pack if you didn't know how long you would be gone, or even where you were going. She looked at herself in the mirror, in the wretched outfit she had spent hours choosing for the launch of her career as an artist, and started crying—less out of self-pity, which she despised, than out of fear. Don't let him be ill, she thought. Dear God, please don't take him away from me in that way. Throughout she kept on studying her face dispassionately. It was amazing how ugly you could make yourself by crying, like scrawling over a drawing. After a while she put her hand into her jacket pocket to try to find a tissue, and felt instead the sharp edges of a business card.

Professor Robert WALTON
Computing Centre Department Head
CERN—European Organisation for Nuclear Research
1211 Geneva 23—Switzerland

12

... varieties are species in the process of formation, or are, as I have called them, incipient species.

CHARLES DARWIN, *On the Origin of Species* (1859)

It was well after three o'clock by the time Hugo Quarry got back to the office. He had left several messages on Hoffmann's mobile phone, which had not been answered, and he felt a slight prickle of unease about where his partner might be: Hoffmann's so-called bodyguard he had found chatting up a girl in reception, unaware that his charge had even left the hotel. Quarry had fired him on the spot.

Still, for all that, the Englishman's mood was good. He now believed they were likely to mop up double his initial estimate of new investment—$2 billion—which meant an extra $40 million a year simply in management fees. He had drunk several truly excellent glasses of wine. On the drive back from the restaurant he celebrated by putting a call through to Benetti's and commissioning a helicopter pad for the back of his yacht.

He was smiling so much the facial-recognition scanner failed to match his geometry to its database and he had to try a second time when he had composed himself. He passed under the bland but watchful eyes of the security cameras in the lobby, cheerfully called out, 'Five,' to the elevator and hummed to himself all the way up the glass tube. It was the old school song, or as much of it as he could

199

remember—*sonent voces omnium, tum-tee tum-tee tum-tee-tum*—and when the doors opened he tipped an imaginary hat to his frowning fellow passengers, the dull drones from DigiSyst or EcoTec or whatever the hell they were called. He even managed to maintain his smile when the glass partition to Hoffmann Investment Technologies slid back to reveal Inspector Jean-Philippe Leclerc of the Geneva Police Department waiting for him in reception. He examined his visitor's ID and then compared it to the rumpled figure in front of him. The American markets would be opening in ten minutes. This he could do without.

'It wouldn't be possible, Inspector, would it, for us to have this meeting some other time? I only say this because we really are feeling pretty frazzled here today.'

'I am very sorry to disturb you, *monsieur*. I had hoped to catch a word with Dr Hoffmann, but in his absence there are some matters I would like to discuss with you. I promise you it will only take ten minutes.'

There was something in the way the old boy planted his feet slightly apart that warned Quarry he had better make the best of it. 'Of course,' he said, switching on his trademark smile, 'you shall have as long as you like. We'll go to my office.' He extended his hand and ushered the policeman in front of him. 'Keep right on to the end.' He felt as if he had been smiling solidly for about fifteen hours that day already. His face ached with bonhomie. As soon as Leclerc had his back to him, he treated himself to a scowl.

Leclerc walked slowly past the trading floor, examining his surroundings with interest. The big open room with its screens and time-zone clocks was more or less what he would have expected in a financial company: he had seen this on the television. But the employees were a surprise—all young, and not a tie between them, let alone a suit—and also the silence, with everyone at his desk, and the air so still and heavy with concentration. The whole place reminded him of an examination hall in an all-male college. Or a seminary, perhaps: yes, a seminary of Mammon. The image pleased him. On several of the screens he noticed a slogan, red on white, as in the old Soviet Union:

THE COMPANY OF THE FUTURE WILL HAVE
NO PAPER
THE COMPANY OF THE FUTURE WILL CARRY
NO INVENTORY
THE COMPANY OF THE FUTURE WILL BE
ENTIRELY DIGITAL
THE COMPANY OF THE FUTURE HAS ARRIVED

'Now,' said Quarry, smiling again, 'what can I offer you, Inspector? Tea, coffee, water?'

'I think tea, as I am with an Englishman. Thank you.'

'Two teas, Amber, sweetheart, please. English breakfast.'

She said, 'You have a lot of calls, Hugo.'

'Yes, I bet I bloody do.' He opened his office door and stood aside to let Leclerc go in first, then went straight to his desk. 'Please, take a seat, will you, Inspector? Excuse me. I won't be a second.' He checked his screen. The European markets were all heading south fairly quickly now. The

201

DAX was off one per cent, the CAC two, the FTSE one and a half. The euro was down more than a cent against the dollar. He didn't have time to check all their positions, but the P&L showed VIXAL-4 already up $68 million on the day. Still, there was something about it all he found vaguely ominous, despite his good mood; he sensed a storm about to break. 'Great. That's fine.' He sat down cheerfully behind his desk. 'So then, have you caught this maniac?'

'Not yet. You and Dr Hoffmann have worked together for eight years, I understand.'

'That's right. We set up shop in 2002.'

Leclerc extracted his notebook and pen. He held them up. 'You don't object if I . . .?'

'I don't, although Alex would.'

'I'm sorry?'

'We're not allowed to use carbon-based data-retrieval systems on the premises—that's notebooks and newspapers to you and me. The company is supposed to be entirely digital. But Alex isn't here, so don't worry about it. Go ahead.'

'That sounds a little eccentric.' Leclerc made a careful note.

'Eccentric is one way of putting it. Another would be stark raving bloody bonkers. But there you are. That's Alex. He's a genius, and they don't tend to see the world the same way we do. Quite a large part of my life is spent explaining his behaviour to lesser mortals. Like John the Baptist, I go before him. Or after him.'

He was thinking of their lunch at the Beau-Rivage, when he had been obliged to interpret Hoffmann's actions to mere Earthlings twice—first when he didn't show up for half an hour ('He sends his apologies, he's working on a very complex theorem'), and then when he abruptly sped away from the table midway through the entrée ('Well, there goes Alex, folks—I guess he's having another of his eureka moments'). But although there had been some grumbling and eye-rolling, they were willing to put up with it. At the end of the day, Hoffmann could swing naked from the rafters playing the ukulele as far as they were concerned, as long as he made them a return of eighty-three per cent.

Leclerc said, 'Can you tell me how you two met?'

'Sure, when we started working together.'

'And how did that come about?'

'What, you want the whole love story?' Quarry put his hands behind his head and leaned back in his favourite position, feet up on his desk, always happy to tell a tale he had recounted a hundred times, maybe a thousand, polishing it into a corporate legend: when Sears met Roebuck, Rolls met Royce and Quarry met Hoffmann. 'It was around Christmas 2001. I was in London, working for a big American bank. I wanted to have a crack at starting my own fund. I knew I could raise the money—I had the contacts: that was no problem— but I didn't have a game plan that would sustain over the long term. You've got to have a strategy in this business—did you know the average life expectancy of a hedge fund is three years?'

Leclerc said politely, 'No.'

'Well it's true. That's the lifespan of the average hamster. Anyway, a guy in our Geneva office mentioned this science nerd at CERN he'd heard about who apparently had some quite interesting ideas on the algorithmic side. We thought we might hire him as a quant, but he just wouldn't play ball at all—wouldn't meet us, didn't want to know: mad as a hatter, apparently, total recluse. We had a laugh about it—quants! I mean, what could you do? But there was just something about the sound of this one that got me interested: I don't know—a pricking of my thumbs. As it happened, I was planning to go skiing over the holidays, so I thought I'd look him up . . .'

$$*\qquad*\qquad*$$

He'd decided to make contact on New Year's Eve: he had figured even a recluse might be forced to put up with company on New Year's Eve. So he had left Sally and the kids in the chalet in Chamonix— which they had rented together with the Bakers, their perfectly ghastly neighbours in Wimbledon— and, ignoring their reproaches, had driven down the valley alone to Geneva, glad of an excuse to get away. The mountains had been a luminous blue under a three-quarters moon, the roads empty. There was no satellite navigation in the hire car, not in those days, and when he got close to Geneva Airport he had had to pull off the road and look at the Hertz map. Saint-Genis-Pouilly was straight ahead, just past CERN, in flat arable land that glistened in the frost—a small French town, a café in its cobbled centre, rows of neat houses with red roofs, and finally a few modern apartment blocks built of concrete in the last couple of years and painted ochre, their balconies festooned with wind chimes, folded-up metal chairs and dead window boxes. Quarry had rung Hoffmann's doorbell for a long time without getting a response, even though there was a pale strip of light beneath the door and he sensed that someone was inside. Eventually a neighbour had come out and told him that *tout le monde par le CERN* was at a party in a house near the sports stadium. He had stopped off at a bar on the way and picked up a bottle of cognac, and had driven around the darkened streets until he found it.

More than eight years later he could still remember his excitement as the car locked with its cheerful electronic squawk and he set off down the pavement towards the multicoloured Christmas lights and the thumping music. In the darkness other people, singly and in laughing couples, were converging on the same spot, and he could somehow sense that this was going to be it: that the stars above this dreary little European town were in alignment and some extraordinary event was about to occur. The host and hostess were standing at the door to greet their guests—Bob and Maggie Walton, English couple, older than their guests, dreary. They had looked mystified to see him, and even more so when he told them he was a friend of Alex Hoffmann's: he got the impression no one had ever said that before. Walton had refused his offer of the bottle of cognac as if it were a bribe: 'You can take it with you when you leave.' Not very friendly, but then in fairness he was crashing their party, and he must have looked a misfit in his expensive skiing jacket surrounded by all these nerds on a government salary. He had asked where he might find Hoffmann, to which Walton had replied, with a shrewd look, that he wasn't quite sure but that presumably Quarry would recognise him when he saw him, 'if you two are such good friends'.

Leclerc said, 'And did you? Recognise him?'

'Oh yes. You can always spot an American, don't you think? He was on his own in the centre of a downstairs room and the party was kind of lapping around him—he was a handsome guy, stood out in a crowd—but he wasn't taking any notice of it. He had this look on his face of being somewhere else entirely. Not hostile, you understand—just not there. I've pretty much got used to it since then.'

'And that was the first time you spoke to him?'

'It was.'

'What did you say?'

'"Dr Hoffmann, I presume."'

He had flourished the bottle of cognac and offered to go and find two glasses, but Hoffmann had said he didn't drink, to which Quarry had said, 'In that case why did you come to a New Year's Eve party?' to which Hoffmann had replied that several very kind but overprotective colleagues had thought it was best if he was not left on his own on this particular night. But they were quite wrong, he added—he was perfectly happy to be on his own. And so saying he had moved off into another room, obliging Quarry, after a short interval, to follow him. That was his first taste of the legendary Hoffmann charm. He had felt pretty pissed off. 'I've come sixty miles to see you,' he said, chasing after him. 'I've left my wife and children crying in a hut on a freezing mountainside and driven through the ice and snow to get here. The least you can do is talk to me.'

'Why are you so interested in me?'

'Because I gather you're developing some very interesting software. A colleague of mine at AmCor said he'd spoken to you.'

'Yeah, and I told him I'm not interested in working for a bank.'

'Neither am I.'

For the first time Hoffmann had glanced at him with a hint of interest. 'So what do you want to do instead?'

'I want to set up a hedge fund.'

'What's a hedge fund?'

Sitting opposite Leclerc, Quarry threw back his head and laughed. Here they were today with ten billion dollars—soon to be twelve billion dollars—in assets under management, yet only eight years ago Hoffmann had not even known what a hedge fund was! And although a crowded, noisy New Year's Eve party was probably not the best place to attempt an explanation, Quarry had had no choice. He had shouted the definition into Hoffmann's ear. 'It's a way of maximising returns at the same time as minimising risks. Needs a lot of mathematics to make it work. Computers.'

Hoffmann had nodded. 'Okay. Go on.'

'Right.' Quarry had glanced around, searching for inspiration. 'Right, you see that girl over there, the one in that group with the short dark hair who keeps looking at you?' Quarry had raised the cognac bottle to her and smiled. 'Right, let's say I'm convinced she's wearing black knickers—she looks like a black-knickers kind of a gal to me—and I'm so sure that that's what she's wearing, so positive of that one sartorial fact, I want to bet a million dollars on it. The trouble is, if I'm wrong, I'm wiped out. So I also bet she's wearing knickers that aren't black, but are any one of a whole basket of colours—let's say I put nine hundred and fifty thousand dollars on that possibility: that's the rest of the market; that's the hedge. This is a crude example, okay, in every sense, but hear me out. Now if I'm right, I make fifty K, but even if I'm wrong I'm only going to lose fifty K, because I'm hedged. And because ninety-five per cent of my million dollars is not in use—I'm never going to be called on to show it: the only risk is in the spread—I can make similar bets with other people. Or I can bet it on something else entirely. And the beauty of it is I don't have to be right all the time—if I can just get the colour of her underwear right fifty-five per cent of the time I'm going to wind up very rich. She really is looking at you, you know.'

She had called across the room, 'Are you guys talking about me?' Without waiting for a reply, she had detached herself from her friends and come over to them, smiling. 'Gabby,' she had said, sticking out her hand to Hoffmann.

'Alex.'

'And I'm Hugo.'

'Yes, you look like a Hugo.'

Her presence had irritated Quarry, and not only because she so obviously had eyes only for Hoffmann and no interest in him. He was still mid-pitch, and as far as he was concerned her role in this conversation was strictly as illustration, not participant. 'We were just making a bet,' he said sweetly, 'on the colour of your knickers.'

Quarry had made very few social mistakes in his life, but this was, as he freely acknowledged, a beaut. 'She's hated me ever since.'

Leclerc smiled and made a note. 'But your relationship with Dr Hoffmann was established that night?'

'Oh yes. Now I look back on it, I'd say he was waiting for someone like me just as much as I was looking for someone like him.'

At midnight the guests had gone out into the garden and lit small candles—'you know, those tea-light things'—and put them into paper balloons. Dozens of softly glowing lanterns had lifted off, rising quickly in the cold still air like yellow moons. Someone had called out, 'Make a wish!' and Quarry, Hoffmann and Gabrielle had all stood together silently with their faces upturned, misty-breathed, until the lights had dwindled to the size of stars and disappeared. Afterwards Quarry had offered to drive Hoffmann home, whereupon Gabrielle, to his irritation, had tagged along, sitting in the back seat and giving them her life story without being asked for it—some kind of joint degree in art and French from a northern university Quarry had never heard of, a masters at the Royal College of Art, secretarial college, temp jobs, the UN. But even she had shut up when they got inside Hoffmann's apartment.

He had not wanted to let them in, but Quarry had pretended he needed to use the loo—'honestly, it was like trying to get off with a girl at the end of a bad evening'—and so reluctantly Hoffmann had led them up to the landing and unlocked his door on to a vivarium of noise and tropical heat: motherboards whirring everywhere, red and green eyes winking out from under the sofa, behind the table, stacked on the bookshelves, bunches of black cables festooned from the walls like vines. It reminded Quarry of a story he had read just before Christmas about a man in Maidenhead who kept a crocodile in his garage. In the corner was a Bloomberg

209

terminal for online home traders. On his return from the bathroom, Quarry had looked in at the bedroom—more computers taking up half the bed.

He had come back into the living room to find that Gabrielle had made room for herself on the sofa and kicked off her shoes. He said, 'So what's the deal here, Alex? It looks like Mission Control.'

At first Hoffmann had not wanted to talk about it, but gradually he had begun to open up. The object, he said, was autonomous machine-learning—to create an algorithm which, once given a task, would be able to operate independently and teach itself at a rate far beyond the capacity of human beings. Hoffmann was leaving CERN to pursue his research alone, which meant he would no longer have access to the experimental data emanating from the Large Electron–Positron Collider. For the past six months, therefore, he had been using data streams from the financial markets instead. Quarry had said it looked an expensive business. Hoffmann had agreed, although the main cost to him was not in microprocessors—many of which he had been able to salvage from scrap—or the cost of the Bloomberg service, so much as in electricity: he was having to find two thousand francs a week simply to bring in sufficient power; he had twice blacked out the neighbourhood. The other problem, of course, was bandwidth.

Quarry had said cautiously, 'I could help you out with the cost, if you'd let me.'

'No need. I'm using the algorithm to pay for itself.'

It had taken an effort for Quarry to stifle his gasp of excitement. 'Really? That's a neat concept. And is it?'

'Sure. It's just a bunch of extrapolations drawn from basic pattern analysis.' Hoffmann had shown him the screen. 'These are the stocks it's suggested since December first, based on price comparisons using data from the past five years. Then I just email a broker and tell him to buy or sell.'

Quarry had studied the trades. They were good, if small: nickel-and-dime stuff. 'Could it do more than cover costs? Could it make a profit?'

'Yeah, in theory, but that would need a lot of investment.'

'Maybe I could get you the investment.'

'You know what? I'm not actually interested in making money. No offence, but I don't see the point of it.'

Quarry couldn't believe what he was hearing: he didn't see the point!

Hoffmann had not offered him a drink, or even a seat—not that there was room to sit now that Gabrielle had taken the only available space. Quarry was left standing sweating in his ski jacket.

He said, 'But surely if you did make money then you could use the profits to pay for more research? It would be what you're trying to do now, only on a vastly bigger scale. I don't want to be rude, man, but look around. You need to get some proper premises, more reliable utilities, fibre optics . . .'

'Perhaps a cleaner?' Gabrielle had added.

'She's right, you know—a cleaner wouldn't hurt. Look, Alex—here's my card. I'm going to be in the area for the next week or so. Why don't we meet up and talk this through?'

Hoffmann had taken the card and put it in his pocket without looking at it. 'Maybe.'

At the door Quarry had bent down and

whispered to Gabrielle, 'Do you need a ride? I'm driving back to Chamonix. I can drop you in town somewhere.'

'It's all right, thanks.' A smile as sweet as acid. 'I thought I might stay here for a while and settle your bet.'

'Suit yourself, darling, but have you seen the bedroom? Best of bloody luck.'

*   *   *

Quarry had put up the seed money himself, used his annual bonus to move Hoffmann and his computers into an office in Geneva: he needed a place where he could bring prospective clients and impress them with the hardware. His wife had complained. Why couldn't his long-discussed start-up be based in London? Wasn't he always telling her that the City was the hedge-fund capital of the world? But Geneva was part of the attraction to Quarry: not just the lower tax, but the chance for a clean break. He had never had any intention of moving his family to Switzerland—not that he told them that, or even acknowledged it to himself. But the truth was, domesticity was a stock that no longer suited his portfolio. He was bored with it. It was time to sell up and move on.

He decided they should call themselves Hoffmann Investment Technologies in a nod to Jim Simons's legendary quant shop, Renaissance Technologies, over in Long Island: the daddy of all algorithmic hedge funds. Hoffmann had objected strongly—the first time Quarry had encountered his mania for anonymity—but Quarry was insistent: he saw from the start that Hoffmann's mystique as

212

a mathematics genius, like that of Jim Simons, would be an important part of selling the product. AmCor agreed to act as prime brokers and to let Quarry take some of his old clients with him in return for a reduced management fee and ten per cent of the action. Then Quarry had hit the road of investors' conferences, moving from city to city in the US and across Europe, pulling his wheeled suitcase through fifty different airports. He had loved this part—loved being a salesman, he who travels alone, walking in cold to an air-conditioned conference room in a strange hotel overlooking some sweltering freeway and charming a sceptical audience. His method was to show them the independently back-tested results of Hoffmann's algorithm and the mouth-watering projections of future returns, then break it to them that the fund was already closed: he had only fulfilled his engagement to speak in order to be polite but they didn't need any more money, sorry. Afterwards the investors would come looking for him in the hotel bar; it worked nearly every time.

Quarry had hired a guy from BNP Paribas to oversee the back office, a receptionist, a secretary, and a French fixed-income trader from AmCor who had run into some regulatory issues and needed to get out of London fast. On the technical side, Hoffmann had recruited an astrophysicist from CERN and a Polish mathematics professor to serve as quants. They had run simulations throughout the summer and had gone live in October 2002 with $107 million in assets under management. They had made a profit in the first month and had gone on doing so ever since.

Quarry paused in his tale to let Leclerc's cheap

ballpoint catch up with his flow of words.

And to answer his other questions: no, he was not sure exactly when Gabrielle had moved in with Hoffmann: he and Alex had never seen one another much socially; besides, he had been travelling a lot that first year. No, he had not attended their wedding: it had been one of those solipsistic ceremonies conducted at sunset on a Pacific beach somewhere, with two hotel employees as witnesses and no family or friends in attendance. And no, he had not been told that Hoffmann had had a mental breakdown at CERN, although he had guessed it: when he went to the loo in his apartment that first night, he had rummaged through Hoffmann's bathroom cabinet (as one does) and found a veritable mini-pharmacy of antidepressants—mirtazapine, lithium, fluvoxamine—he couldn't remember them all exactly, but it had looked pretty serious.

'That didn't put you off going into business with him?'

'What? The fact he wasn't "normal"? Good Lord, no. To quote Bill Clinton—not necessarily a fount of wisdom in all circumstances, I grant you, but right in this one—"normalcy is overrated: most normal people are assholes".'

'And you have no idea where Dr Hoffmann is at this moment?'

'No, I do not.'

'When did you last see him?'

'At lunch. The Beau-Rivage.'

'So he left without explanation?'

'That's Alex.'

'Did he seem agitated?'

'Not especially.' Quarry swung his feet off the

214

desk and buzzed his assistant. 'Is Alex back yet, do we know?'

'No, Hugo. Sorry. Incidentally, Gana just called. The Risk Committee is waiting for you in his office. He's trying to get hold of Alex urgently. There's a problem, apparently.'

'You surprise me. What is it now?'

'He said to tell you that "VIXAL is lifting the delta hedge". He said you'd know what that meant.'

'Okay, thanks. Tell them I'm on my way.' Quarry released the switch and looked thoughtfully at the intercom. 'I'm going to have to leave you, I'm afraid.' For the first time he felt a definite spasm of anxiety in the pit of his stomach. He glanced across the desk at Leclerc, who was regarding him intently, and suddenly he realised he had been gabbling away much too freely: the copper didn't seem to be investigating the break-in any more so much as investigating Hoffmann.

'Is that important?' Leclerc nodded at the intercom. 'The delta hedge?'

'It is rather. Will you excuse me? My assistant will show you out.'

He left abruptly without shaking hands, and soon afterwards Leclerc found himself being conducted back across the trading floor, preceded by Quarry's glamorous red-headed gatekeeper in her low-cut sweater. She seemed in a hurry to get him out of there, which naturally made him slow his pace. He noticed how the atmosphere had changed. Here and there around the room several groups of three or four were gathered in anxious tableaux around a screen, with one person seated, clicking on a mouse, and the others leaning over his shoulders; occasionally someone would point to a graph or a

215

column of figures. And now Leclerc was reminded much less of a seminary and more of doctors assembled at the bedside of a patient displaying grave and baffling symptoms. On one of the big TV screens a network was showing pictures of an aircraft crashing. Standing beneath the TV was a man in a dark suit and tie. He was preoccupied, sending a text message on his mobile phone, and it took Leclerc a moment to recollect who it was.

'Genoud,' he muttered to himself, and then more loudly, moving towards him, 'Maurice Genoud!' at which Genoud looked up from his texting—and was it Leclerc's imagination, or did his narrow features tense slightly at the sight of this figure bearing down on him from his past?

He said warily, 'Jean-Philippe.' They shook hands.

'Maurice Genoud. You've put on weight.' Leclerc turned to Quarry's assistant. 'Would you excuse us a moment, *mademoiselle*? We're old friends. You'll see me out, won't you, Maurice? Let me look at you, lad. Quite the prosperous civilian nowadays, I see.'

Smiles did not come naturally to Genoud; it was a pity he bothered, thought Leclerc.

'And you? I'd heard you'd retired, Jean-Philippe.'

Leclerc said, 'Next year. I can't wait. Tell me, what on earth do they do here?' He gestured to the trading floor. 'Presumably you can understand it. I'm too old to get my head around it.'

'I don't know either. I'm just paid to keep them safe.'

'Well you're not doing a very good job of it!'

216

Leclerc clapped him on the shoulder. Genoud scowled. 'I'm only joking. But seriously, what do you make of this business? A bit odd, wouldn't you say, having all that security and then allowing a complete stranger to wander in off the street and attack you? Did you install it, I wonder?'

Genoud moistened his lips before replying, and Leclerc thought, he's playing for time; that's what he used to do back in the Boulevard Carl-Vogt when he was trying to think up some story. He'd distrusted the younger man ever since the days when Genoud was a rookie under his command. There was, in his opinion, nothing that his former colleague would not do—no principle he wouldn't betray, no deal he wouldn't cut, no blind eye he wouldn't turn—if he could make sufficient money and stay just within the law.

Genoud said, 'Yes, I installed it. What of it?'

'There's no need to get all defensive. I'm not blaming you. We both know you can surround someone with the best security in the world, but if they forget to use it there's nothing you can do.'

'That's true. Now if you don't mind, I ought to get on with my work. This isn't the public sector, you know—I can't stand here gossiping.'

'You can learn a lot by gossiping.'

They moved towards reception. Leclerc said, man-to-man, 'So what's he like, then, this Dr Hoffmann?'

'I hardly know him.'

'Enemies?'

'You'd have to ask him.'

'So there's no one here dislikes him that you've heard about? No one he's fired?'

Genoud didn't even pretend to think about it.

'No. Enjoy your retirement, Jean-Philippe. You deserve it.'

13

The extinction of species and of whole groups of species, which has played so conspicuous a part in the history of the organic world, almost inevitably follows on the principle of natural selection; for old forms will be supplanted by new and improved forms.

CHARLES DARWIN, *On the Origin of Species* (1859)

The Risk Committee of Hoffmann Investment Technologies met for the second time that day at 16.25, Central European Time, fifty-five minutes after the opening of the US markets. Present were the Hon. Hugo Quarry, chief executive officer; Lin Ju-Long, chief financial officer; Pieter van der Zyl, chief operating officer; and Ganapathi Rajamani, chief risk officer, who took the minutes and in whose office the meeting was held.

Rajamani sat behind his desk like a headmaster. Under the terms of his contract he was not permitted to share in the annual bonus. This was supposed to make him more objective about risk, but in Quarry's opinion it had simply had the effect of turning him into a licensed prig who could afford to look down his nose at big profits. The Dutchman and the Chinese occupied the two chairs. Quarry sprawled on the sofa. Through the open blinds he watched Amber leading Leclerc towards reception.

The first item noted the absence, without explanation, of Dr Alexander Hoffmann, company president—and the fact that Rajamani wanted this dereliction of duty officially minuted was, to

219

Quarry, the first indication that their chief prig officer was preparing to play hardball. Indeed, he seemed to take a grim delight in laying out just how perilous their position had become. He announced that since the last meeting of the committee, some four hours earlier, the fund's risk exposure had increased dramatically. Every warning indicator in the cockpit was flashing red. Decisions needed to be taken fast.

He started reading facts from his computer. VIXAL had almost entirely abandoned the company's long position on S&P futures, its principal hedge against a rising market, stranding them with their plethora of shorts. It was also in the process of disposing of all—'I repeat, all'—of its matching pairs of long bets on the eighty or so stocks it was shorting: in the last few minutes alone, the final remnants of a $70 million long position on Deloitte, taken up to hedge their massive short against its competitor Accenture, had been liquidated. And perhaps most troubling of all, as one by one the bets to the long side were lifted, there had been no corresponding move to buy back the stocks that were being shorted.

'I have never seen anything like it before in my life,' concluded Rajamani. 'The plain fact is, this company's delta hedge has gone.'

Quarry maintained a poker face, but even he was startled. His faith in VIXAL had always been unshakeable, but this was supposed to be a *hedge* fund—the clue was in the name, dummy. If you took away the hedge—if you dispensed with all the immensely intricate mathematical formulae that were supposed to ensure that you covered your risk—you might as well take the family silver and bet the lot on the 3.45 at Newmarket. It was true, the hedge put a ceiling on your gains, but it also put a floor under your losses. And given that there wasn't a fund on earth that didn't go through a rough patch every so often, if you didn't put on a hedge, a run of bad calls could wipe you out. His skin felt clammy at the thought. He could taste his lunchtime *filet mignon de veau* rising like bile in his throat. He put the back of his hand to his forehead. I am literally breaking out in a cold sweat, he realised.

Rajamani continued to hammer away: 'We have not merely abandoned our long position on S and P futures, we are actually *shorting* S and P futures. We have also increased our position on VIX futures to something approaching one billion dollars. And we are buying out-of-the-money puts that are so extreme—that presuppose such a massive deterioration in the market generally—that our only consolation is that we are at least picking them up for cents. In addition—'

Quarry held up his hand. 'Okay, Gana. Thanks. We get it.' He needed to take charge of this meeting quickly, before it turned into a rout. He was conscious that they were being scrutinised from the trading floor. They all knew the hedge had gone. Anxious faces kept bobbing up and down from behind their six-screen arrays like targets in a shooting gallery.

Van der Zyl said, 'I'll close the blinds.' He started to rise.

Quarry said sharply, 'No, leave them open, Piet, for God's sake or they'll think we're forming a suicide pact in here. Actually, I'd like to see some smiles from you all, gentlemen, if you don't

221

mind—everybody smile: that's an order. Even you, Gana. Let's show the troops a little officer-class sangfroid.'

He hoisted his feet up on to the coffee table and laced his fingers behind his head in a parody of nonchalance, even though his fingernails were digging into his flesh so sharply the indentations would look like scars for the rest of the day. He glanced around at the personal photographs Rajamani had brought in from home to alleviate the gleaming Scandinavian gloom of the decor: a big wedding group taken at night in a Delhi garden, the garlanded bride and groom in the centre, grinning maniacally; Rajamani as a student graduating from Cambridge, standing in front of the University Senate House; and two young children in school uniform, a boy and a girl, staring sombrely at the camera.

He said, 'Okay, Gana, so what is your recommendation?'

'There is only one option: override VIXAL and put the hedge back on.'

'You want us to bypass the algorithm without even consulting Alex?' asked Ju-Long.

'I would most certainly consult him if I could find him,' retorted Rajamani. 'However, he is not answering his phone.'

Van der Zyl said, 'I thought he was at lunch with you, Hugo.'

'He was. He left halfway through in a hurry.'

'Where did he go?'

'Lord knows. He just took off without a word.'

Rajamani said, 'That is just breathtaking irresponsibility. I'm sorry. He knew there was a problem. He knew we were scheduled to meet

222

again this afternoon.'

There was a silence.

'In my opinion,' said Ju-Long, 'and I would not say this except among us, I believe Alex is having some kind of breakdown.'

Quarry said, 'Shut up, LJ.'

Van der Zyl chimed in: 'But he is, Hugo.'

'And you should shut up too.'

The Dutchman backed off quickly. 'Okay, okay.'

'Shall I minute this?' enquired Rajamani.

'No you damn well won't.' Quarry pointed an elegantly shod toe across the table at Rajamani's computer terminal. 'Now hear me well and good, Gana: if there's any hint in these minutes of Alex in any way being mentally unreliable, then this company will be finished and you will have to take responsibility for that fact to all those colleagues out there, who are right now watching our every move, and to all our investors, who have made a great deal of money thanks to Alex and who will never forgive you. Do you understand what I'm saying? Let me summarise the situation in four words for you: no Alex, no company.'

For several seconds, Rajamani stared him out. Then he frowned and lifted his hands from the keyboard.

'Okay then,' resumed Quarry. 'In the absence of Alex, let's try looking at this the other way. If we *don't* override VIXAL and put the delta hedge back on, what are the brokers going to say?'

Ju-Long said, 'They are just so hot on collateral these days, after what happened to Lehman's. For sure they won't allow us to trade unhedged on existing terms of settlement.'

'So when will we have to start showing them

some money?'

'I would expect we'll need to provide a substantial level of fresh collateral before close of business tomorrow.'

'And how much do you reckon they'll want us to put up?'

'I'm not sure.' Ju-Long moved his neat, bland head from side to side, weighing it up. 'Maybe half a billion.'

'Half a billion total?'

'No, half a billion each.'

Quarry briefly closed his eyes. Five prime brokers—Goldman, Morgan Stanley, Citi, AmCor, Credit Suisse—half a billion to be deposited with each: two and a half billion dollars. Not funny money, not promissory notes or long-term bonds, but the pure crystal meth of liquid cash, wired over to them by 4.00 p.m. tomorrow. It was not that Hoffmann Investment Technologies didn't have that kind of money. They only traded about twenty-five per cent of the cash lodged with them by their investors; the rest they didn't need to show. The last time he looked, they had at least four billion dollars stashed in US Treasury bills alone. They could dip into that whenever they needed it. But my God— what a colossal hit on their reserves; what a step towards the precipice . . .

Rajamani interrupted his thoughts. 'I am sorry, but this is madness, Hugo. This level of risk is far outside what is promised in our prospectus. If the markets were to rise strongly, we would be left facing billions in losses. We might even go bankrupt. Our clients could sue us.'

Ju-Long added: 'Even if we continue trading, it will be unfortunate—will it not?—if the board of

224

the fund has to be notified of our accelerated risk levels just as we are approaching individual investors to put another billion dollars into VIXAL-4.'

'They will pull out,' said van der Zyl mournfully. 'Anyone would.'

Quarry was unable to sit still any longer. He jumped up and would have paced around the office but there wasn't sufficient room. That this should happen now, after his two-billion-dollar pitch! The unfairness of it! He clawed the air and grimaced at the heavens. Unable to stomach Rajamani's expression of moral superiority for a moment longer, he turned his back on his colleagues and leaned against the glass partition, his palms spread wide, staring out at the trading floor, heedless of who was watching. For a moment he tried to visualise what it would be like to manage an uncontrolled, unhedged investment fund exposed to the full force of the global markets: the seven-hundred-trillion-dollar ocean of stocks and bonds, currencies and derivatives that rose and fell ceaselessly against one another day after day, whipped by currents and tides and storms into vast maelstroms that no one could fathom. It would be like trying to cross the North Atlantic on an upturned dustbin lid with a wooden spoon for a paddle. And there was a part of him—the part that saw existence itself as a gamble that sooner or later one was bound to lose; the part that used to bet $10 K on which fly would take off first from a bar table, just to feel the thrill of fear—that side of his personality would have relished it, once. But nowadays he also wanted to hold on to what he had. He enjoyed being known as a rich hedge-fund

225

manager, the cream of the elite, the financial equivalent of the Brigade of Guards. He was ranked 177 in the latest *Sunday Times* rich list; they had even printed a picture of him on the bridge of a Riva 115 ('Hugo Quarry leads the dream bachelor life on the shores of Lake Geneva—and why not, as CEO of one of the most successful hedge funds in Europe?'). Was he really going to jeopardise all that, just because some bloody algorithm had decided to ignore the basic rules of investment finance? On the other hand, the only reason he was on the rich list in the first place was *because* of the bloody algorithm. He groaned. This was hopeless. Where was Hoffmann?

He turned and said, 'We really need to talk to Alex before we put on an override. I mean, when was the last time any of us actually *did* a trade?'

Rajamani said, 'With respect, that's not the point, Hugo.'

'Of course it's the point. It's the whole point and nothing but the point. This is an algorithmic hedge fund. We're not manned up to run a ten-billion-dollar book. I'd need at least twenty top-class traders out there with steel balls, who know the markets; all I've got are quants with dandruff who don't do eye contact.'

Van der Zyl said, 'The truth is, this issue should have been addressed earlier.' The Dutchman's voice was rich and deep and dark, marinated in coffee and cigars. 'I don't mean that we should have thought about it earlier today—I mean we should have done it last week or last month. VIXAL has been so successful for so long, we have all become dazzled by it. We have never put in place adequate procedures for what to do if it fails.'

Quarry knew in his heart that this was true. He had allowed technology to enfeeble him. He was like some lazy driver who had become entirely reliant on parking sensors and satellite navigation to get him around town. Nevertheless, unable to conceive of a world without VIXAL, he found himself rising to its defence. 'Can I just point out that it hasn't failed? I mean, the last time I looked, we were up sixty-eight mil on the day. What does the P and L say now, Gana?'

Rajamani checked his screen. 'Up seventy-seven,' he conceded.

'Well, thank you. That's a bloody odd definition of failure, isn't it? A system that made nine million dollars in the time it took me to shift my arse from one end of the office to the other?'

'Yes,' said Rajamani patiently, 'but it is a purely theoretical profit, that could be wiped out the moment the market recovers.'

'And is the market recovering?'

'No, I accept that at the moment the Dow is falling.'

'Well, there is our dilemma, gentlemen, right there. We all agree that the fund should be hedged, but we also have to recognise that VIXAL has demonstrated itself to be a better judge of the markets than we are.'

'Oh, come on, Hugo! There's obviously something wrong with it! VIXAL is supposed to operate within certain parameters of risk, and it isn't, therefore it is malfunctioning.'

'I don't agree. It was right about Vista Airways, wasn't it? That was absolutely extraordinary.'

'That was a coincidence. Even Alex acknowledged that.' Rajamani appealed to Ju-Long and van der Zyl. 'Come on, you fellows—back me up here. To make sense of these positions, the whole *world* would have to crash in flames.'

Ju-Long put his hand up like a schoolboy. 'Since the subject has been raised, Hugo, could I just ask about the Vista Airways short? Did anyone see the news just now?'

Quarry sat down heavily on the sofa. 'No, I didn't. I've been rather busy. Why? What are they saying?'

'That the crash was not a mechanical failure after all, but some kind of terrorist bomb.'

'Okay. And?'

'It seems that a warning was posted on a jihadist website while the plane was still in the air. Understandably there is a lot of anger that the intelligence authorities missed it. That was at nine o'clock this morning.'

'I'm sorry, LJ. I'm being a bit slow on the uptake. What does it matter to us?'

'Only that nine o'clock was exactly the time we started shorting the Vista Airways stock.'

It took Quarry a moment or two to react. 'You mean to say we're monitoring jihadist websites?'

'So it would appear.'

Van der Zyl said, 'That would be entirely logical, actually. VIXAL is programmed to search the web for incidences of fear-related language and observe market correlations. Where better to look?'

'But that's a quantum leap, isn't it?' asked Quarry. 'To see the warning, make the deduction, short the stock?'

'I don't know. We would have to ask Alex. But it is a machine-learning algorithm. Theoretically, it's developing all the time.'

Rajamani said, 'Then it's a pity it hadn't developed enough to warn the airline.'

'Oh, come *on*,' said Quarry, 'stop being so bloody *pious*. It's a machine for making money; it's not meant to be a sodding UN goodwill ambassador.' He leaned his head against the back of the sofa and looked at the ceiling, his eyes darting, trying to absorb the implications. 'God in heaven. I mean, I'm simply staggered by that.'

Ju-Long said, 'It could be a coincidence, of course. As Alex said this morning, the airline short was just part of a whole pattern of bets to the down side.'

'Yeah, but even so, that's the only short where we've actually sold the position and taken the profit. The others we're holding on to. Which poses the question: *why* are we holding on to them?' He felt a tingling along the length of his spine. 'I wonder what it thinks is going to happen next?'

'It does not *think* anything,' said Rajamani impatiently. 'It is an algorithm, Hugo—a tool. It is no more alive than a wrench or a car-jack. And our problem is that it is a tool that has become too unreliable to depend on. Now, time is pressing and I really must ask this committee formally to authorise an override on VIXAL and start an immediate rehedging of the fund.'

Quarry looked at the others. He was good at nuances, and he detected that something had just shifted slightly in the atmosphere. Ju-Long was staring ahead impassively, van der Zyl examining a piece of lint on the sleeve of his jacket. They seemed embarrassed. Decent men, he thought, and clever, but weak. And they liked their bonuses. It was all very easy for Rajamani to order VIXAL to be shut down; it would cost him nothing. But they had received four million dollars each last year. He weighed the odds. They would give him no trouble, he decided. As for Hoffmann, he took no interest in the personnel of the firm apart from the quants: he would back him whatever he did. 'Gana,' he said pleasantly, 'I'm sorry, but I'm afraid we're going to have to let you go.'

'What?' Rajamani frowned at him. Then he tried to smile: a ghastly nervous rictus. He tried to treat it as a joke. 'Come on, Hugo . . .'

'If it's any consolation, I was going to fire you next week whatever happened. But now seems like a better time. Write it down in your minutes, why don't you? "After a short discussion, Gana Rajamani agreed to relinquish his duties as chief risk officer, with immediate effect. Hugo Quarry thanked him for all he had done for the company"—which as far as I'm concerned, by the way, is sod all. Now clear your desk and get off home and spend more time with those charming children of yours. And don't worry about money—I'm more than happy to pay you a year's salary just for the pleasure of not having to see you again.'

Rajamani was recovering: afterwards Quarry was forced to give him credit for resilience at least. He said, 'Let me be clear about this—you're dismissing me simply for doing my job?'

'It's partly for doing the job, but mostly for being such a pain in the ass about doing it.'

Rajamani said, with some dignity, 'Thank you for that. I'll remember those words.' He turned to his colleagues. 'Piet? LJ? Are you going to intervene at this point?' Neither man moved. He added,

230

slightly more desperately, 'I thought we had an understanding . . .'

Quarry got up and pulled the power cable out of the back of Rajamani's computer. It emitted a slight rattle as it died. 'Don't make copies of any of your files—the system will tell us if you do. Turn in your mobile phone to my assistant on your way out. Don't speak to any other employees of the company. Leave the premises within fifteen minutes. Your compensation package is conditional on your abiding by our confidentiality agreement. Is that understood? I really would prefer not to call in security—it always looks so cheap. Gentlemen,' he said to the other two, 'shall we leave him to his packing?'

Rajamani called after him, 'When word of this gets out, this company will be finished—I'll see to that.'

'Yes, I'm sure.'

'You said VIXAL could fly us all into a mountainside, and that's exactly what it's doing . . .'

Quarry put his arms around Ju-Long and van der Zyl and guided them out of the office ahead of him. He closed the door without looking back. He knew that the entire drama had been played out to an audience of quants, but that could not be helped. He felt quite cheerful; he always felt good after he'd fired someone: it was cathartic. He smiled at Rajamani's assistant: a pretty girl; she would have to go too, unfortunately. Quarry took a pre-Christian view of these rituals: it was always best to bury the servants with the dead master in case he might require them in the next world.

'I'm sorry about that,' he said to Ju-Long and van der Zyl, 'but at the end of the day we're innovators

231

in this shop, are we not, or we are nothing. And I'm afraid Gana is the kind of chap who'd have turned up on the quayside in 1492 and told Columbus he couldn't set sail because of his negative risk assessment.'

Ju-Long said, with an asperity Quarry had not expected, 'Risk was his responsibility, Hugo. You may have got rid of him, but you have not got rid of the problem.'

'I appreciate that, LJ, and I know he was your friend.' He put his hand on Ju-Long's shoulder and gazed into his dark eyes. 'But don't forget that at this precise moment this company is about eighty million dollars richer than it was when we came in to work this morning.' He gestured to the trading floor: the quants had all returned to their places; there was a semblance of normality. 'The machine is still functioning, and frankly, until Alex tells us otherwise, I think we have to trust it. We have to assume VIXAL is seeing a pattern in events that we can't discern. Come on—people are looking.'

They moved off, along the side of the trading floor, Quarry taking the lead. He was keen to get them away from the scene of Rajamani's assassination. As he walked, he tried yet again to get Hoffmann on his mobile number; yet again he was put straight through to voicemail. This time he didn't even bother to leave a message.

Van der Zyl said, 'You know, I was thinking.'

'What were you thinking, Piet?'

'That VIXAL must have extrapolated a general market collapse.'

'You don't say.'

But van der Zyl missed the sarcasm. 'Yes, because if you look at the stocks it's shorting—what are they? Resorts and casinos, management consulting, food and household goods, all the others—these are just right across the board. They are not at all sector-specific.'

'Then there is the short on the S and P,' said Ju-Long, 'and the out-of-the-money puts . . .'

'And the Fear Index,' added van der Zyl. 'You know, a billion dollars of options on the Fear Index—my God!'

It certainly was a hell of a lot, thought Quarry. He came to a halt. In fact, it was more than a hell of a lot. Until that moment, in the general welter of data that had been thrown around, he had rather missed the significance of the size of that position. He stepped across to a vacant terminal, bent over the keyboard and quickly called up a chart of the VIX. Ju-Long and van der Zyl joined him. The graphic showed a gentle wave pattern in the value of the volatility index as it had fluctuated over the past two trading days, the line rising and falling inside a narrow range. However within the last ninety minutes it had definitely started trending upwards: from a base of around twenty-four points at the US opening, it had now climbed to almost twenty-seven. It was too early to say whether this marked a significant escalation in the level of fear in the market itself. Nevertheless, even if it didn't, on a billion-dollar punt, they were looking at almost a hundred million in profit right there. Once again Quarry felt a cold tremble run down his back.

He pressed a switch and picked up the live audio feed from the pit of the S&P 500 in Chicago. It was a service they subscribed to. It gave them an immediate feel for the market you couldn't always get from just the figures. 'Guys,' an American voice

233

was saying, 'the only buyer I have on my sheet here, guys, from about nine twenty-six on, is a Goldman buyer at fifty-one even two hundred and fifty times. Other than that, guys, every entry I have has been sell-side activity, guys. Merrill Lynch I had big-time seller. Pru Bache I had big-time seller, guys, all the way from fifty-nine to fifty-three. And then we saw Swiss Bank and Smith coming in big-time sellers—'

Quarry switched it off. He said, 'LJ, why don't you make a start on liquidating that two-point-five billion in T-bills, just in case we need to show some collateral tomorrow?'

'Sure, Hugo.' His eyes met Quarry's. He had seen the significance of the movement in the VIX; so had van der Zyl.

'We should try to talk to one another at least every half hour,' said Quarry.

'And Alex?' said Ju-Long. 'He ought to see this. He would be able to make some sense of it.'

'I know Alex. He'll be back, don't you worry.'

The three men went their separate ways—like conspirators, thought Quarry.

14

Only the paranoid survive.

ANDREW S. GROVE, president and CEO of Intel
Corporation

Hoffmann had managed to hail a taxi on the Rue
de Lausanne, one block away from the Hotel
Diodati. Afterwards the taxi driver remembered the
fare distinctly for three reasons. First because he
was driving towards the Avenue de France at the
time and Hoffmann needed to go in the opposite
direction—he asked to be taken to an address in the
suburb of Vernier, close to a local park—which
meant he had to perform an illegal U-turn across
several lanes of traffic. And second because
Hoffmann had seemed so edgy and preoccupied.
When they passed a police car heading in the
opposite direction, he had sunk low in his seat and
put up his hand to shield his eyes. The driver had
watched him in the mirror. He was clutching a
laptop. His phone rang once but he didn't answer it;
afterwards he turned it off.

A sharp breeze was stiffening the flags above the
official buildings; the temperature was barely half
what the guidebooks promised for the time of year.
It felt as if rain was coming. People had deserted
the pavements and taken to their cars, thickening
the mid-afternoon traffic. Consequently it was after
four when the taxi finally approached the centre of
Vernier, and Hoffmann abruptly leaned forward
and said, 'Let me out here.' He handed over a

235

one-hundred-franc note and walked away without waiting for the change: that was the third reason the driver remembered him.

Vernier stands on hilly ground above the right bank of the Rhône. A generation ago it was a separate village, before the city spread across the river to claim it. Now the modern apartment blocks are close enough to the airport for their occupants to be able to read the names on the sides of the descending jets. Still, there are parts of the centre that retain the character of a traditional Swiss village, with overhanging roofs and green wooden shutters, and it was this aspect of the place that had stayed in Hoffmann's mind for the past nine years. In his memory he associated it with melancholy autumn afternoons, the street lights just starting to switch on, children coming out of school. He turned a corner and found the circular wooden bench where he used to sit when he was early for his appointments. It girdled a sinister old tree in vigorous leaf. Seeing it again, he couldn't bear to approach it but kept to the opposite side of the square. Nothing much else had changed: the laundry, the cycle shop, the dingy little café in which the old men gathered, the chapel-like *maison d'artisant communal*. Next to it was the detached building where he was supposed to have been cured. It had been a shop once, a greengrocer's maybe, or a florist's—something useful; the owners would have lived above the premises. Now its large downstairs window was frosted and it looked like a dentist's surgery. The only difference from eight years ago was the video camera that covered the front door: that was new, he thought.

Hoffmann's hand shook as he pressed the

buzzer. Did he have the strength to go through it all again? The first time he hadn't known what to expect; now he would be deprived of the vital armour of ignorance.

A young man's voice said, 'Good afternoon.'

Hoffmann gave his name. 'I used to be a patient of Dr Polidori. My secretary was supposed to make an appointment for tomorrow.'

'I'm afraid Dr Polidori spends every Friday seeing her patients at the hospital.'

'Tomorrow is too late. I need to see her now.'

'You can't see her without an appointment.'

'Tell her it's me. Say it's urgent.'

'What name was it again?'

'Hoffmann.'

'Wait, please.'

The entryphone went dead. Hoffmann glanced up at the camera and instinctively raised his hand to cover his head from view. His wound was no longer tacky with blood but powdery: when he inspected his fingertips, they were covered with what looked like fine particles of rust.

'Come in, please.' There was a brief buzz as the door was unlocked—so brief that Hoffmann missed it and had to try a second time. Inside it was more comfortable than it used to be—a sofa and two easy chairs, a rug in soothing pastel, rubber plants, and behind the head of the receptionist a large photograph of a woodland glade with shafts of light falling from between the trees. Next to it was her certificate to practise: Dr Jeanne Polidori, with a master's degree in psychiatry and psychotherapy from the University of Geneva. Another camera scanned the room. The young man at the desk scrutinised him carefully. 'Go on up. It's the door

237

straight ahead.'

'Yes,' said Hoffmann. 'I remember.'

The familiar creak of the stairs was enough to unleash a flood of old sensations. Sometimes he had found it almost impossible to drag himself to the top; on the worst days he had felt like a man without oxygen trying to climb Everest. Depression wasn't the word for it; burial was more accurate— entombment in a thick, cold concrete chamber, beyond the reach of light or sound. Now he was sure he could not endure it again. He would rather kill himself.

She was in her consulting room, sitting at her computer, and stood as he came in. She was the same age as Hoffmann and must have been good-looking when she was younger, but she had a narrow gully that ran from just below her left ear down her cheek all the way to her throat. The loss of muscle and tissue had given her a lopsided look, as if she had suffered a stroke. Usually she wore a scarf; today not. In his artless way he had asked her about it once: 'What the hell happened to your face?' She told him she had been attacked by a patient who had been instructed by God to kill her. The man had now fully recovered. But she had kept a pepper spray in her desk ever since: she had opened the drawer and showed it to Hoffmann—a black can with a nozzle.

She wasted no time on a greeting. 'Dr Hoffmann, I'm sorry, but I told your assistant on the phone I can't treat you without a referral from the hospital.'

'I don't want you to treat me.' He opened the laptop. 'I just want you to look at something. Can you do that at least?'

'It depends what it is.' She scrutinised him more

closely. 'What happened to your head?'

'We had an intruder in our house. He hit me from behind.'

'Have you been treated?'

Hoffmann bent his head forward and showed her his stitches.

'When did this happen?'

'Last night. This morning.'

'You went to the University Hospital?'

'Yes.'

'Did they give you a CAT scan?'

He nodded. 'They found some white spots. They could have come from the hit I took, or it could have been something else—pre-existing.'

'Dr Hoffmann,' she said more gently, 'it sounds to me as though you *are* asking me to treat you.'

'No, I'm not.' He set the laptop down in front of her. 'I just want your opinion about this.'

She looked at him dubiously then reached for her glasses. She still kept them on a chain around her neck, he noticed. She put them on and peered at the screen. As she scrolled through the document, he watched her expression. The ugliness of the scar somehow emphasised the beauty of the rest of her face—he remembered that as well. The day he recognised it was the day in his own opinion that he started to recover.

'Well,' she said with a shrug, 'this is a conversation between two men, obviously, one who fantasises about killing and the other who dreams of dying and what the experience of death would be like. It's stilted, awkward: I would guess an internet chat room, a website—something like that. The one who wants to kill isn't very fluent in English; the would-be victim is.' She glanced at him over her

239

glasses. 'I don't see what I'm telling you that you couldn't have worked out for yourself.'

'Is this sort of thing common?'

'Absolutely, and every day more so. It's one of the darker aspects of the web we now have to cope with. The internet brings together people who in earlier years thankfully would not have had the opportunity to meet—who might not even have known they had these dangerous predilections—and the results can be catastrophic. I have been consulted by the police about it several times. There are websites that encourage suicide pacts, especially among young people. There are paedophile websites, of course. Cannibal websites . . .'

Hoffmann sat down and put his head in his hands. He said, 'The man who fantasises about death—that's me, isn't it?'

'Well, you would know, Dr Hoffmann, better than I. Do you not remember writing this?'

'No, I don't. And yet there are thoughts there I recognise as mine—dreams I had when I was ill. I seem to have done other things lately I can't remember.' He looked at her. 'Could I have some problem in my brain that's causing this, do you think? That makes me do things, out-of-character things, that I have no memory of afterwards?'

'It's possible.' She put the laptop to one side and turned to her own computer screen. She typed something and clicked on a mouse several times. 'I see you terminated your treatment with me in November 2001 without any explanation. Why was that?'

'I was cured.'

'Don't you think that was for me to decide,

240

rather than you?'

'No, I don't actually. I'm not a kid. I know when I'm well. I've been fine now for years. I got married. I started a company. Everything has been fine. Until this started.'

'You might feel fine, but I'm afraid major depressive disorders like the one you had can recur.' She scrolled down his case notes, shaking her head. 'I see it's eight and a half years since your last consultation. You'll have to remind me what it was that triggered your illness in the first place.'

Hoffmann had kept it quarantined in his mind for so long, it was an effort to recall it. 'I had some serious difficulties in my research at CERN. There was an internal inquiry, which was very stressful. In the end they closed down the project I was working on.'

'What was the project?'

'Machine reasoning—artificial intelligence.'

'And have you been under a lot of similar stress recently?'

'Some,' he admitted.

'What sort of depressive symptoms have you had?'

'None. That's what's so weird.'

'Lethargy? Insomnia?'

'No.'

'Impotence?'

He thought of Gabrielle. He wondered where she was. He said quietly, 'No.'

'What about the suicidal fantasies you used to have? They were very vivid, very detailed—any recurrence there?'

'No.'

'This man who attacked you—am I to take it he

is the other participant in the conversation on the internet?'

Hoffmann nodded.

'Where is he now?'

'I'd prefer not to go into that.'

'Dr Hoffmann, where is he now?' When he still wouldn't answer, she said, 'Show me your hands, please.'

Reluctantly he stood and approached her desk. He held out his hands. He felt like a child again, being made to prove he had washed before sitting down to eat. She examined his broken skin without touching it, then carefully looked him over.

'You have been in a fight?'

He took a long time to reply. 'Yes. It was self-defence.'

'That's all right. Sit down again, please.'

He did as he was told.

She said, 'In my opinion, you need to be seen by a specialist right away. There are certain disorders—schizophrenia, paranoia—that can lead the sufferer to act in ways that are entirely out of character and which afterwards they simply can't remember. That may not apply in your case, but I don't think we can take a chance, do you? Especially if there are abnormalities on your brain scan.'

'Maybe not.'

'So what I would like you to do now is take a seat downstairs while I talk to my colleague. Perhaps you could call your wife and tell her where you are. Is that all right with you?'

'Yeah, sure.'

He waited for her to show him out, but she remained watchful behind her desk. Eventually he stood and picked up the laptop. 'Thanks,' he said. 'I'll go down to reception.'

'Good. It should only take a few minutes.'

At the door, he turned. A thought had occurred to him. 'Those are my records you're looking at.'

'They are.'

'They're on computer?'

'Yes. They always have been. Why?'

'What exactly is in them?'

'My case notes. A record of treatment—drugs prescribed, psychotherapy sessions and so on.'

'Do you tape your sessions with your patients?'

She hesitated. 'Some.'

'Mine?'

Another hesitation. 'Yes.'

'And then what happens?'

'My assistant transcribes them.'

'And you keep the records on computer.'

'Yes.'

'May I see?' He was over at her desk in a couple of strides.

'No. Certainly not.'

She quickly put her hand on the mouse to close the document, but he grabbed her wrist.

'Please, just let me look at my own file.'

He had to prise the mouse away from her. Her hand shot towards the drawer where she kept the pepper spray. He blocked it with his leg.

He said, 'I'm not going to hurt you. I just need to check what I told you. Give me a minute to look at my records and I'll go.'

He felt bad seeing the fear in her eyes, but he would not yield, and after a couple of seconds she surrendered. She pushed her chair back and stood. He took her place in front of the screen. She moved

243

to a safe distance and watched him from the doorway, drawing her cardigan tight around herself as if she were feeling cold. She said, 'Where did you get that laptop?' But he wasn't listening. He was comparing the two screens, scrolling down first one and then the other, and it was as if he were looking at himself in two dark mirrors. The words on each were identical. Everything that he had poured out to her nine years ago had been cut and pasted and put up on to the website where the German had read it.

He said, without looking up, 'Is this computer connected to the internet?' and then he saw that it was. He went into the system registry. It didn't take him long to find the malware—strange files of a type he had never seen before, four of them:

u‖2Sq.50‡

/s├■.╫

5⌐qpj.0⊤

⌐╚⁊σɛ‖.o

He said, 'Someone's hacked into your system. They've stolen my records.' He glanced over to where she had been standing. The consulting room was empty, the door ajar. He could hear her voice somewhere. It sounded as though she was on the telephone. He seized the laptop and thumped his way down the narrow carpeted staircase. The receptionist came round from behind his desk and tried to block his exit, but Hoffmann had no trouble pushing him aside.

Outside, the normality of the day mocked him—the old guys drinking in the café, the mother with her pram, the au pair picking up the laundry. He turned left and walked quickly down the leafy street, past the drab shuttered houses opening directly on to the pavement, past the patisserie now closed for the day and the suburban hedges and the sensible small cars. He did not know where he was going. Normally he found that when he exercised—walked, jogged, ran—it focused his thoughts, stimulated his creativity. Not now. His mind was in turmoil. He began descending a hill. There were allotments to his left and then, amazingly, open fields, a huge factory spread out beneath him with a car park, apartment blocks, mountains in the distance, and above him a hemispheric sky filled with an immense grey flotilla of clouds processing like battleships in review.

After a while the road was sliced off by the concrete wall of an elevated autoroute. The road dwindled to a footpath that wandered left alongside the thunderous motorway, taking him down through some trees until he emerged on to the bank of the river. The Rhône was wide and slow at this point, perhaps two hundred metres from shore to shore, greenish-brown, opaque, bending lazily into open country with woodland rising steeply on the opposite bank. A footbridge, the Passerelle de Chèvres, linked the two sides. He recognised it. He had driven past and seen kids jumping off it in summer to cool down. The peacefulness of the view was in weird contrast with the roar of traffic, and as Hoffmann walked out on to the central span, it seemed to him that he had now fallen far outside the run of normal life: that it would be hard for him

245

to get back. At the mid-point of the bridge, he stopped and climbed up on to the metal safety barrier. It would take him only a couple of seconds to drop the five or six metres into the slow-moving current and let himself be borne away. He could see why Switzerland was the world centre for assisted suicide—the whole country seemed organised to encourage one to disappear with privacy and discretion, causing as little trouble as possible.

And he was tempted. He was under no illusions: there would be a mass of DNA and fingerprint evidence in the hotel room linking him to the killing; his arrest was only a matter of time, whatever happened. He thought of what awaited him—a long gauntlet of police, lawyers, journalists, flashing cameras, stretching months into the future. He thought of Quarry, Gabrielle—Gabrielle especially.

But I am not mad, he thought. I may have killed a man *but I am not mad*. I am either the victim of an elaborate plot to make me *think* I am mad, or someone is trying to set me up, blackmail me, destroy me. He asked himself: did he trust the authorities—that pedantic has-been Leclerc, for example—to get to the bottom of such a fiendishly elaborate entrapment any better than he? The question answered itself.

He took the German's mobile phone out of his pocket. It hit the river with barely a splash, leaving a brief white scar on the muddy surface.

On the far bank some children were standing beside their bikes, watching him. He clambered down and crossed the remainder of the bridge and walked straight past them carrying the laptop. He expected them to call out after him, but they

246

remained solemn-faced and silent, and he sensed there might be something in his appearance that was frightening to them.

*　　　*　　　*

Gabrielle had never before set foot in CERN, and immediately it reminded her of her old university in northern England—ugly functional office blocks from the sixties and seventies spread over a big campus, scruffy corridors filled with earnest-looking people, mostly young, talking in front of posters advertising lectures and concerts. It even had the same academic odour of floor polish, body heat and canteen food. She could picture Alex at home here far more comfortably than she could in the smart offices of Les Eaux-Vives.

Professor Walton's assistant had left her in the lobby of the Computing Centre and gone off to find him. Now she was alone, she was strongly tempted to flee. What had seemed a good idea in the bathroom in Cologny after finding his card—calling him, ignoring his surprise, asking if she could come over right away: she would tell him what it was about when she saw him—now struck her as hysterical and embarrassing. Turning round to find the way out, she noticed an old computer in a glass case. When she went closer, she read that it was the NeXT processor that had started the World Wide Web at CERN in 1991. The original note to the cleaners was still stuck to its black metal casing: 'This machine is a server—DO NOT POWER DOWN!' Extraordinary, she thought, that it had all begun with something so mundane.

'Pandora's Box,' said a voice behind her, and she

turned to find Walton; she wondered how long he had been watching her. 'Or the Law of Unintended Consequences. You start off trying to create the origins of the universe and you end up creating eBay. Come to my office. I don't have long, I'm afraid.'

'Are you sure? I don't want to trouble you. I can always come back another time.'

'That's all right.' He looked at her carefully. 'Is it about making art out of particle physics, or is it by any chance about Alex?'

'Actually it's Alex.'

'I thought it might be.'

He led her down a corridor lined with pictures of old computers and into an office block. It was dingy, functional—frosted-glass doors, too-bright strip lighting, institutional lino, grey paintwork—not at all what she had expected for the home of the Large Hadron Collider. But again she could imagine Alex here very easily: it was certainly a much more characteristic habitat of the man she had married than his present interior-designed, leather-upholstered, first-edition-lined study in Cologny.

'So this is where the great man used to sleep,' said Walton, throwing open the door of a spartan cell with two desks, two terminals and a view over a car park.

'Sleep?'

'Work, too, in fairness. Twenty hours of work a day, four hours of sleep. He used to roll out his mattress in that corner.' He smiled faintly at the memory and turned his solemn grey eyes upon her. 'Alex had already gone from here, I think, by the time you met him at our little New Year's Eve

248

party—or was going, anyway. There's a problem, I assume.'

'Yes, there is.'

He nodded, as if expecting it. 'Come and sit down.' He led her along the passage to his office. It was identical to the other, except that there was only one desk, and Walton had humanised it somewhat—put down an old Persian carpet on the lino and some plants along the rusting metal windowsill. On top of the filing cabinet a radio was quietly playing classical music, a string quartet. He switched it off. 'So, how can I help?'

'Tell me what he was doing here, what went wrong. I gather he had a breakdown, and I have a bad feeling it's happening all over again. I'm sorry.' She looked down at her lap. 'I don't know who else to ask.'

Walton was sitting behind his desk. He had made a steeple of his long fingers and had it pressed to his lips. He studied her for a while. Eventually he said, 'Have you ever heard of the Desertron?'

*   *   *

The Desertron, said Walton, was supposed to be America's Superconducting Super Collider— eighty-seven kilometres of tunnel being dug out of the rock at Waxahachie, Texas. But in 1993 the US Congress, in its infinite wisdom, voted to abandon construction. That saved the US taxpayer about $10 billion. ('There must have been dancing in the streets.') However, it also pretty much wiped out the career plans of an entire generation of American academic physicists, including those of the brilliant young Alex Hoffmann, then finishing

249

his PhD at Princeton.

In the end Alex was one of the lucky ones—he was only twenty-five or thereabouts, but already sufficiently renowned to be awarded one of the very few non-European scholarships to work at CERN on the Large Electron–Positron Collider, forerunner of the Large Hadron Collider. Most of his colleagues unfortunately had to go off and become quants on Wall Street, where they helped build derivatives rather than particle accelerators. And when *that* went wrong and the banking system imploded, Congress had to rescue it, at a cost to the US taxpayer of $3.7 trillion.

'Which is another example of the Law of Unintended Consequences,' said Walton. 'Did you know Alex offered me a job about five years ago?'

'No.'

'This was before the banking crisis. I told him that in my view high-end science and money don't mix. It's an unstable compound. I may have used the words "dark arts". I'm afraid we fell out all over again.'

Gabrielle, nodding eagerly, said, 'I know what you mean. It's a sort of tension. I've always been aware of it in him, but especially lately.'

'That's it. Over the years I've known quite a few who've made the crossover from pure science to making money—none as successfully as Alex, I admit—and you can always tell, just by how loudly they insist the opposite, that secretly they despise themselves.'

He looked pained by what had happened to his profession, as if they had somehow fallen from a state of grace, and again Gabrielle was reminded of a priest. There was an other-worldly quality to him,

250

as there was to Alex.

She had to prompt him. 'But about the nineties ...'

'Yes, so anyway, back to the nineties ...'

Alex had arrived in Geneva only a couple of years after CERN's scientists had invented the World Wide Web. And oddly enough, it was that which had seized his imagination: not re-creating the Big Bang or finding the God particle or creating antimatter, but the possibilities of serial processing power, emergent machine reasoning, a global brain.

'He was a romantic on the subject—always dangerous. I was his section head at the Computing Centre. Maggie and I helped him get on his feet a bit. He used to babysit our boys when they were small. He was hopeless at it.'

'I bet.' She bit her lip at the thought of Alex with children.

'Completely *hopeless*. We'd come home and find him upstairs asleep in their beds and them downstairs watching television. He was always pushing himself far too hard, exhausting himself. He had this obsession with artificial intelligence, although he disliked the hubristic connotations of AI and preferred to call it AMR—autonomous machine reasoning. Are you very technically minded?'

'No, not at all.'

'Isn't that difficult, being married to Alex?'

'To be honest, I think the opposite. It's what makes it work.' *Or did*, she nearly added. It was the self-absorbed mathematician—his social artlessness, the strange innocence of him—that she had fallen in love with; it was the new Alex, the billionaire hedge-fund president, she found difficult

251

to take.

'Well, without getting too technical about it, one of the big challenges we face here is simply analysing the sheer amount of experimental data we produce. It's now running around twenty-seven trillion bytes each day. Alex's solution was to invent an algorithm that would learn what to look for, so to speak, and then teach itself what to look for next. That would make it able to work infinitely faster than a human being. It was theoretically brilliant, but a practical disaster.'

'So it didn't work?'

'Oh yes, it worked. That was the disaster. It started spreading through the system like bindweed. Eventually we had to quarantine it, which meant basically shutting everything down. I'm afraid I had to tell Alex that that particular line of research was too unstable to be continued. It would require containment, like nuclear technology, otherwise one was effectively just unleashing a virus. He wouldn't accept it. Things became quite ugly for a while. He had to be forcibly removed from the facility on one occasion.'

'And that was when he had his breakdown?'

Walton nodded sadly. 'I never saw a man so desolate. You would've thought I'd murdered his child.'

15

*As I was considering these issues . . . a new concept
popped into my head: 'the digital nervous system' . . .*

*A digital nervous system consists of the digital
processes that enable a company to perceive and react
to its environment, to sense competitor challenges and
customer needs, and to organise timely responses . . .*

BILL GATES, *Business at the Speed of Light* (2000)

By the time Hoffmann reached his office, it was the
end of the working day—about 6.00 p.m. in Geneva,
noon in New York. People were coming from the
building, heading for home or a drink or the gym.
He stood in a doorway opposite and checked for
any sign of the police, and when he was satisfied
they were not in evidence he went loping across the
street, stared bleakly at the facial scanner and was
admitted, passed straight through the lobby, up in
one of the elevators, and on to the trading floor.
The place was still full; most people did not leave
their desks until eight. He put his head down and
headed for his office, trying not to notice the
curious looks he was attracting. Sitting at her desk,
Marie-Claude watched him approach. She opened
her mouth to speak and Hoffmann held up his
hands. 'I know,' he said. 'I need ten minutes on my
own and then I'll deal with all of it. Don't let anyone
in, okay?'

He went inside and closed the door. He sat in his
expensive orthopaedic chair with its state-of-the-art
tilt mechanism and opened the German's laptop.

Who had hacked into his medical records—that was the question. Whoever it was must be behind everything else. It baffled him. He had never thought of himself as a man with enemies. It was true he did not have friends; but the corollary of his solitariness, he had always assumed, was that he did not have enemies either.

His head was hurting again. He ran his fingers over the shaved area; it felt like the stitching on a football. His shoulders were locked with tension. He started massaging his neck, leaning back in his chair and looking up at the smoke detector as he had done a thousand times before when he was trying to focus his thoughts. He contemplated the tiny red light, identical to the one on their bedroom ceiling in Cologny that always made him think of Mars as he fell asleep. Slowly he stopped massaging. 'Shit,' he whispered.

He sat up straight and looked at the screensaver image on the laptop: the picture of himself, gazing up with a vacant, unfocused expression. He clambered on to his chair. It shifted treacherously beneath his feet as he stepped from it on to his desk. The smoke detector was square, made of white plastic, with a carbon-sensitive plate, a light to show that it was receiving power, a test button and a grille that presumably covered the alarm itself. He felt around the edges. It seemed to be glued to the ceiling tile. He pulled at it and twisted it, and finally in fear and frustration he grasped it hard and yanked it free.

The screech of protest it set up was physical in its intensity. The casing trembled in his hands, the air pulsed with it. It was still connected to the ceiling by an umbilical cord of wire, and when he put his fingers into the back of it to try to shut it down, he received an electric shock that was as vicious as an animal bite; it travelled all the way to his heart. He cried out, dropped it, let it dangle, and shook his fingers vigorously as if drying them. The noise was a physical assault: he felt his ears would bleed unless he stopped it quickly. He grabbed the detector by the casing this time and pulled with all his weight, almost swinging on it, and away it came, bringing down a chunk of the ceiling with it. The sudden silence was as shocking as the din.

*   *   *

Much later, when Quarry found himself reliving the next couple of hours, and when he was asked which moment for him had been the most frightening, he said that oddly enough it was this one: when he heard the alarm and went running from one end of the trading floor to the other, to find Hoffmann— the only man who fully understood an algorithm that was even now making a thirty-billion-dollar unhedged bet—flecked with blood, covered in dust, standing on a desk beneath a hole in his ceiling, gabbling that he was being spied upon wherever he went.

Quarry was not the first on the scene. The door was already open and Marie-Claude was inside with some of the quants. Quarry shouldered his way past them and ordered them all to get back to their work. He could tell at once, craning his neck, even from that angle, that Hoffmann had been through some kind of trauma. His eyes were wild, his clothes dishevelled. There was dried blood in his hair. His hands looked as if he had been punching concrete.

He said, as calmly as he could, 'Okay then, Alexi, how's it going up there?'

'Look for yourself,' cried Hoffmann excitedly. He jumped down from the desk and held out his palm. On it were the components of the dismantled smoke alarm. He poked through them with his forefinger as if he were a naturalist inspecting the innards of some dead creature. He held up a small lens with a bit of wire trailing from the back. 'Do you know what that is?'

'I'm not sure that I do, no.'

'It's a webcam.' He let the dismantled pieces trickle through his fingers and across his desk; some rolled to the floor. 'Look at this.' He gave Quarry the laptop. He tapped the screen. 'Where do you think that picture was taken from?'

He sat down again and lolled back in his chair. Quarry looked at him and then at the screen and back again. He glanced up at the ceiling. 'Bloody hell. Where did you get this?'

'It belonged to the guy who attacked me last night.'

Even at the time Quarry registered the odd use of the past tense—*belonged?*—and wondered how the laptop had come into Hoffmann's possession. There was no time to ask, however, as Hoffmann jumped to his feet. His mind was running away with him now. He couldn't stay still. 'Come,' he said, beckoning. 'Come.' He led Quarry by the elbow out of his office and pointed to the ceiling above Marie-Claude's desk, where there was an identical detector. He put his finger to his lips. Then he took him to the edge of the trading floor and showed him—one, two, three, four more. There was one in

256

the boardroom, too. There was even one in the men's room. He climbed up on to the wash basins. He could just reach it. He pulled hard and it came away in a shower of plaster. He jumped down and showed it to Quarry. Another webcam. 'They're everywhere. I've been noticing them for months without ever really seeing them. There'll be one in your office. I've got one in every room at home— even in the bedroom. Christ. Even in the *bathroom*.' He put his hand to his brow, only just registering the scale of it himself. 'Unbelievable.'

Quarry had always had a sneaking fear that their rivals might be trying to spy on them: it was certainly what he would do in their shoes. That was why he had hired Genoud's security consultancy. He turned the detector over in his hands, appalled. 'You think there's a camera in *all* of them?'

'Well, we can check them out, but yeah—yeah, I do.'

'My God, and yet we pay a fortune to Genoud to sweep this place for bugs.'

'But that's the beauty of it—he must be the guy who put all this in, don't you see? He did my house too, when I bought it. He's got us under twenty-four-hour-a-day surveillance. Look.' Hoffmann took out his mobile phone. 'He organised these as well, didn't he—our specially encrypted phones?' He broke it open—for some reason Quarry was reminded of a man cracking lobster claws—and quickly disassembled it beside one of the wash basins. 'It's the perfect bugging device. You don't even need to put in a microphone—it's got one built in. I read about it in the *Wall Street Journal*. You think you've turned it off, but actually it's always active, picking up your conversations even

257

when you're not on the phone. And you keep it charged all the time. Mine's been acting strange all day.'

He was so certain he was right, Quarry found his paranoia contagious. He examined his own phone gingerly, as if it were a grenade that might explode in his hand, then used it to call his assistant. 'Amber, would you please track down Maurice Genoud and get him over here right away? Tell him to drop whatever else he's doing and come to Alex's office.' He hung up. 'Let's hear what the bastard has to say. I never did trust him. I wonder what his game is.'

'That's pretty obvious, isn't it? We're a hedge fund returning an eighty-three per cent profit. If someone set up a clone of us, copying all our trades, they'd make a fortune. They wouldn't even need to know how we were doing it. It's obvious why they'd want to spy on us. The only thing I don't understand is why he's done all this other stuff.'

'What other stuff?'

'Set up an offshore account in the Cayman Islands, transferred money in and out of it, sent emails in my name, bought me a book full of stuff about fear and terror, sabotaged Gabby's exhibition, hacked into my medical records and hooked me up with a psychopath. It's like he's been paid to drive me mad.'

Listening to him, Quarry started to feel uneasy again, but before he could say anything his phone rang. It was Amber.

'Mr Genoud was only just downstairs. He's on his way up.'

'Thanks.' He said to Hoffmann, 'Apparently he's in the building already. That's odd, isn't it? What's he doing here? Maybe he knows we're on to him.'

'Maybe.' Suddenly Hoffmann was on the move once more—out of the men's room, across the passage, into his office. Another idea had occurred to him. He wrenched open the drawer of his desk and pulled out the book Quarry had seen him bring in that morning: the volume of Darwin he had called him about at midnight.

'Look at this,' he said, flicking through the pages. He held it up, open at a photograph of an old man seemingly terrified out of his wits—a grotesque picture, Quarry thought, like something out of a freak show. 'What do you see?'

'I see some Victorian lunatic who looks like he just shat a brick.'

'Yeah, but look again. Do you see these calipers?'

Quarry looked. A pair of hands, one on either side of the face, was applying thin metal rods to the forehead. The victim's head was supported in some kind of steel headrest; he seemed to be wearing a surgical gown. 'Of course I see them.'

'The calipers are being applied by a French doctor called Guillaume-Benjamin-Armand Duchenne. He believed that the expressions of the human face are the gateway to the soul. He's animating the facial muscles by using what the Victorians called galvanism—their word for electricity produced by acid reaction. They often used it to make the legs of a dead frog jump, a party trick.' He waited for Quarry to see the importance of what he was saying, and when he continued to look baffled, he added: 'It's an experiment to induce the facial symptoms of fear for the purpose of recording them on camera.'

259

'Okay,' said Quarry cautiously. 'I get it.'

Hoffmann waved the book in exasperation. 'Well, isn't that exactly what's been happening to *me*? This is the only illustration in the book where you can actually see the calipers—in all the others, Darwin had them removed. I'm the subject of an experiment designed to make me experience fear, and my reactions are being continuously monitored.'

After a moment when he could not entirely trust himself to speak, Quarry said, 'Well, I'm very sorry to hear that, Alexi. That must be a horrible feeling.'

'The question is: who's doing it, and why? Obviously it's not Genoud's idea. He's just the tool . . .'

But now it was Quarry's turn not to pay attention. He was thinking of his responsibilities as CEO—to their investors, to their employees and (he was not ashamed to admit it afterwards) to himself. He was remembering Hoffmann's medicine cabinet all those years ago, filled with enough mind-altering drugs to keep a junkie happy for six months, and his specific instruction to Rajamani not to minute any concerns about the company president's mental health. He was wondering what would happen if any of this became public. 'Let's sit down,' he suggested. 'We need to talk about a few things.'

Hoffmann was irritated to be interrupted in mid-flow. 'Is it urgent?'

'It is rather, yes.' Quarry took a seat on the sofa and gestured to Hoffmann to join him.

But Hoffmann ignored the sofa and went and sat behind his desk. He swept his arm across the surface, clearing it of the detritus of the smoke

260

detector. 'Okay, go ahead. Just don't say anything till you've taken the battery out of your phone.'

*   *   *

Hoffmann wasn't surprised that Quarry had failed to grasp the significance of the Darwin book. All his life he had seen things faster than other people; that was why he had been obliged to pass so many of his days on long and lonely solo voyages of the mind. Eventually others around him caught up, but by then he was generally off travelling somewhere else.

He watched as Quarry dismantled his phone and placed the battery carefully on the coffee table.

Quarry said, 'We have a problem with VIXAL-4.'

'What kind of a problem?'

'It's taken off the delta hedge.'

Hoffmann stared at him. 'Don't be ridiculous.' He pulled his keyboard towards him, logged on to his terminal and began going through their positions—by sector, size, type, date. The mouse clicks were as rapid as Morse code, and each screen they brought up was more astonishing to him than the last. He said, 'But this is all completely out of whack. This isn't what it's programmed to do.'

'Most of it happened between lunchtime and the US opening. We couldn't get hold of you. The good news is that it's guessing right—so far. The Dow is off by about a hundred, and if you look at the P and L we're up by over two hundred mil on the day.'

'*But it's not what it's supposed to do,*' repeated Hoffmann. Of course there would be a rational explanation: there always was. He would find it

261

eventually. It had to be linked to everything else that was happening to him. 'Okay, first off, are we sure this data is correct? Can we actually trust what's on these screens? Or could it be sabotage of some kind? A virus?' He was remembering the malware on his psychiatrist's computer. 'Maybe the whole company is under cyber-attack by someone, or some group—have we thought of that?'

'Maybe we are, but that doesn't explain the short on Vista Airways—and believe me, that's starting to look like somewhat more than a coincidence.'

'Yeah, well it can't be. We've already been over this—'

Quarry cut him off impatiently. 'I know we have, but the story's changed as the day's gone on. Now it seems the crash wasn't caused by mechanical failure after all. Apparently there was a bomb warning put up on some Islamic terrorist website while the plane was in the air. The FBI missed it; we didn't.'

Hoffmann couldn't take it in at first: too much information was coming at him too quickly. 'But that's way outside VIXAL's parameters. That would be an extraordinary inflection point—a quantum leap.'

'I thought it was a machine-learning algorithm.'

'That's right.'

'Then maybe it's learned something.'

'Don't be an idiot, Hugo. It doesn't work like that.'

'Okay, so it doesn't work like that. Fine, I'm not the expert. The fact is, we have to make a decision rather quickly here. Either we override VIXAL or we're going to have to put up two-point-five bil tomorrow afternoon just so the banks will let us continue trading.'

Marie-Claude tapped on the door and opened it. 'Monsieur Genoud is here.'

Quarry said to Hoffmann, 'Let me handle this.' He felt as if he were in some kind of arcade game, everything flying at him at once.

Marie-Claude stood aside to let the ex-policeman enter. His gaze went immediately to the hole in the ceiling.

'Come in, Maurice,' said Quarry. 'Close the door. As you can see, we've been doing a little DIY in here, and we were wondering if you have any explanation for this.'

'I don't believe so,' said Genoud, shutting the door. 'Why should I?'

Hoffmann said, 'By God, he's a cool one, Hugo. You've got to give him that.'

Quarry held up his hand. 'Okay, Alex, please just wait a minute, will you? All right, Maurice. No bullshit now. We need to know how long this has been going on. We need to know who's paying you. And we need to know if you've planted anything inside our computer systems. It's urgent, because we're in a very volatile trading situation. Now we don't want to call in the police to handle this, but we will if we have to. So it's over to you, and my advice is to be absolutely frank.'

After a few moments Genoud looked at Hoffmann. 'Is it okay for me to tell him?'

Hoffmann said, 'Okay to tell him what?'

'You are putting me in a very awkward position, Dr Hoffmann.'

Hoffmann said to Quarry, 'I don't know what he's talking about.'

'Very well, you can't expect me to maintain my discretion under these circumstances.' Genoud

263

turned to Quarry. 'Dr Hoffmann instructed me to do it.'

There was something about the calm insolence of the falsehood that made Hoffmann want to hit him. 'You asshole,' he said. 'D'you think anyone's going to believe that?'

Genoud continued unperturbed, addressing his remarks directly to Quarry and ignoring Hoffmann. 'It's true. He gave me instructions when you moved into these offices to set up concealed cameras. I guessed he wasn't telling you about it. But he's the company president, so I thought it was permissible for me to do as he asked. This is the absolute truth, I swear.'

Hoffmann smiled and shook his head. 'Hugo, this is total, utter bullshit. This is the same goddamned crap I've been hearing all day. I haven't had one single conversation with this guy about planting cameras—why would I want to film my own company? And why would I bug my own phone? It's total bullshit,' he repeated.

Genoud said, 'I never said we had a conversation about it. As you well know, Dr Hoffmann, I only ever received instructions from you by email.'

Email—again! Hoffmann said, 'You're seriously telling me that you put in all these cameras and never, in all these months, despite all the thousands of francs this must have cost—that never once did we have a conversation about any of it?'

'No.'

Hoffmann emitted a sound that conveyed contempt and disbelief.

Quarry said to Genoud, 'That's hardly credible. Didn't it strike you as bizarre at all?'

'Not especially. I got the impression this was all

264

off the books, so to speak. That he didn't want to acknowledge what was going on. I did try to bring it up with him once, obliquely. He looked straight through me.'

'Well I probably would, wouldn't I? I wouldn't have known what you were talking about. And how in the hell am I supposed to have paid you for all this?'

'By cash transfer,' said Genoud, 'from a bank in the Cayman Islands.'

That brought Hoffmann up short. Quarry was looking at him intently. 'Okay,' he conceded, 'supposing you did receive emails. How did you know it was me sending them and not someone pretending to be me?'

'Why would I think that? It was your company, your email address, I was paid from your bank account. And to be frank, Dr Hoffmann, you do have a reputation for being a difficult man to talk to.'

Hoffmann swore and slammed his fist on his desk in frustration. 'Here we go again. I'm supposed to have ordered a book on the internet. I'm supposed to have bought Gabrielle's entire exhibition on the internet. I'm supposed to have asked a madman to kill me on the internet . . .' He had an involuntary memory flash of the ghastly scene in the hotel, of the dead man's head lolling on its stem. He had actually forgotten about it for a few minutes. He realised Quarry was looking at him in dismay. 'Who's doing this to me, Hugo?' he said in despair. 'Doing this and filming it? You've got to help me sort this out. It's like a nightmare I'm caught in.'

Quarry's mind was reeling from it all. It took

some effort to keep his voice calm. 'Of course I'll help you, Alex. Let's just try to get to the bottom of this once and for all.' He turned back to Genoud. 'Right, Maurice, presumably you've kept these emails?'

'Naturally.'

'Can you access them now?'

'Yes, if that is what you want.' Genoud had become very stiff and formal during the last few exchanges, standing erect as if his honour as a former police officer was being called into question. Which was a bit bloody rich, thought Quarry, considering that whatever turned out to be the truth, he had set up a wholesale secret surveillance network.

'All right then, you won't mind showing them to us. Let him use your computer, Alex.'

Hoffmann rose from his seat like a man in a trance. Fragments of the smoke detector crunched beneath his feet. Reflexively he looked up at the mess he had made of the ceiling. The hole where the tile had come down opened on to a dark void. Inside, where the trailing wires were touching, a blue-white spark flashed intermittently. He thought he saw something move in the crawlspace. He closed his eyes and the imprint of the spark continued to glow as if he had been staring at the sun. A worm of suspicion began to form in his mind.

Genoud, bent over the computer, said triumphantly, 'There!'

He straightened and stood aside to let Hoffmann and Quarry examine his emails. He had filtered his saved messages so that only those from Hoffmann were listed—scores of them, dating back almost a year. Quarry took the mouse and started clicking on them at random.

'I'm afraid it's your email address on all of these, Alex,' he said. 'No question of it.'

'Yeah, I bet it is, but I still didn't send them.'

'All right, but then who did?'

Hoffmann brooded. This was beyond hacking now, or compromised security or a clone server. It was more fundamental, as if the company had somehow developed dual operating systems.

Quarry was still reading. 'I don't believe it,' he said. 'You even snooped on yourself in your own house . . .'

'Actually, I hate to keep repeating myself, but I didn't.'

'Well I'm sorry, Alexi, but you did. Listen to this: "To: Genoud. From: Hoffmann. Required Cologny webcam surveillance units twenty-four concealed immediate . . ."'

'Come on, man. I don't talk like that. Nobody talks like that.'

'Somebody must: it's here on the screen.'

Hoffmann suddenly turned to Genoud. 'Where does all the information go? What happens to the images, the audio recordings?'

Genoud said, 'As you know, it's all sent in digital streams to a secure server.'

'But there must be *thousands* of hours of it,' exclaimed Hoffmann. 'When would anyone ever have time to review it all? I certainly couldn't do it. You'd need a whole dedicated team. There aren't the hours in the day.'

Genoud shrugged. 'I don't know. I've often wondered that myself. I just did what I was ordered.'

267

Only a machine could analyse that quantity of information, thought Hoffmann. It would have to be using the latest face-recognition technology; voice-recognition as well; search tools . . .

He was interrupted by another outcry from Quarry: 'Since when did we start leasing an industrial unit in Zimeysa?'

Genoud said: 'I can tell you exactly, Mr Quarry: since six months ago. It's a big place—fifty-four Route de Clerval. Dr Hoffmann ordered a special new security and surveillance system for it.'

Hoffmann said, 'What's in this unit?'

'Computers.'

'Who put them in?'

'I don't know. A computer company.'

Hoffmann said, 'So you're not the only person I'm dealing with? I deal with entire companies by email too?'

'I don't know. Presumably, yes.'

Quarry was still clicking through the emails. 'This is unbelievable,' he said to Hoffmann. 'According to this, you also own the freehold of this entire building.'

Genoud said, 'That's true, Dr Hoffmann. You gave me the contract for security. That's why I was here this evening when you called.'

'Is this really right?' Quarry demanded. 'You own the building?'

But Hoffmann had stopped listening. He was thinking back to his time at CERN, to the memo Bob Walton had circulated to the chairmen of the CERN Experiments Committees and of the Machine Advisory Committee, recommending that Hoffmann's research project, AMR-1, be shut down. It had included a warning issued by Thomas

S. Ray, software engineer and Professor of Zoology at the University of Oklahoma: '. . . *freely evolving autonomous artificial entities should be seen as potentially dangerous to organic life, and should always be confined by some kind of containment facility, at least until their real potential is well understood . . . Evolution remains a self-interested process, and even the interests of confined digital organisms may conflict with our own.'*

He took a breath. He said, 'Hugo, I need to have a word with you—alone.'

'All right, sure. Maurice, would you mind stepping outside for a minute?'

'No, I think he should stay here and start sorting this out.' He said to Genoud, 'I want you to make a copy of the entire file of emails that originate from me. I also want a list of every job you've done that I'm supposed to have ordered. I especially want a list of everything to do with this industrial facility in Zimeysa. Then I want you to start stripping out every camera and every bug in every building we have, starting with my house. And I need it done tonight. Is that understood?'

Genoud looked to Quarry for approval. Quarry hesitated, then nodded. Genoud said curtly, 'As you wish.'

They left him to it. Once they were outside the office and the door was closed, Quarry said, 'I hope to God you've got some kind of explanation for this, Alex, because I have to tell you—'

Hoffmann held up a warning finger and raised his eyes to the smoke detector above Marie-Claude's desk.

Quarry said, with heavy emphasis, 'Oh, right, I understand. We'll go to my office.'

269

'No. Not there. It's not safe. Here . . .'

Hoffmann led him into the washroom and closed the door. The pieces of the smoke detector were where he had left them, next to the basin. He could barely recognise his own reflection in the mirror. He looked like someone who might have escaped from the secure wing of a mental hospital. He said, 'Hugo, do you think I'm insane?'

'Yes, since you ask, I bloody well do. Or probably. I don't know.'

'No, it's okay. I'm not blaming you if that's how you feel. I can see absolutely what this must look like from the outside—and what I'm about to say isn't going to make you feel any more confident.' He could hardly believe he was saying it himself. 'I think the basic problem we have here is VIXAL.'

'Lifting the delta hedge?'

'Lifting the delta hedge, but let's say also possibly doing somewhat more than I anticipated.'

Quarry squinted at him. 'What are you talking about? I don't follow . . .'

The door started to open and someone tried to come in. Quarry stopped it with his elbow. 'Not now,' he said, without taking his eyes from Hoffmann. 'Sod off and pee in a bucket, will you?'

A voice said, 'Okay, Hugo.'

Quarry closed the door and planted his back against it. 'More than you anticipated in what way?'

Hoffmann said carefully, 'VIXAL may be making decisions that are not entirely compatible with our interest.'

'You mean our interest as a company?'

'No. I mean *our* interest—the human interest.'

'Aren't they the same?'

'Not necessarily.'

270

'Sorry. Being dim here. You mean you think it's somehow actually doing all this itself—the surveillance and everything?'

In fairness to him, Hoffmann thought, Quarry at least seemed to be treating the suggestion seriously.

'I don't know. I'm not sure I am saying that. We need to take this one step at a time until we have enough information to make a full assessment. But I think as a first move we have to unwind the positions it's taken in the market. This could be quite hazardous—and not just to us.'

'Even though it's making money?'

'It's not a question of making money any more— can't you forget about money just for once?' It was becoming increasingly hard for Hoffmann to maintain his composure, but he managed to finish quietly, 'We're way beyond that now.'

Quarry folded his arms and thought it over, staring at the tiled floor. 'Are you sure you're in a fit state to be taking this kind of decision?'

'I am, really. Trust me, please, will you, if only for the sake of the last eight years? It'll be the last time, I promise you. After tonight, you'll be in charge.'

For a long moment they looked at one another, the physicist and the financier. Quarry frankly didn't know what to make of it. But as he said afterwards, in the end the company was Hoffmann's—it was his genius that had brought in the punters, his machine that had made the money in the first place, his call to shut it down. 'It's your baby,' he said. He stood clear of the door.

Hoffmann went out on to the trading floor with Quarry at his heels. It felt better to be doing something, fighting back. He clapped his hands.

'Listen up, everybody!' He climbed on to a chair so the quants could see him better. He clapped again. 'I need you all just to gather round for a minute.'

They rose from behind their screens at his command, a ghost army of PhDs. He could see their exchange of glances as they came over; some were whispering. They were obviously all on edge with what was happening. Van der Zyl came out of his office, and so did Ju-Long; he couldn't see Rajamani. He waited for a couple of stragglers from Incubation to thread their way around the desks and then he cleared his throat.

'Okay, we've obviously got a few anomalies to deal with here—to put it mildly—and I think for safety's sake we're going to have to start dismantling these positions we've built up over the last few hours.'

He checked himself. He didn't want to create a panic. He was also conscious of the smoke detectors dotted across the ceiling. Presumably everything he said was being monitored. 'This doesn't mean we have a problem with VIXAL necessarily, but we do need to go back and find out why it's been doing some of the things it has been doing. I don't know how long that's going to take, so in the meantime we need to get that delta back in line—hedge it out with longs in other markets; even liquidate if it comes to it. Just get the hell out of where we are.'

Quarry said, to Hoffmann and the room, 'We'll need to tread very carefully. If we start liquidating positions this size too quickly, we'll move prices.'

Hoffmann nodded. 'That's true, but VIXAL will help us achieve the optimums, even in override.' He looked up at the row of digital clocks beneath the giant TV screens. 'We've still got just over three hours before America closes. Imre, will you and Dieter help out with fixed income and currencies? Franco and Jon, take three or four guys each and divide up stocks and sector bets. Kolya, you do the same with the indices. Everyone else in their normal sections.'

'If you encounter any problems,' said Quarry, 'Alex and I will be here to help out. And can I just say: don't anyone think for a second that this is a retreat. We took in an additional two billion in fresh investment today—so this shop is still growing, okay? Is that clear? We'll recalibrate over the next twenty-four hours and move on to even bigger and better things. Any questions?' Someone raised their hand. 'Yep?'

'Is it true you just fired Gana Rajamani?'

Hoffmann glanced at Quarry in surprise. He'd thought he was going to wait until the crisis had passed.

Quarry didn't miss a beat. 'Gana has been wanting to rejoin his family in London for some weeks.' A general exclamation of surprise arose from the meeting. Quarry held up his hand. 'I can assure you he's completely on side with everything we're doing. Now does anybody else want to ruin their career by asking me a tricky question?' There was nervous laughter. 'Right then . . .'

Hoffmann said, 'Actually, there is one last thing, Hugo.' Staring out across the upturned faces of his quants, he felt for the first time a sudden sense of comradeship. He had recruited every one of them. The team—the company—his creation: he guessed it might be a long while before he had another chance to speak to them collectively, if ever. 'Can I

273

just add something to that? It's been, as some of you have probably guessed by now, an absolute bitch of a day. And whatever happens to me, I just want to tell you all—every one of you . . .' He had to stop and swallow. To his horror he was welling up, his throat thick with emotion, his eyes brimming. He looked down at his feet, waiting until he had himself under control, then raised his head again. He had to rush to get through it or he would have broken down completely. 'I simply want you to know I'm very proud of what we've done together here. It's never been just about the money—certainly not for me and I believe not for most of you, either. So thanks. It's meant a lot. That's it.'

There was no applause; simply mystification. Hoffmann stepped down from the chair. He could see Quarry looking at him in a strange way, although the CEO recovered quickly and called out, 'All right, everyone, that's the end of the pep talk. Back to your galleys, slaves, and start rowing. There's a storm coming in.'

As the quants began to move away, Quarry said to Hoffmann: 'That sounded like a farewell speech.'

'It wasn't meant to.'

'Well it did. What do you mean, whatever happens to you?'

But before Hoffmann could answer, someone called out, 'Alex, have you got a second? We seem to have a problem here.'

16

Intelligent life on a planet comes of age when it first works out the reason for its own existence.

RICHARD DAWKINS, *The Selfish Gene* (1976)

What was officially logged as a 'general system malfunction' occurred at Hoffmann Investment Technologies at 7.00 p.m. Central European Time. At exactly the same moment, almost four thousand miles away, at 1.00 p.m. Eastern Standard Time, unusual activity was detected on the New York Stock Exchange. Several dozen stocks began to be affected by severe price volatility of such magnitude that it automatically triggered what are known as liquidity replenishment points, or LRPs. In her subsequent testimony to Congress, the chairman of the US Securities and Exchange Commission explained that

> *LRPs are best thought of as a 'speed bump' and are intended to dampen volatility in a given stock by temporarily converting from an automated market to a manual auction market when a price movement of sufficient size is reached. In such a case, trading on the NYSE in that stock will 'go slow' and pause for a time period to allow the Designated Market Maker to solicit additional liquidity before returning to an automated market.* [Mary Shapiro, evidence submitted to Congress. The background detail of what happened on the US financial markets

275

over the next two hours is entirely factual, drawn from Congressional testimony and the joint CFTC and SEC report, *Findings Regarding the Market Events of May 6, 2010.*]

Still, it was only a technical intervention, and not unheard-of, and at this stage it was also relatively minor. Few in America paid much attention for the next half-hour, and certainly none of the quants at Hoffmann Investment Technologies was even aware of it.

* * *

The man who had called Hoffmann over to his six-screen array was an Oxford PhD named Croker, whom Hoffmann had recruited from the Rutherford Appleton Laboratory on the same trip that Gabrielle had hit upon the idea of making art out of body scans. Croker had been attempting to put a manual override on the algorithm in order to begin liquidating their massive position on the VIX, but the system had denied him authority.

'Let me try,' said Hoffmann. He took Croker's place at the keyboard and entered his own password, which was supposed to give him unrestricted access to every part of VIXAL, but even his request for special operator privileges was turned down. He tried to conceal his fear.

As Hoffmann clicked the mouse in vain and tried various other routes into the system, Quarry stood looking over his shoulder, together with van der Zyl and Ju-Long. He felt surprisingly calm; resigned, even. Part of him had always known this was going to happen, just as he always half-expected, every

276

time he strapped himself into an aircraft, that he was going to die in a crash. The moment one surrendered oneself to a machine operated by someone else, one was acquiescing in one's own doom. After a while he said, 'I assume the nuclear option is just to unplug the bloody thing?'

Hoffmann replied, without turning round, 'But if we do that, then we simply cease to trade, period. We don't unwind our present positions: we're just frozen into them.'

Little cries of alarm and astonishment were erupting all over the room. One by one the quants were abandoning their terminals and coming over to watch what Hoffmann was doing. In the manner of bystanders gathered around a big jigsaw puzzle, someone would occasionally lean forward with a suggestion: had Hoffmann thought of putting that there? Might this be better if he tried it the other way round? He ignored them. Nobody knew VIXAL as he did; he had designed every aspect of it.

On the big screens the afternoon reports from Wall Street continued as normal. The lead story was still the riots in Athens against the Greek government's austerity measures—whether Greece would default, the contagion spread, the euro collapse. And still the hedge fund was making money: in a way that was the weirdest aspect of all. Quarry turned away for a few seconds to consult the P&L on the next-door screen: it was now up by almost $300 million on the day. Part of him still wondered why they were so desperate to bypass the algorithm. They had created King Midas out of silicon chips; in what way was its phenomenal profitability not in their human interest?

Suddenly Hoffmann lifted his hands from the keyboard in the dramatic manner of a concert pianist finishing a concerto. 'This is no good. There's no response. I thought we could at least make an orderly liquidation, but that's obviously not an option. The whole system needs to be shut down completely and quarantined until we find out what's wrong with it.'

Ju-Long said: 'How are we going to do that?'

'Why don't we just do it the old-fashioned way?' suggested Quarry. 'Let's take VIXAL off-line and simply call up the brokers on the phone and get them on email and tell them to start winding down the positions?'

'We'll need to come up with some plausible explanation for why we're no longer using the algorithm to go straight to the trading floor.'

'Easy,' said Quarry. 'We pull the plugs and then we tell them there's been a catastrophic loss of power in our computer room and we have to withdraw from the market until it's fixed. And like all the best lies, it has the merit of being almost true.'

Van der Zyl said, 'In fact we only have to get through another two hours and fifty minutes, and then the markets are closed in any case. And the day after tomorrow it's the weekend. By Monday morning the book will be neutral, and we will be safe—as long as the markets don't stage a strong rally in the meantime.'

'The Dow's off a full percentage point already,' said Quarry. 'The S and P's the same. You've got all this sovereign debt crap coming out of the eurozone—there's no way this market's going to end the day up.' The four executives of the

278

company looked from one to another. 'So is that it? We're agreed?' They all nodded.

Hoffmann said, 'I'll do it.'

'I'll come with you,' offered Quarry.

'No. I switched it on; I'll switch it off.'

It seemed to him a long walk across the trading floor to the computer room. He could sense the eyes of everyone like a weight upon his back, and it occurred to him that if this were a science-fiction movie, he would now be denied access to the motherboards. But when he presented his face to the scanner, the bolts slid back and the door opened. In the cold, noisy darkness, the forest eyes of a thousand CPUs blinked at his approach. It felt like an act of murder, just as it had at CERN when they'd closed him down there all those years ago. Nevertheless, he opened the metal box and grasped the isolator handle. It was only the end of a phase, he told himself: the work would go on, if not under his direction then under someone else's. He flicked the handle, and within a couple of seconds the lights and the sound had faded. Only the noise of the air-conditioning disturbed the chilly silence. It was like a mortuary. He headed towards the glow of the open door.

As he approached the cluster of quants gathered around the six-screen array, everyone turned to look at him. He couldn't read their expressions. Quarry said, 'What happened? You couldn't go through with it?'

'Yes, I went through with it. I turned it off.' He looked past Quarry's mystified face. On the screens VIXAL-4 was continuing to trade. Puzzled, he went to the terminal and began flicking between the screens.

279

Quarry said quietly to one of the quants, 'Go back and check, will you?'

Hoffmann said, 'I am capable of throwing a goddam switch, Hugo. I'm not so completely crazy I don't know the difference between on and off. My God—will you look at that?' In every market VIXAL was continuing to trade: it was shorting the euro, piling into Treasury bonds, adding to its position on VIX futures.

From the entrance to the computer room the quant shouted, 'The power's all shut down!'

An excited murmur broke out.

'So where is the algorithm if it's not on our hardware?' demanded Quarry.

Hoffmann didn't answer.

'I think you will find that is something the regulators will also be asking,' said Rajamani.

Afterwards no one was sure how long he had been watching them. Someone said he had been in his office all along: they had seen his fingers parting the blinds, staring out as Hoffmann delivered his speech on the trading floor. Someone else claimed to have come across him at a spare terminal in the boardroom with a mass storage device, uploading data. Yet another quant, a fellow Indian, even confessed that Rajamani had approached him in the communal kitchen and asked if he would be willing to act as his informant inside the company. In the somewhat hysterical atmosphere that was about to overtake Hoffmann Investment Technologies, in which heretics and disciples, apostates and martyrs split into their various factions, it was not always easy to establish the truth. The one thing everyone could agree on was that Quarry had made a grievous error in not having the chief risk officer escorted off the premises by security the moment he had been fired; in the chaos of events, he had simply forgotten about him.

Rajamani stood on the edge of the trading floor holding a small cardboard box containing his personal effects—the photographs of his graduation, his wedding, his children; a tin of Darjeeling tea he kept in the staff refrigerator for his personal use and which no one else was allowed to touch; a cactus plant in the shape of a thumbs-up; and a framed handwritten note from the head of Scotland Yard's Serious Fraud Office thanking him for his help in prosecuting some tip-of-the-iceberg case that was supposed to herald a new dawn in policing the City but which had been quietly dropped on appeal.

Quarry said hoarsely, 'I thought I told you to bugger off.'

'Well I am going right now,' Rajamani replied, 'and you'll be glad to know I have an appointment at the Geneva Finance Ministry tomorrow morning. Let me warn each and every one of you that you will face prosecution, imprisonment and millions of dollars in fines if you conspire in the running of a company that is unfit to trade. This is clearly dangerous technology, completely out of control, and I can promise you, Alex and Hugo, that the SEC and the FSA will revoke your access to every single market in America and London pending an investigation. Shame on you both. Shame on you all.'

It was a tribute to Rajamani's self-confidence that he was able to deliver this speech over a tin of tea and a thumbs-up cactus without any loss of dignity. With a final sweeping glare of fury and contempt, he thrust out his chin and walked steadily towards reception. More than one witness was reminded of the pictures of staff leaving Lehman Brothers with their possessions in boxes.

'Yes, go on, clear off,' Quarry called after him. 'You'll find ten billion dollars buys us a heck of a lot of lawyers. And we're going to come after you personally for breach of contract. And we're going to bloody well *bury* you!'

'Wait!' shouted Hoffmann.

Quarry said, 'Leave him, Alex—don't give him the satisfaction.'

'But he's right, Hugo. There's a lot of danger here. If VIXAL's somehow migrated out of our control, that could pose a real systemic risk. We've got to keep him on side until we can figure it out.'

He set off after Rajamani, ignoring Quarry's protests, but the Indian had quickened his pace. He just missed him in reception. He caught up with him by the elevators. The corridor was deserted. 'Gana!' he called. 'Please. Let's talk.'

'I've nothing to say to you, Alex.' He was clutching his box. His back was to the elevator control panel. He hit the call button with his elbow. 'It's nothing personal. I'm sorry.' The doors opened. He turned, stepped smartly through them and plunged from view. The doors closed.

For a couple of seconds Hoffmann stood motionless, unsure of what he had just witnessed. He walked hesitantly along the corridor and pressed the call button. The doors slid open on to the empty glass tube of the elevator shaft. He peered over the edge, down maybe fifty metres of translucent column, until it dwindled into the darkness and silence of the underground car park. He shouted hopelessly, 'Gana!' There was no response. He listened, but he could hear nobody screaming. Rajamani must have fallen so quickly, no one had noticed it.

He sprinted along the corridor to the emergency exit and half-ran, half-jumped his way floor after floor down the concrete staircase, all the way to the basement and out into the subterranean garage and across to the elevator doors. He jammed his fingers into the gap and tried to prise them apart, but they kept closing on him. He stepped back and prowled around looking for some tool he could use. He considered smashing the glass on one of the parked cars and popping the trunk for its jack. Then he saw a metal door with a lightning-flash symbol and tried that. Behind it was a space for storing tools—brushes, shovels, buckets, a hammer. He found a big crowbar almost a metre long, and ran back to the elevator doors and jammed it into the gap, working it back and forth. The doors parted just enough for him to shove his foot in between them, and then his knee. He wriggled the rest of his leg into the space. Some automatic mechanism was triggered and the doors trundled open.

Light falling from the upper floors showed Rajamani lying face down in the well of the elevator shaft. There was a puddle of blood the size of a dinner plate that seemed to be growing out of the top of his skull. His photographs lay scattered around him. Hoffmann jumped down next to him. Broken glass crunched under his feet. There was an incongruous smell of tea. He stooped and grasped Rajamani's hand, which was shockingly warm and smooth, and for the second time that day tried to feel for a man's pulse, but again he couldn't find one. Behind and just above him, the doors rattled shut. Hoffmann looked around in panic as the elevator car began its descent. The tube of light shrank rapidly as the car hurtled down—the fifth floor went, and then the fourth. He grabbed the crowbar and tried to jam it back between the doors, but lost his footing. He fell backwards and lay next to Rajamani's corpse, looking up at the bottom of the car as it hurtled at him, holding the crowbar upright in both hands above his head like a spear to fend off a charging beast. He felt the oily wind on his face. The light faded, vanished, something heavy hit his shoulder, and then the crowbar jumped and went as rigid as a pit prop. For several seconds he could feel it taking the strain. He was screaming blindly into the absolute darkness at the elevator's floor, which must have been only inches from his face, braced for the crowbar to bend or slip. But then a gear changed, the note of the motor became a whine, the crowbar came loose in his hands and the car began to rise, accelerating rapidly all the way up its cathedral column of glass, uncovering floor after floor of fresh white light, which poured down into the pit.

He scrambled up and shoved the crowbar back between the doors, working it into the gap, parting them a fraction. The elevator had climbed to its highest point and stopped. There was a clunk, and he heard it start to plunge again. He hoisted himself up and jammed his fingers into the narrow opening. He clung there, feet wide apart, muscles straining. He threw back his head and roared with the effort. The doors gave slightly, then flew wide open. A shadow fell across his back, and in a rush of air and a roar of machinery he launched himself forward on to the concrete floor.

*   *   *

Leclerc had been in his office at police headquarters and on the point of going home when he received a call that a body had been discovered in a hotel on the Rue de Berne. He guessed at once from the description—gaunt face, ponytail, leather coat—that it was the man who had attacked Hoffmann. Cause of death, he was told, appeared to be strangulation, although whether it was suicide or murder was not immediately clear. The victim was a German: Johannes Karp, aged fifty-eight. Leclerc rang his wife for the second time that day to say he was delayed at work, and set off in the back of a patrol car through the rush-hour traffic to the northern side of the river.

He had been on duty for almost twenty hours and was as exhausted as an old dog. But the prospect of a suspicious death, of which there are only about eight per year in Geneva, always bucked up his spirits. With flashing light display, a piercing siren and an air of great self-importance, the patrol car roared up the Boulevard Carl-Vogt and over the bridge, cutting into the left-hand lane of the Rue de Sous-Terre, forcing the oncoming traffic to swerve out of its way. Thrown around in the back seat, Leclerc rang the chief's office and left a message that the suspect in the Hoffmann case apparently had been found dead.

In the Rue de Berne there was almost a carnival atmosphere outside the Hotel Diodati—four police cars with flickering blue lights, sharply brilliant in the overcast early-evening gloom; a sizeable crowd on the opposite side of the street, including several glossy black hookers in colourful, minimal clothes, joking with the locals; fluttering lines of stripy black-and-yellow crime-scene tape sectioning off the spectators. Occasionally a camera flashed. They were like fans, thought Leclerc as he got out of the car, waiting for a star to come out. A gendarme lifted the tape and Leclerc ducked underneath it. As a young man he had patrolled this area on foot, had got to know all the working girls by name. He guessed some of them would be grandmothers now; come to think of it, one or two had been grandmothers then.

He went inside the Diodati. It had been called something else in the eighties. He couldn't remember what. The guests had all been corralled in reception and were not being allowed to leave until they had each given a statement. There were several obvious hookers here, and a couple of smartly dressed men who should have known better and who stood apart, surly with embarrassment. Leclerc didn't like the look of the tiny elevator so took the stairs, pausing on each deserted floor to recover his breath. Outside the room where the body had been found, the corridor was crowded with uniforms and he had to put on white coveralls, white latex gloves, and clear plastic slipovers on his shoes. He drew the line at pulling up the hood. I look like a damned white rabbit, he thought.

He didn't know the detective in charge of the crime scene—a new fellow named Moynier, apparently in his twenties, although it was hard to tell as he had his hood up and only the baby-pink oval of his face was visible. Also in the room in

286

their white suits were the pathologist and the photographer, both old hands, but not as old as Leclerc; no one was as old as Leclerc; he was as old as the Jura. He contemplated the corpse, hanging off the bathroom door handle. Above the tight line of the ligature, which was buried in the flesh of the neck, the head had turned black. There were various cuts and abrasions on the face. One eye was badly swollen. Strung up and skinny, the German looked like an old dead crow left out by a farmer to discourage other carrion. In the bathroom there was no light switch, but even so it was possible to see the blood smeared on the toilet bowl. The shower curtain rail was hanging away from the wall; so was the washbasin.

Moynier said, 'A man next door swears he heard sounds of a struggle sometime around three. There's also blood by the bed. I'm provisionally declaring it a murder.'

'Smart work,' said Leclerc.

The pathologist coughed to cover his laughter.

Moynier didn't notice. He said, 'I was right to call you? Do you think this is the man who attacked the American banker?'

'I should say so.'

'Well then, I hope you don't object, Leclerc, but I was here first, and so I must insist that this is my case now.'

'My dear fellow, you're welcome to it.'

Leclerc wondered how the occupant of this squalid room could possibly have come to intersect with the owner of a $60 million mansion in Cologny. On the bed the dead man's possessions had been individually bagged in clear plastic and laid out for inspection: clothes, a camera, two

287

knives, a raincoat apparently slashed at the front. Hoffmann had worn a raincoat like that when he went to the hospital, Leclerc thought. He picked up a mains adaptor.

He said, 'Isn't this for a computer? Where is it?'

Moynier shrugged. 'There isn't one here.'

Leclerc's mobile phone rang. It was in his jacket pocket. He couldn't get at it through his damned rabbit suit. Irritably he unzipped the coveralls and pulled off his gloves. Moynier started to protest about contamination, but Leclerc turned his back on him. The caller was his assistant, young Lullin, who was still in the office. He said he had just been looking at the afternoon log. A psychiatrist, a Dr Polidori in Vernier, had called a couple of hours earlier about a patient of hers showing potentially dangerous schizophrenic symptoms—he had been in a fight, she said—but when the patrol got to her surgery he was gone. His name was Alexander Hoffmann. The psych didn't have a recent address, but she had given a description.

Leclerc said, 'Did she mention whether he was carrying a computer?'

There was a pause, a rustle of notes, and Lullin said, 'How did you know that?'

*   *   *

Hoffmann, still clutching the crowbar, hurried up the steps from the basement to the ground floor, intent on raising the alarm about Rajamani. At the door to the lobby he stopped. Through the rectangular window he saw a squad of six black-uniformed gendarmes, guns drawn, jogging in heavy boots across the reception area towards the

288

interior of the building; following them was the panting figure of Leclerc. Once they had passed through the turnstile, the exit was locked and two more armed police stationed themselves on either side of it.

Hoffmann turned and clattered back down the steps and into the car park. The ramp up to the street was about fifty metres away. He headed for that. Behind him he heard the soft squeak of tyres turning on concrete and a large black BMW swung out of a parking bay, straightened and came towards him, headlights on. Without pausing to think, he stepped out in front of it, forcing it to stop, then ran around to the driver's door and pulled it open.

What an apparition the president of Hoffmann Investment Technologies must have presented by now—bloody, dusty, oil-smeared, clutching a metre-long crowbar. It was little wonder the driver couldn't scramble out fast enough. Hoffmann threw the crowbar on to the passenger seat, put the automatic transmission into drive and pressed hard on the accelerator. The big car lurched up the ramp. Ahead, the steel door was just beginning to rise. He had to brake to let it open fully. In his rear-view mirror he could see the owner, transformed by adrenalin from fear into rage, marching up the ramp to protest. Hoffmann locked the doors. The man began pounding on the side window with his fist and shouting. Through the thick tinted glass he was muffled, subaqueous. The steel door opened fully and Hoffmann transferred his foot from the brake to the accelerator, overstepping it again in his anxiety to get away, kangarooing the BMW out across the pavement and swerving on two wheels into the empty one-way street.

*   *   *

On the fifth floor, Leclerc and his arrest squad stepped out of the working elevator. He pressed the buzzer and looked up at the security camera. The usual receptionist had gone home for the evening. It was Marie-Claude who let them in. She put her hand to her mouth in dismay as the armed men rushed past her.

Leclerc said, 'I am looking for Dr Hoffmann. Is he here?'

'Yes, of course.'

'Will you take us to him, please?'

She led them on to the trading floor. Quarry heard the commotion and turned round. He had been wondering what had happened to Hoffmann. He had assumed he was still with Rajamani and took his lengthening absence as a good sign: it would be better, on reflection, if their former chief risk officer could be persuaded not to try and shut them down at this critical moment. But when he saw Leclerc and the gendarmes, he knew their ship was sunk. Nevertheless, in the spirit of his forebears, he was determined to go down with dignity.

He said calmly, 'Can I help you, gentlemen?'

'We need to speak to Dr Hoffmann,' said Leclerc. He was swaying from left to right, standing on tiptoe, trying to spot the American among the astonished quants who were turning from their computer screens. 'Will everyone please remain where they are?'

Quarry said, 'You must have just missed him. He

290

stepped outside to speak to one of our executives.'

'Outside the building? Outside where?'

'I assumed he was just going out into the corridor . . .'

Leclerc swore. He said to the nearest gendarmes: 'You three, check these premises.' And then to the others: 'You three, come with me.' And finally to the room in general: 'Nobody is to leave the building without my permission. Nobody is to make any phone calls. We shall try to be as quick as possible. Thank you for your co-operation.'

He walked briskly back towards reception. Quarry chased after him. 'I'm sorry, Inspector—excuse me—what exactly has Alex done?'

'A body has been discovered. We need to speak to him about it. Forgive me . . .'

He strode out of the offices and into the corridor. It was deserted. He had a funny feeling about this place. His eyes were searching everywhere. 'What other companies are on this floor?'

Quarry was still at his heels. His face was grey. 'Only us, we rent the whole thing. What body?'

Leclerc said to his men, 'We'll have to start at the bottom and work our way up.'

One of the gendarmes pressed the elevator call button. The doors opened and it was Leclerc, eyes darting, who saw the danger first and yelled out to him to stay where he was.

'Christ,' said Quarry, gazing at the void. 'Alex . . .'

The doors began to close. The gendarme held his finger on the button to reopen them. Wincing, Leclerc got down on his knees, shuffled forwards, and peered over the edge. It was impossible to

291

make out anything at the bottom. He felt a drop of moisture hit the back of his neck, and put his hand to it and touched a viscous liquid. He craned his head upwards to find himself staring at the bottom of the elevator car. It was only a floor above him. Something was dangling off the bottom. He drew back quickly.

*   *   *

Gabrielle had finished her packing. Her suitcases were in the hall: one big case, one smaller, and one carry-on bag—less than a full-scale removal but more than just an overnight stay. The last flight to London was due to take off at 9.25, and the BA website was warning of increased security after the Vista Airways bomb: she ought to leave now if she was to be sure of catching it. She sat in her studio and wrote Alex a note, the old-fashioned way, on pure white paper with steel nib and Indian ink.

The first thing she wanted to say was that she loved him, and that she was not leaving him permanently—'maybe you'd prefer it if I did'—she just needed a break from Geneva. She had been out to see Bob Walton at CERN—'don't be angry, he's a good man, he's worried about you'—and that had been a help because for the first time really she had begun to understand the extraordinary work he was trying to do and the immense strain he must be under.

She was sorry for blaming him for the fiasco of her exhibition. If he still insisted he wasn't responsible for buying everything, then of course she believed him: 'But darling, are you sure you're right when you say that, because who else would have done it?' Perhaps he was having some kind of breakdown again, in which case she wanted to help him; what she did *not* want to do was learn about his past problems for the first time from a policeman, of all people. 'If we're going to stay together we've got to be more honest with one another.' She had only come out to Switzerland all those years ago intending to work as a temp for a couple of months, yet somehow she had ended up staying and fitting her existence entirely around his. Maybe if they had had children it might have been different. But if nothing else, what had happened today had made her realise that work, even the most creative work, for her was no substitute for life, whereas for him she thought it was *exactly that*.

Which really brought her to her main point. As she understood it from Walton, he had devoted his life to trying to create a machine that could reason, learn and act independently of human beings. To her there was something inherently frightening about that whole idea, even though Walton assured her his intentions had been entirely noble ('and knowing you, I'm sure they were'). But to take such a vaulting ambition and place it entirely at the service of making money—wasn't that to marry the sacred and the profane? No wonder he had started to behave so strangely. Even to *want* a billion dollars, let alone *possess* such a sum, was madness in her opinion, and there was a time when it would have been his opinion too. If a person happened to invent something that everyone needed—well okay, fair enough. But simply to gain it by gambling (she had never understood exactly what his company did, but that seemed to be the essence of it), well, such greed was worse than madness, it was *wicked—nothing good* would come of it—and that was why she needed to *get out of Geneva*, before the place and its values devoured her . . .

On and on she wrote, forgetting time, the pen gliding over the hand-woven paper in her intricate calligraphy. The conservatory grew darker. Across the lake, the lights of the city began to glint. The thought of Alex out there with a broken head gnawed at her.

I feel awful going when you're ill, but if you won't let me help you, or the doctors properly examine you, then there's not much point in my staying, is there? If you need me, call me. Please. Any time. It's all I've ever wanted. I love you. G x

She sealed the note in an envelope, wrote a large A on the front and carried it towards the study, pausing briefly in the hall to ask her driver-bodyguard to put her cases in the car and take her to the airport.

She went into the study and propped the envelope on the keyboard of her husband's computer, and somehow she must have pressed a key by accident, because the screen came to life and she found she was looking at an image of a woman bending over a desk. It took her a moment to realise it was her. She looked behind her and above, at the red light of a smoke detector; the woman on the screen did the same.

She tapped a few more keys at random. Nothing happened. She pressed ESCAPE and instantly the image shrank into the top left-hand corner of the screen, part of a grid of twenty-four different camera shots, bulging outwards from the centre slightly, like the multiple images of an insect's eye. In one, something seemed to be moving faintly. She adjusted the mouse and clicked on it. The screen was filled with a night-vision image of her lying on a bed in a short dressing gown, her legs crossed and her arms behind her head. A candle glittered as bright as a sun beside her. The video was silent. She unfastened the belt, slipped off the dressing gown, and naked held out her arms. A man's head— Alex's head, uninjured—appeared in the bottom right quadrant of the screen. He too began to get undressed.

There was a polite cough. 'Madame Hoffmann?' enquired a voice behind her, and she dragged her horrified gaze away from the screen to find her driver framed in the doorway. Behind him loomed two black-capped gendarmes.

*   *   *

In New York at 1.30 p.m., the New York Stock Exchange began to experience such volatility that liquidity replenishment points increased in frequency to a rate of seven per minute, taking an estimated twenty per cent of liquidity out of the market. The Dow was off by more than one and a half per cent, the S&P 500 by two. The VIX was up by ten.

17

The most vigorous individuals, or those which have most successfully struggled with their conditions of life, will generally leave most progeny. But success will often depend on having special weapons or means of defence . . .

CHARLES DARWIN, *On the Origin of Species* (1859)

Zimeysa was a nowhere land—no history, no geography, no inhabitants; even its name was an acronym of other places: Zone Industrielle de Meyrin-Satigny. Hoffmann drove between low buildings that seemed to be neither office blocks nor factories but a hybrid of both. What went on here? What was made? It was impossible to say. The skeletal arms of cranes stretched over construction sites and lorry parks deserted for the night. It could have been anywhere in the world. The airport was less than a kilometre to the east. The lights of the terminals imparted a pale glow to a darkening sky corrugated with low cloud. Each time a passenger jet came in low overhead, it sounded like a rolling wave breaking onshore: a thunderous crescendo that set Hoffmann's nerves on edge, followed by a whining ebb, the landing lights receding like flotsam between the crane spars and flat roofs.

He treated the BMW with extreme care, driving with his face up close to the windscreen. There were a lot of roadworks, cables being laid, first one lane shut and then the other, creating a chicane.

The turning to Route de Clerval was on the right, just past a distribution centre for auto parts— Volvo, Nissan, Honda. He indicated to turn into it. Up ahead on the left was a petrol station. He pulled up at the pumps and went into the shop. CCTV footage shows him hesitating between the aisles, then moving decisively to a section selling jerry cans: red metal, good quality, thirty-five francs each. The video is time-lapsed, making his actions seem jerky, like a marionette's. He buys five, paying for them in cash. The camera above the till clearly shows the wound on the top of his head. The sales assistant subsequently described him as being in an agitated state. His face and clothes were streaked with grease and oil; there was dried blood in his hair.

Hoffmann said, with a terrible attempt at a smile, 'What's with all the roadworks?'

'It's been going on for months, *monsieur*. They're laying fibre-optic cable.'

Hoffmann went out on to the forecourt with the jerry cans. It took him two trips to carry them to the nearest pump. He began filling them in turn. There were no other customers. He felt horribly exposed standing alone under the fluorescent lights. He could see the sales assistant watching him. Another jet came in to land directly over their heads, making the air tremble. It seemed to shake him from the inside out. He finished filling the last can, opened the rear door of the BMW and shoved it along to the far side of the back seat, stacking all the others in a row after it. He returned to the shop, paid one hundred and sixty-eight francs for the fuel and another twenty-five for a flashlight, two cigarette lighters and three cleaning cloths. Again he paid in

297

cash. He left the shop without looking back.

*　　　*　　　*

Leclerc had briefly inspected the body at the bottom of the elevator shaft. There was not much to see. It reminded him of a suicide he had once had to deal with at the Cornavin railway station. He had a strong stomach for that kind of thing. It was the unmarked corpses who looked at you as if they should still be breathing that got under his skin: their eyes always seemed so full of reproaches. *Where were you when I needed you?*

In the basement he talked briefly to the Austrian businessman whose car Hoffmann had stolen. He was outraged, seemed to hold Leclerc more responsible than the man who had committed the crime—'I pay my taxes here, I expect the police to protect me' and so forth—and Leclerc had been obliged to listen politely. The licence number and description had been circulated as a high priority to every Geneva police officer. The entire building was now being searched and evacuated. Forensics were on their way. Madame Hoffmann had been picked up at the house in Cologny and was being brought over for questioning. The office of the chief of police had been notified: the chief himself was at an official dinner in Zurich, which was a relief. Leclerc was not sure what else he could do.

For the second time that evening he found himself climbing multiple flights of stairs. He felt dizzy with the effort. There was a tingling in his left arm. He needed to get himself checked out: his wife was always nagging him about it. He wondered about Hoffmann and whether he had killed his

298

colleague as well as the German in the hotel room. On the face of it, it seemed impossible: the safety mechanism of the elevator had plainly failed. But equally it was a remarkable coincidence, one had to say, for a man to have been at the scene of two deaths in the space of a few hours.

Arriving at the fifth floor, he paused to recover his breath. The entrance to the hedge fund's offices was open; a young gendarme was standing guard. Leclerc nodded to him as he went past. On the trading floor, the mood seemed not merely shocked—he would have expected that, after the loss of a colleague—but almost hysterical. The employees, previously so silent, were huddled in groups, talking animatedly. The Englishman, Quarry, almost ran over to him. On the screens, the numbers continued to change.

Quarry said, 'Any news of Alex?'

'It appears he forced a driver out of his car and stole it. We're looking for him now.'

Quarry said, 'This is unbelievable—'

Leclerc cut him off. 'Excuse me, *monsieur*: could I see Dr Hoffmann's office, please?'

Quarry at once looked shifty. 'I'm not altogether sure about that. I think perhaps I ought to call in our lawyer . . .'

Leclerc said firmly, 'I'm sure he would advise full co-operation.' He wondered what the financier was trying to hide.

Quarry backed down immediately. 'Yes, of course.'

Inside Hoffmann's office there was still debris on the floor. The hole in the ceiling gaped above the desk. Leclerc looked up at it in bewilderment. 'When did this happen?'

299

Quarry grimaced with embarrassment, as if having to confess to the existence of a mad relative. 'About an hour ago. Alex pulled down the smoke detector.'

'Why?'

'He believed there was a camera inside.'

'And was there?'

'Yes.'

'Who installed it?'

'Our security consultant, Maurice Genoud.'

'On whose authority?'

'Well . . .' Quarry could see no escape. 'Actually, it turns out to have been Alex.'

'Hoffmann was spying on himself?'

'Yes, apparently. But he couldn't remember ordering it.'

'And where is Genoud now?'

'I believe he went down to talk to your men when Gana's body was discovered. He also handles security for this whole building.'

Leclerc sat at Hoffmann's desk and started opening the drawers.

Quarry said, 'Don't you need a warrant to do that?'

'No.' Leclerc found the Darwin book, and the CD from the radiology department of the University Hospital. On the sofa he noticed a laptop lying discarded. He went across and opened it, studied the photograph of Hoffmann, then went into the file of his exchanges with the dead man, Karp. He was so absorbed, he barely glanced up when Ju-Long came in.

Ju-Long said, 'Excuse me, Hugo—I think you ought to take a look at what's happening on the markets.'

Quarry, frowning, bent over the screen, switching from display to display. The slide was beginning in earnest now. The VIX was going through the roof, the euro sinking, investors pulling out of equities and scrambling for shelter in gold and ten-year Treasury bonds, the yields of which were falling fast. Everywhere money was being sucked out of the market—in electronically traded S&P futures alone, in the space of little more than ninety minutes, buy-side liquidity had dropped from $6 billion to $2.5 billion.

Here it comes, he thought.

He said, 'Inspector, if we're done here, I need to get back to work. There's a big sell-off underway in New York.'

'What's the point?' asked Ju-Long. 'We're not in control anyway.'

The edge of despair in his voice caused Leclerc to look up sharply.

'We're having a few technical problems,' explained Quarry. He could see the suspicion on Leclerc's face. It would be a nightmare if the police inquiry moved on from Hoffmann's mental breakdown to the breakdown of the entire company. The regulators would be all over them by morning. 'It's nothing to worry about, but I ought just to talk to our computer people . . .'

He started to move from the desk, but Leclerc said firmly: 'Wait, please.' He was looking out over the trading floor. Until that moment he hadn't really registered that the company itself might be in difficulties. But now he noticed, in addition to the anxious groups of employees, several others scurrying around. There was a definite message of panic in their body language, which at first he had ascribed to the death of their colleague and the disappearance of their leader, but now he realised it was separate to that, wider. 'What sort of technical problems?' he asked.

There was a brief knock on the door and a gendarme stuck his head into the room.

'We've got a trace on the stolen car.'

Leclerc swung round to face him.

'Where is it?'

'A guy at a petrol station in Zimeysa just called. Someone matching Hoffmann's description driving a black BMW just bought a hundred litres of fuel.'

'A hundred litres? My God, how far is he planning to go?'

'That's why the guy called. He says he didn't put it in the tank.'

*   *   *

Fifty-four Route de Clerval turned out to be at the end of a long road that took in a cargo-handling facility and a waste-recycling plant before dwindling into a cul-de-sac beside the railway tracks. The building stood out pale in the dusk through a screen of trees: a boxy steel structure, two or three storeys high—it was difficult for him to estimate the height in the absence of any windows—with security lights mounted along the edge of the roof and video cameras protruding from the corners. They turned to follow Hoffmann as he passed. A small slip road led up to a set of metal gates; beyond was an empty car park. The whole site was secured by a steel perimeter fence surmounted with triple strands of razor wire. He guessed it might have been built originally as a warehouse or distribution centre. It

302

was surely not custom-designed: there had not been enough time. Hoffmann drew up in front of the gates. At window-level next to him were a keypad console and an entryphone; beside them the tiny pinkish elephant's-eye of an infrared camera.

He leaned over and pressed the buzzer and waited. Nothing happened. He looked across at the building; it seemed derelict. He considered what was logical from the machine's point of view, then tried keying in the smallest number expressible as the sum of two cubes in two different ways. At once the gates began to slide open.

He drove slowly across the car park and along the side of the building. In the wing mirror he could see the camera following him. The stink of the petrol on the back seat was making him feel ill. He turned the corner and pulled up in front of a big steel shutter, a truck-sized delivery entrance. A video camera mounted above it was trained directly on him. He got out of the car and approached the door. Like the offices of the hedge fund, it was controlled by face recognition. He stood in front of the scanner. The response was immediate, the shutter rising like a theatre curtain to reveal an empty loading bay. Hoffmann turned to walk back to the car and saw, as he did so, in the distance on the other side of the railway tracks, a travelling light show of flashing red and blue moving very fast; a scrap of siren from the police car carried in the wind.

He drove quickly into the bay, lurched to a halt, turned off the engine and listened. He couldn't hear the siren now. It was probably nothing to do with him. He decided he would close the shutter behind him in any case, but when he examined the control panel he couldn't find a light switch. He had to use his teeth to tear open the plastic packaging around the torch. He checked it was working, then pressed the button to close the shutter. There was a warning buzzer; an orange lamp flashed. Darkness descended with the steel slats. Within ten seconds the bottom of the shutter clattered against the concrete floor, extinguishing the thin line of daylight. He felt alone in the darkness, the victim of his own imaginings. The silence was not quite absolute: he could make out something. He took the crowbar from the front seat of the BMW. With his left hand he shone the torch around the bare walls and on to the ceiling, picking out yet another surveillance camera, perched high in the corner looking down at him malevolently, or so he thought. Beneath it was a metal door, again activated by face recognition. He tucked the crowbar under his arm, shone the torch on to his face and tentatively pressed his hand against the pad. For several seconds nothing happened, and then—almost, it seemed to him, reluctantly—the door opened on to a short flight of wooden steps that led up to a passage.

He shone the torch along it to another door at the far end. Now he could hear clearly the faint hum of CPUs. The ceiling was low and the air was chilled, as in a cold store. He guessed there must be under-floor ventilation as there had been in the computing room at CERN. He walked warily to the end, pressed his palm to the sensor and opened the door on to the noise and lights of a processor farm. In the torch's narrow beam the motherboards sat on steel shelves that stretched ahead and to either side, exuding the familiar, oddly sweet electrical scent of burned dust. A computer servicing company had attached its sticker to each of the racks: in case of problems please call this number. He walked on slowly, shining his torch to right and left along the aisles, the beam disappearing into the darkness. He wondered who else would have access. The security company, presumably—Genoud's outfit; building services for cleaning and maintenance; the computer technicians. If each received instructions and payment via email, the place could presumably function independently on outsourced labour alone, without any need of its own workforce: the ultimate Gatesian model of the corporate digital nervous system. He remembered that Amazon in its early days used to call itself 'a real company in a virtual world'. Maybe here was the logical progression in the evolutionary chain: a virtual company in a real world.

He reached the next door and repeated the procedure with the torch and the recognition sensor. When the bolts had slid back, he paused to examine the door frame. The walls were not structural, he saw, just thin prefabricated partitions. He had imagined, looking at it from the outside, that the building would consist of one big space, but now he realised it was honeycombed: it had a cell-structure like an insect colony. He stepped over the threshold, heard movement to one side, and wheeled round as an IBM TS3500 tape robot rushed towards him along its monorail, stopped, plucked out a disk, and whisked away again. He stood and watched it for a moment, waiting for his heart rate to settle down. He detected a sense of urgent activity. When he moved on, he saw that four other robots were racing to complete their tasks. In the far corner his torch showed an open metal staircase leading to an upper floor.

The adjoining room was smaller and seemed to be the place where the communication pipes came in. He shone his flashlight on two big black trunk cables, the thickness of his fist, emerging out of a closed metal box and descending like tuberous roots into a trench that ran under his feet and up into some kind of switch array system. Both sides of the aisle were protected by heavy metal cages. He already knew that the fibre-optic pipes GVA-1 and GVA-2 both passed close to Geneva airport en route to Germany from the fibre landing site at Marseilles in southern France. Data could be transmitted to and received from New York at the same velocity as particles shot around the Large Hadron Collider—a fraction below the speed of light. VIXAL was astride the fastest communications link in Europe.

The beam of his torch traced other cables running along the wall at shoulder height, partly housed in galvanised metal, emanating from beside a small door. It was padlocked. He fitted the crowbar into the U-shape loop and used it as a lever to wrench the shackle free of its housing. It came away with a shriek, the door swung open and he shone his light into some kind of power control room—electricity meters, a big fuse box the size of a small closet and a couple of trip switches. Yet another video camera regarded him steadily. He quickly flipped the handles on the trip switches down to OFF. For an instant, nothing happened, and then somewhere in the big building a diesel generator shuddered into life and, bizarrely, all the lights came on. Hoffmann, in a fury of frustration, took a swing at the camera lens with the end of his crowbar, poking his tormentor in the eye, smashing it to a satisfactory number of pieces, then set about the fuse board, splintering the plastic casings, only finally giving up when it was obvious he was having no effect.

He turned off the torch and retraced his steps to the comms room. At the far end he presented his face to the sensor, struggling to maintain an even expression, and the door to the next room opened—not another antechamber, it turned out, but a huge open space, with a high ceiling, digital clocks to mark the different time zones and large TV screens, obviously modelled on the trading floor at Les Eaux-Vives. There was a central control unit consisting of a six-screen array and separate monitors showing the output of the security cameras in grid form. In front of it, instead of people, where the quants would have sat there were ranks of motherboards, all processing at maximum capacity to judge by their rapidly flickering LEDs.

This must be the cortex, thought Hoffmann. He stood for a while in wonder. There was something about the absorbed and independent purposefulness of the scene that he found unexpectedly moving, as he supposed a parent might be moved by witnessing a child for the first time unselfconsciously at large in the world. That VIXAL was purely mechanical and possessed no emotion or conscience; that it had no purpose other than the self-interested pursuit of survival through the accumulation of money; that it would, if left to itself, in accordance with Darwinian logic, seek to

307

expand until it dominated the entire earth—this did not detract for Hoffmann from the stunning fact of its existence. He even forgave it for the ordeal it had subjected him to: after all, that had purely been for the purposes of research. One could no more pass moral judgement on it than one could on a shark. It was simply behaving like a hedge fund.

Briefly Hoffmann forgot that he had come here to destroy it and bent over the screens to examine the trades that it was putting on. They were being processed at ultra-high frequency in tremendous volumes—millions of shares all held for only fractions of a second—a strategy known as 'sniping' or 'sniffing': submitting and instantly cancelling orders, probing the markets for hidden pockets of liquidity. But he had never seen it done on such a scale before. There could be little or no profit in it and he wondered briefly what VIXAL was aiming to achieve. Then an alert flashed on to the screen.

*   *   *

It was appearing at that instant in dealing rooms all across the world—8.30 p.m. in Geneva, 2.30 p.m. in New York, 1.30 p.m. in Chicago:

The CBOE has declared Self Help against the NYSE/ARCA as of 1.30 CT. The NYSE/ARCA is out of NBBO and unavailable for linkage. All CBOE systems are running normally.

The jargon masked the scale of the problem, took the heat out of it, as jargon is designed to do. But Hoffmann knew exactly what it meant. The CBOE is the Chicago Board Options Exchange, which trades around one billion contracts a year in options on companies, indices and tradable funds—the VIX among them. 'Self Help' is what one US exchange is entitled to declare against another if its sister-exchange starts taking more than a one-second time period to respond to orders: it is the responsibility of each exchange in the United States to ensure that they don't 'deal through'—that is, offer a worse price to an investor than can be obtained at that precise moment on an exchange elsewhere in the country. The system is entirely automated and operates at a speed of thousandths of a second. To a professional such as Hoffmann, the CBOE Self Help alert gave warning that the New York electronic exchange ARCA was experiencing some kind of system breakdown—an interruption sufficiently serious that Chicago would no longer re-route orders to it under the National Best Bid and Offer (NBBO) regulations, even if it was offering better prices for investors than Chicago.

The announcement had two immediate consequences. It meant Chicago had to step in and provide the liquidity formerly offered by NYSE/ARCA—at a time when liquidity was, in any case, in short supply—and it also, perhaps more importantly, further spooked an already jittery market.

When Hoffmann saw the alert, he didn't immediately connect it with VIXAL. But when he looked up in puzzlement from the screen and ran his eye over the flickering lights of the CPUs; when he sensed, almost physically, the phenomenal volume and speed of the orders they were processing; and when he remembered the immense unhedged one-way bet VIXAL was taking on a market collapse—at that moment he saw what the algorithm was doing.

He searched around the console for the remotes for the TV screens. The business channels flickered on at once, broadcasting live pictures of rioters fighting police in a big city square in semi-darkness. Piles of garbage were on fire; occasional off-camera explosions punctuated the chatter of the commentators. On CNBC the caption read: 'BREAKING NEWS: PROTESTERS SWARM STREETS IN ATHENS AFTER APPROVAL OF AUSTERITY BILL'.

The female presenter said, 'You can see police actually hitting people with batons there . . .'

The ticker in the bottom of the screen showed that the Dow was down 260 points.

The motherboards churned on implacably. Hoffmann set off back towards the loading bay.

*   *   *

At that moment a noisy cortège of eight patrol cars of the Geneva Police Department swept down the deserted Route de Clerval, slammed to a halt beside the perimeter of the processing facility, and sprouted along its length a dozen open doors. Leclerc was in the first car with Quarry. Genoud was in the second. Gabrielle was four cars back.

Leclerc's immediate impression as he hauled himself out of the back seat was that the place was a fortress. He took in the high heavy metal fence, the razor wire, the surveillance cameras, the no-man's-land of the car park and then the sheer steel walls of the structure itself, rising like a silvery castle keep in the fading light. It had to be at least fifteen metres high. Behind him armed police were disgorging from the patrol cars, some with Kevlar body armour or blast-proof shields—pumped up, ready to go. Leclerc could see that if he were not very careful, this could only end one way.

'He isn't armed,' he said as he passed among the deploying men, clutching a walkie-talkie. 'Remember that—he has no weapon.'

'A hundred litres of gasoline,' said one gendarme. 'That's a weapon.'

'No it isn't. You four need to deploy to the other side. No one tries to go in without my orders, and absolutely nobody shoots—understood?'

Leclerc reached the car containing Gabrielle. The door was open. She was still in the back seat, clearly in a state of shock, and worse was to come, he thought. He had continued to read the exchanges on the dead German's laptop as the patrol car raced across Geneva. He wondered how she would feel when she discovered her husband had invited the intruder into their house to assault him. 'Madame Hoffmann,' he said, 'I know this is an ordeal for you, but would you mind . . .?' He offered her his hand. She looked at him blankly for a moment, then took it. Her grip was tenacious, as if he was not helping her out of a car so much as hauling her out of a sea that threatened to sweep her away.

Emerging into the cold night seemed to wake her from her trance, and she blinked in amazement at the sight of the force assembled. She said, 'All this just for Alex?'

'I'm sorry. There is a standard procedure for cases such as this. Let's just make sure it ends

311

peacefully. Will you help me?'

'Yes, of course. Anything.'

He led her to the front of the column, where Quarry was standing with Genoud. The company's head of security practically jumped to attention as he approached. What a weasel he was, Leclerc thought. Nevertheless he made an effort to be polite to him; it was his style.

'Maurice,' he said, 'I understand you know this place. What are we dealing with exactly?'

'Three floors, separated by timber-framed partitions.' Genoud's eagerness to help was almost risible: by morning he'd be denying he ever knew Hoffmann. 'False floors, false ceilings. It's a modular structure, each module filled with computer equipment, apart from a central control area. The last time I was inside, it was less than half-occupied.'

'Upstairs?'

'Empty.'

'Access?'

'Three entrances. One is a big unloading bay. There's an internal fire escape down from the roof.'

'How do the doors unlock?'

'Four-digit code here; face recognition inside.'

'Any gate into the compound apart from this one?'

'No.'

'What about power? Could we cut it off?'

Genoud shook his head. 'There are diesel generators around the back on the ground floor with enough fuel for forty-eight hours.'

'Security?'

'An alarm system. It's all automatic. No personnel on the premises.'

'How do we open the gates?'

'The same code as the doors.'

'Very well. Open them, please.'

He watched as Genoud keyed in the number. The gates did not respond. Genoud, grim-faced, tried a couple more times, with the same result. He sounded mystified. 'This is the right code, I swear.'

Leclerc took hold of the bars. The barrier was immensely solid. It didn't budge a millimetre. You could ram a truck at it and it would probably hold.

Quarry said, 'Maybe Alex couldn't get in either, in which case he won't be there.'

'Possibly, but it's more likely he's changed the code.' A man with death fantasies locked in a building with a hundred litres of gasoline! Leclerc called out to his driver: 'Make sure the fire department are bringing cutting equipment. And we'd better have an ambulance, just in case. Madame Hoffmann, will you see if you can speak to your husband and ask him not to do anything foolish?'

'I'll try.'

She pressed the entry buzzer. 'Alex?' she said softly. 'Alex?' She held her finger on the metal button, willing him to answer, pressing it again and again.

*   *   *

Hoffmann had just finished dousing the CPU room, the tape-robot cabinets and the fibre-optic trench with petrol when he heard the buzzer on the control console. He had a jerry can in either hand. His arms ached with the weight. Fuel had slopped over his boots and jeans. It had started to get noticeably

313

hotter—somehow he must have managed to disable the power supply to the ventilation system. He was sweating. On CNBC the headline was 'DOW DOWN MORE THAN 300 POINTS'. He set the canisters beside the console and inspected the security monitors. By moving the mouse and clicking on individual shots, he was able to take in the entire scene at the gate—the gendarmes, Quarry, Leclerc, Genoud and Gabrielle, whose face when he brought it up occupied the entire screen. She looked shattered. He thought: she must have been told the worst of it by now. His finger hovered over the button for a few seconds.

'Gabby . . .'

It was strange to watch on screen her reaction to the sound of his voice, the look of relief.

'Thank God, Alex. We're all so worried about you. How's it going in there?'

He glanced around. He wished he had the words to describe it. 'It's—unbelievable.'

'Is it, Alex? I bet it is.' She stopped, glanced to one side then moved her face closer to the camera, and her voice became quieter, confiding, as if it were just the two of them. 'Listen, I'd like to come and talk to you. I'd like to see it, if I may.'

'I'd like that too. But honestly I don't think it's possible.'

'It would just be me. I promise you. All these others would stay back here.'

'You say that, Gabby, but I don't think they would. I'm afraid there's been a lot of misunderstanding.'

She said, 'Hang on a minute, Alex,' and then her face disappeared from the screen and all he could see was the side of a police car. He heard a

314

discussion start, but she had put her hand over the entry speaker and the words were too muffled for him to make out. He glanced over at the TV screens. The CNBC headline was 'DOW DOWN MORE THAN 400 POINTS'.

Hoffmann said, 'I'm sorry, Gabby. I'm going to have to go now.'

She cried, 'Wait!'

Leclerc's face suddenly appeared on camera. 'Dr Hoffmann, it's me—Leclerc. Open the gates and let your wife in. You need to talk to her. My men won't make a move, I promise you.'

Hoffmann hesitated. It struck him, oddly, that the policeman was right. He did need to talk to her. Or if not talk to her, at least show her—let her see it all before it was destroyed. It would explain everything far better than he ever could.

On the trading screen there was a new alert: 'NASDAQ has declared Self Help against NYSE/ARCA as of 14:36:59 ET.'

He pressed the buzzer to let her in.

18

*The flight crowd is created by a threat. Everyone flees;
everyone is drawn along. The danger which threatens
is the same for all . . . People flee together because it is
best to flee that way. They feel the same excitement
and the energy of some increases the energy of others;
people push each other along in the same direction.
So long as they flee together they feel that the danger
is distributed . . .*

ELIAS CANETTI, *Crowds and Power* (1960)

The fear in the US markets was going viral, algorithms sniffing and sniping at one another along their fibre-optic tunnels as they struggled to find liquidity. Trading volume in consequence was approaching ten times normal levels: 100 million shares were being bought and sold per minute. But the figure was deceptive. The positions were held for only fractions of a second before being passed on—what the subsequent inquiry called a 'hot potato' effect. This abnormal level of activity itself now became a critical factor in the accelerating panic.

At 8.32 p.m. Geneva time, an algorithm had entered the market tasked with selling 75,000 'E-minis'—electronically traded S&P 500 future contracts—with a notional value of $4.1 billion on behalf of the Ivy Asset Strategy Fund. To limit the impact on price of unloading so much, the algorithm was programmed to restrict its trading so that its volume of sales averaged no more than nine per cent of the total market at any given moment: at that rate the disposal was expected to take from three to four hours. But with the market ten times its normal size, the algorithm adjusted accordingly and proceeded to complete its assignment in nineteen minutes.

*   *   *

As soon as there was enough of a gap, Gabrielle slid around the gate and set off across the car park. She had not gone far when she heard shouting behind her and turned to see Quarry breaking free of the group and striding after her. Leclerc was yelling at him to come back, but Quarry's only response was to raise his arm in dismissive acknowledgement and keep on walking.

'Not going to let you do this alone, Gabs,' he said as he drew level with her. 'My fault this, not yours. I got him into it.'

'It's nobody's bloody fault, Hugo,' she said without looking at him. 'He's ill.'

'Still—you don't mind if I tag along?'

She ground her teeth. *Tag along*—as if they were on a stroll. 'It's up to you.'

But when they rounded the corner and she saw her husband standing in the open entrance of the loading bay, she was glad she had someone beside her, even Quarry, because Alex had a long iron bar in one hand and a big red jerry can in the other, and everything about him was disturbing, psychotic—the way he stood perfectly still, the blood and oil on his face and in his hair and smeared down the front of his clothes, the fearful staring expression on his face, the stench of petrol.

317

He said, 'Quickly, come on, it's really getting started now,' and before they had even reached him he had turned and disappeared back inside. They hurried after him, past the BMW, through the loading bay, past the motherboards and the tape robots. It was hot. The petrol was vaporising, making it difficult to breathe. Gabrielle had to cover her nose with the edge of her jacket. From up ahead came a sound like bedlam.

Alex, she thought, Alex, Alex . . .

Quarry cried after him in a panic, 'Jesus, Alex, this place could explode . . .'

They emerged into a much larger room filled with cries of panic. Hoffmann had pumped up the sound on the big TV screens. Aside from the noise of these, a man was ranting somewhere like a commentator in the final furlong of a big race. She didn't recognise it, but Quarry did: the live audio feed from the pit of the S&P 500 in Chicago.

'Here they come to sell 'em again! Nine-halves trade now, twenties trade now, evens trade now, guys, eight-halves trading as well. Once again, guys—eight even offer! Seven even offer . . .'

In the background, people were screaming as if they were witnessing a disaster. On one of the TV screens Gabrielle took in a caption: 'DOW, S&P 500, NASDAQ HAVE BIGGEST ONE-DAY DROPS IN OVER A YEAR'.

Another man was talking over pictures of a night-time riot: *'Hedge funds are gonna try to break Italy, they're gonna try to break Spain. There is no resolution . . .'*

The caption changed: 'VIX UP ANOTHER 30%'. She had no idea what it meant. Even as she watched it changed again: 'DOW DOWN MORE

318

THAN 500 POINTS'.

Quarry stood transfixed. 'Don't tell me *we're* doing that.'

Hoffmann was upending the big jerry can and pouring petrol over the CPUs. 'We started it. Attacked New York. Set off an avalanche.'

'Guys, we are sixty-four handles lower on the day here, guys . . .'

*　　　*　　　*

Nineteen-point-four billion shares were traded on the New York Stock Exchange during the course of that day: more than were traded in the whole decade of the 1960s. Events as they happened were denominated in milliseconds, far beyond the speed of human comprehension. They could only be reconstructed later, when the computers yielded their secrets.

At 8:42:43:675 p.m. Geneva time, according to a report by the data-feed-streaming company NANEX, 'the quote traffic rate for all NYSE, NYSE-ARCA, and NASDAQ stocks surged to saturation levels within 75 milliseconds'. Four hundred milliseconds after that, the Ivy Asset Strategy Fund algorithm sold yet another tranche of $125 million worth of E-minis, regardless of the plunging price. Twenty-five milliseconds later, a further $100 million in electronically traded futures was disposed of by a different algorithm. The Dow was already down 630 points; a second later it was down 720. Quarry, hypnotised by the changing numbers, witnessed it happen. Afterwards he said it was 'like watching one of those cartoons where the guy runs over the edge of the cliff and stays there in mid-air still running until he looks down—then he disappears'.

*   *   *

Outside, three trucks from the Geneva Fire Service had pulled up next to the patrol cars. So many men; so many lights. Leclerc told them to get started. The jaws of the hydraulic cutters, once they were put in place, reminded him of giant mandibles, chomping through the heavy iron fence posts one by one as if they were blades of grass.

*   *   *

Gabrielle was pleading with her husband: 'Come on, Alex, please. Leave it now and come away.'

Hoffmann finished emptying the last jerry can and dropped it. With his teeth he began tearing at the packet of cleaning cloths. 'Just need to finish this.' He spat out a piece of plastic. 'You two go. I'll be right behind.' He looked at her and for an instant he was the old Alex. 'I love you. Now go, please.' He wiped the cloth in the petrol that had pooled on the cover of a motherboard, thoroughly soaking it. In his other hand he held a cigarette lighter. 'Go,' he repeated, and there was such desperation in his voice that Gabrielle began to back away.

On CNBC the commentator said: '*This is capitulation really, this is classic capitulation; there is fear in this market—take a look at the VIX, absolutely exploding today . . .*'

Quarry at the trading screen could barely credit what he was seeing. In seconds the Dow had slipped from minus 800 to minus 900. The VIX was up by forty per cent—dear sweet Christ, that was close on a half-billion-dollar profit he was looking at right there on that one position. Already VIXAL was exercising its options on the shorted stocks, picking them up at insanely low prices—P&G, Accenture, Wynn Resorts, Exelon, 3-M . . .

The hysterical voice from the Chicago pit continued to rant, a sob in his throat: '. . . *seventy-five even offer here right now, guys, seventy even bid and here comes Morgan Stanley to sell . . .*'

Quarry heard a *wumph!* and saw Hoffmann with fire coming out of his fingers. Not now, he thought, don't do it yet—not till VIXAL has finished its trades. Beside him Gabrielle screamed, 'Alex!' Quarry flung himself towards the door. The fire left Hoffmann's hand, seemed to dance in the air for an instant, and then expanded into a brilliant bursting star.

*   *   *

The second and decisive liquidity crisis of the seven-minute 'flash crash' had begun just as Hoffmann dropped the empty jerry can, at 8.45 p.m. Geneva time. All over the world investors were watching their screens and either ceasing to trade or selling up altogether. In the words of the official report: 'Because prices simultaneously fell across many types of securities, they feared the occurrence of a cataclysmic event of which they were not aware, and which their systems were not designed to handle . . . . A significant number withdrew completely from the markets.'

In the space of fifteen seconds, starting at

321

8:45:13, high-speed algorithmic programs traded 27,000 E-mini contracts—forty-nine per cent of the overall volume—but only two hundred of these were actually sold: it was all just a game of hot potatoes; there were no real buyers. Liquidity fell to one per cent of its earlier level. At 8:45:27, in the space of 500 milliseconds, as Hoffmann clicked his cigarette lighter, successive sellers piled into the market and the price of the E-mini fell from 1070 to 1062, to 1059 and finally to 1056, at which point the dramatic volatility automatically triggered what is called 'a CME Globex Stop Price Logic event': a five-second freeze on all trading on the Chicago S&P Futures exchange, to allow liquidity to come into the market.

The Dow was down by just under a thousand points.

*　　　*　　　*

Time-coded recordings of the open channels of the police radios establish that at precisely the moment the Chicago market froze—8:45:28 p.m.—an explosion was heard inside the processing facility. Leclerc was running towards the building, lagging behind the gendarmes, when the bang stopped him dead and he crouched down, his arms clasped over his head—an undignified posture for a senior police officer, he reflected afterwards, but there it was. Some of the younger men, with a fearlessness born of inexperience, never paused, and by the time Leclerc was back on his feet they were already running back from around the corner of the building, hauling Gabrielle and Quarry along with them.

Leclerc shouted, 'Where's Hoffmann?'
From the building came a roaring sound.

* * *

Fear of the intruder in the night. Fear of assault and violation. Fear of illness. Fear of madness. Fear of loneliness. Fear of being trapped in a burning building . . .

The cameras record dispassionately, scientifically, Hoffmann as he recovers consciousness in the large central room. The screens are all blown out. The motherboards are dead, VIXAL extinct. There is no sound except the noise of the flames moving from room to room as they take hold of the wooden partitions, the false floors and ceilings, the kilometres of plastic cable, the plastic components of the CPUs.

Hoffmann gets up on all fours, rises to his knees then lumbers to his feet. He stands swaying. He wrenches off his jacket and holds it in front of him for protection, then runs into the inferno of the fibre-optic room, past the smouldering and stationary robots, through the darkened CPU farm and into the loading bay. He sees the steel shutter is down. How has that happened? He hits the button with the heel of his hand to open it. No response. He repeats the motion frantically, as if hammering it into the wall. Nothing. All the lights are out: the fire must have shorted the circuits. As he turns, his eyes go up to the watching lens and one sees in them a tumult of emotions—rage is there, even a sort of insane triumph: and fear, of course.

As fear increases into an agony of terror, we behold, as under all violent emotions, diversified results.

Hoffmann has a choice now. He can either stay where he is and risk being trapped and burned to death. Or he can try to go back into the flames and reach the fire escape in the corner of the tape-robot suite. The calculation in his eyes . . .

He goes for the latter. The heat has become much more intense in the last few seconds. The flames are casting a brilliant glow. The Perspex cabinets are melting. One of the robots has ignited and is also melting in its central section, so that as he rushes past it, the automaton topples forwards at the midriff in a fiery bow and crashes to the floor behind him.

The ironwork of the staircase is too hot to touch. He can feel the heat of the metal even through the soles of his boots. The steps don't run all the way up to the roof but only to the next floor, which is in darkness. By the crimson glow of the fire behind him he can make out a large space with three doors leading off it. A noise like a strong wind in a loft is shifting around up here. He can't quite make out whether it is coming from his left or his right. Somewhere in the distance he hears a crash as a section of the floor gives way. He puts his face in front of the sensor to unlock the first door. When it doesn't respond, he wipes his face on his sleeves: there is so much sweat and grease on his skin it is possible the sensors can't recognise him. But even when his face is cleaner it doesn't respond. The second door won't open either. The third does, and he steps into utter darkness. The night-vision

324

cameras record him groping blindly around the walls for the next exit, and so it goes on, from room to room, as Hoffmann seeks to escape the maze of the building, until at last, at the end of a passage, he opens a door on to a furnace. A tongue of fire races towards the fresh supply of oxygen like a hungry living thing. He turns and runs. The flames seem to pursue him, lighting ahead the gleaming metal of a staircase. He passes out of camera shot. The fireball reaches the lens a second later. The coverage ends.

*   *   *

To the people viewing it from the outside, the processing facility resembles a pressure cooker. No flames are visible, only smoke issuing from the seams and vents of the building, accompanied by this incessant roar. The fire service plays water on the walls from three different directions to try to cool them down. The concern of the chief fire officer, as he explains to Leclerc, is that cutting open the doors will only feed oxygen to the fire. Even so, infrared equipment keeps detecting shifting black pockets inside the structure where the heat is less intense and where someone might have survived. A team wearing heavy protective gear is preparing to go in.

Gabrielle has been moved back with Quarry to just inside the perimeter fence. Someone has put a blanket round her shoulders. They both stand watching. Suddenly, from the flat roof of the building, a jet of orange flame shoots into the night sky. It resembles in shape, if not in colour, the plume of fire you might see at a refinery, burning off a gaseous waste product. From its base

325

something detaches. It takes a moment for them all to realise that it is the fiery outline of a man. He runs to the edge of the roof, his arms outstretched, then leaps and falls like Icarus.

19

Looking to the future . . . which groups will ultimately prevail, no man can predict; for we well know that many groups, formerly most extensively developed, have now become extinct.

CHARLES DARWIN, *On the Origin of Species* (1859)

It was almost midnight and the streets leading to Les Eaux-Vives were quiet, the shops shuttered, the restaurants closed. Quarry and Leclerc sat in the back of a patrol car in silence.

Eventually Leclerc said, 'You are quite certain you wouldn't prefer to be taken home?'

'No. Thank you. I need to get in touch with our investors tonight before they hear about what's happened on the news.'

'It will be a major story, no doubt.'

'No doubt.'

'Still, if you don't mind my saying so, after such a trauma, you need to be careful.'

'I will be, don't worry.'

'At least Madame Hoffmann is in a hospital, where they can treat her for delayed shock . . .'

'Inspector, I'll be fine, all right?'

Quarry put his chin in his hand and looked out of the window to discourage further conversation. Leclerc stared out at the street on the other side. To think that barely twenty-four hours earlier he had been starting a routine night shift! Truly, one never knew what life would throw at you. The chief had called from his dinner in Zurich to offer his congratulations on 'a swift resolution of a potentially embarrassing situation': the Finance Ministry was pleased; Geneva's reputation as a centre of investment would be unaffected by this aberration. Still, he felt he had failed somehow— had always been that crucial hour or two behind the game. If only I had gone with Hoffmann to the hospital at dawn, he thought, and insisted that he stay for treatment, then none of it would have happened. He said, almost to himself, 'I should have handled it better.'

Quarry gave him a sideways look. 'What's that?'

'I was thinking, *monsieur*, that I could have dealt with things better, and then perhaps this whole tragedy could have been avoided. For example, I could have spotted earlier on—right from the start, as a matter of fact—that Hoffmann was in an advanced state of psychosis.' He thought of the Darwin book and Hoffmann's crazed assertion that the man in the picture somehow provided a clue as to why he had been attacked.

'Maybe.' Quarry sounded unconvinced.

'Or again, at Madame Hoffmann's exhibition—'

'Look,' said Quarry impatiently, 'you want the truth? Alex was a weird guy. Always was. I should've known what I was getting into the first night I met him. So it's nothing to do with you, if you'll forgive me for saying so.'

'Even so . . .'

'Don't get me wrong: I'm desperately sorry it ended like that for him. But imagine it: all that time, practically running an entire shadow company right under my nose—spying on me, on his wife, on *himself . . .*'

Leclerc thought of how often he had heard such

328

exclamations of disbelief from wives and husbands, lovers and friends; of how little we know of what actually goes on in the minds of those we think we know best. He said mildly, 'What will happen to the company without him?'

'The company? What company? The company is finished.'

'Yes, I can see that the publicity might be damaging.'

'Oh really? You think so? "Schizophrenic genius banker goes on rampage, murders two, sets fire to building"—that kind of thing?'

The car drew up outside the office block. Quarry rested his head on the back of the seat and stared at the roof. He let out a long sigh. 'What a bugger it all is.'

'Indeed.'

'Oh well.' Wearily Quarry opened the door. 'I expect we'll talk again in the morning.'

Leclerc said, 'No, *monsieur*, at least not with me. The case has been reassigned to a very able young officer—Moynier. You'll find him efficient to deal with.'

'Oh, okay.' Quarry seemed vaguely disappointed. He shook the policeman's hand. 'I'll wait to hear from your colleague, then. Good night.'

He climbed out of the car, his long legs swinging easily on to the pavement.

'Good night. Incidentally,' Leclerc added quickly, before Quarry shut the door. He leaned across the back seat. 'Your technical problems earlier—I meant to ask—how serious were they?'

The habit of deception still came easily to Quarry. 'That was nothing—not serious at all.'

'Only your colleague said you had lost control of

your system . . .'

'He didn't mean it literally. You know computers.'

'Ah yes, absolutely—computers!'

Quarry closed the door. The patrol car pulled away. Leclerc glanced back at the financier as he entered the building. Some shadow passed across his mind but he was too tired to pursue it.

'Where to, boss?' asked the driver.

Leclerc said, 'South on the road to Annecy-le-Vieux.'

'Your place is in France?'

'Just over the frontier. I don't know about you, but I can't afford to live in Geneva any more.'

'I know exactly what you mean. It's all been taken over by foreigners.'

The driver started to talk about property prices. Leclerc settled down in his seat and closed his eyes. He was asleep before they reached the French border.

*   *   *

The gendarmes had gone from the office building. One elevator was cordoned off by black-and-yellow tape and had a sign stuck to it—'DANGER: NOT WORKING'—but the other was operational, and after a brief hesitation Quarry stepped into it.

Van der Zyl and Ju-Long were waiting for him in reception. They rose as he came in. Both looked badly shaken.

Van der Zyl said, 'It's just been on the news. They had shots of the fire, this place—everything.'

Quarry swore, looked at his watch. 'I'd better start emailing the major clients straight away.

Better if they hear it from us first.' He noticed that van der Zyl and Ju-Long were looking at one another. 'Well, what is it?'

Ju-Long said, 'Before you do, there's something you ought to see.'

He followed them on to the trading floor. To his amazement, none of the quants had gone home. They rose as he came in and stood in complete silence. He wondered if it was meant as some sort of mark of respect. He hoped they weren't expecting a speech. Out of habit he glanced up at the business channels. The Dow had recovered almost two thirds of its losses to close down 387; the VIX was up sixty per cent. The imminent UK election results were being forecast from a nationwide exit poll: NO OVERALL CONTROL. That just about summed it up, he thought. He checked the nearest screen for the day's P&L, blinked at it and read it again, then turned in wonderment to the others.

'It's true,' said Ju-Long. 'We made a profit out of the crash of four-point-one billion dollars.'

'And the beauty of it is,' van der Zyl added, 'that that represents only zero-point-four per cent of total market volatility. No one will ever notice, except us.'

'Jesus wept . . .' Quarry quickly did the calculation in his head of his personal net worth. 'That must mean VIXAL managed to complete all the trades before Alex destroyed it.'

There was a pause, and then Ju-Long said quietly, 'He didn't destroy it, Hugo. It's still trading.'

'What?'

'VIXAL is still trading.'

331

'But it can't be. I just saw all the hardware burned to the ground.'

'Then it must have other hardware we don't know about. Something quite miraculous appears to have taken place. Have you seen the intranet? The company slogan has changed.'

Quarry looked at the faces of the quants. They seemed to him to be both blank and radiant at the same time, like members of a cult. It was eerie. Several of them nodded at him encouragingly. He bent to examine the screensaver.

THE COMPANY OF THE FUTURE WILL HAVE
NO WORKERS
THE COMPANY OF THE FUTURE WILL HAVE
NO MANAGERS
THE COMPANY OF THE FUTURE WILL BE A
DIGITAL ENTITY
THE COMPANY OF THE FUTURE WILL BE ALIVE

*   *   *

In his office, Quarry was writing an email to the investors.

To: Etienne & Clarisse Mussard, Elmira Gulzhan & François de Gombart-Tonnelle, Ezra Klein, Bill Easterbrook, Amschel Herxheimer, Iain Mould, Mieczyslaw Łukasiⵉski, Liwei Xu, Qi Zhang

From: Hugo Quarry

Subject: Alex

My dear friends, by the time you read this you will probably have begun to hear the tragic story of what happened to Alex Hoffmann yesterday. I will call you all individually later today to discuss the situation. For now I just wanted you to know that he is receiving the very finest medical care, and that our prayers are with both him and Gabrielle at this difficult moment. Of course it is too early to talk of the future of the company he founded, but I did want to reassure you that he has left systems in place which mean that your investments will not only continue to prosper, but will, I am confident, go from strength to strength. I will explain in more detail when I speak with you.

The quants had taken a vote on the trading floor and agreed to keep what had happened confidential. In return, each would receive an immediate cash bonus of $5 million. There would be further payments in the future, on a scale to be agreed, dependent on VIXAL's performance. No one had dissented: he supposed for one thing they had all seen what had happened to Rajamani.

There was a knock at the door. Quarry shouted, 'Come!' It was Genoud.

'Hello, Maurice, what do you want?'

'I've come to take out those cameras, if that's all right with you.'

Quarry considered VIXAL. He pictured it as a kind of glowing celestial digital cloud, occasionally swarming to earth. It might be anywhere—in some sweltering, potholed industrial zone stinking of aviation fuel and resounding to the throb of cicadas beside an international airport in South-East Asia or Latin America; or in a cool and leafy business park in the soft, clear rain of New England or the Rhineland; or occupying a rarely visited and darkened floor of a brand-new office block in the City of London or Mumbai or São Paulo; or even roosting undetected on a hundred thousand home computers. It was all around us, he thought, in the very air we breathed. He looked up at the hidden camera and gave the slightest bow of obeisance.

'Leave them,' he said.

*   *   *

Gabrielle was back where her day had begun, sitting in the University Hospital, only this time she was beside her husband's bed. He had been put into his own room at the end of a darkened ward on the third floor. There were bars on the windows and gendarmes outside, a man and a woman. It was hard to see Alex under all the bandaging and tubing. He had been unconscious since he hit the ground. They told her he had multiple fractures and second-degree burns; they had just brought him out of emergency surgery and connected him to a drip and a monitor; he was intubated. The surgeon declined to offer a prognosis: he said only that the next twenty-four hours would be critical. Four rows of glowing emerald-green lines processed hypnotically across the screen in gentle peaks and troughs. It reminded her of their honeymoon, watching the Pacific breakers forming far out at sea and following their progress all the way in to land.

Alex cried out in his sedated sleep. He seemed terribly agitated by something. She touched his bandaged hand and wondered what was passing through that powerful mind. 'It's all right, darling. Everything's going to be all right now.' She laid her head on the pillow next to his. She felt strangely content, despite everything, to have him beside her at last. Beyond the barred window a church clock was striking midnight. Softly she began singing to him a baby's lullaby.